Dead

Secrets

A Jack Mango Murder Mystery

Joy,
Enjoy the read!
Best Wishes!
[illegible]
AKA - L.A. TOTH

Dead Secrets

A Jack Mango Murder Mystery

By

L. A. Toth

Published by:
Linda Toth and Al Toth www.latoth.com
Corpus Christi, TX 78412

DEAD SECRETS – A JACK MANGO MURDER MYSTERY

Published by:
Linda Toth and Al Toth
Corpus Christi, TX 78412
WEBSITE: http://www.latoth.com
FACEBOOK: L.A. Toth

Library of Congress Cataloging-in-Publication Data:
Printed in United States of America
First Edition – Revised and Corrected: October 2016

ISBN-13:978-0692452592
(Alfred S. Toth)
ISBN-10:0692452591

Cover Art & Design: Emily Moravits
Photography: Al Toth and Linda Toth

To our friends in Albuquerque;
We'll always have Vegas.

"We tend to think that the threats to ourselves are outside of us. We fear that some enemy will destroy us . . . In reality, the only thing that can destroy us is within ourselves."

—Chogyam Trungpa; *SHAMBALA*;
The Sacred Path of the Warrior

Dead Secrets

PROLOGUE

ON THE ROCKS WITH A TWIST

"I'm not gonna to do it!" Billy Morton hollered at his nemesis, legs planted wide and arms crossed.

Quietly, "Oh, you will. You know you will. You can't quit and you know it." A low chuckle and quirked smile followed.

Billy cringed. "You make it sound like I can't control my life anymore. I've paid my dues, did my time in the pen and I'm out. You think you hold all the power, but you don't!"

"I *do* control your life, asshole. If you mess with me, you'll regret it," a hardening voice answered.

"How the hell did I get into this screwy predicament?" Billy asked himself.

Eight years ago he was a high level and well paid army psychiatrist, a GS-11 federal civil servant working at Camp Roberts, a half hour northeast of Serrano up and over the Santa Lucia Range on Route 46, then just north of Paso Robles on Highway 101. He counseled soldiers returning with PTSD from Iraq and Afghanistan, as well as their dysfunctional families. He was highly respected in his profession. Now he was little better than a Dalit, an untouchable, his life in shambles with suicide a tantalizing alternative.

Billy thought the worst part of his life was over after spending close to four years of a dime sentence at Soledad Prison, twenty-five miles southeast of Salinas, CA, for sexual abuse of a teenage girl, age fourteen, who looked not quite eleven. That girl just happened to be his adopted daughter, Clare. Little coozie had ratted him right after the first time, too. He ended up (no pun, really), having more sex with Jahrome, his *real* close cellmate for four years, than he ever scored with his scrawny blue-ice veined bitch of a wife Stella. If she'd performed her womanly duties more often and satisfied some of his kinkier fantasies, he'd have ***NEVER*** schtupped Clare and his life wouldn't have degenerated to whale dung.

Billy had been paroled four weeks, six days, and seven hours, and had little choice but to return to Serrano, just long enough to scratch up enough cash to move on. The problem was, where? He would always have to register as a sex offender and who in their right mind would hire him, much less rent to an ex-felon sicko pervert?

In Billy's mind, his only crime was to marry a woman as sexually appealing as Marilyn Manson (hetero-sexually speaking, of course), combined with a wee run of bad luck, which unfortunately continued to this day. He had stopped for a cup of coffee in Tranquility, the next village up the highway on the ridge fifteen minutes north of Serrano. In this paradise along the central California coast where roses bloomed perpetually, all he seemed to do was step into manure. Now he had this piss-ant breathing down his neck.

"Let's go, Billy Bongo. You don't really have a choice. You either do this now, or I make an anonymous call to the cops about those two other girls you diddled at Camp Roberts. You won't get your 'outta jail card' as quickly, going up a second time, same offense; and I betcha your old roomie be happy to see you back."

Sweat dripped down Billy's forehead into eyes and his knees were shaking so badly he thought he would collapse. As he wiped the droplets away with trembling hands, fingers swiping the sheen from his face, he turned around and stared out the bank of oceanfront windows lining the room. In this house above surf and sand, the glass wall framed a cloud shrouded roseate sun sinking toward the marine demarked northwestern horizon. The sun would just miss sinking behind the lighthouse off Serrano Point.

His bladder aching to explode, mouth dry as a ten year drought, and heart pounding like the waves upon the cliffs below him during California's winter storms, Billy decided to bluff. The steady cadence of shore break crashing on the beach and rocks below amplified his quickened pulse and echoed his pounding head.

He glanced behind him, the two eyeballing each other another beat.

"What if I go to the police about *you*?" He countered petulantly, lower lip jutting forward.

Waiting, needing movement, Billy pivoted southward toward the view of Morro Rock rising in solitary grandeur six miles down the coast, guarding the entrance of the imaginatively named Morro Bay and equally creatively titled Town of Morro Bay. One side of 'The Rock' was illuminated, reflecting the waning sun. The sight of that giant, solitary granite volcanic plug only intensified his loneliness and confusion. 'The Rock' had always reminded him of a huge turd some monstrous, prehistoric pterodactyl shat, and then winged away leaving it to petrify for a few million years. Billy wrinkled his nose, amazed that a rock covered in bird poop year round could be turned into a tourist attraction. Such was the nature of Billy.

A Laughing Gull, perched on the deck railing outside the windows, laughing, stared Billy down through the glass. Its head was inquisitively cocked to the side, one beady eye staring at Billy, like it, too, was waiting. Billy could barely focus on the bobbing and darting heads of people on the beach below as they hopscotched along the waterline, jumping and skipping to avoid getting their shoes and pant legs wet. How unfair to be so happy. His sandpaper tongue rolled inside his mouth seeking moisture, while the smell of freshly painted walls burned his nostrils.

"The police? Think again, not gonna happen you piece of shit," came a soft hissed reply.

Smooth movement behind him reflecting off the window panes interrupted Billy's reverie. An arm snapped around his neck, quicker than a Pacific Rattlesnake strike, severely pinching his throat closed. Carotid arteries and esophagus followed form. He twisted and bucked forward to throw the vise from his neck, but taut legs wrapped around his torso and he was rode Jahrome-style, only worse. He reached behind, trying to grab fistfuls of hair but his elbows only bent so far. Billy slapped at the invading arm like a dog pawing at an empty food bowl. His attacker deployed a traditional choke hold, right wrist clasping left arm securely locked around Billy's neck. His attempts to pry either apart were futile. Billy's holiday in prison and constant nail chewing created knobby, grotesque fingertips studded with opaque hunks of hardened skin. Billy couldn't pick up a pencil from a table if his life depended on it, and it was becoming increasing clear to him it did.

"Think Billy!" he admonished to himself. *Christ. Sucker's stronger than I thought!* He collapsed to his knees, thrashing to throw the weight off his back and crashed against a table by the windows, face smeared against glass. The same gull that had watched Billy with such intensity recoiled. It jumped off the porch railing and lifted into the offshore breeze toward the waning sun. Panic increased his heart rate to the point of stroke. He kept slapping around, grabbing for anything, something, but by now blood restriction made it impossible for his brain impulses to reach fingers, much less bend them. His lips and tongue scraped glass as his head slid further down the pane, the taste of ammonia and window cleaner invading his nostrils.

Billy slithered to a splayed mess on the painter's drop-cloth covered floor, head slanted, eyes focusing on the glass reflection of revolving bamboo ceiling fan blades. Air seeped from his lungs and the relentless pressure on his throat prevented him from gathering even a gasp of oxygen. The persistent rotating whoosh above him mocked his inability to breathe and he had nothing else on which to concentrate. Billy's eyesight speckled, tunneled, dimmed. His last thought of such an ignoble demise sparked a last heroic effort (his one and only) to save himself. He squirmed; he twisted, coiled and rolled.

Billy felt euphoric glee. A reprieve! The deadly vise emasculating his throat loosened and he raggedly inhaled a looong breath! Too soon and just as quickly, that same damn rattler wrapped across his face to tighten on his right ear while another gripped a wad of his thinning hair. The popping crack of his fourth and fifth cervical vertebrae shattering under contorting pressure confirmed his suspicion his luck bucket was empty. No pardons.

"Fuck!" Panting. Scrabbling sounds.

"That was harder than I thought, but easy to finish. Ah, Billy. You shouldn't threaten people when negotiation is a non-option," the killer said aloud, making to spit on the body, but stopping mid-pucker.

Ziiiiip! Ziiiiiiip! Ziiiiip! Zipzipzip; swishing of window shades quickly dropped.

"Not that anyone can see in from the beach this high on the cliff, but we don't want any nosy tourists creeping up here peeking in windows."

"What a mess! You were a piece of garbage alive, and you're not much different dead. Sure didn't plan on doing this today! Glad you've got paint tarps on the floor. I'll wrap you up like a burrito just in case you leak."

Scraping sounds of cloth against flooring. Panting.

"Gonna have to come back later and throw you out with the rest of the trash, but right now I've got one more thing to do!"

A whoosh, hinges squeaking, a pause, click, then the irrevocable thunk of a door firmly shut.

Silence.

CHAPTER 1

AS IT ENDS, SO IT BEGINS

Four years and three days before Billy's ultimate departure, the cool March morning of Jack Mango's swearing-in ceremony as Serrano's new Police Chief started out gray, damp and murky. Early morning fog usually gave way to late afternoon sunshine, making the perpetually cold, crystal blue water tolerably surfable, albeit wetsuit clad. Jack stood in the Serrano Community Center parking lot facing the ocean while watching the breakers roll under the pier.

The idyllic seaside community set along the central coast between the southern tip of California's Big Sur range, and in this time-line, a ten minute drive north of Morro Bay, had been strategically established and named by Portuguese traders during the mid-1800s. The local Portugee argued amongst themselves whether the intent was to name the town for its serenity or the common word for foothills. The Spaniards thought the name honored Father Junipero Serra, who settled the Monterey and San Luis Obispo areas during the mid-to-late seventeen hundred mission era.

Appropriately named for any reason, (no, not the chile pepper), Serrano's beachfront was ringed with a sampling of small, quaint clapboard cottages mixed with multimillion dollar getaway mansions. Easily accessible by wealthy dot-comers from the Bay Area north, or movie moguls and actors from Los Angeles, Serrano's crescent sand beach continued unobstructed southward for six miles before smacking up against Morro Rock. This swath offered zones of solitude for contemplation and reflection, as well as remarkable boogie boarding and surf breaks. The offshore waters teamed with kelp, seals, otters, fish, and migrating whales.

Many people who visited Serrano, a town of five thousand residents with an added summer tourist population of up to twelve thousand on weekends, left reluctantly, though rejuvenated. Whether strolling or swimming, finding sand dollars while walking, being pummeled by the breaking waves or piloting a kayak, this was truly an oasis in the midst of a chaotic world.

In stark contrast to Serrano's azure waters, behind Jack and circling north to embrace the south facing bay, golden wrinkled hills with nesting oaks spackled the arroyos, ending at Serrano Point's lighthouse where Highway One disappeared from view through burnt grass hillocks as it wound north to meet Big Sur. Monterey Pine lightly sprinkled the ridge tops.

In this setting, taking advantage of the outdoor vistas, fifty Serranoans gathered to attend the auspicious occasion, happy for an infusion of leadership into their town's protective force. Included in this assembly were most department personnel, (fourteen sworn officers plus support staff), city officials, county politicos, prominent business leaders, various media reporters, and a handful of interested citizens.

Also in attendance was Jack's mother Alexa, as well as fourteen year old daughter Jessica. Not present was Jack's wife, Nancy nee Metzger, who died of melanoma during his tenure with the Los Alamos Police in northern New Mexico. They had fallen in love during seventh grade living in Ligonier, Pennsylvania. They bumped into each other's backs in the lunchroom line, and when both turned to apologize, they froze, recognizing two timeless old souls meeting after eons of separation. Even in their inflamed preteen stage, with little understanding of hormones from hominy, they knew this would be a life-long love no matter what, no matter how. It lasted for a scant fifteen years. That was then.

Daughter Jessica replicated a physical image of her mother with athletic frame, long straight shoulder-length blonde hair and a smile that brightened her green eyes. Much like her grandmother socially, people were drawn to Jessica's personality and energy without quite knowing why.

Alexa played the role of European matriarch, her posture and grace honed by her French lineage. A slight intriguing accent mixed with perfect English worked to pull one deeper into beguiling obsidian eyes. Coal black hair with a hint of salt completed the perfection.

Jack was dressed in one of two sports coats owned, this one a nubby brown Harris Tweed knockoff, blue button shirt, but no tie, (don't want to scare off the natives just yet) offset with a nicely shined pair of ostrich Nocona boots. He stood a trim six foot and one, with wavy dark brown hair, trimmed thick goatee masking his Italian blood line, which gave him a modern, less severe stereotypical persona of what a Chief of Police *should* look like. (No flat tops or buzz cuts, please!) Confirming Jack's ruggedness was a fading three inch scar below his left eye running diagonal across tanned cheek to his earlobe. The thick goatee framing his mouth had been an affectation since his first assignment as a Los Alamos detective, ten years prior. Jack grew it more to irk *his* Chief for lack of any other reason, yet he wasn't shaving it off; he had earned it and was keeping it.

Jack matriculated from the University of New Mexico in Albuquerque after transferring from a small college in Western Pennsylvania. His dream of returning to Pennsylvania with Nancy and becoming a PA State Trooper never materialized when Los Alamos invited him for an interview two weeks after graduating UNM. Jack received his gold detective shield with the Los Alamos Police after spending three years on patrol in the low crime but energetic, upper middle class mountainside community.

Los Alamos is the home of Los Alamos National Laboratory, hidden location for the top secret government Manhattan Project which birthed Little Boy and Fat Man, the two atomic bombs dropped on Hiroshima and Nagasaki which are credited with ending World War II. The town (*Alamo* in Spanish meaning cottonwood) is tucked atop the Pajarito Plateau at approximately 7300 feet, back-dropped by the Jemez Mountains, surrounded by thousands of alpine acreage with vistas of (almost year round) snow-capped peaks across the Espanola Valley clear southeast to Santa Fe.

It annoyed him that most people, even reporters, mixed up Los Alamos with Alamogordo. Los Alamos, a mountaintop community, is where the bombs were conceived. Alamogordo, smack in the middle of New Mexico's Tularosa Basin, a mainly deserted desert, is where the first atomic bomb was tested and exploded.

Being a detective in Los Alamos required him to obtain a top-secret clearance with the United States government which allowed him to liaise with FBI, DEA and Secret Service agencies, all involved periodically with secrets at "The Lab." His security clearance, military background and first degree black belt in Tae Kwon Do helped to exponentially expand Jack's career. Besides acquiring advanced training in sex crimes investigation, arson, child abuse, fraud, embezzlement and unattended deaths, Jack's career encompassed working with the Northern New Mexico Drug Task Force, assignments with visiting presidential and dignitary protection details, acting as the Cerro Grande Wildfire Incident Commander, along with numerous amusing duties guarding Hollywood actors filming in the area. The reason for New Mexico's motto the "Land of Enchantment" was well known by the California movie industry.

July of 2003, Governor Tom Hogan was guest speaker at the usual political stump rally inside Los Alamos's massive glass-walled library. Although the governor's state security detail was present, Jack was assigned to stand on stage behind and off Governor Hogan's left as he spoke from the podium.

Fixed at parade rest, Jack couldn't help but think *chump* speech a more fitting term for the compost spewed by Hogan and the rest of his cronies. As he ruminated upon this thought, scanning the crowd, Mango noticed a man in the second row fidgeting in his seat as if red ants were crawling inside his tighty-whites.

In what seemed like slow motion, but took only a few seconds, the twitching man pulled a small caliber semiautomatic from his belt and pointed it at the governor. Before he heard the shot, or so he thought, Jack powered into a right-footed lunge, caught the governor in a light embrace, twirled 180 degrees, imitated two polka steps, then dragged them both robustly to the floor, slamming down on top of the governor's body. Jack felt a burn along his right side, slightly above the beltline, just before he and Governor Hogan crashed to the floor behind the lectern. While covering the governor, Jack heard a barrage of shots and multiple screams, with galloping footfalls reverberating through the makeshift wooden stage floor. On the day he was shot, Jack had thought life couldn't get much better, and he was correct. He was healthy and happy, father to his beautiful twelve year old daughter Jessica, and contentedly married to his sweetheart Nancy.

Missing his Kevlar vest by a mere half inch, the bullet had punched through Mango's flesh leaving a hole, missing both bone and vital organs. Physically, he healed as quickly as one can after being shot, though for the healee, it can be a long uncomfortable excursion. Governor Hogan escaped unscathed but for multiple aching bruises, which he continued to kvetch about publicly a full three weeks after the incident. An aide eventually pulled the gentleman aside and reminded him it was *Mango* who took the bullet.

Naturally, although not desired, Mango became a brief national icon and state hero for longer than he cared. The average citizenry of Los Alamos and those within his own department started treating him differently. Many old friends became enemies. Maybe not true enemies, but no one invited him and his wife to dinner or out for drinks any more after work. Envy, jealousy, and insecurity took center stage in the smallness of people's minds in the small town. His immediate supervisor cold shouldered him while the younger officers continually asked him to rehash the shooting, teasing him about his fancy dance moves.

His own chief had sarcastically asked, "You plan on running for Mayor, boy?"

Three months later, with wound healing well and life returning to mundane, Jack's rebuilt happy bubble ruptured. Nancy was diagnosed with Stage III skin cancer; the bad kind. Doctors gave hope she would live another four to five years, and vowed to help them scour the range of treatments available to 'beat the rap'.

Six months after Nancy's diagnosis, Jack held Nancy's hand while she lay *in situ*, oxygen plugs up nose, bipping machines preventing deep sleep, and liquid filled plastic lines meandering down and over, dripping who knew what at this point into her veins.

Her eyelids fluttered. A soft, "Jack?"

"Here, bunny honey," head snapping up from his slight doze. "What can I get you?"

"Time is it?"

"I don't know, seven? Does it matter?"

"Hmmm. Wanted to see one more."

"What?"

"Sunset"

"Sun's already behind the Jemez. We'll bundle you in the truck, get you up top another evening," Jack encouraged.

Both turned their heads to gaze out the west facing hospital room window at the shadowed mountains.

"I'm so sorry about all this," she rasped.

"Nothin' to be sorry about, Nan," he said, trying hard to hold the surge of moisture filling his eyes.

Everything there was to say had already been said. Goodbyes. Jessica's future. Reminisces of all the good times and those few silly fights. Funeral arrangements.

Jack dropped Nancy's hand and reached over to smooth a lock of hair off her forehead, a reflex gesture of affection, forgetting there *was* no hair. Stopping mid-reach, he caressed her cheek instead.

"I don't regret a thing. We've had the perfect life together, more than I ever hoped, and you gave me a gift which I'll cherish more than my own life: Jessica. I'll take good care of her, I promise."

"I know you will." A tear spilled down her cheek. "*I* have a regret," she sighed.

Flustered and mute, Jack looked her.

Whispering, she confessed, "My one and only regret about our marriage. I should have forced you to take lessons with me and learn how to dance. You didn't even waltz with me at our wedding. I didn't care because we were so in love."

Smiling, remembering, she continued. "I watched you once after we first wed. You practiced in front of a mirror and didn't know I was watching. You were right; the man can't dance!" She coughed, trying to laugh. "I thought we'd have enough time to learn together."

Persisting, a rueful tinge in her voice, "And then you danced with the governor, but it took a bullet to make you. I would have liked to sway my way 'round a dance floor in your arms just once."

"You'll marry again. Some hot chile pepper will snap you up. You're too good a man to run loose on his own for long. Just make sure you dance with the next one." Nancy groped around, searching for his hand, found it, and brought it to her lips. Exhausted, breathing shallow, she closed her eyes.

Stunned, Jack leaned forward, his brow against the rails of her hospital bed and silently wept. Three hours later, the alarms jerked him upright, right hand slapping hip coming up empty.

Jack shook his head. *Gun home in safe. Wife in hospital.* The blaring helped him focus as green clad blurs skidded around the corner into the room like cats on linoleum.

Yelling. Scrambling. "Crash cart! STAT! Move!"

Ever the unflappable cop in the face of death and chaos, Jack stepped up, unclipped his wife's chart from the bedrail and calmly waved the top sheet at them which stated in bold red letters: "Terminal. DNR."

All activity ceased. Plugs were pulled, switches flipped. Four heads swiveled to look at Jack, and then in unison to his wife. Tiptoeing shuffles. The door wisping closed.

Silence.

Unable to go home and face his daughter, Jack drove out of the hospital parking lot and in mere minutes was up over the ridge, curving into the Jemez's darkest section of mountain road. Turning off the main pavement, he bumped down a dirt track, pine limbs scraping against truck paint as if to impede his forward momentum. The trace ended at his and Nancy's favorite elking spot, a viewing meadow where they had spent many a chilly autumn evening bundled together, spying through branches at rutting elk and bugling bulls.

Jack parked, grabbed the ever-waiting fleece blanket, climbed into the bed of his truck and lay down, hands cradling head. New moon. Santa Fe and Albuquerque, the nearest city lights too far away or blocked by summits to dim the span of Milky Way arcing above him. He didn't need to turn his head to know the radiance was bright enough to throw shadows.

Silence.

After his induction, the ceremony dragging on longer than necessary, Jack confidently worked the crowd, shaking hands and slapping backs, playing the role of welcoming warrior. Having already met most of the major players, he anticipated some would eventually become friends, others opponents. He was astute enough to realize both would critically influence his career and life.

His small family stood to the side engaging in obligatory chitchat with the locals. Most of the town's politicians and business people, their tenure spanning multiple generations, mingled in private little groups discussing plans for Serrano's future.

Mayor Percival, "Percy," Hathaway held court at the edge of the crowd with Sheriff Stanislau, "Stan," Sederwall of the San Luis Obispo (SLO) Sheriff's Office and a smattering of county commissioners. Hathaway was most likely greasing palms, opportunistically angling for favors. A former actor who supposedly made his small fortune playing bit parts in "B" movies, his prosperity actually trickled in from subtitled Japanese info-mercials as well as foreign film and commercial voice-overs. He was a politician who would spend a thousand dollars to save a nickel, taking credit for glorified yet worthless civic projects.

Mango eyed Sheriff Sederwall thinking he'd like to know the man better. A former Los Angeles Police officer who had spent too many years working the filth and vice in its glitzy Hollywood division, Sederwall had needed a change. He ran for and won the top spot in the sheriff's department six years prior. In real life, he was a cowboy, horseman and small time rancher; all grown-up from a bad boy escaping a hole-in-the-wall Missouri river town. He only played at being a successful twenty-five year police veteran.

Thankful that the power-shakers had moved on, Mango shifted toward those people not yet met standing along the edges. One man, a healthy fiftyish, Irish-Asian who was making a point to wait until no one would interrupt before introducing himself. Reaching out his hand to shake, Mango recognized the digits of a fellow martial artist; calloused knuckles, sinewy fingers and firm tight grip.

"Chief Mango. Lee Cavanaugh at your service. Glad to have you in town. I've heard much about you."

"All good, I hope," Mango answered with a warm, friendly smile.

"Very much so. I hear you have martial arts experience?"

"Only a first degree black. I wasn't able to test for second when my schedule was interrupted by moving here," Mango answered.

"I'm pleased you're from a good school and an old school. Not one that wraps fourth degree belts on nine year olds, sending them out thinking they're Jackie Chan," he responded, studying Mango's expression.

"Nothing extravagant, sir. Fifteen basic moves with meticulous training and excellent instruction. Los Alamos is home to some of the country's highest IQ's and dedicated over-achievers. We of non-rocket science intelligence make up for our humble inadequacies by giving a hundred and ten percent in Tae Kwon Do class."

"I teach here in Serrano," replied Lee. "Nothing heavy duty, but our school has been in existence for over twenty years, ever since my partner and I moved from San Francisco in the early Eighties. We also own and operate Dickies over by the pier."

"Thought you looked familiar. You were working behind the bar when my family and I ate lunch there a couple days ago. Excellent food and quite the historical setting. I understand the building is an historical landmark."

"It was built in the late 1860s and was Serrano's epicenter. In fact, deals are still cut there; many that affect local politics with some deals cut under the table," Lee paused. "But we won't go there. I know you're a busy man today. Please accept my invitation to bring your family in for dinner soon, and I'll fill you in on more of the building's history. I'd also like to see you continue your martial arts training with me. We have a wonderful group—"

A stunning redhead walked up and nudged into the conversation, her laser green eyes appraising Jack intensely. "Chief Mango. I'm Randi Shirazi. It is my pleasure to meet you," she said, right hand extended, hand gripping his firmly. "I own the jewelry store across from Lee's place in the old bank building. I also own several vacation rental properties.

I could broker a good deal for you if you're looking for a place to live."

"Don't believe a word she says," Lee Cavanaugh shot back, evaluating Mango's reaction to Randi. "And don't let those eyes fool you. While you're gazing deep, she'll rob you blind, and then hit you with a left side-kick severely damaging your vital body parts."

"Mr. Lee! We don't want to frighten away our new chief before he gets settled in," Randi demurred, full lips faking a pout.

"I'll take that under advisement," Mango laughed, eyes locked on Randi's.

"We do have evening class Tuesday and Thursday, and Saturday mornings. Tomorrow is Tuesday. Come and join us?" Lee asked. "It'll be good for you."

"Sure. Where?"

"Other side of that door," Lee said, pointing to the entrance of the community building. "There's a recreation and banquet room in the back. I was able to work out, shall we say, *an arrangement*," Lee smiled slyly.

"Just like they did in the 1860s," Mango grinned. "Okay. Deal. And, you are right; I do need it."

"Speaking of deals," Randi spoke up, "I really can help you with housing. If you're looking to buy, I know all the real estate agents in town. What are you looking for?"

"I like space, dirt and trees. I'd love to find a couple acres if possible. Maybe a fixer upper considering the price of real estate here, with enough room for my mom and daughter, too. I'm pretty easy to please. Running water, heat; not too many leaks in the roof. Electricity would be a plus," Mango joked, while grinning a practiced smile. "I got a good price selling my house in Los Alamos. Plus, I received some hardship money from New Mexico, so I should be able to afford something decent."

"Shut the front door!" Randi exclaimed. "I thought your name sounded familiar. You're the cop who got shot saving the governor's bacon a while back. I read about that. You're the real deal, a living hero."

"Uhmm, I really don't want that advertised here. All I need is for some punk to show up thinking he can finish the job . . . especially now that I'm Chief," Mango warned.

"That was rude of me; my apologies. I *am* glad to see you're still a healthy specimen of a man. Now, back to business. Let me see what I can do about finding your dream property, Chief Mango. But I'll be honest with you. A place with electricity might cost you—" Randi tilted her head at Mango artfully.

Beaming, she shook his hand again, adding, "I have an appointment, so I've got to run. *Caio,* and welcome to Serrano!" She slid her fingers reluctantly out of Mango's hand, turned quickly and walked breezily toward the parked cars.

Randi stopped and twirled, saluted Mango, and then resumed her stride.

"Powerful woman," Mango exhaled to Lee, mesmerized. "And that's an understatement."

"That's what makes, Randi, Randi. She's super smart, a go-getter, and always operating at full speed. Her *chi* is definitely energized," Lee said to Mango with a bemused shake of his head and arched eyebrow. "By the way, I wasn't exaggerating about that side-kick."

Mango and family were finally able to finish their official day by late afternoon and return to their beachfront house rental. Since it was still a full month before tourist season, they were able to secure a month-long lease at a realistic rate from a town council member. After a nap and still full from the snacks throughout the afternoon, instead of dinner, they opted for a walk along the beach.

Fleece jackets, shorts, and sandals were appropriate attire for a sunset stroll. A mild onshore breeze gently moved palms fronds that dotted the beachfront properties. Soft waves crawled up the sand and softly shushed away. Lights glimmered from the sporadically occupied homes sitting atop the sand and granite bluffs twenty feet above. A half mile north, the pier was partially lit, sparkling like a string of brilliant diamonds over the water.

"Sure is quiet and laid back here, Dad. Just like Los Alamos in a way. Everything closes right after sunset."

"Safe, too. Don't think I'll have to worry *too* much letting you run around town alone."

"Only reason it's safe is because you have a nine millimeter gun under your jacket!" Jessica laughed, jumping away from the shore break. She sprinted back to Mango and Alexa, tightened her arm around her father's waist and patted the Glock in its concealed holster.

"Don't touch the hardware, young'un," Jack growled.

"Sorry, I forgot." Contrite, she continued, "I really like all the different birds; and the sea otters are so cute, especially the babies. The way they roll around and play is so cool!"

"They are, kiddo," Jack answered gazing off at the rolling swells.

Seeing her dad preoccupied, watching the water, she stopped walking and asked, "Are these waves good enough to surf?"

"Not right now. See how they close out quickly and crash? You want waves that will curl left or right, which are much easier to ride and a heck of a lot safer. Waves like these will send you over the falls, or into a jack-n-slap."

"What's that?"

"It's when you think you've got a great ride, and all of a sudden the wave jacks up, sucks you up, and then smacks you down into the sand. Really hard. You can get concussed or even break your neck and die.

"Surfing still looks fun, though. How come you know so much about it? It's not like they had waves in New Mexico," Jessica joked, poking Jack playfully, careful to avoid the gun.

"I was stationed up the coast at Ft. Hunter Liggett when I was in the Army. Some of the enlisted guys taught me. They'd blast down-mountain every chance they'd get, just to hit the waves," Jack replied. "Lots of times we'd drive right past Serrano all the way into Morro Bay to find the best surf, and then camp on the beach. (It was allowed back then.) We'd have to wake up before dawn and beat-butt back to camp so we wouldn't be considered AWOL," Jack reminisced.

"Really? How come I don't know any of this?"

"Not much to tell, and way before your time, sprout. When I was much younger—"

"Were you good at it? Do you think I'll ever be?" Jessica pondered while watching her toes and feet sink into the sand.

Jack snorted. "We'll have the pros teach you. After trying to teach me, my surf buddies are the ones who coined the term 'jack-n-slap.' Just like anything else in life, being good at something means trying your best and most importantly, practice, practice, practice."

"Can people be good at everything they do?" Jessica asked.

"Nah. Sometimes no matter how hard you try, you just can't get it right."

"But not you, Dad. You're good at *everything*, huh?"

"Hardly, Jess. Hardly," Jack laughed.

"Yes, you are! What aren't you good at?"

"Dancing. Hmmmph. We'll discuss that later. Like, in about twenty years." Jack looked back at his mother.

Alexa threw Jack a pointed look, her eyes wide and eyebrows lifted into exaggerated commas.

"Whaaaat?" Jack feigned as he stepped in a mound of sea kelp which had broken loose from its moored depths, deposited by breaking surf onto the sand. "Let's head back to house. I'm beat."

After a pooped Alexa and Jessica dropped into bed, Jack put on a long sleeve fleece, wool socks and sweatpants. He made a nest of blankets in a lounge chair on the back porch, snuggled in, and listened to the endless lapping waves creep up the sand and hiss lazily back. Looking up and expecting muzzy fog, he was pleased to see clear sky and the Milky Way, a bright ribbon spinning down the horizon into pacific dark. *Out of chaos comes continuity.* He was now formally

Serrano's Chief of Police. His pondering of past, present and future settled him into contented sleep.

Three nights later, as Mango snoozed in the same spot, his cell phone would buzz and rouse him. He was needed downtown. A fourteen year-old girl. Signs of sexual assault. The first case of his new career. A case where the perp was packed off to jail, pronto. A case which would blow wide open four years later.

CHAPTER 2

TAE KWON DO

Chief Mango's first year in Serrano flew faster than a gull caught in Santa Ana Winds. Getting to know his people, their personalities and quirks was basic stuff and just good PR. He made it a point to walk around Serrano's downtown almost every day, building relationships and checking the pulse of the town. Jack did not dress in uniform except for formal functions. Attired in cargo pants, Teva hiking boots, police insignia polo shirt with a pocket, and belt mounted badge next to his ever present Model 27 Glock strapped to his side, Jack enjoyed the late morning for his walks. Sweet scents from the cookie shop competed with ocean brine and the pungent tang from the fish market.

His sanctuary from work, his *hacienda*, was a deal that Randi with her connections scoped before it hit the open market. He offered and they accepted. A litter box bigger than three acres, Jack renamed it *Alamosta Rancho*. Tucked back on the far reaches of old McFarland's spread off the back road to Atascadero, in a hidden valley dotted with grasses, oaks, eucalyptus, and a smidgen of cottonwoods, the driveway was a quarter mile long. Providing peaceful privacy to Jack, Jess, & Alexa were a ranch house, small barn, workshop and stable. Half the acreage was fenced pasture with plenty of space for a couple horses. The house was rustic wood frame, a fusion of ranch and contemporary, definitely California style, pine tongue and groove floors, and lots of natural light flooding the rooms through massive windows.

Mango closed in and renovated a large back porch into a complete guest suite and living area for Alexa, allowing her to have her own space and privacy when needed. Jessica's two cats, Kiawe (pronounced key-**ah**-vee) and Pono, gifts from Detective Kiana de la Cruz, roamed never far from the house's perimeter. Two smart cats very aware those sweeping ground shapes were really hungry hawks. A newly constructed chicken coop and run, all with protecting wire, housed Jack's laying hens. Jessica insisted they take advantage of stalls and pasture, so two spunky horses, Dakota and Sammy joined the menagerie.

When he had time, Jack continued to upgrade and remodel the rancho's buildings, but reserved two evenings a week for Tae Kwon Do. Both provided meditation and therapy, and the class helped him establish friendships away from the department. He had learned the hard way that contacts outside of work helped keep one balanced. Tae Kwon Do's biggest benefit, the concentration required on pure movement, performing each form to perfection allowed Jack (for an hour) to free his mind completely of outside clutter.

Jack enjoyed the dozen or so people who showed up for Lee's evening classes, who was known as Master Lee inside the community building's dojo, but commonly called Mr. Lee publicly, and just Lee to good friends. He had practiced and taught Tae Kwon Do and Kung Fu for more than thirty years, absorbing the arts while attending undergraduate school at Berkeley.

Of Irish and Asian descent, he was sired by an unnamed soldier stationed in Korea, hence his unique mixed heritage. Mr. Lee's piercing moonstone wolf-eyes with slightly curved eye lids, exuded compassion, but missed little. A short yet sinewy man, forearms thick and veined, he had the build of a construction worker. You definitely didn't want to rile the man up. His short thirty-two inch legs could break seven inches of wood and his gnarled hands do equal damage, quicker than the flicker of a hummingbird's wings.

Master Lee's martial arts classes were taught mostly Korean style, but Jack preferred the defensive moves and attacks of the Kung Fu form. Ever focused, he absorbed every detail, edge, and advantage taught by Lee. As an officer of the law who strictly adhered to enforcement protocols, Mango never used these tactics during normal police situations. When faced with deadly force, though, his motto, "always cheat, always win" galvanized within him into an added edge of confidence.

As a student, Mango practiced humility by volunteering to sweep the floor clean before each class; a traditional way of honoring his instructor. Jack sniggered at the martial arts shows on television. Arrogant guys taking six groin kicks and four direct strikes to the throat, popping back up like plastic clowns. From the martial artist's viewpoint; one punch or one kick; fight over. Anything more, it's time for extra training.

Mr. Lee quickly became mentor and confidant to Jack. He was a rare person; honest, trustworthy and shrewd. Lee was also gay, "from birth" as he told Jack. He and partner,

Roscoe Rae, met while 'working' the nascent porn industry during the mid-1970s, before drugs, disease and AIDs decimated the industry. Lee and Roscoe grabbed their earnings, quit the biz, quit college, and explored options to buy a restaurant in The City. Not thrilled about locating a business where the growing and wild gay lifestyle was rapidly displacing the crumbling hippie scene, they embarked on a three day jaunt down the coast, a vacation to plan their future together. Stopping in Serrano for gas and food, Roscoe received a sign. Literally. A plastic "For Sale" sign smacked him in the head, blown from the building across the street by the sea breeze, hitting him as he pumped gas into the car. The restored derelict structure became Dickies, with Lee and Roscoe resurrecting the historical location and becoming unofficial hosts to Serrano's social core.

Randi Shirazi was also a frequent attendee at Master Lee's classes. The dedication and energy, strength and precision she brought to class were contagious. While sparring, her drenched red hair would snap across her forehead spraying opponents with fans of perspiration, sweat oozing down her white *gi*. Her *ki-up*, a roaring bellow emanating deep from within her center made even her most experienced competitors flinch, conjuring Valkyrie visions of their imminent annihilation.

Randi and her husband, Emil, moved to Serrano in the late Nineties, buying the old bank building and refurbishing it into a jewelry store of distinction. As a young apprentice in Persia, Emil trained with artisans who used unique cutting methods and unusual heating techniques to treat precious stones, producing astonishing gem colors and brilliance. He and his two older twin brothers immigrated to the United States during the Shah's fall from power in 1979 and settled in Los Angeles. The two brothers supplied the uncut stones; Emil designed and produced the jewelry. Randi's life before her marriage was mostly unknown in Serrano. She simply didn't talk about it much. Her volunteer work for sexual abuse victims in San Luis Obispo County, though, confirmed what most people thought. Randi volunteered her whole heart.

That heart was broken a year before Jack arrived in Serrano, as Emil was killed in a tragic auto accident driving home from a San Francisco business trip via scenic Route One through Big Sur. His car went off the road, plunging five hundred feet onto the rocks and into the waiting Pacific. Randi's only consolation being he would have died instantly upon impact. Emil's body was never found. Since the convertible top was ascertained to be locked open, it was theorized he was smashed to guacamole upon impact and into the sea or possibly ejected. Either way, it appears the fishes ate the remains because nothing ever washed ashore. Unable to replicate Emil's designs, she hired local artisans to keep the store operating, but their best work palled compared to her husband's.

Detective Kiana de la Cruz, Mango's lead investigator, would periodically attend class but was more interested in the journey, not the black belt destination. Master Lee's self-defense tactics were her main focus although she did enjoy the comradery of group practice. Kiana's life as a single woman in her late twenties was too active with surfing, hiking, bicycling and yoga to limit to one routine.

A native from Molokai, Kiana's Hawaiian, Filipino and Spanish ancestry combined to make her a stunningly beautiful; a long, shiny black-haired, hazel-eyed *wahine*. Kiana had watched too many of her *ohana*, her extended family succumb to a life of smoking *pakalolo*, indolence, and government handouts. Opportunities were scarce on the rural (some say backward) island, further stigmatized by its leper colony history. Spending lazy days surfing and fishing may be fine for the rich; her kind usually ended up cleaning luxury hotel rooms or if lucky, hawking rental cars and timeshares to the tourists. Professional high paying jobs went to the *haoles*, white MBA types in suits shipped in from the mainland.

Fresh out of high school and determined to not end up with two *keikis* by age twenty (or pregnant with a third), Kiana tapped her extensive *ohana* connections and found a family living in Santa Maria related to her mother's cousin's wife's brother's auntie who helped Kiana establish California residency. Living out of their cramped garage (no apartment here), Kiana worked as a cashier at Albertson's by day, studied criminal science by night, and brought discarded groceries and produce home for her relatives. Any remaining cash from her job after paying for rent and necessities, she saved.

The day after her twenty-first birthday, she borrowed her auntie's junker and for two weeks, road tripped a circle from Santa Barbara to Santa Cruz and back, stopping along the way in every small-town law enforcement office. One month later, after returning home to Molokai for one last visit, Kiana flew a final ticket into LAX wearing shorts, T-shirt and flip-flops, her two surfboards replacing checked luggage. Folded into a side pocket of her pack lay an official document directing her to Allan Hancock College Police Academy, Santa Maria, CA; registration commencing in seven days. Another notice declared a 'commitment to hire' from the Serrano Police Department upon academic completion, plus full reimbursement of her training expenses after two years of employment.

Tenacious and disciplined, Kiana shaped a life for herself in Serrano and lived by Hawaii's state motto, "*Ua Mau Ke Ea O Ka Aina I Ka Pono,*" ("The Life of the Land is Perpetuated in Righteousness.") She would always yearn for Molokai, but California was her *pono* now, her land. Her *mana*, her power, her integrity was tied to the Pacific Ocean, a cooler version in Serrano but still her native waters. She was at peace. She was happy. She was grateful.

Eight other adults attended Master Lee's classes regularly, including two goofy Cal-Poly students. They drove in twice a week combining martial arts with surfing, always bringing their boards, just in case. On the rare evening when the stars lined up with Jupiter, moon waxing, southwest swells rolling, *and* Mango and Kiana were both off duty; the two cops joined the two undergrads. The kids, tickled to be surfing with law enforcement, ribbed Kiana and Mango unmercifully.

"Duuuude. Want me to swim back to the beach and get some muh, muh, mari-wah—uhhh, mac-nuts from the car?"

"Wait a minute dude, I can't find my car!"

"Yo! Who ya' gonna call? Cop busters!"

Such was the nature of Serrano.

CHAPTER 3

TWENTY-ONE FEET DON'T FAIL ME NOW

Well equipped to guide Serrano's police force, Mango settled soundly into small vacation-town life, overseeing his officers who dealt with the usual run of traffic accidents, DUI's, disorderly conduct, larcenies, vandalism, and the occasional burglary. By the start of Jack's second year he had completely restructured the department, (as much as a fifteen person force could be) as well as open communications to liaise and coordinate State, SLO County and Morro Bay police operations. Extra blue was always needed to help with crowd control and emergency events. With only two to three officers plus a commander on duty during any eight hour shift, (and that's if no one was sick, in training or on vacation), it was imperative to anticipate additional staffing needs.

As the first of many major changes, Detective Kiana de la Cruz was promoted to detective and six months later bumped to lieutenant, making her the 'go to' officer. Highly respected, she possessed that sixth sense which made a good cop exceptional. Kiana's promotions were well received. Everyone knew she deserved them and no one complained, whined, or filed a grievance about her advancement. It not only boosted the entire staff's morale but kept a solid, valuable employee on team.

To further strengthen the chain of command, Mango also promoted Officer Jorge Pacheco to Operations Sergeant, much like a platoon sergeant in the army. His attitude and professionalism set a positive example for the younger officers, and his family values and local boy status enhanced Jorge's mentoring significance.

When Mango took charge, the Serrano police department had been stuck in a time warp. The departing Chief Williams was a nice enough guy, but leaned toward keeping a low profile and a *laissez faire* management style (more like *don't make waves*) of policing. Milking a second retirement, he hadn't been inclined to innovate or put much effort into training, leadership or progressive policing concepts. For ten years, the town had remained a quaint, seaside village of mainly second homes, but its population had doubled, excluding the exponential growth in visitors. During Mango's first Fourth of July weekend as Chief, an estimated influx of twenty thousand visitors celebrated the famous beachside fireworks, filling business coffers but creating a logistical headache for the small force.

The world had changed, and law enforcement needed to be at the forefront of technology and training. Serrano was a high traffic destination during summer months and through early autumn, hosting tourists from around the world, some bringing their problems with them. During busy season, officers responded to a smattering of drug and alcohol issues, moving traffic violations, and the rare felony. During the remainder of the year, Mango's officers rode around fighting crimes of complacency and monotony.

A squat, windowless cinderblock building situated on Main Street, closer to Serrano's sewer plant than downtown, housed police headquarters and three holding cells. Functional, it was as appealing as the town's public bathrooms near the pier, and only slightly cleaner. Both were designed and built in the early 1930s, apparently by the same architect who could not differentiate between a cop shop and an outhouse. Funded by the Public Works Administration (PWA), a New Deal agency which administered building programs during the Great Depression, neither building had been upgraded much since their construction.

Chief Mango's first priority was to spend money on his staff, turning a defunct storage area into a small athletic room with lockers, free weights, a couple benches and a treadmill. He also remodeled the briefing room and kitchen, buying two new coffee makers, microwave, refrigerator, a large conference table, and comfortable armless chairs so officers could sit without their guns and service belts mashing into their sides and backs. Full spectrum lighting replaced decades old fluorescents, and air purifiers and filters were installed into the outdated ventilation system. Many a new police chief would immediately remodel their offices, never a smart move to win support or increase morale. The entire town council, except for the Honorable Mayor Percy Hathaway quickly endorsed the funds and supported the changes.

Briefings were conducted daily, and Mango's admin assistant and part time dispatcher, Dora, organized a real-time call log electronically distributed to all personnel with twelve hour updates. Training became mandatory, (met with much groaning and grumbling initially), but Mango made sure the drills were relevant and fun, filling more than just minimal state requirements.

"Listen up! Everyone have their guns secured in a lock box? Double check your holsters and make sure your gun is *plastic***.** I've had a really good day and don't need to end it with someone getting shot. Plus, I would hate to see Lt. de la Cruz writing reports all night and conducting interviews," Chief Mango half-kidded to the group.

Kiana shot back, "Thanks, Chief."

"No problem, Lieutenant. You earned ***it***."

"What is ***it***, I earned, sir?"

"***It*** is only half a word, Lieutenant."

"Great, Chief. I think I can smell the ***it*** coming."

"***It*** happens!" Mango yelled.

"Stop it with the one-liners, already," complained Officer Skibitski, rolling his eyes.

"Humor is an essential part of the job, Patrolman. As long as ***it's*** not pointed at me," teased Mango, motioning the officers to follow him outside into the parking lot.

Once outside, Mango continued. "Gather round. Tonight we work on nighttime car stops. This includes the officer's approach, demeanor, conflict avoidance, and controlling the situation."

Kiana moved a 'civilian' car into place, and then she parked a marked unit into proper position to simulate a vehicle stop.

"You always maintain control of the stop and you attempt to do it verbally while using an authoritative approach," Mango instructed. "You *always* ask *only* to see driver's license, registration and proof of insurance. If people try to discuss why you stopped them, you keep repeating your three requests. This helps to prevent a pissing match with the driver and keeps you in control of the stop." Mango started the scenario.

"What if they keep refusing?" queried Skibitski

"You repeat at least three times with major emphasis on the third. If they refuse, you take it up a notch."

Mango continued, "Sir, I have asked you three times for proper identification. We will not discuss anything else until that occurs. The choice is yours, but nothing will be discussed until you comply with my request. Now, please give me your . . . "

Each officer enacted the scenario, with Mango and Kiana switching turns as they played compliant, but most of the time acting like assholes. Afterwards, they practiced nighttime felony car stops; clearing two people out of a vehicle and using a backup officer.

During one scenario, Patrolman Baker asked about the proper response if a passenger or driver gets out of the vehicle with an edged weapon, not a gun. "What do we do, Chief? Especially if it's not a gun, but a knife? I mean a knife can kill you just as dead as a gun."

"Yes, a knife can kill you." Mango agreed. "An excellent question and I have a particular training exercise specifically for that. I've watched a training video from guards who taped inmates in a prison yard. One inmate would run toward a standing inmate from a short distance away. The stationary inmate pretended to pull a holstered gun, while the rushing man tried to stab him with an imaginary knife. The prisoners were training, calculating the maximum distance before a cop could react and shoot a knife-wielding assailant. For the *unprepared*, the distance turned out to be twenty-one feet."

"Twenty-one feet! That's a hell of a long way, Chief. Are you sure?" questioned an astonished Skibitski.

"Well, *grasshoppa'*, that's what we're going to find out," sagely replied Mango. "Most people don't realize one or two seconds is a long time. In a life-threatening situation, blood rushes away from your small blood vessels, slows your reaction time down and tightens you up. Some people freeze, unable to move. Vision will tunnel and sphincters pucker."

"However," he continued, "The guy with the knife will usually win within twenty-one feet. You will not be able to clear leather and hit target unless you practice. Think of Billy the Kid, depicted in those old-time movies practicing his draw, over, and over, and over. Only practice will reduce your on-target effectiveness to fifteen feet. When the bad guy is still six feet away you might have time for two shots— if you're really fast. And lucky."

"Now line up in pairs about twenty feet away and make like those inmates!" Mango commanded. "And, don't forget to alternate the good cop, bad guy roles."

Mango and Lt. de la Cruz stood off to the side, observing the action and making suggestions for improvement.

"They seem to enjoy this exercise, Chief. This is real! You'd never think someone that far away could kill you." Shaking her head, Kiana added, "I'll go home tonight and reevaluate every tetchy situation I've been in which could have turned bad. Not that I've been in many, but you do remember every single one, with that pucker factor creating such clarity of memory."

"Especially in this town, we need to remember to stay on guard," Mango agreed. "We rock and roll only a few times a year so it's too easy to become relaxed."

"The serenity of living here, ya' know?" Kiana joshed.

"Ever told you I've been shot?"

"Never told me," Kiana responded, "But I read about it."

"Hurts like a mother! Don't let anyone tell you different; it's the ultimate anti-orgasm. Been stabbed once, too. Actually, cut more than stabbed."

"That how you got the scar on your face?" Kiana asked.

"Nah. That was something stupid I did as a teenager," Mango grinned. "Let's keep that our little secret. Don't want to disillusion the troops about my dangerous aura."

He continued, "On a domestic I got wedged in a bathroom doorway with a wacked out meth-head. Stupid situation to get myself into. Came up under my vest with her boyfriend's hunting knife like she's gonna cut her way dead-on through me. Thought I was having open heart surgery right then and there. Baker's right; both weapons can kill you. It's why I'm so big on training and practice. This isn't a video game we're playing."

Mango clapped hands twice, "Alright! Let's wrap it up. Good practice tonight! Go back in and collect your weapons and I'll see you all on your regular duty rotations this week. Situational awareness out there!"

Mango required his officers act professionally, and to achieve this objective he treated them as such. This created a confident, efficient, and dedicated officer, resulting in fewer mistakes and many less headaches for him. He applied his mantra, "practice, practice, practice," to policing, a phrase Mango stole from his New Mexico Tae Kwon Do master. Practice was the journey to perfection, and perfection a mastering of skill.

As Mango and Kiana followed the men inside the station, lights striped across the training cars, and a large metallic colored SUV pulled into the fenced parking lot and stopped, engine and lights killed. Mango looked over and admired the set of legs preceding the rest of Randi Shirazi as she dropped to the ground from her champagne gold Land Rover.

"Kiana, go on in and check with Sergeant Pacheco and the other officers, to see what dates will work to schedule a field sobriety testing class in a few weeks. I'll be there in a minute."

"Right, boss."

Mango walked to where Randi stood by her Rover. "What brings you here this late?"

"Just getting back from LA. Had to pick up some stones from Emil's brothers. They are such pigs! I have no idea how Emil turned out to be such a nice guy while his brothers would murder their own mother if it would turn a profit."

"Pretty harsh. What did they do?"

"I don't want to talk about it right now. Not here."

"Do you need to talk about it?"

"I don't know what I need, Mango, except a couple stiff drinks and a shower. Preferably in that order."

"So go home and unwind."

"I don't want to go home. The last thing I need is to sit at the house and drink alone. Can you meet me at Dickies?"

"Sure. Mom and Jessica are probably sound asleep by now. They don't usually wait up for me on training nights."

"Thanks. I might even pay! See you there in a half hour. I need to run home and at least change clothes."

CHAPTER 4

AN APPLE AN EVENING

Taking the opportunity at the station to also change clothes, Jack walked into Dickies a few minutes after 10:30 p.m. dressed in jeans, sandals and a white *Surf Serrano* logo sweatshirt. He made sure his .380 was concealed and securely locked in the gun safe hidden inside his police unit, a specially equipped forest green Jeep Wrangler 4-Door Sport Unlimited hardtop.

Jack wasn't by nature a drinker, but appreciated the occasional alcohol buzz and guilt of the morning after. "Sometimes a guy just needs to hurt himself," he grinned, thinking he was supposed to meet Randi to talk about her problem, but just maybe he needed to talk to someone about *his* problems. Jack noticed the dining area mostly empty, the bar still active with a few locals and tourists swapping lies. Three young techies from probably the bay area, stood under the flat screen, "*oohing*" and "*ahhing*" at March Madness basketball antics.

At the opposite end of the bar, Hizzoner Percy Hathaway was involved in an animated discussion with Lee and Roscoe. To their right was an office access, a store room area and 'The DP'. This was the historical cave in which the elite of Serrano sealed deals and shaped the history of their town's livelihood since its founding. The unofficial meeting room for the City Council, Serrano Port Authority, and local Kiwanis was now Serrano Police Chief Mango's lunch room and satellite office. The uninitiated assumed DP meant Department of Police. Those in-the-know were aware that DP stood for "the room at Dickies Place," and the drab police station just that, the station.

The proprietors and mayor took note of Mango. Seeing him out on a weeknight this late in non-investigative mode was a rarity.

"Hey, Mango! Come on over. Belly up! We were just talkin' 'bout you," a somewhat intoxicated Hathaway called more loudly than needed. "All good, too, for a change," he guffawed, waving the ever present glass of single malt in his right hand. "Buy you a drink?"

Definitely pushing his early seventies, Hathaway, none the less, sported a full head of slicked-back jet-black hair and matching eyebrows. A thick herringbone gold rope dripped from his neck and a Cellini Dual Time Rolex, (to keep track of when those Japanese info-mercials aired), accented the massive gold rings bedazzling each hand. His liberally applied cologne was clouding the large mirror lining the wall behind the bar.

"Hold those good thoughts Mayor. Back in a sec," Mango answered while studying the reflected images of those seated bar-side.

Smiling at Hathaway and growling to himself, "Shit, the last thing I want is to sit here and talk shop with that prick. Maybe this wasn't such a good idea, but I'm over forty and definitely allowed out past dark." Mango hung a hard left toward the restrooms halfway between bar and dining room, making time to consider staying or leaving.

Walking back into the tavern after his 'duty call', Mango watched Randi walk through the front door. Dressed in tight, faded jeans and equally snug grey V-neck cashmere sweater, she winced and hesitated a step after spotting Hathaway sprawled on a barstool.

Mango quickly glided over to Randi. "I wasn't sure I was going to stay, but seeing you arrive to rescue me, I've changed my mind," Mango murmured.

"One condition, though," she countered, her emerald green eyes high-lighting a cat-like appearance. Mango admired how her flaming red hair and dash of freckles trailing into cleavage enhanced her exotic appearance.

"Condition?" Mango, standing too close, inhaled Randi's recently applied perfume, a welcome counterpoint to the mayor's aroma.

"Let's go sit in a far booth so we don't have to subject ourselves to that idiot," she countered, nodding her head subtly toward the bar.

"Good plan. Grab a seat and I'll get us a drink."

"A bottle of chilled Sobieski vodka and bowl of olives are good enough for me. What are you drinking?" she asked giving Mango a wary eye.

"Ah-ha. A connoisseur. If you don't mind, I'll share your choice. I've never tried that brand."

Back at the bar Mango acknowledged Hathaway, "Sorry Mayor, but I'm going to pass on your offer."

"Well, don't that beat all? But I agree I'd 'a done the same given the circumstances. Agreed, Lee?"

"As a good bar-keep, I observe but make no comments about my patrons. Besides, wouldn't want to ruin my reputation as a devoted husband," Mr. Lee rejoined, winking at his partner, Roscoe Rae.

"Your loss, Chief. We cudda solved most of the world's prol-lems tonight, but I'm at the point where my communive skills are slowin' drown," slurred Hathaway. He stood a little unsteadily but made an effort to stand straight and act sober. He was after all, the mayor.

"No problem, Sir. Want me to call a unit and have them run you home?"

"Nahhhhh. I'm fine. 'Sides, I'm good friends with the Police Chief," he bragged, listing slightly to the left as he walked, gait straightening five steps from the front door.

"Good friends with the Chief, hmmm?" mocked Mr. Lee. He glanced at Mango as Hathaway shoved the door open. "It's what I love about the bar business. I learn something new every day."

"I should have the SOB arrested for DUI, but that would break a promise I made to myself a half hour ago."

"What promise?"

"That I wouldn't get involved in, or talk work if I came here tonight."

Mr. Lee said, "Sounds like a promise you shouldn't break. Go back and sit with Randi. I'll bring your order in a minute."

"Didn't order anything yet."

"No need. I know what she wants, alcohol wise at least, and knowing you, you'll be polite and drink the same."

Mango walked back over to Randi, the booth closest to the dining room entrance which was still within sight of the bar area. Softly lit lanterns accented the dark walnut walls and comfy black leather cushioned seats.

"Think we'll start a rumor?" Mango asked nervously as he slid into the booth opposite Randi.

"Not at Dickies. If we were drinking together in SLO or Pismo, the rumor drums would be deafening."

Mango and Randi both chuckled. Their paths had crossed numerous times at the SLO county courthouse where they opportunely lunched together, schedules permitting. Situated in downtown San Luis Obispo, the courthouse was a stroll away from Higuera Street and San Luis Obispo Creek, a restful leafy setting, and home to countless culinary marvels, some of the best in central California. The location offered them a welcome hour's respite from the more unsavory aspects of their court ordered responsibilities.

As the arresting and senior officer during Billy Morton's sexual assault case, Chief Mango spent hours testifying as well as heel cooling. Randy Shirazi, the CASA (Court Appointed Special Advocate) volunteer for Billy's adopted daughter, Clare Brandon, followed the case. Randi ensured that victims of child abuse did not get lost in the shuffle, making sure Clare received help as well as acting to coordinate the diverse agencies involved with her care.

Mango and Randi maintained a professional yet friendly rapport during their lunches, appropriate to the matters in which they were linked. Their discussions rarely touched upon much detail regarding their personal lives beyond Jessica's teenage angst, widow and widower status, and the banalities of local politics; their banter occasionally infused with a mere hint of innocent flirtation. Both dressed for the job, Mango smartly outfitted in his infrequently worn uniform; Randi impeccably attired in subdued silk skirt suits and moderate heels. Mango, ever aware of his surroundings, noticed their fellow diners glancing surreptitiously and enviously at them as if wishing their own lunch mates displayed such panache.

Except for group martial arts class, neither Randi nor Mango had made any extra effort to socialize together in Serrano until tonight.

"Now that I've convinced you we aren't inciting a scandal, I'm off to the ladies room to do something about my puffy eyes," Randi said without humor.

Mr. Lee saw Randi get up from the table and hurriedly shuffled over to Jack, "What's going on?"

"Don't know. May be work related, actually," Jack considered. "She showed up at the station parking lot. Said something about Emil's brothers in LA, and obviously upset."

Lee gave Jack a "we'll see what we see," look, and walked back to the bar, smiling in encouragement at Randi when she returned to Mango's booth.

She sat down but remained silent for a moment. Mango couldn't help but notice her breasts rise and fall under the grey sweater as she sighed deeply. Randi concentrated, squeezing her hands together as if she was prepping to break boards in class.

Mr. Lee rematerialized, balancing a tray holding four neat chilled vodka shots and a bowl of locally grown olives. He placed each item deftly atop the scarred wood and said, "Enjoy you two. If you need anything else . . . " He walked off, eternally the discrete barman.

Throwing a generous mouthful and allowing the vodka to massage her throat, Randi exhaled very slowly, enjoying the smooth burn, the warmth oozing down into her chest and belly. Setting the glass down but keeping both hands on her drink, she looked across the table at Mango, her head down, brows scrunched together.

"What I'm about to tell you, no one else in town, or central California knows. Scout's honor, Mango, you can't breathe a word of this."

"You know I can't promise that from a legal and police perspective, but from a personal standpoint you have my word. If there's something big that you're into and it's illegal, you'd best not tell me. If this is a good 'cry on my shoulder' session, I'll support you as much as I can," he answered, leaning his body back and away from Randi, not wanting to give the appearance of pressing her. Waiting, Mango allowed her to relax and take another deep breath.

"Shit. Okay, here goes," started Randi, blowing out a puff of air. "I was a hooker in LA for a few years. That's how I met Emil. More towards the end of my 'career' as a top shelf escort, the Vueve Clicquot of pleasure. If Neiman Marcus could have legally sold my services in their Christmas Fantasy Catalog, they would have."

Randi stopped. "You still with me?"

"Go on."

"Whether a weekend in Paris with an entrepreneur, or a night with a tycoon at the L'Ermitage Beverly Hills, I averaged five thousand a week excluding tips and gifts. I got lucky, although skill, brains, and beauty did play a part. Not bad for poor white trash from Flour Bluff, Texas."

"Continue."

"Emil was my first Paris trip and my first time overseas. He took me with him during a jewelers' conference attended by most of the heavy hitters from Belgium along with a shitload of Saudis. Heady stuff; the City of Love, River Seine, Eiffel Tower . . . all I had to do was act like the Madonna in public and fuck like the harlot I was. I didn't do the saintly part well, but the Whore of Babylon would have been proud," Randi snorted, raised her glass in salute and downed her second shot.

"You sure you want to continue?"

"Be quiet, Jack. Don't you know anything about women?"

He sipped at his first drink judiciously and nibbled an olive. Looking down, he scrolled his index finger along the tabletop making crop circles. "Honestly? No. I've only had one love. Never had a chance to date anyone else besides my childhood sweetheart. Kind of a clichéd cliché."

"That is so amusing, you only having one love."

"Why's that so funny?"

"Because it's one more than I ever had, and both of us such experts in our fields. Now, that is just snot-slinging hilarious."

Mango remained quiet. Randi stared into her empty glass. Mr. Lee, attuned to his customers, breezed past their table, plopped down two more shots and disappeared.

"Emil initially managed the California connection of his family's import-export business based out of Turkey. Many of his relatives remained in the Middle East choosing to settle there after the Shah's fall. I became his addiction; well, that and making jewelry. When Emil's work visa neared expiration, I entered into an arranged business marriage with him allowing him to not only stay in the country, but to also own his private version of Scheherazade. He paid me $25,000 for the marriage. I expected a typical quickie divorce after immigration law requirements were met, but we surprisingly discovered our marriage was a good fit."

"Nothing wrong with that. Surely there must have been a little love there somewhere?"

Ignoring the question, Randi continued. "Emil eventually helped his two older twin brothers, Mikhail and Hafid, to immigrate here permanently. The three started their own business in LA specializing in rare gems, stones and gold jewelry. Emil was the creative one with the twins procuring the raw product. I've told you during our lunches about Emil's technique to heat and polish stones which lightened, darkened or completely change their color, as well his mastery in gem cutting. Affluent customers, especially the entertainment crowd clamored for his unique creations."

"So what was, or is the problem?"

"Emil's brothers are assholes. *Mikhail* means 'Allah's angel' and *Hafid* means the 'wise one.' What a load. The angel is vile and the wise one is still trying to find his brain like the *Wizard of Oz's* scarecrow. They bullied Emil horribly, stealing much of the profits from their partnership."

"Did either one hurt you tonight?"

"Shhhhsh. Let me finish the story. It does have a happy ending. Sort of. At least for a while. Emil became a home-body, content in our marriage, while his brothers traveled, trading and probably smuggling stones between Asia Minor and the U.S. After ten years of servitude, Emil tried to convince his brothers to quit their international deals and buy into real estate here in Serrano. They refused, so Emil and I left and did it alone."

"How?"

"With the money Emil stashed from his share of the LA jewelry business. We opened the Serrano store, Shirazi Jewels, and expanded our trade through the internet while selling custom trinkets to wealthy tourists. We invested the profits from the store into real estate and I now own six properties in Serrano, some of them oceanfront. The vacation renters cover what mortgages are still outstanding, and then some."

"Sounds like a good plan, so far," Mango observed.

"Emil wanted to go straight, so I took accounting classes and made sure the properties were purchased with legitimate funds and not traceable to the twins. And, how shall I say, their dealings?"

"What do you mean, straight and legit? You're scaring me here, Randi."

"Don't get your boxers in a wad, Chief," Randi teased, obviously catching a high from her quick drinks. "This is something in which Interpol would have to be involved. Wouldn't you rather teach Jessica how to surf than get tangled up in global intrigue and gem smuggling?"

"Good point, but keep this story completely out of my jurisdiction. Preferably California."

"We assumed some of the rough stones the twins supplied were either stolen or smuggled, but there was no way to determine which ones. They always provided us with authentic, at least valid looking, receipts and invoices for the stones they forced us to buy from them. The mark up of the finished jewelry was unbelievable, a thousand percent in some cases, but the brothers still fleeced Emil out of a lot of money by skimming the LA profits and inflating their gemstone expenses.

"So Emil turned the questionable stones into polished jewelry making the gems virtually untraceable," Mango reflected, while smoothing his goatee.

"Exactly. Then Emil died in that stupid accident and the evil twins' platinum laying goose vanished."

"I heard his body was never found."

"When he didn't arrive home Sunday night from an Independent Jewelers' Expo in San Fran, I called and reported him missing. Serrano Police transferred me to county and state, but they didn't start seriously looking for him until Monday evening. When nothing came up on accident reports matching his silver Miata convertible, I was told not to worry my pretty little head, since he was probably being a naughty husband and would turn up drunk and debauched. I tried to tell Chief Williams he wasn't like that, but he wouldn't listen!"

"I would have taken you seriously, Randi."

"I know," she replied, reaching over to squeeze his hand.

"From what I understand, his vehicle was found along Big Sur at the bottom of a cliff."

"Only after I insisted they search the PCH. Highway One from Carmel to San Simeon, and only after a tourist reported seeing what they thought was the backend of a car sticking out of the water, half submerged on some rocks. God only knows why Emil decided to go that way. We normally took that route together, since it's so dangerous and curvy." Randi shrugged. "He called me from Salinas and said he was on his way home. Who knows? Maybe he got tired of traffic and took the cutoff on Highway 68 to the coast. It's the last one before you reach Paso. Maybe he just wanted to enjoy the sunset. Either way, that's the last time I talked with him."

"So, you were able to, ahh, identify any remaining, ahh, remains?" Jack tried to tactfully ask.

"Once they recovered the Miata, his wallet, driver's license and cell phone were found in the console."

"That's it?"

"When they sawed the crushed little trunk open, his weekender packed with clothing and his travel cases with cloth rolled pouches full of his jewelry samples and gems were intact, along with a plastic baggie of cash, credit card receipts and design orders."

"I was asking more along the lines of biological residue," Jack delicately inquired, "Which could be tested?

"There was no trace of Emil except blood on the leather steering wheel cover and splotches throughout the interior and along the rim of the crumpled windshield frame. They surmised the top was down and he wasn't wearing his seatbelt, so after the first midair roll he banged around in the car and was ejected. I always yelled at him for not wearing his safety strap," Randi ruefully added.

"Was the M.E. able to match his blood type or DNA?"

"I was told they could confirm it was blood but not if it was his, and that saltwater can prevent positive testing sometimes; especially since seven days had elapsed from the time his car was pulled, from when it *allegedly* crashed into the sea. I've been in limbo ever since."

"How's that?"

"We were beneficiaries and executors of our respective wills, so the court appointed me as administrator of his assets until he or his body parts turn up. A missing person in California can be declared dead only after five years have passed, and I've got two more to go. I keep expecting to find him on my doorstep one morning, saying he'd been bonked in the head so hard he'd had amnesia. But," Randi made a moue, "That only happens in movies."

"I'm assuming hospitals were contacted, missing persons reports filed, the coast guard kept an eye out, etcetera?"

"Sure. I personally took out ads in the newspapers, posted on the internet, and drove up and down the coast looking for him practically every other day for a year. Nothing. It seems like he's been gone ten years, not three, what with his relatives breathing down my neck. They still blame me."

"How can they? Sounds like he did a Roberto."

"A what?"

"Robert Clemente. Any good Yinzer worthy of the name knows of the Pittsburgh Pirate, the greatest ballplayer ever, who died in a plane crash off San Juan International Airport's runway. Happened back in 1972, New Year's Eve, when he was ferrying supplies to earthquake survivors in Nicaragua. They never found his body. Now that I think about it, there were serious concerns about the air-worthiness of the plane."

"His relatives made sure the cops grilled me for weeks, insinuating I either tampered with the car or somehow caused the crash. I was also investigated on how much and when any life insurance had been purchased and if I was the beneficiary," Randi fumed.

"That is standard procedure."

"Not the way his two brothers kept egging them on! The police also questioned me extensively about whether Emil would have faked his own death or committed suicide."

"What do you think?"

"Emil and I had a comfortable life. We were happy and he definitely was not depressed. Besides, he'd have never walked away from his jewelry kit, much less his life's work."

"So what happened tonight to make you so upset?"

"Order some more vodka and I'll tell you. Better yet, I've lots more at my house. I run a tab with Lee, so we can just go. By the way, what's a Yinzer?"

"It's a Pittsburgh thing. It's equivalent to the Texan 'ya'll,' except we say 'you-in's,' ergo, 'yinz.' As in *yinz* ready *ta* leave, yet?"

Dickie's was empty when Jack and Randi headed for the door. Mr. Lee threw Jack a questioning look with one arched eyebrow.

"Goodnight Mr. Lee," Jack called, waving away Lee's concern. "Just taking a lady friend home who imbibed a tad too much of your fine spirits."

Mr. Lee's facial expression didn't change. "Choices, Jack," Lee rejoined, "Life is about choices, my friend."

Randi's cats were waiting patiently in the grand foyer, sitting on the bottom step of a sweeping curved set of stairs to their left, as Jack and Randi walked into her home. Zeba, an orange/black tiger striped male with white paws, eyes matching Randi's, stretched languidly, and then hopped to the floor to figure eight between Randi's legs. Zulu, an orange-eyed white female with randomly odd patched Dreamsicle swirls along her flanks, ogled Jack suspiciously and remained aloofly seated at attention, tail wrapped around toes.

"And who do we have here? Jack queried playfully, as he closed the door and shot the deadbolt.

"Zeba and Zulu, my two rescue cats. Someone dumped them at the Highway One underpass near Serrano Bridge. Found them during my evening jog about three years ago and took them home, got them fixed when old enough, shots, the works. Poor kittens weren't much older than two months and starving. The vet thinks they're brother and sister, too. Makes my blood boil and want to hurt people who'd do such a thing.

"Lucky cats, and you're a kind-hearted woman."

"A lot you know," she joked back. "I had an ulterior motive. Emil and I never had kids. His family definitely doesn't deem me kin and I don't consider any remaining birth relatives alive. The cats are my family, now that he's gone. Kind of sad, actually."

"I don't think you're sad. I think you're beautiful."

In response, Randi grasped Jack's hand and pulled him into the den to their right. Trailing behind her, he noted the long wide foyer was designed to lead one's eyes past the two doors on the left wall. On the wall were hung three huge abstract paintings, pulling one into an immaculate open concept cook's kitchen with an impressive glass slider; a straight shot from the front door opening to what he assumed was the backyard. An arch in the wall at the far end of the den led back to the kitchen, completing a well-planned entertainment circle. Randi sank down next to him into a butter soft Italian leather sectional and regarded him, eyes searching, apprehensive yet expectant.

"So, you wanted to talk about—"

"Why are you here, Jack?" Randi interrupted.

"You invited me."

"No. Why are *you* here with *me*?

"You seemed upset tonight," Jack replied. "And lonely. "I've been lonely, too, ever since Nancy died. It's been almost five years . . . "

"Kind of had that figured. But why me?"

Taking a moment, Jack proceeded. "You're a safe bet. We've come to know each other from our work and Mr. Lee's class, and I know you're probably not going to run around town blabbing our private business. Besides, I know your secret now."

"Ohhhh. So, now I'm business and you're going to blackmail me for sex?"

"God." Jack closed his eyes, put his hand to his forehead and squeezed. "That's not what I meant. That didn't come out right," he stammered. "Guess that wasn't a very romantic thing to say, huh? I think I just blew it and should be going," Jack glumly finished, rising from the couch.

"That's it?" Randi shook her head. "My, you are an idiot when it comes to women. Sit down and let me tell you another secret. I liked your answer because you're safe too. Ditto. I'm not supposed to be a widow at this age. In this town, finding a man with scruples while keeping my reputation intact, (which I've worked too hard to build) is near impossible. Let's just say I don't get much action these days, either."

Zulu jumped atop the couch back, startling Jack backwards into the cushions. She perched there making little *mrrphh* sounds, rubbing against his shoulder.

"Cat scared the shit outta me!"

"Thought you have cats on the ranch?"

"They're Jessica's. Kiana gave them to her and she takes care of them. I don't have time to give 'em much attention besides throwing crunchys at them. Nancy was allergic, so I've never been around cats until now."

"Oh, ho. So the perfect wife had a flaw?"

Jack's head snapped back and he reared up to full sitting height as if slapped, yelling, "Don't you dare—"

Randi immediately slid to the floor at his feet, arms wrapped around his calves, head bowed onto Jack's knees shouting, "*Mi dispiace, Mi dispiace*! Forgive me!"

Shocked by the unexpected action and language, he stopped in mid-tirade, blinking at Randi in confusion. "I didn't know you spoke Italian."

Randi unwound one hand from Jack's legs and said, "*Piccolo*," holding up her thumb and finger half an inch apart. She looked up imploringly, "To quote you, 'I think I just blew it.' Can we start over? I never meant to dishonor your wife's memory."

"Please get up, Randi," Jack answered sheepishly, reaching out and pulling her back on the couch. "Guess I'm still a little raw when it comes to Nancy. I think tonight we're both allowed a do-over."

Settled back into leather, Randi exhaled a sigh and eyed Jack speculatively. "I do have a stipulation."

"Ground rules?"

"More like titties for tat."

"What?"

"If you expect to see my tits, you have to give me tat. I've told you my secret, more than one essentially, so now you have to tell me a secret about you."

"Okaaaaay," countered Jack, thinking. Finally settling on, "I haven't been with anyone else."

"You already told me that, and that's no secret."

"No, I mean I've never been with any woman except for Nancy."

Mouth open, Randi stared at Jack.

"Cat got your tongue?" chided Jack, glancing briefly to where both cats now sat observing them from the far end of the couch.

"I'm, I'm," she stuttered. "Never? Not even before you married?"

"Nope."

"I've never met a man like you, Jack. Someone so principled."

"Don't give me a halo just yet. I have, to cite a famous president, "lusted in my heart" many times while I was married," he laughed, "And before."

"Why not do anything before?"

"I dated Nancy through high school, and when I was in the army, even though we weren't officially engaged, we were promised. Believe me, I thought about it. I wasn't into the one night stands, though. Looking back, I probably could have taken advantage of a few situations if I had known how. I was a gangly, skinny country kid from the Pennsylvania Appalachians. What did I know?"

Randi scooted closer to Jack, nestling up under an arm. "And after you married, you were the faithful husband."

"After I married, all other women became forbidden fruit I could admire but never taste."

"I envy you your commitment."

"Told you I'm not a saint. I did regret not sampling from the produce bin while I had the chance. A lifetime of juicy sweet peaches is nice, but I sometimes craved something different. Cherries maybe . . . "

Randi crawled up and over, straddling her legs around his. Sitting astride, breasts firmly planted against his chest, she wriggled her pelvis deeper into a snugger fit. Jack's arms involuntarily rose, one hand to cup her buttocks even closer, the other to the back of her neck pulling her face toward his.

As their lips met, Randi murmured, "No cherries here, Jack." She dipped her head slightly to the right, found the spot where his collarbone met corded neck muscles and sucked. His head dropped back against the sofa-top, eyes closed, hand tightening on Randi's rump as a reflexive moan escaped his throat.

Randi looked up at Jack, slitted jade eyes glittering. She trailed a line of hot wetness up his neck with her tongue. Stopping to nip his earlobe, she dipped the moist appendage into an ear and breathed, "Tonight, I *can* offer you an apple."

CHAPTER 5

BUSTED WAVE-O'S

Mango clumped heavily through Dickie's back door into the kitchen, calling, "Hey Lee! I know you're not open for breakfast except on weekends—"

"Ahh-ha. Look what Zeba and Zulu dragged in," Lee kidded, stepping away from a prep area, wiping hands dry.

"Huh? What about Randi's cats?" replied a muddled Mango. "I'm late to the station, but I really need something to eat. Can I talk you into some scrambled eggs?"

"To go with your brain?"

"Huh?"

"You are now officially Serrano's latest juicy buzz. In fact, you're the best one in ten years, since the high school prom king and queen got so drunk on chardonnay they ended up naked at the end of Serrano Pier doing the nasty. Half the town lined up for a quarter mile along the beach with binoculars. They had at it for so long, both showed up in Morro Bay's urgent care next morning to get the splinters picked out. Red cheeks and I'm not talking face!" Lee doubled over guffawing.

"Thought you didn't gossip about your regulars?"

Lee, still snorting and gasping, straightened and mopped his tears using the same rag on which he dried his hands.

"Not the same. Story's in the public domain and not a secret, and so long ago nobody cares. Moreover, they're married now. They come in to drink, and we all have a good laugh remembering the story."

"I wasn't outside *or* on the pier."

"No, but you're in that domain now," snapped Lee, waving a spoon at Mango, "A public figure. You have any idea how many people've been trying to get into Randi's panties since Emil died, and I don't mean just men? Everyone in town saw where you parked your police Jeep into the wee hours, and tales be wagging."

"Thought that was tongues," barked back Mango, cranky.

"I guarantee yours was last night."

"Okay," Mango conceded, holding out his hands, palms up. "I deserved that, and yeah, I smacked myself upside the head when I saw my Wrangler parked in the middle of Randi's driveway this morning. Figured it was early enough, no one would notice."

"Such naiveté from such a smart guy."

"Humph. That won't happen again."

"Jeep?"

"Both."

"Oh, really? Don't forget she's *my* friend, too," warned Lee.

Mango exhaled. "Randi's a world-wise woman. Last thing she said after kissing my forehead goodbye and flopping back down dead-asleep was, "don't be a stranger." Not like she jumped up at the crack of dawn making me pancakes, singing words of undying love," Mango grumbled.

"We barely got to sleep by daybreak. I think this was more a mercy fuck for both of us."

Lee waited for Mango to continue, head cocked to the side, arms folded.

"Guess she's leaving it up to me, but I don't know if I can survive another night like that." Mango rubbed both hands down his face. "Our paths do cross on juvie cases, and there's class here with you, so it's not like I'll never see her again. We'll see what develops in the future. Again, I thought you said you don't talk about your paying customers?"

"You're talking. I'm listening. I'm talking to you, not about you. We're not open for business and you're not paying. And, I'm not the one naming names or divulging details."

"I gotta sit down or I'm gonna fall down," Mango griped, moving towards the dining room.

"Yeah, you look like dog shit. You need the hair of."

"I am not hung over. I barely finished my first drink last night and never had anymore. I go on duty in an hour, so no alcohol."

"Go into the bar and sit, Mango. I've got something guaranteed to perk you right up," Lee winked. "Roscoe and I have been working on a new combination slash signature dish and drink. You'll get a virgin version, trust me."

"Don't forget coffee! And eggs! Please?" Jack whined.

Lee snorted. "You look like you've been around world. Twice. And to the moon and back," he chortled. Turning towards the kitchen, Lee hollered, "Roscoe honey! Bring Mango a sample of our new creation: Pearl necklace and two shooters. Also, three eggs scrambled, biscuits, and a pot of coffee."

A moment later, Roscoe sashayed into the bar and deposited in front of Mango a silver plated tray of a half dozen oysters with two full shot glasses nestled in the middle, parsley garnished artfully along the edges. "The rest in a minute, Mango," he explained. Lips quirking, he hurried back into the kitchen where a burst of laughter filtered back at them.

Mr. Lee picked up one of the tumblers lined along the bar face and polished.

Mango glared down at the glistening, gelatinous saltwater and ice pooled array of mollusks and the murky, lumpy bloody contents of each shot glass. "I can't eat this on an empty stomach! This is disgusting!"

Behind the bar, Mr. Lee put the glass quietly down on wood and placed a hand over his heart. "You insult me, Mango," he chided in a gentle voice. "These are locally sourced Morro Bay oysters from the finest purveyors on the central coast, trucked in each morning if available. They've been out of water barely three hours. I hand-pick the finest specimens of the lot for this dish and the ones not meeting my high standards get fried or chowdered.

Mango stared at Mr. Lee. Neither budged.

"We're still tweaking the recipe and trying to come up with a catchy name for an ensemble of menu items along this theme. This is one of many versions. Roscoe and I think it will be a hit if we market correctly. This is what we used to eat after a hard day in the biz, back in the city. A pick-me-up."

"Don't you mean *before* a hard night's work? I thought this stuff was an aphrodisiac?"

"Some people do. Oysters are high in vitamin E and zinc, along with being an incredible source of protein, sodium, potassium, calcium, manganese, phosphorus, iodine, and many other vitamins and trace elements. We found they balance the electrolytes better, *after*.

"You're killing me here, Mr. Lee."

"Plus, we've come up with a secret sauce with a twist.

"What's in it?"

"If I tell you, I'll have to shoot you."

"Lee! Don't ever say that to a cop, much less to one whose been shot."

"Good advice. Though I'll apologize only if you eat," Lee bargained, pointing at Mango's plate. "I promise you'll feel better."

Reluctantly, Mango raised an oyster to his lips and slurped, eyes opening wide in surprise. "Mmmmmm, good. You're right."

Lee resumed polishing glasses, watching as Mango sucked down the contents of each remaining oyster in quick succession.

"I do feel better!"

Lee turned, faced the bar mirror and proceeded to stack the polished beakers in a pyramid. Frank Sinatra's *Strangers in the Night*, in whistled form, wafted into the air between the two.

"Lee."

"Hmmmmm?"

"Put on some music?"

Lee walked from around the bar and pointed at the two, still full, shot glasses with their red, grisly, viscous contents. "Drink."

Standing in front of the vintage looking (but strictly digital) jukebox, Lee contemplated the menu, then pushed two buttons. Annie Lennox's voice belted out the opening lyrics to *I Need a Man*.

"Really?"

Lee danced back toward Mango, arms pumping in time with the thumping, double-bass beat, while Annie wailed she needed a man and where she needed his fingers.

"You would rather I had played Julie Brown's, *I Like Them Big and Stupid*?"

Before Mango could reply, Lee held out one stop-sign hand. "Shush! What's that?" he shouted, cupping the other hand to his ear, a look of surprise playing across his face.

Instantly on high alert, Mango kicked the bar stool out from under him, trigger hand hovering over his gun holster, neck cranking one direction and then the other, knees bent and ready for action.

"I do believe I heard your *huevos* busting." Throwing back his head and laughing gleefully, Lee boogied into the kitchen.

CHAPTER 6

JACK GOES UP THE HILL TWICE

Jack woke early. Again. Sighing, giving up on sleep and fidgety, Jack swung his long legs to the floor, stood and stretched, fingers scrubbing scalp as he padded from bedroom to kitchen. Snagging a plain t-shirt draped over a wooden chair, he pulled it over his head, extra insulation against the chill and a compliment to the loosely draped scrubs hanging low on lean hips.

Shuffling to the kitchen counter and punching the coffeemaker button, he stood backside against the blue tiled worktop surveying his living area, wondering where Pono and Kiawe had hidden his sheepskin slippers this time. Yawning, jaw cracking and still bleary-eyed, Jack spied a slipper wedged underneath his well stuffed recliner, the other he tripped over as he crossed the kitchen to snag his favorite cup, a red New Mexico Zia logo against a yellow background, hanging from its regular hook under the cabinets.

While waiting for coffee, Jack tiptoed to Jessica's bedroom and silently eased her door open a crack. Comforted to observe two upside down, comma curled cats bracketing a golden-haired covered pillow, Jack closed the door softly and retraced his steps.

Miracle brew in hand and trailing the ever-present fleece blanket behind him, Jack shambled outside onto the front covered porch, grimacing as he let the screen door whack loudly behind him. After a quick reassuring scan of the surrounding shaded acreage and driveway, he settled gratefully into his right-sized rocking chair, closed his eyes and sipped, rising steam relaxing his tense facial muscles.

Opening his eyes, Jack noticed the stars had vanished; darkness was fading to light. A faint nicker from the far pasture drew his attention to the horses standing together, Sammy occasionally nuzzling Dakota, tails flicking serenely. Jack gazed longingly at them, then further downslope to a silhouetted barn. A growing glow to the southeast bounced off fog underbelly to cast a ruddy hue over the immediate hills.

"Red sky at morning, sailor's warning," he pondered, lowering his gaze to the two horses still rubbing muzzles.

"You two aren't much interested in ancient mariner poetry, yet seem to have a better love life than I do," Jack murmured, shaking his head and sipping more coffee.

"The department is shaping up, work is slow right now between Easter and Memorial Day, Jessica and Mom are settled into life here, and I keep making up excuses," Jack reflected, kicking legs out straight to stop his measured rocking. "What the hell. It's time," he decided, throwing coffee dregs into the flowerbed below the porch while making to rise.

"Time for what and why are you poisoning my wood roses with good coffee?" Alexa's voice rang behind him. "Who are you talking to?"

"And *bon matin* to you, *Maman*," replied Jack, inflecting the last word to French form. "Still sneaking up on me like a good mother." Amused, he leaned over and kissed Alexa's cheek as she relaxed into her own custom rocker.

Alexa, her eyes clear and intense, clad in long flannel gown, sheepskin booties, and checkered wool robe, her thick hair braided down her back, conjured fleeting images of a vanished world; a simpler time now lost to wars and progress. Refilling Jack's mug and setting the coffeepot between them atop a rough-hewn table, Alexa smiled and raised her own cup in salute, "You still haven't answered my questions."

"I was thinking it's time you and Jess take a holiday up to the city. This could be an early 16th birthday present for her, and I'm sure you could use a break, too. How does San Francisco sightseeing, eating at five star restaurants, and staying a couple nights at a ritzy hotel sound?"

"Sounds wonderful, but what about the shopping?" Alexa objected.

"What shopping?"

"Exactly."

Puzzled, head slanted to one side, Jack looked at Alexa in confusion.

"Tch'tch," Alexa clicked her tongue as only the French can, "Forty-two years old, living with your mother and daughter, and you still don't know all women heading to any big city go shopping? That's a given," finished Alexa, winking at Jack. "We'll go easy on your wallet and only eat at *four* star restaurants."

Jack chuckled, "You drive a hard bargain, *Maman.* Shopping, too. I figured you could leave today since it's a Friday and come back late Sunday afternoon. Jessica's grades are good, and final testing doesn't start for another three weeks at school. I don't think she'll be too disappointed to skip class today, just this once."

"Are you not coming with us? Are you trying to get rid of us?" Alexa's eyes widened in sudden understanding and fear. "Is something bad going to happen in Serrano and you want us gone?"

"No, no. Nothing like that," he replied soothingly. "I just thought you two might like to leave the old homestead for a while and go do some girl bonding without Dad's looming male presence. I know that living in the outback, even here in paradise, can drive anyone a little stir crazy. And it's probably time Jess starts making new positive memories without her mom."

"Don't you lie to me, Jacques Antonio Mango," Alexa warned, lips crinkling with tiny laugh lines, but eyes flashing steely black. "I know you. Out with it," she persisted, shaking a finger in his face. "Something's up. Why are you not coming with us?"

"Nothing's up," answered Jack kindly, folding both his hands over her finger. "I just need a few days of private time for myself."

"Please tell me what's going on," Alexa implored as she pulled her hand away from his, using it to gather folds of robe close against her neck.

Jack exhaled slowly, saying, "I never told you any of this, but I think at this point I owe you the truth."

Alexa listened attentively, absorbed in his story, waiting until Jack finished speaking. "Well! I always wondered . . ."

"About what?"

"When you arrived home from California you were . . . changed, and I don't mean from being in the Army. I could never quite pinpoint the exact word to describe it. Not melancholy; more like wistful with a faraway look in your eyes at times. Now I know why."

Nonplussed, Jack asked Alexa, "You think Nancy noticed?"

"If she did, she never mentioned it and we never discussed it, if that's what you're asking."

Not wanting to pursue that particular dialogue, Mango questioned Alexa, "So what do you think about what I just told you?"

"I think we've both been blessed in love."

Surprised at her answer, he blurted, "How can you say that when both our spouses died young? Papa died in 1977 during the Johnstown Flood in the Alleghany Mountains when was I twelve. Those valley walls were so steep he never had a chance. Then, Nancy dies before we had the option to grow old together. Blessed? I feel like there's a family curse following us!"

"We've both endured tragedy in our lives but it's not a curse. Don't you dare call it that!" Alexa scolded.

"You know the story of how I met your father, Antonello Mango," Alexa smiled indulgently at Jack. "He was a bus boy at a ski resort in the French Alps; so brash, confident, and cocky, with those dark Italian good looks, and ahhh," she sighed, "Such sparkles in his eyes."

"When he followed me back to our home in Nice, my parents, textile fabricators for all the haute couture houses in both France and Italy, did not approve his pursuit of me," Alexa continued. "Thinking he was lured by my heiress status to the family fortune, they forbade our union and threatened to disown me. Much to their chagrin, we ran off together to America, penniless, with only our dreams and our love to sustain us."

Jack eyed his mother incredulously, "And you think that ended well? Alone, a single mother with a young son, trying to make a living as a French teacher at Ligonier High School?"

"I didn't plan on being a widow before I turned thirty but for the short time I was with Antonello, it was worth it. If I had known what the future held I would have made the same choice! You don't feel the same about Nancy and cherish your time together?"

"I've always been angry that dad died so young, and when Nancy died it felt like the universe was conspiring against us. I also felt guilty when you took emergency leave, moving to Los Alamos to help us and never returned to teaching. Now you're retired and living here in Serrano and still taking care of us, just a continuation of our family misfortune."

Alexa leaned her head back, laughing at him fondly, shaking her head. "I'm glad I was able to help you and Jess. And of all the places we visited on our road trips together after your father's death and before you joined the army, New Mexico and here in Serrano, were my favorites. This area reminds me somewhat of the Mediterranean where I grew up. I secretly schemed to move here when I retired but never thought I'd be able to afford it. So here we are in paradise, you, me and Jess. Have our lives turned out so poorly?"

"You know the reason I moved here," Jack apologized. "I did have my own secret and ulterior motive."

"Nonetheless, I think it's a good idea for you to pursue this. It is time. It's been two years since we moved here and almost four since Nancy died."

"So," Jacked chided Alexa, "You're ready to get rid of us and move on with your life?"

"I'm saying it's no longer healthy for you to stay single, and I've been hoping you'd get on with your life. Over the last couple years you've gone out with friends, tried to stay balanced with the martial arts, played both dad and mom to Jessica, and whipped the Serrano force into shape, but there's still a hole in your life."

"What about your life, *Maman*?" Jack inquired earnestly. "And why have you never remarried?"

"My life revolves around my family and always will. But I think at this age in her life, Jess needs (*ahem*), a slightly younger role model than what I can provide. As far as my love life, I've never found anyone to outshine, much less equal Antonello. From what you just told me, even though you can never replace Nancy, you may have a second chance at love. Go pursue that chance, Jacques."

"Should I tell Jessica about my plans?"

"I'd wait until after; see what happens after your first meeting." Alexa advised.

"We're agreed," Jack decided, slapping his knees. "Go make reservations for a hotel down by Fisherman's Wharf. I'll check with Amtrak, and see if I can get you two a superliner bedroom on the Coast Starlight on the 12:30pm out of Paso Robles and a roundtrip back home on Sunday. Travel from Paso to the Wharf by train, even with transferring into the city from Oakland on their dedicated bus, takes less than six hours. Hell, it's four hours to drive it and that's if traffic is moving. You won't need a car in the city; they have the trolleys and BART. You and Jessica should be checked into your hotel tonight with time enough to have a late dinner on the Wharf."

Jack stood up from his rocker, offering a hand to Alexa. "Go tell Jess and get packed. I have a few errands to run, but I'll meet you back here at 10:30 to make the train. After that, I'll be driving up to the King City area, but I may, or may not, come home tonight depending on how things go," Jack grinned sheepishly.

As Alexa bustled into the house, Jack called to her, "Remember to text me. Let me know how the trip is going and when you get checked in. You have any trouble at all, make sure you call me!"

As Jack drove his Jeep down the driveway into town he heard Jessica shrieking with joy, and watched in his rear view mirror as she burst through the front door, both arms waving, "Thanks Dad, see you at 10:30!"

Mango slipped into Dickie's back kitchen entrance and waved at Roscoe. He continued into the dining room to find

Lee taking liquor inventory behind the bar before opening for the lunch crowd rush.

Hearing a footstep, Lee looked up and spied Mango's image before him in the mirror. Turning around, Lee greeted Mango with a smile. "Haven't seen you in class for a couple weeks. Avoiding anyone?"

"Nope. Busy."

"Uhnn-huh. Same with a certain someone else. You attending class tonight?"

"No. I'm heading out of town for a day, maybe more. Got some business near King City. I'm dropping Jess and Alexa in Paso so they can spend the weekend up in San Fran. I was wondering if you or Roscoe can feed the cats, chickens and horses for a day, maybe two?"

"Sure, no prob. You're dressed casually today so I assume your business is personal?"

"Actually, I stopped by because I need your advice, Mr. Lee."

"You know I don't give advice as it usually comes back to bite my ass."

"Well, you *are* the old wise-ass barkeep."

"I am wise and I listen. Old is a matter of perspective, and should Roscoe be worried you're admiring my ass?"

Mango gave him a look "Seriously?"

"Alright, alright. What's this about?"

"It's about a girl."

"At your age I'm hoping you mean a woman."

"If you'll let me finish, it's about a girl I met a long time ago."

"Stop right there, Mango."

"What, you don't want to talk to me?"

"Go on into The DP. I'll be back in minute. Sounds like this may take a while."

A few minutes later Lee pirouetted into The DP, kicked the door closed and deposited a tray on the table in front of where Mango was seated. It was stacked with a coffee pot, two white mugs, matching small plates, a butter tub, and a loaded platter of blueberry scones. "Okay, spill it," said he, flashing a wicked smile and rubbing large knuckled hands together.

"Don't know where to start."

"Beginning?"

"Like I told you earlier, I met a girl—"

"Not a woman?"

"I met a beautiful California rancher's daughter over twenty years ago when I was an MP in the army stationed at Fort Hunter Liggett," Mango huffed.

"Now I'm really confused."

"You keep interrupting. I thought you were the great listener?"

"Sorry." Lee circled his hand twice motioning Mango to continue. "I knew you were in the army, but how did you end up stationed near here and how did you meet this girl?"

"While growing up in the mountains near Ligonier, Pennsylvania I was brainwashed by Beach Boy music and became determined to move to California and learn how to surf. I joined the army after high school so I could use the GI Bill to finance my way through college. I scored so well on the aptitude testing I was deployed as military police and given a choice of three postings. I chose Ft. Hunter Liggett which, as you know, sits in a high mountain valley on the eastern backside of the Big Sur range deep in the Los Padres

National Forest. A couple hours north of Serrano, it seemed the perfect place for a hillbilly boy like me to feel comfortable and be close enough to the Pacific to learn surfing."

"What were the other two postings?" asked Lee.

Mango rolled his eyes, took a bite of scone, a sip of coffee, and continued wryly, "Germany or the Philippines. Don't even say it."

Lee said nothing but looked down, smirked, and shook his head sadly.

"Anyway, at the end of my enlistment a four year long drought broke with a vengeance. While on patrol one torrentially, rainy afternoon a few miles from the center of base, I drove past an old rancher who flagged me down. Back then, most of the open range, even on base, was leased through the National Forest Service to adjacent landowners who ran cattle. One of the rancher's calves was stuck in a mud bog near the road and he needed help. I stopped and we spent two hours pulling the animal free using his truck winch while that dumb cow bawled and fought us the whole time! After coaxing it into the trailer and slamming the door closed we both fell down hooting at the sight of each other, encrusted in great gobs of muck with only our eye whites and shining teeth visible. The rancher's name was Grant Brewster, and in gratitude he invited me to his hacienda for a home cooked meal later that week."

"Brewster name sounds vaguely familiar," Lee mused stroking his chin. "Continue, please."

"Four nights later I arrived at his ranch and was invited into his cavernous, Mission style home and ushered into a rough beamed, though very well appointed, Spanish tiled living room to find the most beautiful California girl I have ever imagined or seen since. She was stoking the embers and adding logs to a walk-in fireplace, dressed in tight faded jeans and button-down white shirt, blonde hair flowing like swirled gold silk, framing a face embracing bluer than Pacific Ocean eyes."

"Love at first sight?" predicted Lee.

"I experienced that with Nancy. This was different; more, shall we say . . . incendiary, to the point where I felt like every time she walked near it that evening, the fireplace flames roared higher. When Grant introduced me to his sixteen year old granddaughter, my throat was so dry I stammered and could barely croak out a "hello." I had never met a 'Kate Brewster' before or felt such a craving for someone. Even at that young age she was an amazing combination of poise, beauty, toughness, and intelligence. I think it was her cobalt eyes that pierced right through to my heart which snagged me, though."

"Now I remember!" exclaimed Lee. "A young blond missy, just as you described, used to stop by here to eat, parking her horse trailer behind the building in the alley. Said she brought her horses down from her Santa Lucia area ranch to ride along the beach when she needed a change of scenery. Could have been her, but it's been a good eight years since I've seen her in town. Interesting. So what about Nancy; weren't you engaged to her?"

"Formally, no. Promised, yes. That niggling detail was in the back of my mind the whole evening. Sparks flew between us and smoldered along with moments of awkward shyness, but we ended up having a relaxing meal after Grant told our story of the calf, the rain, and the mud. Throughout dinner, Kate and I stole blazing glances at each other across the table while trying to be discreet in front of her grandfather. I realized later that Grant Brewster knew exactly what he was doing when he invited me out to his ranch."

"So what happened next?" a captivated Lee asked.

"We all took coffee and dessert on the back portico. It was twilight and a beautiful, crisp cool evening with the stars just starting to show through against a plum to indigo ink sky. 'Granddad, can I take Jack up the hill trail to show him our spread?' Kate asked. Grant looked at me and said, 'It depends. So, what exactly are your intentions towards my granddaughter, Mr. Mango?'"

"To which you replied?" prodded Lee.

"'All honorable, sir,' of course," countered Mango.

"Then Grant growled at me, 'Good answer. Make sure it stays that way, soldier boy.' He excused himself for a moment then came back outside and eased himself into a rocking chair, placed a cut-glass tumbler of amber liquid on the table next to him, and said, 'I'd offer you a drink, Jack, but I want to make sure you escort Kate safely down that hill. I got my night binoculars right here. Do anything funny and I'll know. Here's a flashlight in case you need rescuing.'"

"And?" an enthralled Lee prompted.

"We climbed the hill and talked. Kate told me she was spending the summer at Grant's ranch before going back to high school in Sacramento, graduating a year early with plans to earn a double degree in animal sciences and business management at Cal-Poly in San Luis Obispo. She wanted to help Grant run the ranch. Kate's dad never wanted anything to do with the ranch, nor her aunt, uncle or any of her four cousins. Both her parents were doctors in Sacramento and never visited Grant except briefly during Christmas holidays. According to Kate, the other relatives treated the place like a glorified dude ranch and visited only to race four-wheelers around the range terrorizing cattle."

"Unlike her father and the rest of the crew it sounds like she definitely inherited her granddaddy's ranching gene," Lee observed.

"Kate passionately conveyed to me she hated the city and loved everything about ranching to such an extent it made her heart beat fast and burned in her soul. She became so ardent describing everything about the estate she stopped mid-sentence and apologized, saying, 'Guess I'm babbling like an idiot.'"

"So then you two came back down the hill?" quizzed Lee.

"Not quite yet. Kate drilled me with those eyes, looked slyly down at the dirt, drew a couple figure eights in the dust with the toe of her cowboy boot like she was judging what to say next, looked up and pointed to the heavens saying, 'Look at all those stars, Jack! Sometimes during the dead of night, the Milky Way will burn so bright you'll be able to see your shadow from its glow. I could never live anywhere else, could you?' I didn't say much as we walked down the hill together holding hands, as I was too busy envisioning the life I could have with this girl. When we stepped onto the porch, only then did I see the high powered rifle with attached scope leaning against the door frame behind Grant's rocker."

"Cagey old fart. Did you see her again?"

"I regret that I did not. Grant asked Kate if she wanted me to visit for dinner soon. She nodded her head quite enthusiastically. I wanted to say yes, but I couldn't. My fantasy ended abruptly when, before I could stop myself, I revealed I was mustering out in a month, committed to college that summer in Pennsylvania and needed to move back home to help my mom. I stuttered a bit explaining that ever since my dad died, my mom needed my help and that I'd been away too long. It was the truth but I never said anything about an almost fiancé waiting for me."

"I'm sure the grandfather understood your predicament. What was Kate's reaction?"

"Like fire brutally extinguished with a bucket of ice water and my words drifting away like smoke in the air. I awkwardly shook Kate's hand, wanting so badly to at least kiss her cheek, but couldn't. I shook Brewster's hand, made an inane joke about bovines, thanked them both for a fine dinner and enjoyable evening, climbed into my car and drove too fast down the ranch road until I could no longer see their house. I didn't trust myself to drive slower for fear I'd turn around, drive back and say I was joking, and of course I'd come to dinner again! I guess I drifted around the backroads for almost five hours until I got tired and parked the car on a gravel pull-off near some oaks. I got out and lay on top of the hood. Above me the Milky Way sliced across the sky, a splash of light painting the black void so vividly, individual stars seemed dimmed by its glare. She was right, you know. I could see my silhouette."

"So, you did the honorable thing and moved home, helped your mom and married your intended," Lee stated softly.

"In that absolute silence with the stars scorching overhead, my forearm hairs stood on end. I couldn't catch my breath and my eyes watered so painfully it felt like someone had flung salt in my face. I was so dumbstruck by the sheer stupidity of what I had just tossed away, I howled like a wolf whose mate had just been slaughtered. The old coot had practically thrown his granddaughter at me. Kate was definitely smitten and the feeling was mutual. If I had pursued that relationship, my mother and I would have been set for life. No more scratching for scholarships, working two jobs, seeing her shop at Goodwill for clothes or scrimping on food," Mango finished bitterly.

"You would have chucked your whole life *and* Nancy away because of a chance meeting with a rancher and an infatuation with his granddaughter he wanted to marry off, both of whom you had only known for, what, four hours? You made the right decision to return home," Lee counseled.

"It didn't seem like it at the time. I was feeling stuck in that proverbial rut with my life planned out ahead of me, together with Nancy. No one ever conceived of us *not* being together, least of all me. I was a month away from leaving the army to return home; Nancy was starting her last year of college, and even with the GI Bill it would be another four years of debt and bills to get through college, more grinding work to stretch that dollar. It would have been so easy for me to stay in California, marry the rancher's daughter a year or so later, have five kids and be king of a ranching empire!"

"So what stopped you?"

"I genuinely loved Nancy. I could have never hurt her like that. So I went home, married her, helped my Mom, moved to New Mexico, graduated college, became a cop in Los Alamos, did all the 'right' things, and well, you know the rest. But the whole time I was married to Nancy I thought about Kate probably more than I should have."

"That's quite a story. Nancy and Alexa never knew?"

"I've never told anyone until this morning. I told my mother an abbreviated version of meeting Kate, but nothing to Nancy. I always felt guilty fantasizing about Kate, almost to obsession, and what my life would have been like if I had stayed."

"You would have been an exceedingly different man," Lee admonished. "If you had decided to stay to win the girl and the ranch, think about the type of person you would have become. One who follows his own selfish desires, a man without honor in love and maybe without scruples in business? Would the guilt of jilting Nancy eaten into the core of your soul, turning it so rotten your life with Kate would have been miserable? Would you be the honest and excellent cop you are now, or would you have become the guy who drives past an old man out in the rain desperately trying to pull his cow out of the mud?"

"That one choice changed the course of my whole life, and even though I knew it would have harmed Nancy, I sometimes think I picked wrong, selecting obligation over opportunity. I never considered the damage staying in California would have done to my life," Jack contemplated.

"We all daydream about the choices we should have or might have made. That's the conundrum of being human. The hard part is recognizing the honorable path to integrity no matter how difficult the route. It may not be the easiest road and probably won't make you rich, but it does make you a better person and able to look yourself square in the face in the mirror each morning. Honestly Mango, has your life turned out badly?"

"No, but I spent a good portion of it thinking the bovine scat on the other side of the fence smelled sweeter. Pretty stupid; I'm learning though."

"And you just happened to end up back in Serrano as Police Chief?" quizzed Lee.

"It was obvious I couldn't live in Los Alamos after Nancy died, so I started searching the internet for jobs, and yeah, I clicked on Serrano for the fun of it. Shocked the shit out of me when I hit on the town's website and stumbled over the Chief's posting, and was further stunned when I was actually offered the job. I came back to Serrano for not only the waves and scenery, but to follow-up on a wild hope and the odd chance that Kate's still single and might be interested in me."

"Your relocation to Serrano sounds more like a move to the past than a move to the future," Lee observed.

"As a cop I'm supposed to think logically and practically, not uproot my family and move a thousand miles to pursue an apparition of passion that occurred one night, twenty years ago. I had a wonderful marriage with Nancy and wish I could click my heels and return to my old life. But as my mother observed, there is a hole in it and I can't change the fact that Nancy's gone. If I can chase Kate now with a clear conscience, wouldn't it be a positive for both my family and theirs?"

"You moved out here on blind faith hoping to pick up where you left off?"

"Of course not; I may be stupid but I'm not dumb," Mango answered drolly. "I used my investigative knowledge and connections to search through personal and public records and easily figured out Kate's still using her maiden name. Her mail is delivered to the ranch and I never found any marriage license records in Monterey or San Luis Obispo counties. There's still a possibility Kate could have gotten married somewhere else and kept her maiden name, though from the corporate filings I found, I doubt it."

"You could glean that from business records?"

"Kate's schooling seems to have paid off. She and Grant integrated his holdings into Brewster Ranch, Inc. about fifteen years ago, making themselves vice president/secretary and president/treasurer with Grant's children listed as subordinate officers. Additionally, all officers and their offspring and spouses are shareholders, in diluted portions. I couldn't find anyone remotely resembling Kate's spouse listed in any of the documents. Kate's also designated as the ranch's Operational Supervisor and contact person."

"I thought using police sources for personal reasons was imprudent, devious and rather illegal?" Lee reproved, lifting an eyebrow.

"You caught me on that one," Mango confessed, "But I could have pulled the same information off the internet, though it would have taken me longer and cost more. It's not like I accessed sealed records or private archives; everything I learned is recorded in the public domain," he equivocated.

"I'm surprised you've lived here two years and haven't reintroduced yourself."

Jack grimaced, "Grief, guilt, uncertainty, but mostly fear has held me back."

"Fear of what?"

“What if I contact her and she doesn’t want to see me or her grandfather hates me? What if the life I’ve always wanted with this woman doesn’t happen. Again?”

“Then you’ll have your answer and you can get on with your life, either way. You just going to stroll up to their front door and say ‘hi?’”

“I’m thinking about it; be less awkward than phoning. That’s why I’ve not been to class for a couple weeks. In my spare time I’ve been driving up to the Jolon, Lockwood, and the King City area, the closest towns to Ft. Hunter Liggett and Brewster’s ranch, stopping at local diners and saloons, getting a feel for the area from locals.”

“Research just shy of stalking?” Lee questioned.

“No good cop goes into any uncertain situation without some knowledge, and it’s not like I sat on a hillside watching their ranch through binoculars! I did learn Grant Brewster is very much alive and living in the main house while Kate lives alone in the guest quarters. Kate manages the ranch with advice and guidance from the old man, who is well thought of by all. Everyone I spoke with agreed that she’s learning from the best in the business; a generous and fair rancher who would give you the shirt off his back but you’d have to work it off to reimburse him or owe him a favor.”

“This information settled your doubts?” asked Lee.

“Breathe easier, at least. I’m ready to drive up to the hacienda today, scope the place out one last time and if it feels right, go knock.”

“And this is what you really want, a life with Kate?”

“I’m not sure anymore, but I think so,” Mango deliberated. “I’d like to be in love again and even though I’m in no hurry, eventually married.”

"About time, too! You must be getting lonely with nothing but all those chickens up at the house," Lee cackled.

"Don't be dissing my chickens. I love those chickens, and they prefer to be called hens," Mango faked offense, smiling back at Lee.

"What about you and Kiana? You two work well together and in your personal lives, you have the same hobbies and interests, even the same energy."

"But not the same age; a five year difference with Kate is still feasible but a fifteen year difference with Kiana? Besides, she's my best officer and banging your second in command isn't the greatest way to instill stability and professionalism in a department."

"Good point. What would Kiana do with you when you're too decrepit to dance?" Lee jested as he reached for the remaining pastry then dribbled the last of the coffee into his mug. He didn't see Jack wince at the remark.

Jack pushed back from the table. "Thank you for listening, Lee, and for the coffee and scones. I need to head up to my rancho and see mom and Jess off. Any last minute words of wisdom before I go Kate hunting?"

"To walk back in time twenty years will be a test of your conscience and faith. Like many journeys in life, your intended destination may not be the one you reach. Be careful what you wish for," Lee intoned.

Before Jack could knock on the old, ornately carved double pine doors, they were flung open to reveal a grinning Grant Brewster. "Thought you'd never get your ass back up here, Jack, or should I say Chief Mango? Don't you think waiting twenty-two years a little extreme even for a cautious cop like you? Dang, boy, I've seen three legged heifers move faster'n you!"

Jack gaped at Grant, seeing a frailer but still robust man standing with an elkhorn-tipped cane, looking not much older from their last meeting. A regal presence clad in pressed, dark jeans and pearl buttoned, grey cowboy shirt with red piping, longish white hair pulled into a ponytail with a rawhide thong, blue eyes glittering as they surveyed Jack.

"Pleased to see you, sir. My apologies for taking so long," replied Jack formally, holding out a hand.

Grant shook it firmly. "Come set a spell on the front porch. Kate's not here. She got edgy waitin' for you to show, just like a young calf on a frosty morning. I suggested she get off the mountain and head into King City or Paso to price feed and run errands. Boy, is she gonna chew my butt," he said laughing hard, slapping his thigh.

Jack followed a slightly limping Grant to a set of padded Adirondacks. "She knew I was coming?"

"Oh, don't look so astonished. You think we wouldn't know about your little recon missions these last weeks? Even though this land is vast, strangers do tend to stick out. When we heard about someone looking like Serrano's police chief sniffin' 'round these parts, it was only a matter of short time before you turned up."

"How do you know I'm chief in Serrano?"

Grant sat up straighter and beamed. "Internet's a marvelous tool. Lost your trail after you moved from Ligonier to Albuquerque, but caught your tracks when you hired onto the Los Alamos police. Didn't need the web to hear about your to-do with the governor. That played over the national news. I also make it a point to keep up with who's who in every town, no matter how small, within a 100 mile radius of the ranch."

Grant added, "I am sorry to hear about your wife's passing and your loss. My condolences. I do understand it takes time to overcome grief. I still miss my Lizzy after all these years. I'm glad you finally came to visit."

"Thank you. I appreciate it. So how did you know it was me before you answered the door?"

"Kate's put in all kinds of electronic gadgets. Hell, I've got a picture of you drivin' through the main gate in your truck and one of your license plate, all taken by the security camera at the cattle guard, and then wi-fi'd to my laptop."

Bemused, Jack said, "Maybe I need to hit Serrano's town council up for more funds and upgrade our surveillance equipment and hire Kate as a consultant."

"She's done an outstanding job of bringin' us into the 21st century. Streamlined operations, got all the records computerized; the works. Put in RFID, radio frequency tags on all the cattle so we can track vaccine schedules and which range, feedlot or stockyard the cows are at; practically anything you need to know about each animal."

"Sounds like Kate's turned into quite the modern rancher. You must be very proud of her."

"That's not all. She's in the process of negotiating with them tel-com companies to build a cell tower in the middle of the ranch. She wants a geo-enabled, fully integrated GPS data based collection system for field work using cameras and PDA's that are dust, water and shock resistant, along with virtual fencing and electronically controlled paddocks.

I had to memorize that last bit and have no idea what most of it means, but Kate says the technology should be "integrated seamlessly" within a few years which would allow us to become even more efficient."

"I'm impressed."

"From the time when my great, great, granddaddy started this ranch, all anyone needed to run cattle was a horse, rope, rifle and a branding iron until about twenty years ago. It's 2007 and all this virtual stuff is run by computer geeks who can't even spell the word cow. Don't know if I'm bragging or just an old man wistful for the 'good ole days'," Grant finished, pursing his lips.

"I'm sure there'll always be a need for real people to unstick real cows from real mud," Jack kidded. "So, how is Kate?"

"Still single and just as pretty as a sunflower back-dropped by blue sky," he replied. "You interested?"

"She never married? Why not?"

"I tried settin' her up with some of the neighboring rancher boys. Woulda been nice to enlarge the spread, combine families, expand our influence and all. Got her engaged to one but it didn't stick. She never met anyone in college, and doesn't meet many eligible men workin' the ranch, riding range, or fussin' with her computer gear, neither," Grant sighed and shrugged. "Said none of 'em had that twinkle in their eyes she was lookin' for.

Grant peered at Jack speculatively and continued. "Funny. Over the years we'd laugh when hoping something good would happen but thought it unlikely: Like beef climbing a couple dollars a pound right before selling or winnin' a scratch-off lottery ticket so we could afford new gears on the windmill. She's the one who'd always say, 'Or when that soldier boy shows back up . . .'"

"And here I am. Should I wait for Kate to get back, or call later and try another day?" Jack asked nervously.

"She should be home soon and never forgive me if I let you leave again. Come inside and have that drink I ought to have offered you last time." Grant stood up and placed his hand on Jack's shoulder. "Anything else you'd like to know?"

Jack inhaled deeply and asked, "If Kate's agreeable, may I have your permission to court your granddaughter?"

Grant grinned and slapped Jack's back. "Thought you'd never ask, son."

CHAPTER 7

BILLY SPOILS THE PARTY

Mango flung out his right arm, fumbled his hand over the night stand and finally found his buzzing cell phone wiggling towards the table end. The room was well-lit by a setting full moon at five in the morning, but that didn't make it easier finding the cause of his abrupt awareness. Kate Brewster rolled over; her tan face appearing in profile from under the quilt, eye open and brow upraised, mouth quirked. A flash of blue fluoresced from that one eye as she punched her pillow, let out a small snort, fell onto her back and let her long, wavy blond hair fall seductively across her breasts.

"Mango," he barked into the phone, ogling his bedmate while pretending alertness. He was exhausted after only a few hours of sleep preceded by hiking three hours along Nacimiento Lake, and then another three hours of spine numbing *wiki-wiki.* He wasn't fooling himself but hoped the caller was.

"Chief, it's Kiana. Sorry to interrupt your time off, but we have a body. Billy Morton, sprawled at the bottom of the bluff down near the Sixth Street beach access. Looks like a homicide."

"Hope you rot, Billy! Why'd you have to pick this morning?" Mango muttered testily to himself, seeing his image reflected back at him from laser blue eyes. Kate crossed her arms against her breasts, pulled the sheet up tight and continued to glare at him.

Mango sighed. "On my way. Have you reached Doc Kno, our one and only over-worked M.E.?"

"Yeah, but no rush. He's way out Route 58 finishing up a fatal rollover at the sharp bend at Topaz Solar Farm. Said he probably won't make it here for a couple hours."

"At least there won't be much crime scene contamination since it's so early."

"Don't bet on it. With the full moon illuminating the beach, we already have half a dozen gawking walkers plus their dogs, all milling around the body with a mishmash of tracks. We aren't sure what the high tide washed away, if anything. Even looks like a dog may have piddled on Billy's head."

Mango grimaced, and then whistled. "Talk about having a bad hair day. Protect the scene with the usual protocol for unattended death and homicide, but let's not make assumptions. You have anyone else coming in to help?"

"Skibitski's on his way and should be here in a few minutes. He's more excited than a big wave surfer hearing Waimea Bay's going off. First dead body and all," Kiana snickered.

"Keep a leash on him and rein in that enthusiasm. We don't want more doggie accidents. See you in about twenty."

Mango put the phone down, switched on the nightstand light, turned and looked at Kate. Raising his palms to her in supplication, he said "I know, I know, I'm sorry! We've got a possible homicide; that child molester from four years back, Billy Morton. And, he just got out of Soledad a month ago."

"This was supposed to be our anniversary weekend! Oh, never mind. Duty always calls, huh?"

"You know with a death like this I have to be there. Kiana's good, but my support staff is too inexperienced for me to trust them with everything, especially a case with his history," Mango said, as he unwound his six-foot and one athletic frame from their comfortably toasty bed. Rising, he trailed a finger along her temple, tucking a stray lock of golden hair behind her ear.

Heaving himself off the bed, praying his legs would hold after his vigorous night, he stumbled into the master bathroom, slapping for the light switch.

"Sometimes I think you spend more time with Kiana!" Kate hollered in his direction. Jack heard a pillow pouf against the bathroom doorframe as he leaned his powerful forearms against the sink. He rolled his eyes at himself in the mirror.

"Don't you be rolling those big brown eyes around, *Jacques Antonio* Mango!"

"How does she do that? The woman can see through walls!" he thought, but answering aloud, "Kate, I love you more than anything. We've been together two years now, which I think is fantastic, considering we live a hundred miles apart. You're the love of my life, darlin'."

"Then let's get married. Move up to the ranch and make a life together with me. We can elope to Reno or Vegas next month."

"Kate, we've talked about this before, and you know I can't tell a heifer from a mare," Jack responded in a smile tinged voice.

"Mares are female horses, not cows. Jeez!"

"See what I mean? You know I'm not a cowboy. I'm a cop. I'm too young to retire; what would I do, arrest cows?" Jack regarded his reflection, straightened his back, smoothed his thick goatee and ruffled his brown, wavy hair off his forehead with his fingers. He decided he wouldn't offend Billy Morton with his morning stubble.

Kate jumped nimbly off the bed, more energetically then Jack's recent heave-ho, crossed the room in two strides and leaned against the bathroom doorjamb. Jack eyeballed her naked, muscular yet lusciously curvaceous image in the mirror, shook his head and flashed his best scallywag grin, "You just want me for my tight butt!"

"Don't change the subject. You can retire now and I'll be your sugar momma. Granddad's ten thousand acres, seven hundred head, plus his gas and oil royalties should be enough to keep us happy for at least a year or two," she teased.

Jack turned on the water and washed his face using the action to remain silent.

"My clock is ticking out of time and I want a family with you, Jack! Ranching isn't that bad now that I've got the whole place wired. We could have anything we ever desired and the time in which to do it. I can hire a foreman. And you weren't complaining too much about the rancher's daughter last night," she purred as she wrapped herself against his naked flanks.

Jack disentangled himself, took Kate's hand and walked them back to the bed where they both sat on the edge. Kate pulled Jack back down to lay beside her, propped one elbow up, and kissed him deeply while grazing her fingernails up his thigh.

"Lordy woman, if we had more time like you want, your lovin' would kill me! Do you have any idea where my clothes are, much less where my brain is? I think I lost both," Jack groaned as he scooted on his belly to the edge of the bed and peered over the side, looking for at least his socks.

"I thought Frenchmen could make love all night long."

"Ahhh, remember? I'm not all French. I'm half Italian, too."

"Even better! With all that hot blood, you should be able to last for days," she cooed, running one hand down his back and the other up to his dangling things while he struggled to pull on his socks.

"Hold that thought," he groaned as he bent over and nuzzled her neck. "Now be a good little rancher woman and help me find the rest of my clothes. I have a date with dead guy."

"Such romantic talk. Don't you forget, you're talking to the ranch foreman *and* vice president." She slapped his ass, climbed out of bed and with a sigh of exasperation, pulled a purple silk robe off the wall hook, shrugged her arms through the sleeves and tied it around her lithe torso. "Fine. You don't get any more of *this* for a while, not until we talk more," she huffed, jerking the bow at her waist for emphasis.

Softening her voice, Kate said, "You better feed your animals if you have a few minutes. I'll make you a quick bowl of oatmeal and fruit. But we still have things to discuss when you get back. You are coming back soon, right?"

This was supposed to be their anniversary weekend. Alexa, Jessica, and Kiana, sensing Kate and Jack's need for privacy, schemed together to purposely give them a few days alone to celebrate their two year reunion, and used Jessica's pending eighteenth birthday as an excuse for the trip. Alexa and Jessica graciously vacated the Alamosta Ranch and sacrificed their time to fly to the Big Island of Hawaii to spend five days at the Mauna Kea Beach Hotel on the Kohala coast. Kiana's cousin, an assistant general manager, obtained *Kama'aina* air and lodging rates to help defray their expenses.

Walking onto his expansive front porch, Jack slipped his feet into his mucking boots. He stretched by gripping a roof beam and arching his back, trying to convince stiff muscles to move, and talk himself into concentrating on a possible murder investigation instead of recalling the feel of warm Kate and his soft bed. He lumbered down the steps and out to the barn thinking aloud, "Damn! Every time I try to make this work, something happens; and the more I try to force it, the more it doesn't."

He and Kate's long distance relationship was somewhat solid, at least as solid as the San Andreas Fault could rattle but not collapse. He knew Kate was perplexed as to why he'd not 'popped the question' yet. She was brainy, beautiful, shrewd yet kindhearted, and everything he'd dreamed about for so many years; but he wasn't ready to commit to becoming a fulltime cowboy. He chided himself, thinking Lee had been right, 'careful what you wish for.' Knocking on mid-forties, his love life was as stable as a brick building in an earthquake zone, and he wondered how he could make critical police decisions with such conviction, but not reconcile the quandary of keeping the job *and* the woman, both he dearly loved.

Jack knew Kate's life was the ranch, and as the last Brewster who showed any inclination to keep it active and successful, she was passionate in her calling. To ask her to leave the fields of wildflowers and roving wildlife, and the panorama of the Santa Lucias was inconceivable. With no traffic, crime or outside interference, where most would have seen boredom, monotony and bleakness, she beheld peacefulness, purpose, and space to breathe. Now what little extra time either of them squeezed into their busy lives was spent driving four hour roundtrips between Serrano and Brewster Ranch.

After feeding chickens, horses and cats, Jack walked to the fence and leaned in, propping a booted foot on the lowest rung. He gazed lovingly across his small three acre ranchette, the morning glow of rising sun silhouetting his two horses, tails flicking and friskily chasing each other in the chilly pre-dawn air. Jack understood Kate's sentiments regarding her ranch because he felt the same way about Alamosta. The difference though, was his place was a hobby, a refuge from work and a place to unwind, not a completion of his whole being and a way of life. "Great," he addressed the horses, "You two are showing me up again and making me feel even more confused."

"Jack! Come on. Breakfast is ready."

Mango was able to drive in a mere ten minutes from his hillside ranchette to shore access, near the corner of Sixth Street and Pacific Avenue at the southern outskirts of Serrano. Jeep parked at the trailhead, portable radio in hand, he bounded down the steep sandy composite-wood stairway to the beach, the shrill staccato cry of gulls punctuating the morning ambiance. Two hundred feet offshore a dense fog blanketed Serrano Bay, a combination of salt particles and evaporation creating dampness in an otherwise arid locale. Streams of sunlight peaking over the eastern hills behind him created an eerie contrast of illuminated beach and azure water, the shafts of light being abruptly swallowed into the grey-black void of mist. A fragrant, salty tang smothered Mango's sinuses like syrup.

Seeing the chief arrive, Officer Joe Skibitski peeled away from the small group of beachcombers he had been keeping away from the body and rushed to meet Mango like a puppy welcoming his master home from work. Mango hoped he hadn't given out preliminary information better left classified for now.

Skibitski was a conscientious cop but young, and in his exuberance had sometimes overlooked critical elements or angles of a situation. He lacked life experience but was eager to learn. When Mango hired him around the same time he promoted Kiana to Lieutenant, it was understood he would walk in Kiana's shadow for unofficial continuing education and extra on-the-job training.

Skibitski was the millennial Barney Fife. A little geeky, slightly goofy, with loose gangly joints and white blond hair cropped military style. Whatever experience he lacked was made up for with enthusiasm and energy. A local kid from the area's farming stock, he'd never been north of San Francisco, south of Santa Barbara nor east of the state line, but his dream to get off the dirt and into policing was a constant motivator and he didn't want to blow his chance.

Ski was different. With his blue eyes in sunlight which turned gray green with the fog, people tended to underestimate him and mistook his plodding simple logic as thinking in black and white, an either/or mentality. In his methodical fashion, he saw decisions as if on a compass; once you determined where north lay by where the needle pointed, you had 360 choices in which to pick the correct course. The answer, "You tell me," to Mango's query of whether he was nicknamed *Ski* for his surname or the shape of his nose was the deciding factor in Mango's decision to hire him.

"Morning Ski. Thanks for coming in on your day off."

"No problem. Guess what?" Ski nodded his head towards the body. "It's that molester you busted a few years back. Karma, man. He deserved this."

"Not sure anyone deserves to die like this, but I won't disagree with you on the karma." Mango eyeballed the crime scene behind Ski. "So, anybody in that group you corralled we need to be concerned about, or piques your interest?"

"Not really. Early walkers are all. I did get everyone's name, address, and contact info."

"Good work and good thinking."

"That was Kiana's idea. This is my first murder. I hope I don't screw anything up."

"First thing right now is confidentiality and second, let's not jump to conclusions about this being a murder, though we will investigate it as such."

"Kiana said that, too. And I didn't say a thing to those folks."

"Good, there's hope for you yet, Officer Skibitski."

"You think so, Chief?"

"Nah. Just thought I'd say something nice," Mango answered with a straight face before looking past Ski to address a grinning Kiana de la Cruz, senior officer and de facto head of criminal investigation. She was walking towards them from the crime scene and stopped to stand beside Ski. Mango was pleased to see she had cordoned off the area where the body was grotesquely splayed.

"Nice morning, Lieutenant."

"That it is. Boy, you look like you were shot at and missed, and shit at and hit. Sir."

"Thought we were supposed to be talking dead body/crime scene, not analyzing my appearance," Mango replied.

"Just making an observation. But it does look like you had an interesting night."

"A minor lack of sleep. And, Ski, not one word."

"I didn't say anything!"

"I heard you thinking it."

"You know they have medication for that," Kiana snickering, jumping in before Ski could speak.

"I'm not into drugs, Lieutenant. I rely on holistic self-medication techniques."

"Not sure if your methodology is working."

"Let's change the subject to Billy since he's having a worse day than I am."

"Barely, but let's," Kiana laughed loudly, while Mango blushed and coughed once.

Kiana and Ski turned around to face Billy Morton's body ten feet in front of the base of the cliffs which lined the beach. He lay prone, backside down, with arms extended above his head like he was about to jump off a diving board backwards, but more probably someone dragged him through the sand to the water's edge at high tide and dropped his arms thus, when finished with their task. If there was a killer, the perp didn't consult a tide chart, as what water Billy dove into was now shoreline thirty feet closer to the horizon. His head was twisted upward grotesquely, the left side of his chin almost touching the inside of his left elbow giving him the appearance of trying to look over his left shoulder, mouth agape in surprise. Billy's legs were fully extended, his long tan pants covering his tattered sneakers and riding low on his hips gangsta style, polka-dot boxers exposed, probably more from being pulled down while being dragged rather than from affectation. Missing were drag marks, erased by the receding high tide or his assailant, with any leftovers subsequently trod on by dogs and walkers who found the body. Sand was sprinkled on the upturned face, most likely from prancing canines hoping for a juicy bit of rotting flesh with which to roll on.

"What have we got so far, Kiana?" queried Mango.

"Pretty sure it's Billy Morton, but I don't remember him being able to turn his head completely around and upended." Kiana stepped back one pace and craned her neck, owl-like in imitation of Billy's position. "Guess four years in Soledad would make a child molester watch his back."

"Don't we have a sense of humor this morning," Mango retorted.

"You appointed me morale officer this month. Just doing my job, sir," smirked Kiana.

Mango knelt down and closely studied the pile of dead flesh, concentrating on head, neck and simple brown, short sleeve T-shirt clad upper torso. "His neck looks like a pelican's with a small fish stuck sideways in his throat. Do we agree on a broken neck theory?"

He bent over further to view Bill's upper arms. "Could be bruising on the triceps, and maybe under the arms, but I can't see past the material. Then again, it could be livor mortis. If it is, then it's a given he was killed somewhere else and deposited here. We'll know more when we have better light and when the pathologist gets here."

Kiana slapped her forehead. "I missed that on the arms. I did look closely at his hands and fingernails. Nothing I could see out of the ordinary and I did note that nasty cut above his right eye."

Mango backed away from the body making sure he stepped in his same footprints of approach to eliminate any further contamination.

Pointing to the top of the cliff, Mango asked, "Isn't that one of the houses Randi Shirazi rents out?"

"Sure is. I saw Stella Morton's piece of crap Taurus parked there yesterday afternoon while I was on patrol," volunteered Skibitski, now standing off to the side, not sure of his rookie status in his first murder case. "And guess who lives in the house next door on the left?"

"Shit. Hizzoner Percy, probably sleeping off a bottle of scotch and I'll bet the ranch he's been oblivious since he staggered home from Dickie's, just like every night," blurted Mango. "I'll talk to him later. You say you saw Stella's car here yesterday? Was she in it?" Mango continued quickly, trying to steer his outburst away from Hathaway.

"Car was parked off street in front of the house. Stella and/or Billy could have been working there. I sometimes see Billy driving Stella's car, but not often. Surprised that POS even runs," replied Ski.

Much to the dismay of the community, after Billy was remanded to Soledad for his ten year sentence, Randi hired Stella Morton to clean houses. Townspeople did not understand how Randi could be Clare's advocate yet still employ Stella, Billy's wife. Stella testified at the trial that she was innocent and unaware of the abuse, claiming to also be a victim of Billy's warped exploitations, but people just didn't buy it. Most thought Stella could have stopped the girl's ill-treatment. Many felt it was okay for Randi to be sympathetic about Stella's predicament but not enough to do favors, much less hire her.

"You sure Stella's car was there yesterday and not the prior day?" Mango double checked.

"Sure as I'm standing next to you right now. I stopped for a mahi sandwich at Dickies then figured I'd cruise Pacific Avenue and check the construction workers' license plates on their pick-ups over at the McMansion being built, there on the corner of Fourteenth Street. It was there when I drove past. Lordy, you don't think she killed her own husband do you?"

Mango swiveled his head quickly both ways to ensure no one had overheard the comment. Ski was a good patrolman but he sometimes didn't put his brain in gear before engaging his mouth. "Shh-h-h, for God's sake, don't give anyone a reason to start rumors. You don't know who might be standing around eavesdropping."

"Sorry, just thinking aloud."

"No harm no foul; just be careful 'cause big ears are always listening." Switching gears, Mango quizzed Kiana. "When will the M.E. get here?"

"Thirty minutes? He's coming in from Santa Margarita. Been helping CHP with that fatality on Route 58 last night. Possible DUI involving a carload of teens not making one of the ninety degree curves near the Solar Topaz Farm. Only one dead; a passenger in the front not wearing a seatbelt, was thrown during the rollover and ended up wrapped around the guard rail." Kiana replied.

"Ski, go back over to the gathering crowd of looky-loos and continue to take names whether they saw anything or not. Maybe if we make them think they're getting sucked into a murder investigation they'll decide it's better to leave and go home. And I repeat, don't volunteer this is a possible murder scene or volunteer anything at all. Just the facts, ma'am; we have a body. Period."

"You want me to start knocking on doors at the houses above the beach?" Ski anxiously asked, hoping to play a major role in the investigation with Kiana.

"Not yet, it's still pretty eye-cracking early, so let's give it an hour at least. Most of these are rentals and are probably empty anyway."

Mango observed Kiana, who was leaning over the body and doing that owl thing again, rotating her upper shoulders and neck mostly upside down. "Billy's head and neck sure look twisted."

"Well, his mind was twisted to begin with, but I agree, most necks don't have the Adam's apple in the back left, below the hair line." Mango countered.

"Not much evidence visible," Kiana commented.

"Nothing obvious. Remind me to make sure the M.E. scrapes DNA residue from Billy's neck. So, what do we know about Billy since he was released?"

"Very little. He registered as a sex offender and hasn't missed an appointment with his parole officer. He's been working for Randi painting, cleaning, yardwork and doing handyman stuff. Doesn't that seem a little unusual, what with Randi being Clare's advocate?" pondered Kiana.

"It does. It's hard to figure Randi out at times, though I know she likes to help the underdogs of this world, or maybe she just wanted to keep tabs on Billy for Clare's sake. I guess she has her reasons and we need to find out exactly what those are. You two keep a lid on things here. Ski, when you finish encouraging the gawkers to leave, get a couple of cloth tarps and have the EMTs help you set up a barrier to keep people from taking pictures of the M.E.'s post mortem exam. Kiana, poke around the cliff top edges, but be wary. If you do see anything, back off, contact me and wait. Technically, we need a search warrant or owners' consent since it's private property. In fact, call in a search warrant for Randi's rental where Billy may have been working. Tape up access to the property and post a guard. I'm heading Uptown to see if Randi's awake yet."

"Careful Chief. Don't get caught serving breakfast in bed," Ski ribbed.

"Didn't I just give you an order? Keep your lips buttoned with any remarks inside your noodle, or you'll find your butt back on patrol."

"I am on patrol."

"I meant patrol on another department, smart guy." Mango turned on his heel, caught Kiana's eye and winked before heading up the to the road.

CHAPTER 8

TRES MUJERES

Randi Shirazi stepped out of the shower and toweled herself dry. She turned one shoulder, then the other, craning her neck to catch her rear-end reflection from the large mirror hanging above double-basin copper-vessel sinks. Zeba and Zulu studied her from their pillows perched on the far end of the marble counter.

Dropping the towel on the counter, Randi cupped her still firm breasts, lifted them up and inward and appraised her forty year-old body. Shoulder length, razor-cut red hair and penetrating emerald-green eyes fit nicely on top of a firm and unblemished physique, toned by fifteen years of martial arts and thousands of miles of bicycle touring and jogging. Her trapezius and deltoid muscles narrowed into sinewy defined biceps framing solid pectorals. Abdominals ripped and tight, sat atop equally taut obliques forming an inviting "V" to her groin. It was not easy, but a three hour regiment five times a week of combined martial arts, aerobic and weight training were worth the results.

"Not bad for an old widow, she murmured to herself in the mirror, "Not bad at all." Her two admiring felines squeezed their eyes shut as if in agreement.

Randi looked out her eye-level, clerestory windows at the ubiquitous post-sunrise morning sea fog blanketing Serrano's shoreline. Cormorants, gulls and pelicans were at work skimming effortlessly along the glassy Pacific, occasionally rising and then diving in kamikaze fashion to grasp unsuspecting baitfish schooling just below the surface. She didn't worry about being naked in front of the high horizontal windows because her home was one of the most elevated in town, backing up to a hill where it and a little known walking trail separated her backyard from the Pacific Coast Highway. The confined backyard was in stark contrast to the southwesterly panorama of the Pacific Ocean leading into infinity. The view was framed by the Montano de Oro foothills and Morro Rock to the south, with the highlands or *serranos* leading north into the awe-inspiring coast of Big Sur.

Randi ran away from home at age fifteen. Her mom walked in while daddy was molesting her, and could no longer deny the fact that he'd been doing it to her since age ten. There was no getting around the truth that for five long years the money and whiskey had been more important to her mother than her daughter's welfare. Daddy took off three weeks later, never to be heard from again. Mom started rolling through boyfriends with the intensity of Grant taking Richmond, bringing home drunken copycats more interested in Randi than her mom. Randi figured since she'd been spreading her lips and legs for free all these years, it was time to make some money from it and heeded the siren call of Los Angeles to become a teenage street hooker, secretly hoping to become the next celebrated movie star.

South Texas was a dead end, so Randi bought a one way bus ticket and never looked back.

While her acting talent was legendary, it had never landed her anywhere but on her back, eventually with Emil. Using her persona as the respected wife of a successful business owner propelled her into the heart of Serrano where she was accepted for herself, her sordid past a secret. She volunteered at the Morro Bay Animal Shelter where she met the sister of the District Attorney from San Luis Obispo. Within a year she was a volunteer Court Appointed Special Advocate, representing kids who ended up in the system through no fault of their own due to abandonment, neglect or abuse. These were categories in which Randi excelled.

Fixated in self-reflection, Randi started when she heard the doorbell chime. "You've gotta be kidding. It's 6:30 in the morning!" The chimes sounded again. "Coming, coming," Randi bellowed, knowing the sound wouldn't reach the front door from her second story master bath. Slipping into a seafoam colored silk negligée and covering herself modestly in a warm, pink fleece bathrobe, she trotted down the curved stairs to the white marble floored foyer.

Glancing at the small monitor on the wall next to the front door, she beheld a bedraggled image of Clare, head hanging and clutching a backpack to her chest, hair disheveled, absent of a jacket, shivering noticeably.

Randi opened the door and stared at the girl, who looked up at her through the tops of her tear-filled, red-rimmed eyes. Clare's sweater and jeans were smeared with grime. Her matted, russet bronzed hair showed evidence of a night spent outdoors sleeping on the ground, and her naturally thin, frail physique made her dishabille look even worse.

"Oh sweetie, what happened?" fretted Randi, holding out her arms as Clare tripped forward, buring her face into Randi's chest sobbing uncontrollably. Randi wrapped her arms around the waif, feeling the young woman's body shudder as she cried. Zeba and Zulu crouched on the stairs, blinking knowingly up at the arrival of another injured stray.

Clare took one step backwards out of Randi's arms and wailed, "I blew it, Randi. It all went to shit. That bastard showed up at the bar in Tranquility, can you believe it? I snapped. I snapped bad!" Clare howled and wept. "I couldn't handle it!"

"Who? Who showed up and what happened?"

"Billy! He walked right into the coffeehouse and ordered a latte like I was some faceless servant. I don't think he even knew it was me. But I saw red, started throwing things, and the customers scattered out the door like roaches. I think I beaned Billy with a coffee cup. Then Harry pissed me off. He wouldn't listen or let me explain. I thought if anybody would understand, he would; but all he cares about is making money. He fired me! I ended up sleeping under the highway at the Serrano Drive Bridge. I have nowhere else to go. I fucked up and I'm scared. I couldn't control my anger. Why can't I be normal?"

"Let's get you cleaned up first," Randy said, walking Clare past the staircase to a first floor bedroom suite tucked between her office and the kitchen. "While you take a shower I'll make breakfast. You need food. Then we'll go find Harry and see if we can get you your job back. He probably freaked out at your freak out, and fired you in the heat of the moment. Everything will be okay."

Randi heard the distant muffled spatter of the guest shower while she cracked eggs into a bowl. Just as she pulled the lever to toast two English muffins, the door chime declared another visitor. “Jeez! Did the whole flippin’ town sleep under the bridge last night and decide I’m running a homeless shelter?” Randi fumed, slapping a wooden spatula down onto the granite island counter. She turned the fire off under the pan she’d been heating and stalked through the den to open the front door. Again.

Chief Jack Mango’s image filled the security screen. Randi let out a deep breath, loosened the belt of her fuzzy robe just enough to allow the green silk and a bit of cleavage to peek out, and opened the door wide. “Well, well, let me guess, you saw the error of your ways and woke this morning with thoughts of marching down here to ravish me.”

When the door swung open, Mango, (God forgive him) roamed Randi’s body bottom to top. First noticing the tan sinewy legs disappearing under the robe, then the partially open wrap exposing transparent silk indicating it was her only piece of clothing underneath, to finally the swell of rising breasts, the invitation of welcome punctuated by luscious lips.

“Mmmm-hmm, earth to Mango. Are we going to stand here and give the neighbors proof the Serrano cops are serious about community policing, or would you like to come in? I was making breakfast,” Randi continued. Even in a bulky bathrobe, she was able to twitch her hips in a seductive sway to invite entry.

That sway chimed deep in Mango’s synapses, a primal urge to continue the biological mission of the male species in regard to propagating the human race. Not that Mango thought about it in quite those words. He smiled and stepped over the threshold while holding Randi's gaze.

"There's nothing more tempting than to take you up on your offer of a hot breakfast . . . " Mango cleared his throat and started again. "Actually, we had a possible homicide last night. I have a couple questions."

"I don't remember offering you anything hot," Randi purred, with a slight raise of her eyebrows. "And surely you aren't insinuating that I'm a suspect and need to handcuff me, are you?" she drawled, offering arms out, wrists together. "I won't fight you as long as you're gentle."

Jack swallowed hard, remembering; feeling his Adam's apple click and thinking it felt like the size of a stuck grapefruit. He turned his eyes downward to his shoes, groaning silently, feeling that sudden spark of unspoken desire; in other words, trouble.

Jack loved Kate, and Randi shrewdly understood not only male desires, but was perceptive enough to know she could never hold Jack's affection in competition against Kate. Their trysts were in the past, and after the initial awkwardness had worn off, they remained friends; whether sharing drinks and talking philosophy at Dickies, practicing forms with Mr. Lee, or the occasional pedal along the PCH together. Randi though, couldn't pass up the opportunity to tease Mango, just a little.

Fighting the rising blush, he looked up to meet Randi's searing scrutiny, he stuttered, "Yeah. Where was I?"

"Murder?"

"Billy Morton found dead on the beach this morning right in front of your Sixth Street rental. I hear Stella works for you, and her car was seen there yesterday afternoon. I also hear you've hired Billy for odd jobs since he got out."

"Billy's dead? Couldn't have happened to a nicer guy! And you think Stella did it? Can't blame her."

"I'm not saying, I'm just saying, know what I'm saying?" Jack smiled as he recited his well-practiced maxim. "Just need to know when and if Stella and/or Billy were working at your rental. We may have a motive but are still way short on means and opportunity," Mango answered, trying hard to return to a professional state of mind. The adage, "If you could do something and not get caught, would you do it?" kept swimming through his head. At the moment he hated himself for allowing Randi to scramble his brains but that's what Randi excelled at and enjoyed.

"Stella was scheduled to clean, and Billy to paint the place yesterday afternoon, but not on any specific timetable or necessarily together. As long as a job is completed by a certain time and date, I never worry about when the work is actually done. I'm not exactly sure when either of them was working, but I was there yesterday morning with Billy showing him what needed to be painted and helping to move furniture. I was going to run by there this morning to check that it's finished. They knew that. I'm assuming they were both in the house together in the afternoon finishing up."

"I'm afraid you can't inspect the place. It's being taped off as part of the crime scene and we're in the process of getting a warrant to gain entry."

"Hell Jack, I'll give you access right now. All you need to do is ask."

"Best we keep this official and do it by the book. Don't want any of our procedures to be questioned in court, if it comes to that."

Randi jerked when a loud thump reverberated from inside the house.

Mango craned his neck to look behind Randi. "Sorry. Didn't realize you had company," he said, thinking, "Lucky SOB." He noted the spare bedroom door was closed, and in the kitchen down the hall he could see the cook's island prepped with breakfast fixings and two places set on the attached eating bar.

"Just my grandma in town from Toledo," Randi said, a little too quickly. "Probably let the toilet lid slam shut with her arthritis and all. You know how family can be when they get old, showing up unannounced," Randi glibly added.

"Well, I better get going. Wouldn't want your grandmother to think any funny business is going on out here. One more question, though. Do you know of Stella making any threats or saying anything negative about Billy?"

"What do you think? A screwed up marriage from the get-go, finding out your hubby likes little girls, the mortification and humiliation, and four years alone cleaning toilets and washing dirty sheets for a living. Then the bastard prances back here acting like he should be forgiven? Other than that, I wouldn't see any reason for her holding a grudge," Randi shrugged.

"I get it. I will need you to come down to the station, make a statement regarding your whereabouts yesterday, and sign some paperwork. I'm outta here. See you later and thanks for your help." Mango turned to go, stopped and turned back to Randi. "By the way, you realize you have a bunch of dirt all over the front of your robe?"

Randi's eyes opened wide and she looked down, one hand trying to swipe away the soil. "Cats," she stammered, "Got into something. Uh, didn't know I'd gotten it all over me."

"Better cinch that robe. Wouldn't want you catching cold." Mango stepped outside and walked back to his jeep, tugging surreptitiously at an important juncture of his uniform, the better to rearrange a choice bit of anatomy.

Randi slowly closed the heavy, handcrafted oak door, leaned back heavily against it and listened to Mango's jeep rumble away. *What the hell! Did Jack know Clare was here and he just didn't lead on?* She was going to have to think on this. This was starting out to be one weird morning.

She walked back into the kitchen and fried up bacon while finishing the eggs, waiting for the English muffins to pop from the toaster. *Why did I just lie about Clare? Stupid, Randi. Really, really stupid.*

"Did I hear some guy's voice?" Clare asked, leaning around the corner from the guest suite toweling her hair, now dressed back in her dirt stained clothing.

"We need to get some clean clothes on you! *And*, we need to talk. That voice you heard was Chief Mango. Someone killed Billy last night."

"You're shitting me! No way! Oh, my God! They think I did it because of the fight yesterday?"

"I wouldn't call that a fight, more of an overreaction. Sit down, girl. You need to eat and boy, do we need to talk," Randi stressed, placing two dishes filled with scrambled eggs, bacon and muffins on the counter, adding a glass of orange juice next to each. Randi sat and pointed at Clare with a strip of bacon, "From the beginning, tell me what happened it."

"Can you freakin' believe it? I kinda go bananas on him and the next morning he's dead! Billy waltzed into the Hill o'Beans yesterday during lunch hour. The place was filled with tourists and that bastard strolls right up asking for a fuckin' latte! *And* called me honey. I *hate* that word! I guess I shouldn't have screamed, 'Get the hell away from me, you sicko pervert or I'll cut your balls off.' He did die with his balls, didn't he?"

"Um, don't know. Mango never mentioned his balls, whatever good they did for him."

"Like, anyway, Billy started screaming back at me, saying how *I* ruined *his* life, and then I started cussing and throwing anything I could grab. Glasses, mugs, knives, spoons, dishes. I think I busted the mirror behind the bar, one of the plate windows, and maybe nailed Billy with a coffee mug in the head. He ran out the door after that." Clare abruptly stopped talking, started moaning, rocking back and forth in her chair, hyperventilating. "They're gonna think I did it. No! Billy's gonna fuck me again!"

"Shhhh, Clare. Breathe! Keeping telling me what happened."

"Harry came running over and we got into it. I was mad enough to slap the piss out a junkyard dog and make him drink it!"

"Clare!" Randi gasped, holding her hand over her mouth to hide a bit of un-chewed egg.

"I told Harry to mind his own business or I'd rip his balls off too! I guess he didn't appreciate me sayin' that in front of what was left of his customers. One guy spit his Frappuccino all over the back of the espresso machine. I turned around and stomped off before I did something really outrageous. I'm like, you know, tryin' to work on my anger issues. Harry followed me, fired me, and told me I had twenty minutes to get out of town on the next PCH bus. Who the hell does he think he is, John Fuckin' Wayne?" Clare paused to breathe, finally shoveling a large portion of eggs and muffin into her mouth.

Clare, chewing with her mouth open, continued. "I was gonna catch the shuttle into town but it always runs late. I got tired of waiting and no way was I gonna hitch a ride. I hid behind some trees near the bus stop, and once I saw the cop leave and Harry almost get run over walking across the highway back to his house, I snuck back to the coffee shop and, well, you're not gonna like this."

"Like what?"

Clare lowered her eyes. "Like, that I borrowed a bike and helmet from the rack. Nobody ever bothers to lock them in T-ville."

"You stole a bike?"

"Borrowed. I'll put it back, I swear! Besides, I needed, to ya' know, get outta Dodge?" Clare cocked her head and with one eye closed, squinted up at Randi.

Randi shook her head and softly said, "You could have called me. I would have come for you."

"Yeah, I figured that out later. Wasn't thinking real straight."

"Then what?"

"I was gonna hang out in that shack by the lighthouse, but it gets creepy out there at night, so I rode down Highway

One into Serrano. It's all downhill. I got off on Serrano Bay Road by the surf shop and the skate park. The last thing in the world I wanted to do was hang out pretending to chat nicely with people. So, I know a place up Serrano Creek where no one goes. I walked with the bike up the creek past the last set of homes, and where it widens out there's a nice spot. Like, the only thing you can hear are birds, the breeze and an occasional barking dog. Ended up sleeping there all night, and then went up the ridge to your place before dawn. I sat between your Range Rover and garage for an hour until I finally rang your bell when it started to get light. I didn't kill him, Randi, but I'm not sad he's dead. In fact, I am outright thrilled. Except for the part about him keeping his balls. But, I didn't kill him!"

"I don't think the police are disagreeing with you at this point. Chief Mango is actually looking for Stella. Someone saw her car at my Sixth Street rental yesterday afternoon. The bad thing is, Billy was supposed to be painting the living room for me. They found him dead at the bottom of the cliff in front of my rental house this morning! I did see Stella yesterday afternoon while I was out on my bike. She was in the Taurus and she passed me at the edge of town, driving towards Tranquility like she was in a hurry. Probably heading out to see Harry Henderson. Rumor has it her car's been parked behind Harry's house a lot."

"Now that you mention it," Clare mused, "there have been afternoons where Harry disappears for a couple hours. When he shows back up he has that *drained* look. You know, shuffling around all quiet-like and grinning a lot," Clare laughed, her wet hair drying to damp. Sipping juice, she eyed Randi. "I didn't kill him; why would I? You gotta believe me!"

Stella Morton lay under a light quilt in her apartment, her head angled into the pillow, facial skin stretched taut, eyeballs racing back and forth under her lids. Her brain was busy; sprinting and circling, spooling bad visions.

"How the devil did I ever get in this position? My entire life has been nothing but a rapid descent to nowhere . . . and it just keeps getting worse."

From outside her apartment came the cry of scavengers and predators; a distant gull's cry and swish of a hawk gliding by, both out looking for breakfast. The upper canyon road leading to her complex was sprinkled with oaks as it wound next to an intermittent Serrano Creek. Above the road, rising hills covered by burnt golden grasslands with occasional stands of more oaks scattered across the rounded ranges. Stella's apartment was located in a small wood-framed, eight-unit complex surrounded by some pine and eucalyptus. It was perched near the top of the canyon, each unit having a wide-angle view of Serrano Bay and the undulating knolls. She had moved in and started renting there immediately after Billy went to prison. They lost the house and she lost everything else.

Stella struggled with sleep, being almost too tired to fully drift off. In addition to her lack of deep REM, when she did dream, the images were vivid and terrifying. In one loop, she was running down the beach in Serrano chased by townies, some carrying pitchforks. They were shouting and chanting, "Why didn't you do something, Stella? When are you going to make it right?" Under the blanket her slight body jerked; feet kicking and hands slapping back at the pursuing demons, snorting and moaning guttural laments in mental agony.

CHAPTER 9

CLARE'S STORY

Clare Brandon was a life-long product of the California Child Protective Services System, shuttled through more than a dozen different foster homes by age fourteen. Abandoned at birth by a father unknown and crack addicted mother, (both assumed long since deceased), she was malnourished, mentally neglected, and projected the physical body of a nine year old; skinny hips, tiny bumps for breasts, chocolate rich hair, and dark, puppy-dog eyes too large for her pale, slender face.

Those eyes landed her in a local KSBY-TV human interest story, not unlike segments about starving children in Africa or kittens at the pound waiting to be euthanized. Clare was profiled as a sweet but bedraggled and forgotten orphan child hoping a kind and responsible family would take pity and adopt her. No mention was made of her temper which rivaled a New York City cab driver's with attitude. She maintained her composure most of the time but could twist off in a heart-stutter with a take-no-prisoners resolve.

Billy and Stella Morton watched the report during a late night newscast and decided they were in agreement; they wanted to adopt this youngster, though each secretly for different reasons. Billy saw an opportunity and solution to every pedophile's wet dream: a teenager with the physical characteristics of a fifth grade prepubescent girl. Stella on the other hand, saw the opportunity to acquire a family pet which would absorb Billy's attention. She had no interest in her husband or his twisted sex games.

Theirs was not a happy marriage of almost fifteen years. Stella hated having sex with a man who wanted her to dress up in 'tween clothes, knee socks, and sometimes even diapers. Billy craved sex more than once a year, his jerking off techniques and kiddie porn habit no longer satisfying. Both hoped the pretense of a blissfully married couple unable to have children, hoping to adopt, would solve their problems. Billy thought Stella frigid, but didn't know Stella spent her afternoons in Tranquility exchanging mutual gratification with Harry Henderson while Billy was hard at work counseling traumatized military families.

Stella was once not quite attractive in her youth. However, ageing had deleted the 'quite' from her current mien, leaving dull watery eyes and equally lackluster shoulder length, frizzy, darkish hair which if labeled *windswept* would be a kindness. With a body that quit without getting started, she chose to conceal her small breasted, thin physique and usually wore Laura Ashley type dresses which led many to think she was much younger. Raised by parents who never expressed affection, Stella was wary of people and chose quiet and introverted as her persona. She occasionally felt guilty for not indulging Billy with his fantasies, but with no inducement of passion on Billy's part, her skin crawled whenever he touched her.

When Billy and Stella applied for the adoption they appeared the perfect match for Clare: a respected psychiatrist with a federal security clearance and a demure, self-effacing housewife. No criminal records or civil offenses, their finances were secure, and they passed all interviews, reference checks and psychological testing. Right before Thanksgiving, they were awarded custody of Clare Brandon Morton, which set in motion events from which maybe only one of the three would recover.

Family life progressed slowly leading up to the Christmas holidays; dinner together in the evenings, fun walks on the beach, and lounging in the den to watch shows and movies on a giant flat screen. Billy lavished Clare with presents for Christmas, gifting her with an iPhone as well as a long oversized purple fleece robe, frilly underwear and shear nightgowns. Although Clare thought Billy and Stella a bit eccentric, she eventually relaxed and figured she had finally gotten lucky, and maybe the rhetoric the foster people spouted about waiting for the right family to find her were true. Even the students at her school in Morro Bay accepted her openly, thinking she was just another new kid and didn't pry into her unknown past. Clare's irritability seemed to dwindle and when bad days happened, Billy the psychiatrist seemed to know the right things to say and do to put her at ease.

By January, Clare was snuggled next to Billy on the couch while watching movies, and they would wrap themselves in a soft *Finding Nemo* quilt while snacking on popcorn or ice cream. Clare never had a father-figure and was enjoying this slight, small statured, slightly balding, soft spoken man who cared for her like no one had before. Being daddy's girl was an extreme change from living in a foster house with four to six kids all scrambling for a piece of attention.

Stella though, was a different ball of yarn and gave Clare bad vibes. After Christmas, Stella quit joining them on evening walks and became somewhat aloof. Her only involvement with Clare being polite feeding and watering with distant courtesy lacking any signs of affection. While Clare nestled with Billy on the couch, Stella would sit across the room in her knitting chair peering over the tops of her reading glasses at them. Initially, Clare thought Stella jealous, but realized Stella just didn't give a shit.

One damp, foggy evening in the middle of January, after insisting Clare wear her fleecy robe, Billy wrapped an arm around Clare and pulled her close during one of their movie-with-the-blanket rituals. Her thigh pressing tight against his, she was forced to lean onto Billy's chest and rest her arm along his waist. Stella's feigned indifference chilled Clare more than Billy's attention.

For the first few weeks it wasn't so bad. Billy occasional rested his hand on her thigh under the comforter, and then slowly glided it further up to part her robe, the better to brush his forearm softly across her skin. Clare knew exactly what was happening, as other foster girls had talked of men who had crossed the line. The older girls, fifteen to seventeen, insisted fondling was a given.

"Lots of sicko bastards out there," declared Zoe, a fellow foster inmate. "They all pretend it's natural and just part of growing up. Some aren't as bad as others, but the ones who drink are just fucking mean. Bastards; they think they're being nice."

"No one's ever touched me like that."

"Don't worry, they will. You stay in the system long enough, even adopted, it'll happen. Wait 'till you grow boobs. They can't keep their hands off you."

Clare was pretty sure Zoe's declaration was coming true. *Maybe I've got the one who thinks he's being nice.*

At the end of January, Clare changed places and watched TV sitting more toward the end of the couch opposite Billy, but he would lift up the quilt and pat the cushions, coaxing Clare to slide closer.

"Come on, honey, scoot over and keep me warm," he would wheedle in a thin boyish voice.

Stella in her chair, would look up quickly, narrow her eyes in a nasty glare and grip her *People* magazine so hard it crinkled, but after a moment, with bored indifference and a shoulder shrug, look back down to read, as if to say, "Go ahead, doesn't bother me one bit."

The week before Valentine's Day, Billy became bolder and would rest his hand higher up and periodically, *accidently,* press Clare's mound through the robe. He kept reminding Clare that Valentine's Day was coming up, and asking if there was anything special she wanted.

"I don't know. No one's ever given me anything for Valentine's before."

"Well, guess I'll have to surprise you with something nice."

That *something nice* was a silk pajama set, the top a V-neck button front, one size too large, so if she bent over it poofed out to expose her chest. She found the gift puzzling since Stella wore baggy sweat pants and flannel shirts with long sleeves bunched up at the elbows. The fuzzy robe disappeared, but the lurid comforter remained, its motif eternally etched in Clare's mind; Bruce's toothy white shark leer, Marlin the clown-fish's constantly anxious expression, and ingenuous little Nemo staring up at her while the right hand of Billy Morton pawed between her thighs. After a lifetime spent in the system, it never occurred to Clare to seek help, since the foster child's code was, "Keep your head down, fight your own battles with the kids, and for heaven's sake, never ever make waves against the adults."

At the start of Spring Break in mid-March, Stella left to visit her supposedly ailing mother in Visalia. Billy took leave from work and promised Clare a fun-filled week; just the two of them.

Stella left the house right after breakfast on Saturday. Car all packed and ready, she pushed back from the kitchen table and breezed out the back door with one parting remark, "Enjoy yourselves," said with as much emotion as, "Don't forget to take out the garbage." Clare, still in her silk PJ's, sat quietly beside Billy at the table.

"Don't worry about us," Billy called after Stella, leaning over to drape an arm around Clare's shoulders.

"We'll take care of each other, won't we, honey," Bill winked at Clare, giving her a little squeeze.

Clare was positioned to see through the kitchen window as Stella opened her car door, climbed in and drove away without a backward glance. *Too weird. Aren't they supposed to hug or kiss goodbye?* But, thinking about it, she couldn't remember seeing Billy or Stella show any warmth towards each other. Clare was the only one who received affection, and only from Billy.

Clare and Billy spent the afternoon walking through San Luis Obispo de Tolosa Mission near downtown SLO.

Throughout the day, Billy pointedly held Clare's hand as they walked through the church and later while they dined on baked rigatoni at Vieni Vai Trattoria. During the drive back to Serrano he rested his hand on Clare's leg just above her knee, occasionally sliding his palm up and down her thigh.

The two spent their evening beach-walking, listening to the surf breaking, and finally stopping to sit on a large granite outcrop to admire the sunset. Billy absent-mindedly rubbed Clare's back. "You're going to be old enough to drive in a year. We need to start thinking about what kind of car you'd like."

"You don't have to buy me a car."

"Sure, I do! You've been a really good girl. Plus, you know I'd do anything for my little movie buddy."

"How would I ever pay you back?"

"Silly," Billy joked, nudging her, "You don't have to; you already do enough for me."

"Wouldn't Stella be angry?"

"Let's not worry about Stella. I know she's been kind of a sourpuss lately, but she *does* like you. She just doesn't have that special connection with you, like you and I do."

Arriving back at the house, Billy insisted they both shower. "Go rinse and get the day's funk off and clean up. You wouldn't believe how much one can sweat walking around town all day. Run along, get washed up and put on your silk pajamas."

When Clare showed back up showered and dressed as told, she found Billy in the kitchen making hot chocolate. She peeked into the living room to see if the set was on and was relieved to see a blank screen, and the Nemo blanket folded over the back of the couch.

"Come into the kitchen. I bet you're tired. I know I am," Billy stretched his arms back, exaggerating a yawn.

She sat down at the table; her damp shoulder length hair draped to one side over the collar of her top. Billy walked over and handed her a cup of cocoa. "This cup is especially for you, honey."

Clare noticed his eyes focus on the front of her pajamas, her small pointy nipples outlined through the silk top. She leaned forward quickly to swing her hair forward as camouflage, and with the same movement plucked the clammy material away from her chest.

"Thanks," she whispered softly, eyes downcast. She straightened her back quickly, accepted the proffered cup and took a small sip. Billy reached behind for his own cup on the counter.

"Bottoms up! Make sure you drink it all. Waste not, want not," he teased, turning to observe her without making eye contact.

"Are we watching TV tonight?"

"No, I think we're both too tired. Go crawl into bed and we'll get an early start tomorrow. Think you'd like to go up to Big Sur or Hearst Castle?"

Clare breathed a sigh of relief; she'd been dreading a session on the couch. Alone. She'd been obsessing about it all day, and now he just wanted to go to sleep. Maybe, just maybe, she had him wrong; and maybe the things Zoe told her were making her loony. Reassured, Clare sipped her drink while Billy sat and smirked at her like a coach on the sidelines getting ready to call a trick play.

After a few minutes of discussing their day, Billy stood, stretching and yawning again. "My, oh my! Am I sleepy.

Let's wash these cups out and hit the sack. Finish up, now. Make sure you drink it all."

Clare dreamt about bad things that night. She didn't remember falling asleep, but as she awoke, recalled a dream where someone was hurting her, lying on top of her, grasping her arms and legs and not allowing her to move. She vaguely remembered crying over and over, "Please, don't. Stop. No! Noooo—"

She opened her eyes slowly and carefully squinted, scanned the dark room, pretending to still be asleep just in case someone was there. She saw nothing, heard nothing. Clare was frightened, as the dream had seemed all too real and painful. In fact, it still hurt. She slid her hands down to her crotch.

"Oww-w-w!" She fingered the raw and swollen skin between her legs. Clare sat bolt upright in bed, threw her covers off, rolled left to let her feet hit the floor and after a moment of hesitation, leaned over and clicked on her nightstand reading lamp. Blood covered her fingertips and now the lamp. Her period had finished a week ago.

Clare whipped around and stared at the entrance to her room. The door was closed. She looked down at herself and felt a popping sound inside her head, like a balloon detaching from its tether. Naked from the waist down, her jammy bottoms lay in a slick crumpled heap on the floor next to her bed.

She stood and quietly tip-toed to the door, clicked the lock, and ended up standing in front of her dressing table and wall mirror. Woozily, Clare regarded her reflection, pulled off the clingy top, wiped her hands on it and threw the shirt next to the pants. She turned on the table lamp, picked up a hand-mirror and in its reflection observed her red and swollen labia, blood still trickling from her vagina, and red smeared inner thighs. What appeared to be a bite mark indented her skin at the very tender top of where meaty inside thigh meets groin. Even her butt felt raw, like being rubbed in one spot for too long.

"That fucking prick-ass bastard!" Zoe had been right all along. Clare's first impulse had been to sneak into Billy's room, cave his miserable head inside-out with a baseball bat, then continue downward until his probing dong had been reduced to nothing but Cuisinart pulp.

Ironically, it was Billy who saved his own life that night, having taught Clare to control her rage. *Don't act out violently. Don't react negatively. Don't make it worse for yourself.* He had encouraged her to analyze her emotions, to calculate a rational response and take a proper course of action, even if it meant separating herself from her target and walking away. *Think it through. Let some time pass.*

Clare kept reciting Billy's mantras the entire time she silently dressed, snuck out the window and ran to the police station, collapsing outside on its sidewalk, numb. She used the cell phone Billy had bought her and dialed 911. Then with a sucking sound only she could hear, she slammed back into her head and sobbed onto her kneecaps as the wail of an ambulance dopplered its way across town to her. The only female on duty, the police dispatcher, ran outside to help. Through tears of embarrassment and fury, she lay on the gurney in the back of the ambulance, reciting over and over, "Zoe told truth, Zoe told truth."

CHAPTER 10

A SHITTY HARRY DAY

Two hours after Billy Morton licked his last on a glass window and slid to the floor, Harry Henderson was four miles north of Serrano near Highway One, furiously pumping his skinny knees up and down, burning off tension. He was pedaling the old lighthouse trail heading south from his house, which wound up and over the ridges dividing Serrano from the roadside hamlet of Tranquility. Harry was the overseer of Tranquility, an old ranching homestead from the 1800s, now a private village owned by a consortium of investors.

Tranquility, or T-ville to the locals, could be seen from the highway and was a day-tripping pit-stop back in time for tourists visiting the area with its isolated beaches, elephant seal viewing areas, and opulent Hearst Castle tours. Back in the day, it served travelers on the Pacific Coast Highway with a livery stable, blacksmith, mercantile, post office, and produced some of the finest butter, cream and cheese in all of Central California.

The colony now consisted of an assortment of artists' galleries, the aptly named Hill o'Beans Coffee Bar, curio shops and a glass blowing foundry housed in a collection of wood-framed farm homes, whitewashed buildings, leaning shacks, and rustic barns renovated into reasonably good condition. Seemingly stuck in the Sixties with gray haired, goat-milk yogurt slurping hippies in tie-dyed shirts plying their crafts, the town also enfolded a population of hybrid wannabe Gen Xers and Millennials; strawberry-blonde maidens sporting copious piercings wearing micro-skirts and razor-haired, sleeve-tatted hipsters, all living the ideal communal existence. Residents referred to themselves as Tranks.

Harry's today had not gone well. Right at the end of lunch rush, one of his baristas in the coffee shop had gone berserk. Shocked tourists ran for their cars. Harry had been busy bussing tables and straightening chairs on the patio outside the bookstore when he heard yelling and crashing glass.

Two elderly, blue-haired women imitating wind sprinters blasted past Harry to the parking lot. He dropped some chair cushions and rushed towards the bar to intervene, but crashed into an angled row of bicycles and tumbled across the brick courtyard, grabbing at his spasming lower back.

A pale-skinned, bleeding from the head guy, who looked vaguely familiar to Harry, bolted past him to an old model red Ford Taurus parked in front of the post office-cum-museum, yanked open the door, threw himself inside, and once the engine caught, spun gravel leaving Tranquility. Harry tiptoed into the shop and cautiously approached Clare, noting the wildly disarrayed chestnut hair, tears running down her cheeks and ping-ponging eyeballs. Breathing heavily, she was finished with her meltdown but looked close to blowing again.

"What the hell happened here?"

Even with his back continuing to spasm, Harry attempted to put an arm around Clare's shoulder, hoping to lead her to the rear of the bar as he eyed the broken mirror, cracked window, and crockery shards. Talking in a soft voice, Harry coaxed her from the few brave patrons who chose to stick around (now also viewing their phone vids to see if any juicy bits were good enough to post on YouTube) to see how the whole thing played out.

"Don't touch me, damn you! Get your fucking hands off me, you bastard!" Clare's tirade restarted. "You're just like the rest of them!"

She wrenched away so suddenly that Harry tumbled to the floor, hard enough to crack the back of his head. Seeing stars swirl, he saw her staring down at him, hands to mouth, then turn and flee. Using an overturned table to hoist himself upright, he followed at a distance, one hand to his back and the other to the growing bump forming on his skull. She ran into her one room shack behind the glass blower's shop, situated on the eastern rear side of the village at the back of the valley, and slammed the door shut. Harry, loping along at a distance, traversed the curtilage slowly, and upon reaching the threshold, head throbbing, stopped and courteously knocked.

Clare yanked the door open and screamed, "Leave me alone, you fucker, and go away before I kill you!" Quite a number of milling sightseers turned to stare.

Past his patience and in an equal fit of anger, Harry terminated her on the spot, yelling, "Get your stuff and get the hell out of here! You're fired! The bus will be by in another twenty minutes. Make sure you're on it." He threw two twenties on the door mat at her feet, and said, "I'm keeping the rest of your pay for damages. And remember, this is private property. You even think about coming back to buy a cup of coffee, I'll have you arrested!"

Harry hurried back to the coffee bar, limping all the way. He needed to see if he had any customers left and if he could get someone from one of the other businesses to fill in. *Jeez, what a crazy little snot! When Randi talked me into hiring her, she said Clare might have a few issues, but I can't operate a business this way. Good riddance!*

Around four p.m., Harry had given up trying to reopen the bar and finished talking with the lone county Deputy Sheriff who stopped by in response to a disturbance report called in by a concerned tourist. After assuring the police all was well, that Clare had vacated the premises and he was not pressing charges, he locked up and trudged across Route One to his two-story rancher's house, which was separated from the village back when they paved the Pacific Coast Highway. Hobbling onto the asphalt, tender head down and mind preoccupied, he startled at the sound of a blaring horn and screeching tires. Diving backwards off the edge of the roadway, he tumbled onto his already aching back. The car swerved, regained control and sped onward, but not before someone yelled an unintelligible expletive and trailed a middle finger at him. *Holy Moly, Harry, watch what you're doing before you get yourself killed!* Arriving at the sanctity of his kitchen, Harry slumped into a chair, massaging his beltline trying to relieve his tight muscles.

Grumbling, he grabbed a Longboard Lager and shuffled outside to the adjoining porch. "Shitty, shit day! Look what I get in return for trying to do a good deed."

When the second and third beers didn't soothe nerves nor loosen his pulled lumbar muscles (and now shoulder and neck from his second and third fall), Harry walked back over to Tranquility proper, making sure the businesses were locked up. Slogging back to his house (after looking both ways this time), he crossed the road and decided to climb on his black Cannondale mountain bike, hoping a view of the ocean and some cardio work would calm his headache and loosen the kinks.

The trail he biked was mostly a hiker's path. Although it was predominantly downhill, he still had to traverse three hills before he hit the flats where the trace veered away from running parallel with Highway One, down onto the promontory leading toward a small, day use only state park and the old lighthouse. As he neared the point, Harry stopped and gingerly climbed off his metallic green bike and inhaled deeply. He was sweating moderately from the beer and finally starting to feel better. The sound of nearby waves helped relax him as he walked through a grove of eucalyptus trees, the smell overwhelming as it bled directly from the trees into his aura; aroma therapy for the soul.

Harry loved this particular eucalyptus stand, especially when migrating monarch butterflies roosted in the trees during their generational journey to and from Mexico. Many an evening was spent sitting in the copse contemplating what a lucky life he'd led. He never looked forward to the muscle screaming uphill peddle back to his house, but he always enjoyed the reward of the trip, knowing he had just communed with nature at its finest while doing his body a favor.

Saddled back up, he peddled out of the trees around a bend and spied a dark colored, well used cargo-style, Ford F-350 Econoline extended-van, parked where a seldom used service road dead-ended near a strip of sandy beach in Lighthouse Cove. The van was backed in, like it had turned around so it's nose pointed toward the highway. *Odd. Wonder how they got it here through the chained gate?*

After leaning his bike gently against one of the bigger rocks and leaving his helmet dangling from a handlebar, he walked carefully to the van and cupped his hands against the driver's window. Wincing as he stretched his neck, he concentrated on peering beyond dark glass.

"Huh. I'm gonna call this into the cops after I get a picture of the license plate. Vehicles shouldn't be out here. This is a bike-and-hike trail only," Harry fumed silently.

Two airborne squabbling gulls interrupted Harry's focus, causing him to jump ever-so-slightly. Chicken skin prickled his sweaty biceps and trickled up his shoulders to his neck, and scalp. Giggling at his foolishness, sound masked by ocean and birds, he stepped back and pulled his new iPhone from a pocket, intending to walk along the van's length to its back double doors. Head down, fiddling with camera functions, he didn't hear the faint skitter of pebbles. He smacked full-on into another person wearing a cycling helmet and mirrored glasses.

Off balance from the impact, Harry had one moment to glimpse a portion of a bicycle wheel leaning up against the van's rear bumper before he was twirled and face slammed against the window into which he had just peeked. An arm wrapped tightly, firmly, around his neck, cutting off the flow of blood to his brain.

"What are you doing? You're going to kill me! Stop!" Harry tried to hiss, pulling vainly, slapping and clawing at the arm, desperately spitting and spluttering with cat brawl instinct. A five mile peddle, three beers, and stiff neck and back worked to his disadvantage restricting his ability to react. The assailant locking his windpipe in a constricting vise made it impossible for Harry to breath.

Because of his recent shoulder injury, he couldn't reach behind to rip the attacker's arm away. Staring at his bulging eyes and gaping mouth, a large leach on his back and a sea serpent locked around his neck, all reflecting back at him from tinted glass, Harry disbelieved the vision; not only of himself, but whoever perched on his left shoulder. The sun-blocked lenses of his assailant slipped. He knew those eyes.

Maybe if he'd been getting enough oxygen to his brain he would have thought to fall backwards and crush his foe, but he'd become so very tired of falling this afternoon. As he slumped forward and oozed down the van's door to dusty earth, he realized his day had taken a fatal turn past *merde* and his toilet bowl was flushing.

The monkey on Harry's back lowered their entwined bodies into a sitting position, and then quickly pressed his face into grit while pinning his upper body to ground. His mouth buried in fine dust and sand of drought-stricken trail, he tasted powdery particles scrape down his esophagus as he struggled to inhale. Not realizing his eyes were closed, he couldn't understand why fireworks were flashing over the Pacific. *Thought they only shot those off during holidays?*

Harry finally ceased struggling when he felt his esophagus crunch. His sparkling skyline faded with the final sunbeams of dusty dusk. Tonight, Harry didn't have to worry about his uphill trek home or calling his chiropractor in the morning. His shitty Harry day had just turned into a crappy day in paradise.

Out on the PCH, a bright yellow mountain bike picked up speed, rider blasting south on the declining straight-away into Serrano. A white Bell helmet and wrap-arounds shaded concentrating eyes, the owner's adrenalin long gone, muscles burning, with breathing slow and steady. Not much to hear wearing a helmet blocking the sound of whooshing wind.

Silence.

CHAPTER 11

BILLY STILL BE STIFFIN'

After questioning Randi about Billy's last day on the job, Mango detoured to The DP and ordered a flat of coffee and a dozen breakfast tacos to go.

"A misnomer," Mango pondered while waiting for his order.

In New Mexico, they are called *breakfast burritos*, with one stating *red*, *green*, or *Christmas* to denote which chile pepper sauce(s) should be ladled inside to complete the innards, which never, ever contained jalapenos. In Texas, they are known as *taquitos*, and are usually accompanied by little plastic cups of *pico de gallo*, red salsa containing jalapenos or green salsa with tomatillos. In California, they are breakfast tacos or wraps. No matter the name, and paired with the regional sauce *du jour,* they remain the Southwest's staple for breakfast on-the-run; a flour tortilla stuffed with scrambled eggs and one's choice of bacon, sausage, chorizo, potatoes, cheese, onion, or whatever else is available, all wrapped up burrito style in tinfoil. Thinking about their many incarnations made Mango's mouth water.

Arriving back at the beach where Billy still lay, Mango navigated down the stairs juggling the bag of leaking breakfast in one hand and a tray of coffees in the other. He noticed roughly a dozen gawkers still milling about the yellow police tape a hundred feet south of Billy. Skibitski, standing guard at the cordon, looked toward Mango and then down toward the bag, puppy-dog eyes imploring, begging for a treat. Mango shook his head imperceptibly and motioned a stay command with the bag, cocking his head toward the tape barrier at the same time. Amused, he watched as Ski sighed, resigned to obey, standing firm.

A tarp and granite outcropping concealed the scene from the north, nobody bothering to rubberneck from the cliffs because much of it was private property, the view better at beach level anyway. The rental houses were vacant at the moment, but were all booked with guests soon to arrive for the weekend. The medical examiner, Dr. Novak, circling the body and photographing it from different angles, waved when he spotted Mango walking toward the crime scene. Mango waved the bag of tacos back at him.

Still snapping pictures, he tersely greeted Mango, "Morning Chief. Starved. Haven't eaten since last night's dinner. Not since before the wreck up by Topaz. Kids."

He inhaled abruptly, and then recited rapidly as if he were in the morgue and speaking into a recorder, "Too fast, too much beer, not enough brains. Didn't leave an inch of skid-marks. Never made the last ninety degree. Just straight offa the runway, ya' know? Airborne, then rolled. Phish. One without a seatbelt? Go figure out the rest."

Dr. Nick Novak, commonly known as "Doc Kno," was in his mid-sixties and sported a thinning crown of closely cropped white hair. He stood with a slight slouch and bowed legs acquired from a lifetime of squatting over and leaning across his dead clients. At times, he seemed less medical doctor and more mechanical engineer, analyzing a catastrophic bridge failure to determine what fatal flaw caused its collapse.

Satisfied with his shots, knees popping, Novak stood from his crouch. He short-stepped around Billy toward the proffered bag and accepted two tacos, snapping off plastic gloves and stuffing them into a plastic baggie hanging from his waist, rinsing his hands from a squirt bottle of alcohol, seeming to appear like magic from one of his many cargo pants pockets.

"Thanks for breakfast. Any with chorizo?"

"You know better than that, Nick. Plenty of onion and salsa, too. I wouldn't forget my favorite M.E. So, what do you think? Initial thoughts?"

"Don't think he was killed here. Hard to tell with the shading, but I think I see faint livor mortis where it shouldn't be."

"Upper left arm, triceps?"

"Yeah, you caught that too. Good eyes. Probably broken neck. Surprised if it isn't. Effing dog prints scrambled everywhere like they found a pound of hamhock. Looks like urine on the back of his head and neck, sand mysteriously washed away at the hair line, and indented sand dots where it dribbled off. Talk about having a bad morning. Let's hope he wasn't sodomized!"

"After four years in Soledad that would be a little difficult to determine," quipped Mango.

Kiana, who had silently sidled up next to Mango and filched a coffee from the cardboard tray, snorted into her cup before taking a sip. "Funny! That's sick, but funny!"

Doc grinned and winked at Kiana as he chewed through his breakfast, dabbing red salsa away from the corner of his mouth with his tongue.

"One good thing going for Billy is, we can't smell the difference between him and all the reeking kelp around him. The flies don't seem to either," Mango retorted wryly, pointing at the tangled heaps of seaweed covered in swarming clouds of black kelp flies.

"Whew," Kiana waved her hand in front of her face, "Stinks. Beach is covered in this stuff all the way to Morro Bay today. Happens more often than I'd like, but it's a part of living here. Feeds the sea life, birds, maintains the ecosystem and all that, but I hope the next high tide washes it back out! Guess if we didn't have all the flies we'd deal with the stench a lot longer. Price we pay for life in our corner of utopia, huh?"

Kiana pointed at the large, wet stain centered on Billy's pant crotch. "The other good thing is we're outside. Hate it when they die inside a building. Nowhere for the smell to go."

"Except up your nose," piped up Doc.

"Seems the flies are more interested in the sea kelp," quipped Mango.

"Smart flies," dead-panned Kiana.

Kiana sipped at her coffee and hid her smile at Mango over the rim of her cup. She was even worse with gallows humor than he, and was considered just one of the guys who enjoyed similar interests in common. In their four years working together they had become surfing, hiking and biking buddies, but never bed buddies. She knew there was a mutual attraction. *But why screw-up a good thing*? Both loved their jobs, were comfortable being single, and enjoyed the bond of not only their friendship but the respect and camaraderie which came with policing in a small department. It also helped that Mango was dabbling in widower therapy called Kate Brewster.

"Thoughts on the perp, Kiana?" Jack queried.

"Could be Stella; she had reason enough. An empty marriage. Hell, an empty life and now her predator husband is back in town. Guess she never divorced him. Can't even fathom how you get into a situation like that. Lot of people out there just like her leading dysfunctional lives, plodding along like zombies, a razor's edge away from the tipping point from cracked to purely insane. Maybe with Billy back it became too much?"

"Randi voiced the same sentiments. She also confirmed that Stella and Billy could have been together at the house," he nodded to the top of the cliff, "Billy painting and Stella cleaning up for the next renters. That and Ski's visual of the car, but we've no confirmation both were there at the same time."

Mango was reaching for his cell phone just as Dora's voice crackled through his radio,"Central to Chief, central to Chief."

He stopped speaking, raised his finger in a wait-a-second manner, and answered, "Good morning Dora, thought you had Saturday off."

"Did, but heard you might be busy."

"Thanks. It is appreciated. What have you got?" Mango replied into his hand-held.

"I'm gathering print-outs of all involved, assigning case numbers, and briefing day shift. And, we just got a call from a hiker about a panga boat, on the beach just south of Lighthouse Point on the left trail that runs past the eucalyptus trees. Sheriff's office has a unit enroute but it may take twenty minutes."

Mango liked Dora. When dispatching, she was a second set of eyes for the officers. She was also a lot of fun, great for morale and not to be messed with. It was an unspoken, unofficial rule, that when Dora told someone to jump, they did. A veteran on the force longer than anyone, she knew every single soul in Serrano. Third generation local, combined with twenty years at the PD, she had the salt to keep the entire department in line. Thorough, professional, and an efficient administrator with a keen business sense, Dora was one thing old Chief Williams had done right.

"Chief to Serrano Three. Ski. Come over here a second," Mango said, motioning to the young rookie.

"Yes, sir?"

"Head out to the boat and preserve any evidence at the scene until SLO-SO arrives. If it's like a usual drop point, there's nothing left but the odor. Take some pics, secure the scene and wait for the deputy to get there. Use caution; just because the boat looks empty doesn't mean there aren't any bad guys around."

Mango sighed and said to no one in particular, "Those stripped down, open-hull fishing boats with simple outboard motors coming up from Mexico are getting way too common along this coast. Used to be they'd motor clear up Big Sur into a nice secluded cove to offload their tons of pot. Then they figured out the Hearst Castle coastline was easy pickings. Getting lazier and greedier, they've discovered our little inlets make perfect dumping grounds. Looks like we're gonna to have to step up our coastal patrols!"

Mango, Kiana, and Doc watched as Ski jogged as best he could through the soft sand, policing accoutrements on his service belt jingling as he headed for the stairs. Pausing, he turned, putting his hands together in a praying motion, and then pointed to his open mouth. Mango tossed him a tinfoil bound burrito which Ski caught one-handed and resumed his stride.

"Thanks, Chief!" he called back to them.

"Looks like a busy morning, so we better distribute the rest of breakfast," Mango said.

"And I was about to see if I could take the day off and go surfing," Kiana pouted.

"I promise, as soon as we get this case wrapped up, you can go surfing and I'll join you. Deal?"

"Shoot. Now I bet you want me to go with you to see if Stella's home."

"And the lady wins a stuffed bunny! You'll make a hell of a detective someday, de la Cruz."

Doc Kno cleared his throat. "Not to break up the comedy act, but I'm about dead on my feet and I still have work to do."

Standing up a tad straighter, the M.E. recited formally, "It would appear you have a homicide, but it is possible, even with the slightest degree of possibility, he could have done a header off the cliff. His neck does appear to be broken but we should expect a more pronounced crater effect from the fall. His body should be a little deeper in the sand, don't you think?"

Not waiting for a response, he continued, "I will have more later on the tox levels. The livor mortis has me questioning. If it is livor, that means he died a few hours back and was then moved. But again, with the cool fifty-five degree night, I will have to estimate accordingly. But yes, he could have been killed yesterday afternoon and then moved here over night. I'll have more info for you later."

Mango and Kiana looked at each other. "All we need is a call from Dora saying Stella's at the station and wants to write out a signed confession. We should have this done up by noon," Kiana hooted.

"I wish you would not joke like that, Lieutenant. My overtime budget is taking a hit already without you adding bad juju to the mix."

"My apologies, Doctor Novak," responded Kiana, with a slight bow from the waist.

"Accepted. Chief Mango, I await the deceased at the morgue within a respectable time, so I may assist you with your official investigation." Dr. Kno turned and strode imperiously away.

"Somebody got cranky in a hurry," Kiana whispered to Mango.

"Maybe the salsa in his taco gave him heartburn," Mango whispered back.

CHAPTER 12

DING DONG

"Serrano Three to Chief, come in," patrolman Skibitski called on his radio.

"Go ahead, Three."

"Chief, we have us a drug panga. There're still a few bales left near the boat. Either they got spooked or just ran out of room. Got tire tracks and looks like someone cut through the padlocked chain at the cattle guard leading onto Highway One."

"Preserve as much as you can and then walk out to the gate and wait. SLO-SO is on the way. One more thing. Make sure they bag the padlock and section of chain that was cut. Not only do we want to dust for prints, but striations from a bolt cutter are sometimes very distinct and identifiable.

"10-4. I walked in. Nothing is disturbed."

"10-21 this number," said Mango, meaning *call him.*

When Mango's phone rang, he told Skibitski that Doc Kno was finished with the on-site examination of Billy and EMTs were transporting the body to the San Luis Obispo morgue. Mango relayed that he and Kiana would be driving up to Stella Morton's, and once the SO showed and was briefed on the panga, Ski was to rendezvous with them at

Stella's. Ski was to keep his ears open to radio chatter and for sirens, just in case the visit with Stella went bad and a pursuit ensued, and was reminded of the Stop-Strip in his trunk.

"However," Mango cautioned, "This is an informal visit and welfare check. We don't have enough evidence to rush out and get an arrest warrant for her."

Phone conversation finished with Ski, as he and Kiana walked to their vehicles, Mango continued, "We play this nice and easy. Let's not come off too abrupt as she may or may not be involved with Billy's death. Either way, be nice to keep her calm for safety's sake and more willing to talk, so we can get some questions answered.

Mango and Kiana took their own units. Kiana's Dodge 300 had lots of go juice under the hood in the off chance a vehicle chase came into play. It was a marked unit with a cage in back, just in case Stella needed to be transported.

Leaving both vehicles street-side, they walked down the driveway across a culvert into the small parking lot to the back of Stella's complex. The apartments faced the seasonally dry Serrano Creek which provided a garden ambience; trees, birds, and rustling leaves giving tenants a soothing view from their living room windows.

"One door into each apartment from the parking lot with the creek cutting off access out windows. Let's just knock and tell her we have some bad news and we'd like to step in and talk. Can't inspect her apartment, but keep your eyes peeled for weapons or obvious evidence. We can always come back later with a warrant. Make sure your shoulder microphone is on. We don't want an attorney to come up with any reasons for an exclusionary defense. Since she's next of kin, we'll tell her about Billy and wait for her reaction," Mango instructed.

After Mango knocked three different times, Stella slowly opened the door a few inches, left hand firmly holding the inside doorknob, right forearm cocked above her head perpendicular to the frame. She wore a plain, faded grey, plaid house dress, greasy hair disheveled like it had been combed back with her fingers thirty seconds ago, but then maybe not. She unconsciously wiped her right shoulder against her nose and cheek. She smelled of stale wine.

Mango declared, "Stella, we need to speak with you. Can we come in for a minute?"

"About what? What are you doing here and what time is it?"

"It's about Billy. Something's happened. May we come in?"

"What about Billy? What did that bung-hole do now? Whatever it is, it's not my fault! Can't believe Randi's having him work for her, which means working with me. Says it's only for a few weeks 'til he gets money together to move on to LA. I don't want that dickhead in my life anymore. Nobody understands that?"

Stella inhaled a breath to say more but before she could, Mango interrupted, "You don't have to worry about Billy. He's dead. He was found on the beach this morning with a broken neck, in front of Randi's house where you two worked yesterday."

Mango paused, waiting for Stella's response. She stood still a few seconds then shook her head back and forth as if flies were buzzing her face.

"Dead?"

"Can we come in so neighbors don't get an earful?" Mango asked, wondering if this was a delaying tactic, stalling for time to concoct a story or was her mind so muddled in merlot her cognitive processes were pickled.

"Uhh. Sure. Guess so. I need a smoke," Stella stuttered, raking fingers through her hair while stepping back, turning to reach for a pack on the cluttered table around the corner from the door.

"Go right ahead," Mango soothed as he and Kiana stepped inside the tiny foyer, shuffling forward as much as possible until Stella refused to back up further. Kiana frowned at Mango. He knew how much she hated cigarette smoke.

Mango shrugged back at her while Stella concentrated on her cigarette, tossing the lighter back on a table next to a tray overflowing with ashes and butts. Mango still couldn't decide if Stella was playing it cool and buying time to gain composure, or she really didn't know a thing about Billy's death and was trying to appear coherent after sleeping off a drunk.

"Billy's dead," cackled Stella, throwing her head back and spewing a stream of smoke. "Ding dong, the little turd's gone; my nightmare is over! Do you have any idea what it's been like for me? The way people have looked at me, always whispering and pointing? Like I've got some kind of disease; that skin stuff from Hawaii? Leap-rosy?"

"Leprosy. It's called leprosy, Stella," corrected an irritated Kiana, waving smoke away from her face, using the motion to crane her head forward, the better to scan the sparsely furnished studio.

"Whatever. I was the sicko's wife. Now I'm the widow. They all looked at me like it was my fault. No one knew what that little slut was like. She wanted it. I could tell. She made him do it!"

Mango interrupted, "Stella. Enough. When did you last see Billy?"

"Yesterday at Randi's Sixth Street rental. I was there cleaning. He took a break from painting and used my car to run a couple errands. When he came back there was a bad cut on his forehead and he was pretty upset. Told me he had a run-in with Clare up in T-ville. Said he went to see Harry about some odd jobs and when he went into the Hill o'Beans for a coffee, Clare was the barista. Said she went nuts, screaming and throwing stuff at him like he was the reincarnation of Freddy Krueger. All the customers ran for their bikes and cars; Billy, too. My car, actually. Hell, you don't think Clare killed Billy, do ya'?"

Up to that point, their main person of interest had been Stella. Neither knew of the recent brew-ha in Tranquility which now put a new spin on possible suspects. Lieutenant De la Cruz and Chief Mango quickly flicked each other a *holy shit* glance and hoped the bombshell would go unnoticed by Stella, who was busy with her own flicking of ash.

"What time did Billy return your car?" asked Kiana, much relieved to see the ciggy, sucked down to filter finally stubbed out. Stella wiped the ashes from her finger-tips into the threadbare material of her dress.

"Not sure. Two, maybe three o'clock? Not sure."

"What happened after Billy finished telling you about the fracas?" Mango asked.

"The what-us?"

"The disturbance with Clare?"

"I was peeved at him for being that stupid. But then, I'm the one forgot to tell him Clare works there." Stella shrugged one shoulder and continued. "Billy still had some touching up to finish. I was done cleaning so I took my car and left soon after he got back. Can you believe it? That idiot made it four years in the pen but was dead within four weeks of living on the outside."

If Stella was lying, she was doing a fine job. Mango reminded himself to remain open and objective, although twenty minutes ago he was fairly sure he had a crime of passion, a suspect and a motive with opportunity. Now he wasn't so sure about the suspect.

"Where did you go, after you left Billy at Randi's rental?" Mango queried.

"Here."

"Anywhere else between when you left and now?"

"Nope. Came right home and stayed here 'til you both showed up."

"Can anyone corroborate that?"

Stella looked at Mango quizzically.

"Did anyone see you coming, going, or staying home until now, or did you talk with anyone who could attest to your whereabouts?" Mango rephrased.

Stella lifted both shoulders and shrugged. "Don't know and no."

"Stella, do you have any plans or know what you're going to do next?"

Confused, Stella wrinkled her brow and asked, "What do you mean? Like what?"

"Like leaving town," de la Cruz interjected.

"Whoa, stop right there you two! You don't think I killed Billy!" Stella backed up two steps; arms stretched forward, palms out. "I've been done and over that bastard for years, and if I had wanted to kill him I sure as shit wouldn't have left the bugger lying out on the beach in front of a house I just cleaned! Christ, give me a little more credit than that."

"We're not sure what to think, but then the day just started. I am going to leave an officer parked out on the street. If you need anything or you hear anything strange, we'll have an officer right here for your safety," Mango appeased.

"Am I free to leave?"

"Technically, yes. I'm not detaining you. However, if what you're telling us is true and you didn't kill Billy, then the killer is still out there and you could be next."

"I didn't kill Billy. Trust me; I could do a helluva' lot worse than just kill him. I knew enough to send him back to jail. But now we don't have to worry about him diddling more kids," Stella huffed.

"I thought at Billy's trial you were unaware of what he was doing with Clare, and you're saying you know about more kids?" asked an incredulous de la Cruz.

"No! What I mean is people told me things. After the trial."

"If you learned of other children he abused, why didn't you report it?" asked Mango.

"Report gossip? Report so-and-so told me their friend's daughter's friend said something? With my ruined reputation? Yeah right."

"Were you blackmailing Billy?" pushed de la Cruz.

"Huh? No! Look at how I live. And besides, Billy didn't have a pot to fart in much less money I could squeeze. It's something I threatened him with to keep him from bothering me, since that bitch Randi made us work together. Now leave me alone. I've done nothing wrong."

Mango asked Kiana as they walked down the steps from Stella's apartment, "You see the mirror lying on the coffee table?"

"Oh yeah. Though she probably uses it for putting on makeup."

"She needs a bigger mirror than that for makeup," Mango replied.

"We can't all be beauty queens, you chauvinist. Though it almost makes you feel sorry for Billy."

"Almost."

"The white powder on the mirror. Coke or crystal meth?" asked Kiana.

"My money's on meth since it's cheap and easy to make from Sudafed. If we have cause to search in the near future, make sure we get a sample."

In the parking lot, Mango pointed his chin at Stella's red Taurus. "Let's go take a simple plain-view peek into her car to be thorough."

Mango inspected the driver's side while Kiana peered in through the passenger side windows. On the backseat sat a small bucket, a box containing cleaning supplies, a couple brooms, and a mop angled across the bench seat. On the rear floorboard, handles half hidden under the passenger seat, lay what appeared to be hedge clippers.

"Didn't know she did landscaping, like trimming shrubs and hedges for Randi," commented Kiana.

"Not clippers. Those are bolt cutters," Mango determined after studying the tool a moment. "Let's make sure both the car and Ms. Stella don't disappear on us. You watch the car. I'll go back up, talk to Stella and see what she knows about these."

A couple minutes later Mango and Stella hustled down the stairs and joined Kiana at the Taurus. Stella was upset.

"I don't own bolt cutters. I don't know nuts from bolts. Why would I need something that? I'm a maid."

"They're just called that, but are used for cutting through things like padlocks, chains and other thick metal objects," Mango clarified.

"So?" Stella glared back at him, mystified.

Kiana pointed at the device in the car, "Right there Stella, those are bolt cutters."

"Never seen them before. Maybe they're Billy's and he forgot them when he returned my car, but they're not mine," Stella persisted.

"Then you don't mind if we take them with us?" Chief Mango asked. "We'll give you a receipt for them."

"Whatever. Don't mean a thing to me. You want 'em, take 'em."

Mango pulled one nitrile glove from a cargo pant pocket and retrieved them, careful to not disturb anything else.

Stella studied Mango's face, then asked, "You think they're connected to Billy's murder?"

"Right now I'm not sure what to think. But if you say they're not yours and have no idea how they got there, it would be best for us all if we preserve them without additional contamination.

"Lt. de la Cruz," Mango continued, "Kindly fill out a property receipt and consent search form, and provide a copy of each to Ms. Morton."

Cutters in possession, they observed Stella climb the stairs back to her apartment before they strode to their own cars. Mango watched as Kiana carefully wrapped the utensil in large paper sheeting and then locked them in her trunk.

"Think those have anything to do with the panga boat?" she asked.

"Don't believe in coincidences. Pretty suspicious we stumble upon a tool which can cut a chain and padlock; right after Ski calls us about that very occurrence on the trail to where the panga boat was found."

"And where *is* Ski, by the way?" Kiana mused. "He was supposed to meet us here."

"One of many exponentially increasing questions to which we need answers. Doc Kno cautioned you about jinxing this case. To paraphrase, 'We'll have this wrapped up quicky-quicky with time enough to go surfing.' Right," Mango grunted.

"Proper term is *wiki-wiki* and has nothing to do with swiftness," retorted Kiana.

"Guess we better find Harry and Clare; try to figure out what happened in T-ville and what chaos Billy stirred up. Call in and have Dora check yesterday's duty reports, see if anyone answered a call about a ruckus at the Hill o'Beans."

Both their car radios sounded, "Chief Mango, this is Central. 10-19 the station," meaning *return.*

"10-4," he replied. "Wonder what that's about. Maybe Doc Kno has good news for us."

They looked at each other knowing the opposite. You could sense it in Dora's voice. The day also had a certain feel about it. The fog was extraordinarily dense and should have burned off long ago. It was causing a damp chill to penetrate their padded jackets to the point of making them shiver. The only thing missing was a flash of lightning followed by its crack of thunder. Spooky organ music was more likely, as the region was stuck in serious drought going on three years.

"Hang out here a few minutes in case Stella gets frisky and wants to come out and play," Mango instructed. "She leaves, you follow. I remember a windshield crack and tires a little thin on her car. Seems like a good excuse for a safety violation stop. Bottom line, she can't leave the town limits, but no pursuits. We'll call SLO-SO if it looks like she has rambling fever past that point. If she stays put, I'll have someone relieve you soon; I need you for more than babysitting. Be careful."

"Don't worry about me. I'm good. But something's brewing; I can feel it in my bones. Bad karma, Brah. I'll keep an ear to the radio."

CHAPTER 13

STELLA SCATS AND CAT TRACKS

Jack drove back down Serrano Canyon Road heading for the station. He checked his watch. Nine o'clock. He should call Kate. She was probably packed and headed home by now. Not the perfect anniversary weekend, ending before it began.

"Hey darlin'. Had a few minutes and thought I'd call. I'm sorry about this morning, but we have a murder and I have a feeling it's gonna get worse before it gets better."

"So it really is a murder? I do understand. It's just, it was supposed to be our—" She sighed. It was hard being in love with a cop, much less Chief of a small resort town, what with all the constant interruptions. On the other hand, conversations were never dull and his police humor made her laugh like no other. She comprehended too well, working from dawn to dusk on her ranch, how easily one's daily life could be interrupted by emergencies; the early birth of a calf, a machine breaking down, or a life threatening accident from farm equipment.

"Who was it again? A local?"

"Old Billy Boy Morton found this morning napping on the beach, except he had a broken neck which may have happened elsewhere. I'm heading back to the station now. Also, a panga boat was found near the park on Lighthouse Beach. Ski should still be there and Kiana's up at Stella's apartment, just in case. So, how's your morning going?"

"Let's see. Stayed in bed until seven-thirty crying in my pillow. Made a pot of coffee then forced myself out onto the deck to watch the sunrise. By myself, I might add."

"Boo-hoo! Some people have it rough," Mango laughed, but she was right. He wished for the memory of that languid morning which didn't happen, which was not happening with increasing frequency. They lived more than a hundred miles apart, subsisting on together-time during weekends and the rare weeknight. He could retire tomorrow with a decent income and move up to the ranch. But Jack wasn't a rancher and that was a problem for him. He'd romanticized living the dream of riding pasture on horseback, the original American West's profession. He'd a fair taste of it in New Mexico due to his friendship with a family who owned a fifteen by fifteen square mile Mexican Land Grant, home to black bear, mountain lion, mule deer and a herd of nearly ten thousand elk. Louie Grider, foreman of the Hernandez Ranch, allowed him and a few choice compadres to explore it on horseback with access to places rarely seen. The property was now a federal preserve with vistas of Louie's cabin immortalized in a show, filmed there about a contemporary western lawman working the hinterlands. The thing about ranching; it was hard work and not very exciting. He enjoyed working hard and a job done well, but agreed with his mother's advice, "Work is work, but don't kill yourself over it. Nobody ever said on their deathbed, 'Gosh I wish I had spent more time digging ditches.'"

Mango pulled up to the station and saw Dora outside, flirting with Marshall Cormac, a San Luis Sheriff's Deputy and Canine Officer. Marshall was leaning casually against his black 'n white, while his dog, Buster, confined in the back seat, hung his head through the half-lowered window vying for Dora's attention. Mango had met Marshall a week after moving to Serrano, out for a joyride in his personal red F-250 with New Mexico plates, hauling ass up a back road past the Nacimiento and San Antonio lakes. Marshall had clocked him at seventy-five mph. A lifelong friendship was born.

"Guess you're about to tell me what brings you here," Mango preempted. Giving Dora a perceptive wink, he gripped Marshall's hand and shook it solidly. A fellow New Mexican, Marshall's barrel-chested, muscled torso was the result of a mixed Mexican-Irish heritage. Standing an unanticipated close to six feet on such a stout mid-body, the female deputy sheriffs wondered if his long legs 'up to there' included an 'as long up there.' None had found out. Yet. A fine head of thick dark hair, long black eyelashes and a smile dimple, mixed in with a severe five o'clock shadow always in evidence by one o'clock, added to his allure.

Marshall worked six years with the Las Cruces Police Department on canine and drug interdiction before getting into a shootout with two dope transporting bangers on the I-10 interstate. Civil rights groups and media hammered him, saying the Mexican Nationals were profiled and killed without cause. When the case was finally resolved and Marshall cleared of wrong doing, he promised himself he would get the hell out; twenty miles north of a busy border crossing was just too damn dangerous. He researched California's central coast and found it had just enough action to satisfy his adrenalin addiction, but not enough to make him paranoid. Since he was also U.S. Army, he viewed Mango as a brother in arms, if not in blood.

"You have a dead body, Chief."

"I know that," Mango said. He looked over at Marshall's German shepherd, head still straining, staring at all three in anticipation.

"Let me rephrase that. You have another dead body."

"And how do you know that?" a peeved Mango asked Marshall, turning his head to look at Dora.

"Why do you think I called you back to the station?" replied Dora, rolling her eyes.

"I was in the area. Thought I'd stop by to visit, but just as I arrived I was dispatched to give assistance. Dora here filled me in," soothed Marshall.

"Yeah. Sorry I snapped at you both. It's been a kick-ass morning, and looks like my butt's gonna hurt even worse, sooner than later. Let's go talk in my office. Bring Buster with you, too. Dora, could you bring us coffee and then sit down and brief us?

After receiving additional detailed information from Skibitski from the panga scene, Jack brainstormed with Marshall and Dora. The second victim appeared to be Harry Henderson, though initially there had been some doubt since much of his face was missing, courtesy of the local bird, coyote and miscellaneous critter population. After a quick discussion, Dora left to run NCIC checks on possible suspects and Mango called Kiana on her cell.

"Heads up. We have another body. Probably Harry Henderson, but since his face is gone we can't be absolutely sure. We're waiting for SLO-SO to send a couple more units to Lighthouse Trail, and once Pacheco gets in, we'll rendezvous with you and pick up Stella, then go take a look at the late Harry."

"She's officially a suspect?"

"Still unofficially and a POI, but I'd rather we handle this as a safety precaution for her well-being. There's obviously a connection, but *what* is the big question."

"Both her ex- and her bed-buddy dead. If she's not responsible, someone's sure trying to make it look like she is."

"No argument there. Watch your '*okele*, Kiana. If it is Stella, she'll be desperate. No telling what she'll do next, especially if she's snorting that junk on her mirror."

Mango waved Sergeant Jorge Pacheco into his office. "Okay, Jorge is here. We'll be leaving in five."

Jorge, of average height and a firm two hundred thirty pounds of muscle, was an ex-parole officer. Burned out by the bullshit where seventy percent of his parole violators were given a wrist slap, he was Mango's enforcer. A fourth generation local boy, born and bred in Santa Margarita on his family's cattle ranchette and modest farm just north of SLO, Jorge was the first of his people to receive a college degree. He could change his calm stockman's demeanor easily and transform into a tough guy when needed, which is exactly what Mango needed now.

"Glad you could join us Sergeant! Don't bother to sit. I'll update you as we leave. We'll meet up with Kiana and brief her together, make sure we're all on the same page. You know Sheriff Marshall Cormac? Good. Let's ride."

Chief Mango, Sheriff Cormac, and Sergeant Pacheco parked their units off the corner of the entrance of Stella's apartment complex and walked in to meet a waiting Lieutenant de la Cruz.

"Here come the three dudes. You look like escapees from a hokey *Magnum, P.I.* episode; Thomas Magnum and his two sidekicks, ready to kick ass and fight for justice," she laughed.

The three men stopped in a line facing Kiana and gazed at each other. Mango preened and said, "It's obvious I'm Magnum since I'm the Chief; besides, I do kind of resemble him."

Keeping a straight face, Kiana cleared her throat, and pointed at Sheriff Cormac and Buster. "That must make you Higgins, what with the dog and all."

"Absolutely not! I'm the suave, good looking Italian guy named Rick, not some prissy English bloke," barked Marshall.

"Touché," replied Kiana.

They all turned as one and regarded Sergeant Pacheco nervously. "I'm T.C., the guy who owns his own business *and* a helicopter!" chuckled Jorge.

With a sigh of relief, and glad Kiana had eased the tension to a potentially squirrely custody detention, Mango continued in a more serious tone. "We think it's Harry Henderson who was found dead, lying under some brush at the eucalyptus grove near the lighthouse. A panga boat with product strew around it was also nearby on the beach. That's why Ski isn't here yet and why we are. We also know Billy was murdered. Stella is connected to both men and is unable to account for her whereabouts after leaving work yesterday afternoon, as well as bolt cutters found in her vehicle. The chain allowing a transport vehicle to enter the trail was cut. We need to take Stella into custody. If she is not the perp in at least one of these deaths, she may know something, be involved in the dope boat and/or be in danger."

"Today is your lucky day, girl!" Marshall beamed at Kiana. "But, any day you get to hang with me is a lucky day. Right, Jack?" Mango pretended he didn't hear.

"I didn't catch leprosy today either, *haole*," Kiana countered, throwing Marshall a stink-eye, a '*what in the hell was that*' look. Turning to Mango, she asked, "What do you mean, you think it's Harry? You said that earlier."

"Coyotes and such apparently like soft tissues like cheeks, tongue, eyeballs, ears, and nose cartilage. We're pretty sure it's Harry. Same body type, dressed like Harry when riding his bike, was known to frequent the Lighthouse Trail, and has a cursive tattoo on his right forearm reading 'Tranquility'. You know I'm not a guessing man, but we are pretty sure. Almost. Dental records and prints will confirm ID, and if we can't find next of kin, I hear Stella knew him well."

"*Madre de Dios!*" Jorge gasped, making the sign of the cross. "I hope he was dead before he was chewed on."

"Any sign of Stella?" Mango asked. Looking at the three officers, he kept reminding himself that murders happened rarely here. Except for the odd vehicle fatality, neither Kiana or Jorge had extensive experience with dead bodies, much less homicides, and Cormac had probably seen one too many. One was freaking over the description of Harry's corpse, another was doing a bad flirt job on his lieutenant, and the flirtee had just smacked him down royally. Normally, everyone bantered and ribbed each other with good natured camaraderie or resorted to sick humor, which showed Mango just how on edge they all were.

"Not a peep, Boss. I walked along the apartments, went around the building after you called, saw nothing, and haven't heard anything but birds singing," Kiana stated.

"Let's go knock and get this done. I'm thinking Kiana and myself at the door. Marshall, you and Buster down below by the steps and Jorge, you watch the parking lot."

Everyone quickly moved into position. With thumps on Stella's door unanswered, Mango found the apartment manager and had him give them access. Mango and Kiana entered first, it being their jurisdiction and case. They quickly cleared the entire one-bedroom to discover nothing. Stella had vanished.

"Marshall, get Buster in here and a scent going. I see a blind spot out back that heads down Serrano Creek, or where the creek used to be," Mango instructed, noting the drought. "Five years ago the water would have been too deep for her to go that way."

Mango glanced at his Lieutenant. She was mumbling, "Well, suck my toes. Bet she skunked out the door when I walked around the building."

She looked up to see Mango watching her and grimaced. "Sorry, Chief. Screwed the pooch on this one. Didn't think she'd rabbit."

"It happens. Can't be everywhere all the time. At least we know she didn't take her car. Let's go looking."

The group searched the immediate area to make sure Stella wasn't hiding nearby and waiting until everyone left. Back in her abode, a dusty bike was noted leaning up against a wall in the bedroom. It was probably too noisy and rusted for Stella to have used to make a quiet getaway, though it still looked street worthy.

"She may have made it to Route One by now, depending on when she left, which was probably right after I did. Stella didn't waste a minute," Mango hypothesized.

"Buster and I will do our best to track her. I'll switch down to channel seven for direct contact to you, but will text with general info," Marshall said as he picked out several personal items to wave in front of the dog's nose.

"Let's get the apartment locked up and taped. Kiana, call out a BOLO on Stella and one more officer to sit here on scene. Jorge, you take up watch here and respond to Marshall if he runs into any trouble. Otherwise, stay right here. We can't afford to have Stella's apartment contaminated and lose any possible evidence, if we need it. Keep in mind everyone, we do *not* have a felon loose, we have a *person of interest* and only a possible suspect. Watch your triggers and be careful. We have no idea what we just stumbled into."

Officer Skibitski on site with Harry was amazed how not having eyeballs, nose or lips made the deceased look so altered, and noted how extremely white were the cartilage, bones and teeth. No exceptionally strong odor yet, but flies were starting to arrive en masse, circling the prone figure lying like a wax dummy in an outdoor diorama. Ski made sure that no one but the M.E. would be allowed near the body.

Sheesh, not even ten o'clock and the body count is already two. Skibitski had posted SLO Deputy Sheriff Christy Cervantes on watch at the trailhead's cattle guard next to the parking lot. This freed him up to walk around the edges of the crime scene clicking off multiple photos; too many were never enough since film was digital these days. He'd like to come back later and shoot when the setting sun would angle better shadows on the tracks. There were vehicle tire and two sets of bicycle tracks about thirty feet from where Harry lay. The panga was discovered by a morning hiker. Harry was located by Officer Joe Skibitski with a little unexpected help.

Mango and de la Cruz pulled into the lot at the Lighthouse Trail and parked their police units next to a waiting Christy Cervantes.

"Hey, Deputy," hailed Kiana. "Lucky you got assigned to this side of the county. We heard that wreck at Topaz was brutal and the kid driving didn't make it."

"There's a lot of that going around today."

"This guy's dead, too, though by a different process," Mango informed her.

"Yeah, anyway, Sheriff Sederwall said that I'm all yours and anything you need, just ask. Well, almost anything."

"I hear you, Christy. Make sure you send my thanks to Sederwall. Do you mind staying here by the gate until we get back or until more units arrive?"

"Not at all. Skibitski's waiting for you. The sheriff also told me to tell you to not worry about jurisdiction. Both crimes are in yours, but we'll still assist. If it turns into something completely different, he'll call you later to discuss."

Jack appreciated the cross-departmental assistance. Many agencies would be bickering over who would take control of not one, but two major felony scenes. Jack played a pivotal role in this cooperative attitude three years back when he suggested the Serrano Council donate a small plot of land, with power and utilities, so SLO County could build an EMS sub-station at the north end of town. Not only did it lessen response time to numerous vehicle accidents on Route One, but also served as a safe haven for patrols to rest while still on duty having to cover such a large county. Sederwall had responded by donating a secured channel, one which regular scanners could not read, a huge aid when discretion regarding a delicate incident was needed.

Mango and de la Cruz stepped over the cattle guard and walked the extreme edge of the path so as to not disturb evidence. "Kiana, think we can get some casts of the tire tracks? Notice how one track appears a little deeper than the other?"

"Good in theory, but with such dry conditions and sandy, powdery soil, the casts wouldn't be of good enough quality for court or trial. But I did see the depth discrepancy, like the vehicle was much heavier going one direction than the other. I wish we had soft squishy ground so we could get a better tread impression! You know something else," she continued as they slowly strolled and observed, "There's only one set of bicycle tracks. It's possible to exit the trail elsewhere, but these look more like touring or road tires, not mountain bike tires."

Kiana didn't miss the cast query from Jack. He knew damn well they wouldn't be sharp enough as evidence for trial, and that the defense would tear their condition apart in court. Another one of his little tests, always checking for perception. But lately, she had noticed he was scrutinizing her summations at bit less often.

"True, but some of the mountain bikes I see these days are getting away from rough tires and are a hybrid off-road/street tire," Mango countered.

Kiana huffed. So much for her theory of decreasing oversight, especially after Stella slipped past her.

Mango adjusted his cap and sunglasses. The fog still hung above them, but with the sun higher, a glaring whiteness hard on the eyes now bounced off the shroud. The movement was used to hide a smile behind his hand. He knew Kiana was turning into one fine ace investigator under his tutelage.

They arrived at the eucalyptus grove to find Skibitski still photographing the crime scene, and Mango noted with approval, from beyond the yellow-taped perimeter. Harry lay on his side, but with torso twisted so his shoulders, neck, and head rested horizontally on the ground. If he'd retained his orbs, he would have been enjoying the view of sky and eucalyptus trees above, albeit with his jaw hanging open. Partially concealed under some brush, he obviously had been dragged there, whether by coyote or human remained to be determined. A tornadic cone of flies now buzzed atop Harry's ravaged face and around the halo of bloody gristle strewn onto surrounding dirt. This image, along with his intensifying aroma, negated the grove's soporific fragrance and soothing vibrations of nearby shore break, for which the trail was locally famous.

Lifting his gaze from this tableau, Mango looked at Ski then nodded down the trail toward the distant panga. "How long has he been here?"

A large, shiny coal-black cat paced back and forth in the sand in front of the boat, padding with a swaggering gait, hips rolling rhythmically as if comfortable at sea, yet limping slightly, favoring his left rear leg with each step. His wide dark face accented by a white goatee added just a dash of panache to his bearing. Weighing in at close to twenty pounds, he was obviously not timid nor overtly aggressive; he just was. With each turn, he seemed to be studying his surroundings, thoughtfully looking at the boat then the humans, rotating his sizable ears as he swiveled his head to gaze up the coast, then in the opposite direction, as if to say, *Where am I and what am I gonna do now*?

"Ever since I got here," answered Ski. "Found him sniffing what we're assuming is Harry, which is actually how I discovered him. Scared the shit outta me; I thought it was a frickin' panther chowing down on a deer!"

"He disturbed the body?" asked Mango.

"More like on-point with nose twitching, one paw batting at an arm but not connecting, jumping back with each swipe. I shooed him away and he seemed to understand about staying outside the crime zone. Acts like he's comfortable around people and been mostly sitting behind me while I took pics. He may have heard you two walking up the trail before I did, because a minute before you arrived he went back to the boat and started pacing. He's also obviously a male."

"He appears to be well fed. That is one big kitty cat! I bet he goes three feet when he's stretched out," admired Kiana.

The large cat stopped his patrol and sat, watching the hominids speak. He slowly blinked his eyes once.

"He behaves like he belongs with the boat. Make sure we bring him back to the station. We'll have a deputy drive him over to the county shelter. I may even take him if no one claims him," Mango contemplated.

"Ski, you check out the panga yet?" Mango asked.

"Kind of busy with Harry here. I did scope it from the top of the bluff with binoculars, just long enough to see there wasn't any activity. I couldn't see too much detail as it was foggier than it is now. Does appear to be some broken bundles lying next to the boat, like they got rushed."

"Or ran out of room," countered Kiana, glancing at the distant feline as its head bobbed up and down twice. "You see that? I think that cat agreed with me. He's starting to weird me out!"

All three giggled uneasily. Skibitski cleared his throat and continued, "A few strange things I've noticed about all the tracks. If Harry did ride in, I haven't seen his bike or helmet anywhere. Then you have one set of real knobby, which might be Harry's, coming down the hill from T-ville which disappear near where a different smoother bike tread starts and leads back to the parking lot. Then in the middle of the two different treads, it looks like someone groomed the area near the two sets of truck tire tracks where the transport vehicle sat."

"Show me," Mango instructed.

As the cat sat up straighter, craning his neck higher to monitor their movements, Skibitski led Mango and Kiana to the nexus of imprints which he had cordoned off earlier.

He pointed along the tape to where large tire tracks stopped after turning around in a circle, and at several scuffed sets of footprints behind these tracks where marijuana bales would have been loaded. He also pointed out a lone set of prints through the smoothed area which abruptly disappeared when the driver climbed into the vehicle. The dirt circling where the vehicle had been parked was brushed, resulting in a donut of flat sand circling a hole of windblown grit, which also matched the surrounding landscape.

"The single disappearing prints look like a person ran; definitely not walked. And," Skibitski added, "Why would someone go to the trouble of wiping the area around the vehicle but then leave footprints after loading and driving away? I'm pretty sure no one walked out of here. They rode out in the vehicle and maybe someone on a bike, but it sure wasn't Harry."

"Good observations, Ski." Mango continued, "Make sure you get lots of pictures, especially tread design and pattern. Don't forget to photograph the boat, beach and trail, and shots to give perspective on distance. Let's keep the trail, the road and beach closed and turn back any hikers who might filter in from feeder paths. Tell 'em they'll be open for use tomorrow."

Mango and de la Cruz's phones both pinged with a text from Marshall and Buster, "*No sign down canyon, back to unit.*"

Speaking to Kiana, Mango ordered, "Tell him to meet us at Dickies, and have Mr. Lee lay in a supply of sandwiches. Call Dora and have her advise all on-duty about the food available there, get someone to deliver here for Ski and Christy, and don't forget Jorge. Call Christy, fill her in and make sure she can hang until we get Harry tagged and bagged."

Focusing back on Skibitski, Mango instructed, "Doc Kno's on his way back and should be here by noon. He's not real happy about it, though he did perk up when I told him Harry's face was gone. Don't rile him, but make sure you jot down every remark he utters. There's got to be a connection here; we don't get random crime to this degree in Serrano. We need to start figuring out who came from where and why."

"Kiana," Mango added, "When you're done, let's go look at that panga and interview our only eye witness: a cat who probably speaks *no ingles*."

"Almost ready. FYI, Cervantes just radioed a couple more Sheriff's Deputies are hiking in."

"Excellent. Ski, when they get here, send them over to Serrano Lighthouse," Mango directed, "And have them check and clear the buildings and environs, plus bag anything that looks remotely like evidence. I doubt anyone would be foolish enough to hide out near a drug boat or dead body, but hey, anything's possible the way this day is going."

Walking towards the shore, they examined a wide trace of drag marks plowed into the trail, which Kiana theorized were made from canvas movers' skids used to tow marijuana bales. Churned sand, pebbles and dirt along with numerous footprints were scattered over and beside the smoother tow line, and paw prints crossed back and forth over the impressions. Mango hovered his size twelve above a giant boot indent and found his entire foot fit inside.

"Guess Kate wasn't thrilled you were called out," commented Kiana as they hiked down the bluff toward the boat, each constantly scanning the path and adjacent area.

"Yeah, she was pretty hacked. But she knows I wouldn't be here unless it was important, and two dead people in one day plus drug runners in this part of the world are definitely major. Wish we lived closer to each other so I could be the rancher's husband and still be Chief of Serrano. I can't quit and just be a cowboy. Without this job I don't know who I'd be."

"Same here. I feel so in control of my life here, and I like knowing that everyone from Dora on up to Sheriff Sederwall has got my back. This job, especially here, lets me live in the moment and help others; you can't beat the people, location or the waves. Be hard to give any of it up."

"There's not much surfing up at Brewster Ranch. Besides, who would you hang out with if I left?" Mango quipped.

"I'd probably go back to the Islands, see if I could get on with Maui County Sheriff's Department. I couldn't be a cop on Molokai. I'd end up arresting too many *ohana*."

"They have cops on Molokai? Hard to have a police department when you don't have traffic lights."

"They do too! Have police I mean; a small Maui County sub-station. They have crime; drugs, larceny, sex predators, alcoholism fueled spouse abuse, even murder. All the same fun stuff here on the Mainland. So, why when I try to talk to you about Kate, we always ends up on a different subject?"

"I thought we were talking about how distraught you'd be if I left the department and how you'd stumble tearfully back to Hawaii to console yourself."

"Ugghh, see what I mean? And now you're trifling with me. Yes, we were talking about you and Kate. What are going to do?"

"About Harry?"

"Kate. Your mom and daughter went to Hawaii to give you two some privacy. Did you buy a ring? Are you going to pop the question? That! You've told me this was one of the reasons you moved here. Now another anniversary has rolled around, so what are you waiting for? I thought Kate was your second chance at love, but you're no closer to being engaged much less married to the woman."

Mango stopped walking, removed his sunglasses, pinched the bridge of his nose, dropped his arm, looked up and contemplated blue sky now that the fog had finally burned off. Kiana stood with arms crossed and studied him.

"You're not going to ask her, are you?"

"I'm afraid I can't, Kiana."

"I've never known you to be afraid of anything."

"I'm not sure any more about who or what I want," he sighed, still not looking at her.

"For someone who preaches *carpe diem* and following the path of integrity, you are so full of bullshit. You want it all but won't make compromises in your life for the woman you love? Or are you are afraid of living, enjoying what the gods have blessed upon you, but are afraid of another loss? I'm not getting it, Jack. You and Kate can't work out the logistics? Sorry, but from a woman's perspective you're pissing me off. You're a fake."

"What?" Insulted, Jack finally dropped his eyes down to meet hers.

"Yeah, you heard me! Talking the talk, but can't walk it. You're the cleverest man I know, but when it comes to love you ain't even crawling. You're leading Kate on and I betcha she knows. You know it; shit, everyone knows. But you continue to play your little game by refusing to commit. For *Pele's* sake, at least have the balls to tell her you can't pull the trigger so she can move on with her life, with or without you. You owe her that!"

"You sound like my mother."

"Your mother is a smart woman. Maybe you should listen to her, if not me. I'm telling you this as a friend. If I didn't know you better, I'd bet you're having an affair with someone else."

Jack stood motionless, staring down at her like a lost puppy, eyes betraying a secret.

Kiana inhaled sharply. "That's it! There is another woman!"

"Kind of," he murmured.

"But how? When you're not with Kate, you're with me, or at the department, or with Jessica."

"She doesn't know that I'm in love with her." Jack looked like he wanted to say more, hunching his shoulders like a kid caught coloring a wall with crayons.

"Surely, it can't be Randi?"

Jack shook his head no.

"If it's not her, then who?"

He remained silent, nodding his head forward, a guilty smile playing along the corner of his lips.

Slow realization widening Kiana's eyes was quickly replaced by open mouthed horror.

"Me?"

Jack nodded once and continued to watch her hopefully.

Kiana whipped her sunglasses off, dark eyes glaring; face rippling into a façade of pure fury. She turned suddenly, facing away from Jack. Hands shaking, buying time, she fumbled at her breast pocket to hang her shades there.

Turning slowly to confront him, she cocked both fists on her hips below her duty belt.

"Right in the middle of an 'effing pervert's murder investigation? In the middle of another murder with a freaking drug boat and a bizarre cat watching us like we're both nuts? You bombshell me now?"

"You started this conversation."

"I asked you about Kate."

"I answered and told you the truth."

"As opposed to lying to Kate? Oh, no you don't. You're not making me the reason you dump her. Leave me out of it; I'm not going to be your excuse!"

"I've never lied to her and I certainly don't want to hurt her. But, I'm finding you and I are . . . more in sync. I've been trying to find the right time and place to tell you how I feel about you."

"Really? So you'd abandon Kate for me and then what? You're balking at marrying her because you'll have to resign as Chief and move up to her ranch? You know we can't be an item unless one of us leaves the department, and I guarantee you it's not gonna be me. And if you're not giving up your job for the woman you supposedly love, then you're certainly not gonna do it for me!"

"You have haven't told me if you return my feelings," Jack tentatively queried.

"You want it with both barrels? Fine. It doesn't matter what I feel because it doesn't matter. Neither of us is quitting. If I resign, I'd have to find a lateral transfer to a different department, probably many hours away. Ooops! Same problem you have with Kate, and you and I both know it's a freezing day on Kauai that I'd find such a job. Most likely I'd have to start at the bottom and work my way up again. Not doing it. If you resign, you better marry Kate. I told you, I'm not going to be the reason you two split up."

"You've got to admit, we make a good team," he chided. "You're my BFF, my surf buddy, my confidant, and my lieutenant. I love you and we love the same things. Why not have a life together?"

"Is this how it starts?" hissed Kiana.

Confused, Jack shook his head slightly. "How what starts?"

"You write me up for losing Stella? Then the nit-picking about every little error begins? Followed by substandard performance reviews, officer in need of training status and then probation, until you recommend to the town council I should be terminated? The age old story of the subordinate spurning her supervisor's advances only to be booted out the door?"

"I'd never do that to you. I'm appalled you'd even think that of me," Mango declared. "You're the best officer I have on the department. I rely on your good judgement and I'll put all that in writing!"

"Glad you said that." Kiana pulled the phone from her breast pocket and waggled it at Mango. "Anything else you'd like to say?"

"Guess I've said enough. I feel like an idiot. And I was wondering why you weren't spewing real cuss words."

Kiana clicked the record function off. "Very observant. Jeez, Jack. They have a word for this in Hawaiian."

"Which is?"

"I don't know, but I bet they have a word for it. Can we put this on the back burner and get back to work? Chief."

Mango raised an eyebrow. "This mean you're not my surf buddy no more?"

"Put your professional cap back on and let's go to work. We'll talk about surfing later." She sighed. "Do we need to talk!" Kiana turned and continued toward the abandoned panga and cat.

"But—"

"Later!"

"Yes, ma'am. You're the boss."

"Men," Kiana snorted, "Or should I say boys. "*Hupo pupule haole*," she mumbled under her breathe for emphasis, "Stupid, crazy white guy."

Arriving at the boat, Kiana concentrated on the crime scene, remarking, "I still can't get over how big these things are. When you look at photos they appear to be dingy sized. It's larger than the rowboats used to chase whales, back in colonial times."

Almost thirty feet in length, six at beam and four feet tall at gunwale, the prominent bow was buried in a deep sand furrow carved from an open throttle landing, leaving the panga leaning slightly to starboard. The dirty white hull of thick fiberglass with matching sun-bleached bench seats tied the sides together. Three 250 horsepower engines mounted on the transom at the stern were buried a foot in sand, their bent propellers hidden from view. It was simple yet efficient, designed to slice easily through ocean swells and carry up to five thousand pounds of cargo.

"If the bales were standard fifteen kilos each they probably dragged three kilos per person up to the truck. Supposing three men at nine kilos per trip makes ten trips back and forth. Probably took two hours before the vehicle pulled onto Route One," Mango postulated as he and de la Cruz pulled on their ubiquitous nitrile gloves. "We don't know what type of transport, but panel vans are usually their vehicle of choice; no windows except in front."

After Mango finished his conjecture, the cat jumped gracefully onto the tilted gunwale, tippy-toed to a rear compartment under the transom and parked himself beside a knapsack. Mango followed awkwardly, prodded, then reached for the bag and upon inspection inside, found three cans of Friskies cat food and a bottle of water, no label. Shadowed by the hungry feline, he scrambled back onto the beach, strode to a flat outcropping of black igneous basalt, chose a tin, popped the ring and peeled off the top, up-ended it, and while the cat ate, poured fresh water into a nearby eroded depression.

"You get one can Mr. Cat. The other two are evidence and will be dusted for prints. Let's hope I didn't pick the wrong can." Gazing into the cat's emerald green eyes, he was amused to note that their color was exactly the same as Randi's.

"I estimate they left five bales, and at twelve to fifteen thousand per, they left behind sixty to seventy-five thousand dollars," Kiana assessed as Mango returned the empty can into the knapsack. "Not a bad gratuity to leave behind."

"Something happened which made them drop and leave quickly. Even sixty grand's a pretty penny to throw away, no matter how successful a distributor. Most of this weed will end up far away. Mexican weed is not nearly as potent as what's grown in California legally, for medicinal purposes only, of course. This dope is for people who can't afford the high end stuff and will be sold on the street."

"Personally, I think the Feds should just make *pakalolo* legal nationwide and regulate it like alcohol for both recreational and medical purposes. Turn the Alcohol, Firearms, & Tobacco Agency into the ATWF, the "W" for weed. They could pronounce it 'At Woof.' It would become more profitable to grow and sell legally, put the drug runners out of business, and the taxes collected wouldn't hurt, either," Kiana opined. "Look what ending Prohibition did not only for the economy but also in convicting mobsters for tax evasion."

"No argument there. Legalization is already occurring in a few states, but I'd like to see it done at the Federal level, too. Ridiculous that cannabis is listed under the U.S. Controlled Substances Act as a Class I drug, right up there with heroin, peyote and LSD. It's considered to have a high potential for abuse, no accepted medical use, and is not considered safe even under medical supervision. Hell, Class II drugs such as cocaine, raw opium, and hydrocodone are considered suitable for medical treatment, and even anabolic steroids, phenobarbital, and Xanax type depressants are considered less dangerous than pot and listed in Classes III and IV. At the very least, bumping weed down to Class IV would make sense; low potential for abuse and acceptable for medical use with limited physical or psychological dependence. The people who need it for pain, seizures, and PTSD wouldn't have to sneak around like criminals, and we could concentrate on the real drugs; crack, meth, and the burgeoning oxy trade or hillbilly heroin."

Kiana shook her head side to side in frustration. "They keep saying marijuana's a gateway drug for harder stuff. That's a misconception. I bet the 90% who try stronger drugs all started with booze and cigarettes. And have you *ever* been on a domestic where someone's gone berserk after smoking pot, smacked the spouse around or punched holes in the walls? Violence happens when they're drunk, high on meth, or whacked out on prescription drugs. You smoke pot, you get happy, eat too much, go to sleep, and don't wake up with a hang-over."

"Though," Mango reminded her, "Marijuana does still impair, so just like alcohol, it would need to be regulated, restricted from minors, and DUI laws enforced."

De la Cruz nudged Mango's elbow. "The cat's licking his whiskers and finished. We better get going or Ski's gonna think we stashed a couple boards down here and grabbed some waves," Kiana joked, gazing at the nicely formed rollers.

"Knowing Ski, he'll be thinking other things."

"Don't start. Chief."

"Not me, Lieutenant. My mind is clear and guilt free."

"You never lie, either."

"No comment, Lieutenant. Off we go with cat in tow before Skibitski starts reading your thoughts."

"My thoughts? If I remember correctly, I asked a pertinent question about Kate and got two-by-foured," Kiana groused. She turned and clambered up the embankment to the main trail, putting a slight more rotation into her hips and stomp to her step.

Mango followed close behind chewing on his own thoughts. Behind him followed the cat.

After a quick briefing with Skibitski, Mango leaned over, trying to catch the cat. It kept backing away just out of reach.

De la Cruz suggested they resume their trek to their units and the cat would continue to tail them. They did and it did.

Halfway back, alert for nuance, Kiana stopped and stared intently at the tracks they had followed in. Mango waited. The cat sat.

"Chief, have you noticed the bike treads leading to the parking lot cross *over* the incoming van tracks? They are also crossed *by* the van's deeper impressions when it left and was heavier with cargo. Since the bike treads originate or end at the van, maybe the bike was in the van and someone biked out before the van left. Or, someone biked in, stopped at the van, and was in the van with the bike when it left. Whoever, they erased their footprints, too. And, if we can't find Harry's bike, I bet *his* bike went with the van, too. Was Harry in the wrong place at the wrong time or was he part of this drug transport but expendable? We need to figure out which way these bicycle treads lead. In or out?"

"Ahhhh, I've been waiting for you to figure that out, my leetle cricket," replied Mango. "Excellent analysis."

Back in the parking lot, after updating Deputy Cervantes, Mango touched base with Dora, then instructed de la Cruz to transport their feline stalker to the station to await transfer to the animal shelter. He opened his Jeep's door and the cat jumped immediately into his driver's seat, licked a paw once then curled up into a large, furry black ball.

Kiana laughed. "Looks like he trusts you now."

"Yeah, but do I trust him?"

CHAPTER 14

DICKIES AND DATS

Jack, Kiana, and Marshall Cormac with Buster, and Jorge Pacheco and Dora arrived at Dickies within seconds of each other. They walked in together, each face showing the strain, their red eyes puffy and darkly ringed. Lee, poking his head out the swinging kitchen door to watch the procession to the back room, realized he hadn't been making extra sandwiches for a simple police training session. Dora stayed behind at the bar, rounding up take-out orders. A California Highway Patrol Trooper, DeWayne Smith, nattily attired in a crisp tan uniform complete with *Smokey the Bear* hat, sauntered through the front entry.

"Hey, s'up good lookin'! Dispatch said Chief Mango's here." Smith winked at Dora, recognizing her from previous visits to the station. "How come you're not holding down the proverbial fort? We all know you're the one who's really in charge."

"Keep the flattery coming, Trooper! How you been Smitty?"

"Livin' the dream every day," grinned DeWayne.

Dora grinned in return, throwing a thumb behind her shoulder toward The DP. "They're in there, may be a few more uniforms on the way. Go on in. I have to get this food out to the people still in the field." She leaned across the bar and whispered in his ear, "Two deaths, probably connected, and a possible suspect on the run."

Trooper Smith tipped his hat to Dora, strode across the room, knocked on the closed door before entering and observed Mango, de la Cruz, Cormac, and Pacheco seated around a large oval table. Steaming coffee mugs, glasses and a water carafe decorated the tabletop, with de la Cruz and Pacheco sitting with pens poised above note pads. Serious business was being addressed. Smith's arm hairs stood on end raising chicken skin. He wondered if the stories were true.

Throughout the building's vortex swirled the particular rhythms of Serrano for over a hundred fifty years. In the past, politicians, businessmen, and clergy had determined Serrano's future in this same room. An essence of their auras remained, including those murdered within. People such as Kenny "Kona" Davenport, a young trader of mixed heritage, who in 1878 became embroiled in an altercation with a clerk, who refused to allow a darky to use his indoor privy. The clerk, if not for the good fortune to be nephew of an influential shipping magnate dealing in redwood timber, would have been tried for homicide. Both clerk and trader mysteriously disappeared, never to be heard from again.

Kona's ship lifted anchor the next morning and sailed west into the Pacific without him. Legend has it he was part *Ali'i*, of royal Hawaiian blood, and walks Serrano's waterfront at night; others say he plugs Dickies toilets regularly to overflowing.

When asked, Kiana's reply is "Surely you don't believe in my old *tutu's* fairytales, made up to scare little kids, do you?" But no one has ever seen her on the beach alone after sunset. After all, in Hawaiian lore, nightwalkers are dangerous, and if looked upon can turn one to stone. No use taking chances in case the tale is true.

Trooper Smith slid into a chair, nodding to Mango as Mr. Lee arrived to serve up breakfast; a continental array of hardboiled eggs, cheeses, prosciutto, croissants, olives, avocado, and juices. Lee also deposited a large bowl of water next to Buster's dish of special dog chow while surreptitiously dropping a few freshly cooked bacon bits atop the mix.

"I hope you don't mind the cold food. You guys did show up unexpectedly, and in numbers," Lee kidded as he topped Mango's coffee. Lee's lightly slanted eyes searched the Chief's. A returned stony stare confirmed Lee's worst suspicions. Someone was likely dead.

Once Mr. Lee departed and closed the door firmly, Mango summarized the morning's events, then said, "We have a shit storm and everything is on the table. I want to know what each person thinks, no matter how trivial; any outlandish idea, suggestion, rumor, or question. Lieutenant de la Cruz, you first."

"My thoughts lead to Stella now on the run; her relationship with the dead husband and the maybe dead lover. But it doesn't feel right, like it's too easy. The bicycle tracks are throwing me off, what with two different sets. Then there's Harry's possible broken neck and Billy's obviously. Is Stella strong enough to do that? If the powder on her mirror is any indication, she'd be jacked enough. I'm also intrigued that each victim was found where they were supposed to be; Billy near his work site and Harry at the bottom of a trail we know he rode almost daily. Harry had to be in good shape, but he was extremely passive; a milquetoast who couldn't handle a complaint from a seventy year old tourist without becoming a sniveling boy."

Mango observed, "He had no acumen for verbal confrontation, much less violence, and in my experience with the man, not much of a spine."

Kiana continued, "From what Stella told us, Harry was shocked by Clare's little monkey-in-the-closet episode with Billy and very intimidated by her ferociousness in their subsequent encounter. Old Billy, though not the brightest crayon in the box, you'd think he would have suspected a double cross, especially after watching his back for four years as a child molester in the pen. But as a psychiatrist, probably thought he could outwit and manipulate people. We need to find Stella. We have to wait on info from Doc Kno. And, we are looking for a large van or truck. My guess would be van, as it's not good smuggling technique to be driving down Route One at night with the back cargo bed mimicking a Cheech and Chong episode."

After the snickering died down, Mango looked at Deputy Cormac. "What can you and Buster do about Stella?"

"Not much unless we pick her trail up again further down the canyon. It's senseless for me to pursue, since patrols are on side streets waiting for her to get flushed out. Maybe we can at least determine if she made it into town or if she caught a ride with someone. I can perhaps give you a 75% probability of either scenario. Sure would be nice to have another officer looking over my shoulder above the arroyo. Never know when you might spook a critter from cover."

"Pacheco?"

"I can go with Cormac. I know the neighborhood and also a few areas we can access quickly on foot. It's the Injun in me."

"You have Native-American blood?" Kiana asked, head cocked slightly, mouth quirked.

"Well, maybe not Indian, but I do have four generations of Mexican. That doesn't count?"

Marshall interrupted. "Maybe your grandma had an Indian in her?"

"Don't be dissing *mi abuela*! Remember, I'll be the Mexican watching your back when Stella comes from behind a bush trying to stick you with a knife. What happens if I am distracted by one of your jokes about *mi familia*, God rest their good Christian souls. Mmmm, *gringo*?"

"O-kaaay. On that note, I think we need a break. Go smell some salt air," sighed Mango, pushing his chair away from the table. After watching the two men interact for four years, their sarcastic banter hadn't changed. A stranger would have thought the two loathed each other as much as cats hated dogs, when in reality they enjoyed the opportunity to tag-team.

Taking Mango's hint, they trooped outside via an always locked, private door onto a small open-air deck surrounded by a windbreak wall. Mango leaned against the wood and breathed deeply, enjoying the view through one of four, large one-way glass porthole windows lining the outside wall; the kind in which those inside the enclosure could watch the beach and beyond, concealed from prying eyes, but no one could see in.

The town was now in full swing. Tourists were strolling, many of them tired but smiling parents, herding energetic offspring running amok in the sand like ants without a mission. Some sightseers noticed the five marked police units, three from different jurisdictions, angle-parked facing the seawall which separated the beach from Front Street. They thought the bubbled wall and nondescript door was an unidentified back entrance to Serrano's police station. The main entrance of Dickies faced the opposite side of the building on Main Street. Across from Dickies entrance, in what used to be a bank building, were Shirazi Jewels and a property rental agency.

Kiana and Jorge stood off to the side looking through a porthole, observing a slightly overweight, middle-aged mom pushing a stroller with baby. The husband lagged behind, busy ogling the crotch of a twenty-something in skinny jeans walking towards them.

Kiana turned to Jorge and declared, "Men are such pigs."

"Slap me with a whip, woman! I hope I'm not in that group."

"Sorry. My thoughts keep wandering back to Clare, and what that bastard, Billy, did to her."

"No offense taken. But, you have to admit, all things being equal, fat chicks do use more soap," Jorge deadpanned.

"Uggg-h-h-h! I work with a bunch of Neanderthals!" Kiana turned and popped him smartly upside the back of his head with two fingers.

"Play nice, children," Mango chided, then asked Jorge, "How do you come up with that shit?"

"Born funny, I guess," he shrugged with a wink at Kiana. She pulled a face at him.

Trying to suppress a smile, Mango asked Trooper Smith, "For how long do we have you?"

"Already spoke with my shift commander. There are three units on duty: one from Nipomo, another from Solvang up to Paso, and me. Two more on duty at noon, and they'll work the general area until late tonight, depending on developments. Whatever you need."

"Perfect, Smitty. Have both available troopers concentrate on the loop between Atascadero, Morro Bay, and Tranquility searching auto rental companies, rest stops, motels, and side roads. Don't forget off-the-grid spots for transfer points, and make sure they run plates for time stamps and progress."

Mango continued, "Meet with Cervantes at the Lighthouse Trail parking lot and make sure her two other Deputies stay and protect the scene. You two head up to Tranquility, tape off Harry's house and have your incoming two troopers talk to T-ville employees. I'm not waiting for confirmation on Harry from Doc Kno."

"Let's not forget Clare Brandon," Kiana added. "She lives in a cottage, backside of the village center toward the old stables. She's a Tranquility employee, also. We need to make sure she's okay. Clare was Billy's victim and the reason he went to prison. There were supposedly more kids he abused but no one else came forward. You've all been briefed about her clash with him yesterday, per Billy's version from our talk with Stella earlier."

"Unfortunately," Mango interjected, "No report was filed, since the disturbance was finished by the time an officer arrived, no arrests or charges, just a note in the logs requesting a 'call for service'. The sheriff who responded is off duty for the next few days, but I've a call back in so we can get more information from him. Try to find and hold Clare on site, as we need to talk with her about the incident. Hell, I doubt she knows that Billy is dead, much less Harry."

"Is she a suspect, and do we bring her in for questioning?" asked Smitty.

"Technically, yes," Kiana answered, "She is under suspicion, as anything is possible right now. The relationships are there; Harry was her boss and well, Billy, that's obvious, so we can't rule her out. We're more concerned for her safety because of Stella, who disappeared after we talked. Did Stella kill Billy and possibly Harry, and will now go after Clare? On the flip, maybe Clare killed Billy and Harry, and Stella flew because she knew Clare would come after her?"

"Clare could be the culprit, but Kiana and I know this girl," Mango hedged. "Treat her kindly. She's got a mouth on her, but it's mostly bluster. She's a good kid. We've known her since the trial and with Randi's help have looked out for her. Be careful when you find her, as with any suspect. If you need to, hold her in a unit and tell her Kiana or I will drop everything and be there within fifteen minutes to speak with her."

"Meanwhile, we have no idea if Stella's on foot, catching rides, or what," groused Kiana, knowing she's the one who let Stella slip away.

"We have regular officers on patrol canvasing the town and perimeter for her." Addressing Jorge and Marshall, Mango snapped his fingers. "If you don't pick up Stella's scent or direction, break that off after a half hour and cruise Main Street. Contact every business which has a security cam and have them save their tapes starting from yesterday. Better yet, the day before, if possible, for a full 48 hours. Jorge, station yourself at the bottom of Serrano Canyon by the overpass. Marshall, pick a concealed spot at the opposite end of town and keep your eyes open."

Mango checked his wrist watch. "Almost noon. This is going to be a bear of a case, and we need to jump start it or we'll be chasing our tails for days. De la Cruz and I will pull together preliminary paperwork and follow up on leads as new info comes in. Anything else? Then let's get going and see what turns up. Be careful. Situational awareness; one of those things we don't know could bite us."

Mango opened the deck door and strode down the stairs onto Front Street with the group ghosting behind. They walked to the seawall and stood gazing at the infinite loop of shore break. Mango closed his eyes and inhaled sharply through his nose, absorbing a last peaceful moment before perpetual chaos ruled for who knew how long. Marshall and Smitty nodded their heads intuiting Mango's thoughts.

The group split up. Jorge and Smitty went back inside The DP to gather their notes, Marshall following to retrieve Buster.

De la Cruz and Mango stood an extra minute to view the action. A gaggle of teenagers in identical blue wetsuits gathering under the pier. The lifeguard in charge bellowing test instructions for life saving certification into a bullhorn. Helicopter moms, slurping organic coffee from recycled cups, hot footing across the sand juggling beach chairs, coolers, and color coordinated towels, searching for the choicest spot in which to proudly cheer on their graduating progeny. Watching this idyllic locals' scene, recognizing faces, the two cops knew those lives contained secrets: alcoholism, depression, infidelity, drug use, financial woes, sexual and spousal abuse, or all of the above. All had secrets. Some, more than others.

"What do you think?"

Turning slowly to face Mango, Kiana replied, "Something in this puzzle is missing. Like I said before, the Stella thing is almost too obvious. The panga boat and Harry is a lot of coincidence. The cat. Explain that! Dora said it fell asleep under her desk like he's lived there his whole life. Said he even allowed her to pet him to make sure his limp wasn't a new injury. He has many old scars, and a knot on his right rear hip that may have been a previous break, but acts like he still has eight lives to go. And where's Harry's bike?"

"That all?" prodded Mango.

"Back to the panga. Not only is it a helluva coincidence, but a serious case of connect-the-dots. Those empty boats are found further up the coast once every what, two, three months? This time they're right in our backyard with a few bales left behind, either rushed or plum ran out of room. Bolt cutters in Stella's car and a sheared lock and chain link at the trailhead. We can place Stella in the vicinity of Billy, but that's reasonable (or convenient) since Stella and Billy worked for Randi. Stella and Harry's affair is old news, townie gossip, but we don't know if she was with Harry yesterday."

"Anything else?"

"Sure. Why was Billy in Tranquility yesterday? For a job, or because he finally found out about Stella and Harry? Did Billy kill Harry? Did Harry kill Billy? Do we have two killers or one? Was Harry riding his usual trail, or was he delivering a transport vehicle? Did he see more than he should have? And if Stella has bolt cutters, was she in on it, too?" Kiana placed both palms against her temples. "I think my brain is about to burst. Gaaa."

They watched the surging waves roll under the far end of the pier, visible now that the marine layer had risen.

"Supposed to be a northwest swell coming in. Might create a nice right break. Be good longboard action tomorrow morning," Mango contemplated.

"Yeah, but it means nothing to us if we don't get started on those reports. We need to get the major players listed and double check timelines with a chronological summary of events so far," Kiana urged.

"Let's see how much we can document before heading back out," agreed Mango.

Sighing deeply, he scanned the rollers, gaze stopping on the collection of future life guards as a whistle blew. Mango watched blue suited lemmings sprint across sand and seaweed, swarming as one body into the surf, paddling single-mindedly. One lone instructor floating on a surfboard at the pier's terminus acted as their return cue, protecting the flock from infinite trajectory over the horizon.

"Now, that guy has the right idea," Mango said, watching the bobbing coach. Stifling another sigh, he turned and nodded his head in the direction of Dickies. "Back to The DP."

"Keep in mind, Chief," Kiana mocked, as she fell in step beside him, "Most cop shows say the case needs to break within the first forty-eight hours."

"Glad to know you're augmenting your training with crime programs, Lieutenant," Mango quipped back. "But therein lies a grain of truth. As a small town in a rural county, we don't have the luxury or privilege of waiting on fiber and hair analysis from the lab. Unlike CSI shows, it takes days to weeks, sometimes months, for examined and processed evidence to be returned. We have at least one killer we need to find. Now. And, I agree, it's a little too cut and dried for the Stella connection only. I'm thinking we need to examine your theory that Harry was involved with the panga boat delivery. I mean, he *was* found dead at the scene."

"Not hoping for too many miracles, are you?" Kiana quipped.

"I pray for too many every day I live."

"How's that working for you?"

"Way I see it, we should be the ones sitting out there on our boards under the end of the pier," Mango confessed, taking one last backward glance at thrashing arms circling the solitary lifeguard.

"We can do that every day in Hawaii. All we have to do is quit our jobs, forsake our loved ones and catch a one-way ticket to Honolulu. Easy."

"How about right after we solve these murders?"

"Okay, I'll hold you to it. What will Kate say?"

"The way our relationship has been going, she may boot me over the Pacific herself, especially after how this anniversary's turned out. I'm going to end up spending it with you and not her."

"I hope that's not too hard on you."

"There's no one else in the world I'd rather spend Kate's anniversary with, than you," Mango half-jested.

"Way my love life's been going, I'll take that as a compliment," said Kiana.

"Didn't know you had a love life."

"That's what I thought about you," she razzed back.

"We have each other, then."

"Yes, we do, Jack. We do," admitted Kiana.

"You want to talk about it now?"

"No."

"When?"

"After we go and catch us a killer or two. Chief."

"God, I love it when you talk tough!" Mango laughed as they reached the stairs to The DP's backdoor, Kiana in the lead.

"Stirs my loins when you talk that way," Mango thought to himself, watching her hips rock with each step up.

"I heard that," Kiana murmured, not turning around as she punched in the keycode to unlock the door.

Just then a blue 1995 Jaguar XJS Convertible roared up and screeched to a stop behind them. Its occupant threw the driver's door open and shut it just short of a slam. Hizzoner Percy Hathaway strutted purposefully toward Mango until he stood barely two feet away.

"We need to talk, Mango."

Mango groaned silently and thought, "Third person that's said that to me today."

Kiana grabbed the opportunity to slip through the porch access door and close it silently behind her. A second later, Marshall Cormac walked out, took one look at the mayor and his car, wisely tugged Buster's lead and the two of them took off down the seawall at a trot. Three seconds later Jorge Pacheco and DeWayne Smith did the same.

"Mayor, I've asked you to address me professionally when I'm with my officers. I'd appreciate that same courtesy I give you."

"I'm the mayor of this town and I'll address you any damn way I please. I understand a dead body was found on my beach this morning and you didn't call me about it." Stale scotch coated each out-blown syllable and his red eyes blinked almost as fast as hummingbird wings.

"Hathaway. I guess I forgot who the police chief is. I was going to call you when I had the time and when I had answers. Right now I have neither."

"You do realize Memorial Day is in almost three weeks and starts the summer season? I will not—"

"Yeah, I think I heard something about that," Mango interrupted.

"I want this cleaned up ASAP. If not, I will personally bring in the Highway Patrol."

"CHP is already here. In fact, you're double parked in front of all of our units."

"Double parked? That's your main concern, me double parking?"

"No, my main concern is that you're oozing alcohol all over the sidewalk, your eyes are bloodshot and glassy, your speech is slightly slurred, and you're operating a motor vehicle in an area of families with small children walking about. Plus, you're illegally parked. You really want to push this, Hathaway?"

"You wouldn't dare!"

"My advice is you climb your ass back into your car and go home before you really irritate me. I have two murders to solve. So, if you will. Mayor."

Hathaway blanched. "Two murders?"

"That's right, Billy Morton and Harry Henderson. Our main suspect is on the run and we're trying to locate a possible second."

"So, why aren't you out there catching these people?"

"We're here at The DP taking a much needed break from running all over God's green acres, between two towns and everywhere else in between for the past eight hours, in order to plan our investigation. That's all I've got for you right now, so I highly suggest you go home, shower and make sure you brush your teeth."

Mayor Percy poked Mango in the chest. "You can't talk to me like that." He poked again. "I'm the mayor!"

"Then start acting like it and let me do my job. You're drunk at lunchtime in public, *and* driving. Do you want me to arrest you? Here, in front of all these people? And if you touch me again like that, I'll add assaulting a peace officer to the charges."

They glared at each other.

"Go home. Carefully. You live six blocks away and the speed limit is 25 mph." Mango's eyes narrowed and his lips tightened as he continued to stare down the Mayor.

Hathaway opened his mouth.

"Go home, sir. Please."

"You find these people. Find them! This shit doesn't happen in Serrano."

"I will and it does. Now, for the last time, Mayor, go home."

Hathaway, seething, knew he was too drunk to push it. Scowling, he turned around and climbed back into his Jaguar. As he pulled away, he rolled down his window and yelled, "Find them, Mango!"

Mango stood and watched the purring car idle slowly down Front Street and turn the corner, then walked up the steps to The DP's patio door. It clicked open as he reached for the code box, so he pushed it and walked in.

Kiana, gazing out through a port window, held a hand over her mouth trying hard not to laugh. "Would you really have arrested him?"

"Bear shit in the woods? Little turd was drunk and wanted to play big man." Trying hard to play it cool, he couldn't hide his flushed cheeks and the throbbing, engorged vein at his temple.

"You okay?"

"Just fine. For being such a pompous ass, how does that guy keep getting elected?"

"From what I've heard, it's the voice. When he turns on the juice it's like the velvet throat of Zeus decreeing on high from Mt. Olympus. Especially at campaign rallies, I've seen people mesmerized; their eyes glazing over, and then they forget and vote for him again. He's good at it.

"He obviously forgot to use it on me." Mango shook his head to clear out the cobwebs. "So, you find those killers while I chatted with Percy?"

"Stuffed and cuffed, Boss. Just waitin' on the hangman."

CHAPTER 15

RANDI CONFESSES

Back at The DP's conference table, Mango dropped into his swivel chair. "Let's knock this out so we can close up shop, get back in the field, do some first class interviewing and finish up with another debrief for shift change. If we're lucky, we'll catch Stella and find Clare okay," said Mango, more to himself than directly to Kiana.

Without her help during the Billy Morton enquiry, he truly felt a guilty verdict might not have been handed down. Although Mango was highly skilled in child abuse investigations, Clare's history with males was either nonexistent or extremely negative. She needed to be interviewed by a woman.

Interrogating children of sex crimes is unlike any other type of criminal examination, as kids could easily be misled or their statements misinterpreted. One improperly asked leading question could trigger an attorney attack in court which would spiral an air-tight case down the tubes. Victim secondary trauma was another major concern; simply by being interviewed, an injured juvenile re-experiences the molestation. One mistake and a child could be psychologically damaged even more.

Kiana, under Mango's tutelage and the District Attorney Office's guidance, with no formal training in child abuse interview techniques and only a few days to prepare, had been instrumental in pulling essential information from young Clare. A strong circumstantial case was built culminating in a conviction due to Kiana's insightful and patient questioning of courageous Clare Brandon.

Realizing Kiana de la Cruz was exceptional not only as a police officer but as an individual, Mango viewed her as his professional protégé and sounding board, as well as personal confidant. Projecting the persona of stern cop with the added stress of Police Chief, he never shared his doubts or limitations with other officers, much less civilians. With Kiana he was able to vent frustrations and expose his flaws. She was also the one person who'd ever seen Jack Mango cry. True, Kate was an extraordinary woman whom he loved deeply, but their mental intimacy paled when compared to his and Kiana's, and left Jack shamefully feeling vaguely dissatisfied with his virtual fiancé.

Mango and Kiana had reached a stopping point with data entry and case reports, (the unglamorous side of policing which none of the cop shows reveal) when voices from just outside the door filtered into the room. Mr. Lee knocked before opening the door, apologizing for the interruption before allowing Randi Shirazi to enter.

Making sure the door was closed and she was alone with them, she exclaimed, "Jack, I messed up this morning and have a confession. That wasn't my grandmother you heard in the bathroom."

"I know that, but this isn't the time or place to discuss your love life. It's really none of my business," Jack brusquely replied, not sure where the conversation was heading.

Kiana was the only person who knew Randi and Jack had shared additional secret rendezvous since their first publicly noted assignation. Their subsequent trysts had been extremely discreet; two single, consenting adults enjoying late night tête-à-têtes, usually when Jack's frustration of living a hundred miles away from Kate collided with Randi's availability and carnal magnetism. Those encounters had ceased more than a year ago once Jack realized Kate should not be trifled with, and Randi understanding she was out-classed.

"Damn it, Jack. I'm here to tell you I lied this morning and shouldn't have. Clare was the one making noise in my bathroom. I was afraid for her and wanted to protect her when you told me about Billy. They had a serious blow-out in T-ville yesterday when he showed up at the coffeehouse. Clare then pissed Harry off, so he fired and evicted her and ordered her out of town. She slept under the Serrano Canyon Bridge last night but showed up at my house this morning an hour before you."

Mango and Kiana looked each other, mouths ajar, turning their heads simultaneously towards Randi. An expectant silence hung in the room.

"Will you both please shut your maws? I had no idea until I talked further with Clare, after you left, Jack, that she may have been angry enough to do something stupid," Randi defended, chest heaving.

"And you waited all morning and didn't call me right away? You know you're harboring a possible felon?"

"Cut me some slack, will you? Your news of Billy's death shocked me and I wasn't thinking straight. I just wanted to calm her down and get a hot meal into her. Poor kid slept rough all night. Clare's mixed up, but not a felon. You really think she's capable of murder?"

"You're the one who's come to me with concerns, relaying how she warped out on Billy and Harry. Maybe she snapped; it happens!"

"You know how I've looked out for her. Between the three of us, we've made sure she didn't get lost in the system, stayed safe, got counseling, and when she turned eighteen had a job and place to live. I consider her the daughter you and I never conceived." Randi stabbed a finger at him. I'm going to protect her, even from you!"

Kiana threw a pointed sideways look at Mango which he ignored.

"Have a seat, Randi. Let's go over everything Clare told you," he said, motioning to a chair on the opposite side of the table. "Mind if we record this?"

Randi, staring down at the tabletop, shook her head no.

Kiana stood and poured her a glass of chilled water with lemon, reached into a briefcase, pulled out her phone, hit play, noted a verbal permission, place, person, time, and date stamp and placed it on the table in front of Randi. She stood against the wall with arms crossed while Randi conveyed her conversation with Clare.

When finished, Jack asked, "Is Clare still at your house?"

"She was in the spare bedroom when I left, trying to sleeping. I think she knew I was lying when I told her I had to check on some rentals."

"I need to talk with Clare. I'd also like voluntary consent to search your house. If you don't give permission, I will go for a warrant. I'd rather have your cooperation, especially if she was involved with Billy's death; we need to play by the rules on this one. We also can't ignore her mental condition. The girl has been through hell and a person can only absorb so much, so she may not be too friendly to cops, even Kiana and I," Mango said, leveling a stern look at Randi across the table.

"I understand," she whispered, "You have it." A spilling tear from one bright eye traced down her cheek. "I'm sorry. I didn't intend to mislead you."

"You're involved in this even more, so I need to ensure your safety and safeguard your rights."

"Okay." Turning to Kiana, Mango blew out a breath and rubbed a hand down his face. "Call Cervantes in Tranquility and have her contact Sederwall in SLO. We need a search warrant for Harry's house, which is technically out of our jurisdiction and falls under the Sheriff's department. Advise her and Smitty that Clare may be here in town at Randi's home. I need Smitty to meet us back at the station and Cervantes to stay put preserving Harry's house. No radio traffic, use your cell," Mango directed. He stood and stroked his goatee, deep in thought while staring out the window to the porch's bubble view of ocean.

"That all, Chief?" asked Kiana.

"No. Unless Cormac and Pacheco are hot on our suspect's tail or are running down new evidence, have Dora 10-19 them back to the station. Have her do the same with Ski, and release the deputies at the lighthouse scene once Harry is on route into SLO with Doc Kno, but send both to assist Cervantes. I need to pow-wow with everyone at the station while we're waiting on Randi's consent form to search her house. Finish up here and meet me at the station."

"Jack?" Randi timidly asked, without her usual bravado, "What's going on with Harry?

Mango turned to face her, "It would have been nice if you hadn't waited all morning to tell me about Clare; someone else, maybe you, could have been hurt. We have two dead bodies and I don't want to see you as a third!"

"Two?" She gasped, pulling back into her chair, jade eyes blinking away more tears.

"Harry is dead, too. Possibly by the same person who did Billy, or not, in the same way; neck wounds from choking maneuvers. We also have an abandoned panga near where Harry was found, three to five thousand pounds of marijuana in transit, and our only witness is a twenty pound, psychic black cat who walks with a limp.

"Harry's dead?"

"Pretty sure it's Harry. Still waiting on a positive ID since his face was eaten away overnight."

Mango watched her flinch. He probably shouldn't have disclosed all that, but he wanted to make an impact. Once she knew of Billy's death and Clare's fight with him and then Harry, she should have come forward immediately.

"Everything I just told you is confidential. You say one word of it; I'll arrest you for obstructing an investigation." Mango's tone softened, "Come on, Randi, I'll drive you to the station so you can sign that form. I'd like to find Clare before something else happens."

Kiana pushed off from the wall, retrieved her phone and turned off the recorder. Pressing buttons on the device, she texted Mango, "***Y not print form off laptop here, go Rndiz hse now?***"

Mango held up one finger signaling Randi to wait, then manipulated his own phone and replied, "***Cuz R alredy protectd C 1x 2day. Want R @ HQ & us n control f situ.***"

Kiana's texted reply of ***ah*** buzzed Mango's phone as he hustled Randi out the door.

CHAPTER 16

MEANWHILE, BACK AT THE STATION

Time ticked quickly forward into mid-afternoon as the players trickled into Serrano's police station. Mango ensconced Randi into a conference room to wait, and then instructed Dora to list only Clare Brandon plus personal belongings on Randi's consenting search form. Kiana rolled in a few minutes later signaling thumbs up to Mango, grabbed the documents, showed Randi where to sign along with the other documents she should have signed earlier that morning, and instructed her to stay put until notified.

Deputies Marshall Cormac and Buster Dog arrived shortly thereafter, followed by CHP Trooper DeWayne Smith. They congregated in the breakroom searching for donuts and coffee. Officer Joe Skibitski blasted through the lobby to his desk to busily download digital photos, and inventory the sparse evidence he was able to collect from the lighthouse scene. Sergeant Jorge Pacheco returned from Main Street after searching for security cams which could have recorded a large cargo vehicle driven through town.

Deputy Christy Cervantes, still in Tranquility awaiting a warrant authorizing entry, clicked photos of the surrounding area, and secured Harry's house and north side trailhead with tape. Rookie Patrolman Ron Baker continued to guard Randi's rental house, waiting for a senior officer to arrive with a warrant, allowing an inside evidence search connecting Billy's murder to the premises. Serrano's remaining regular duty officers continued their routine patrols, enjoying the rare opportunity for hyper-vigilance above the norm.

Sitting at the head of the briefing room table as his crew assembled and waited to hear updates, Mango, eyes closed, chair tipped back and fingers steepled under his chin, assessed his recent command decisions. The two homicide/crime scenes were not messy enough to consume hours of meticulous evidence collection, which translated into overtime savings from a perpetually tight budget. The Harry/Panga site, while still taped, had yielded such scant evidence that Mango felt the officers were needed more at Tranquility. Additionally, Billy's final resting spot had been swept clean by a rising tide, and since the front yard of the rental exhibited no verifying evidence, Mango decided to forgo the decorative strands of eye-catching crime tape. He saw no point in antagonizing Mayor Hathaway further by turning the man's neighborhood into a bloody circus, hordes of tourists circling, snapping pictures of nothing. Additionally, his first instinct had been to rush over to Randi's and bring Clare into custody. Wanting these investigations to proceed at less than a helter-skelter pace, he had opted to bring his troops together to plan a more methodical course which would also cover his ass. He did have Dora dispatch two patrolman to her neighborhood on the off chance Clare was still in Randi's home. He was now second guessing these choices.

Sighing deeply, Mango swiveled his chair forward, ready to address those gathered. Kiana, last to arrive, slipped into her chair right-side of Mango. "Chief, after viewing magnified images, Ski confirmed the bicycle marks each side of the donut hole (or where the drug transport vehicle was parked) are definitely different," she said displaying side by side slides via a new multimedia projector.

Mango observed, "Those on the north, from the direction Harry would have arrived are fatter, knobby mountain bike prints. The ones south, leading to the parking lot are a smoother hybrid variety."

All heads in the room nodded agreement. "Lieutenant, text the knobby tire pictures to Cervantes and have her search for similar tracks on Harry's property. Receipts showing payment for bike and tire purchases or repairs, would also be helpful to confirm whose bike made those tracks."

"I'm no tracker, right, Jorge?" Marshall piped up, manifesting chuckles, "But I'm assuming whoever killed Harry left the scene with his bike by either carrying it out or sticking it in the van and driving it out."

"Typical white man, always jumping to conclusions," scoffed Jorge. "Could mean a passing hiker or biker saw an opportunity and stole the bike after seeing dead Harry. Though, I guess it also could be tied to the drug drop."

"There were no additional foot or bike prints except the ones we've noted," reminded Kiana, "And a bike like that is too heavy to lug. Plus what we assume is Harry's trail stops at the donut hole, so I say the drug runners took the bike with them. Why leave extra evidence if they offed Harry, but then again, why take the bike and not scrub their footprints from around the transport vehicle?"

"Good point. Why conceal some evidence but ignore others? It's as if we're looking at two different crime scenes— Mango stopped mid-sentence, watching all eyes widen in chorus, realizing his deduction explained the perplexing scenarios.

"We have three distinct crimes, all high degree felonies, all separate, but all related," Kiana interpolated.

"Love it when an investigation proceeds smoothly with suspects and evidence dropping into our laps like bunnies conjured by magic," spoke an exasperated Chief Mango.

"We cannot find our one person of interest, another one just turned up and we think a dead man's bike was hijacked. We have two dead bodies and thousands of pounds of marijuana tripping across the state," summarized Kiana.

"We need answers and progress, and we have neither," Mango banged the table for emphasis. "Jorge, what's up with surveillance video in town?"

"There are three businesses and two residences which have cams. They can save and review their tapes for the past forty-eight hours and mark anything which matches our parameters of a large transport vehicle driven through town. It will initially save us time reviewing everything ourselves. They'll also deliver copies so we can analyze them here and look for additional or suspicious activity."

"Any word on Stella or Clare?" Smitty ventured.

"Nothing on Stella," Mango replied, "Disappeared right off the grid. I guarantee everyone in town knows about Billy by now, and if anyone sees her word would get out. Let's not forget Dickies, the gossip establishment of Serrano. If something happens in this own, it's heard there first."

"Kiana," requested Mango, "Recap our conversation with Randi about Clare, her activities, and whereabouts."

"So no one knows Clare is in town except Randi," commented Skibitski once she finished.

"We think Clare may have pedaled into town via Route One on a yellow bike she stole from the coffee shop, which would have taken her past the Lighthouse Trail, then went off road up Serrano Canyon to spend the night," reminded Kiana.

"I reviewed the logs with Dora," added Skibitski, "And confirmed a stolen bicycle report from T-ville within the correct timeframe, although spotting it could be a problem. With only three cycle shops in a thirty mile radius, half the people in Serrano own yellow bikes. They show up well in daylight and glow at night."

"Ask Dora to check the shops and the National Bike Registry," suggested Kiana. "Lots of people register them nowadays since a good bike can cost in the thousands."

Mango snapped his fingers. "Kiana, something you mentioned about Serrano Canyon reminds me about our search for Stella." Turning to Marshall, he resumed, "Did you check only downhill into the canyon from her apartment?"

"Mostly. We assumed she'd have taken the easiest route to the highway. Maybe she's smarter than we think, especially if she committed a murder or two. Guess she outfoxed us and headed for the hills," replied a sheepish Marshall.

"Don't assume. Be perceptive. I've seen too many investigations compromised because we thought we had it figured out," stated Mango.

"Where do we go from here?" asked Marshall.

"Three teams. Ski, check with Dora for the warrant on Randi's rental which should be ready by now, and lead that crime scene investigation with Officer Baker. You both have good eyes for detail. See if you can determine if Billy was killed inside or not."

Ski, eyes shining, nodded once.

"Smitty," Mango continued, "You and Jorge do a general search for Stella at local hang outs: beach parking lots, trailheads, parks, and overpasses. Any place you think of where a person could mix in with others and be lost in the crowd, hiding in plain sight. If you turn up nothing, we'll think about searching the hills next."

Jorge and Smitty turned and smacked their palms together.

"Marshall and de la Cruz are with me to Randi's," Mango continued, "To interview Clare who should be exhausted and scared." He shouted down the hallway to Dora, "Have we heard anything from the two officers up at Randi's?"

"Nothing," she yelled back.

"I just can't see her involved in all this," Mango said.

"I'm following your advice," Kiana interrupted. "I'm not eliminating that possibility. She has a strong motive for both murders and fair opportunity."

"On the *Mango Who-Done-It-Meter*, she scores five out of nine points, with minimal being one point," he quipped. "Two each for motive and opportunity and one for means."

Ski laughed. "What does Stella rate?"

"Three, three and two. I don't know how physically capable either woman would be to pull off one or two murders. But, mix in adrenalin with a dash of psychosis and a lot of snorted meth in an opportunistic crime of passion, and *wha-laa*!"

"Wha-hah? Sounds like something John Wayne would say," as he slapped his knee and guffawed.

"*Wha-laa* is Hawaiian for 'haole who laugh at chief, soon find himself in deep *lepo*,'" interpreted Kiana.

"Got it. Sorry," Skibitski said quietly, blushing faintly.

Mango stood up. "Time to go hit the road again. Deputy Cormac, before we leave for Randi's, check in with Sheriff Sederwall and get me an update on that search warrant for Harry's house. Make sure it's been expedited and en route to Deputy Cervantes."

Mango stopped talking, leaned over and knuckled the table. He took a serious moment to look at each person seated. "Some Zen wisdom: "If you understand, things are just as they are. If you do *not* understand, things are just as they are. In other words, don't see things the way you think they should be. Complacency kills. What's my mantra?"

"Situational awareness, sir!" they sang in unison.

CHAPTER 17

WHERE, OH WHERE, IS CLARE?

In position at Randi's house, Mango stood near the hinges of the front door while Kiana on the adjacent side, did the knocking. Marshall and Buster flanked them from around the corner, fifteen feet away, crouched low out of obvious neighbors' sightlines. Buster, tail wagging, was ready to play 'catch the perp'.

Kiana knocked a second time. Nothing. She reached over and inserted the key Randi had given them and then the key code. The door swung silently open and held at two inches ajar.

"Clare, it's Lieutenant de la Cruz and Chief Mango. Are you okay? We need to talk with you. Answer me, please. Clare?" Kiana called out.

"Clare, if you don't answer or show yourself, I will have to send in a K-9 dog unit. None of us want that," Mango tried. He waited another thirty seconds, called again, then signaled to Deputy Cormac to send in Buster.

A complete search of the house and grounds yielded an unmade bed in the downstairs guestroom and condensation inside the shower stall. A note on the nightstand by the phone read, "I didn't kill Billy."

"Damn it!" exclaimed Mango. He walked outside the house, called station dispatch and had Dora discreetly announce in 10-code to other units that Clare had not been found where last seen. He directed Randi to be transported on-site so she could determine if anything was missing or askew.

"Damn it!" he repeated. "I waited too long, but didn't want to rush over here without a plan. Kiana, grab your camera and take pictures of the bedroom, show the note placement and then bag it for evidence. We'll use the coffee bar's receipts for handwriting comparison. We should be able to get some prints off the note, too."

"You notice she wrote she didn't kill Billy, but not that she didn't kill Harry," Kiana said, as she walked by carrying evidence bags and camera.

"True. But, she may not know Harry is dead, so how could she deny it if she didn't know about it," countered Mango.

"Or, knew that we know Harry is dead, so why tip her hand," Kiana stopped walking to counter Mango's counter.

"Now you're making *my* head hurt. We've one more hour before dusk, two suspects missing and not a freakin' clue. Check with Ski and see if he's found anything at Randi's rental. If not, send him to Harry's to help Cervantes. We need both evidence searches completed ASAP. Tomorrow we go hunting."

"Right. Off to gather more evidence!" replied a saluting Kiana, resuming her trajectory into the house.

He turned to a waiting Cormac, "Can Buster get a whiff off that bed?"

"Yeah, but it'll be faint. Be better if we had a piece of clothing worn for a longer duration, though we might be able to determine a travel direction from here," Marshall answered, hoping to redeem his tracking prowess after the directional Stella blunder.

The K-9 strained against his lead, prancing like a Lipizzaner once he realized play time wasn't over. Marshall tugged once, "Come on boy; let's go bust her, Buster!"

Mango watched as Randi was delivered to the curb and strode up the sidewalk, red hair bouncing with each step as she approached her front door. The two walked around her house searching for items missing or out of place. He followed, enjoying the rear view of her smooth, seductive gait across white marble flooring. Finding nothing gone, they ended up in the kitchen as Kiana emerged from the guestroom.

"Done here. I have the note pad and photos."

"What pad?" asked Randi.

Kiana held up the quart size baggie and jiggled it.

"Oh, no!" exclaimed Randi, pointing to an ornate, drop-top secretary tucked into a kitchen nook. "She took that out of my desk."

"So?" Mango asked, looking past Randi's finger.

Before Mango could stop her, she rushed to the old desk and jerked open the first lower right-hand drawer. "Shit! This is where I keep my .22 Mag, and it's gone!"

"Are you absolutely sure?" asked Kiana.

"Of course I am! I last used it when you two took me and Mr. Lee shooting two months ago. I cleaned it, put it back and it's been there ever since because I do check it regularly. You know I don't have a concealed permit. I keep it for home protection," she answered, running nervous fingers through her hair. She wrapped her arms tightly around her shoulders as if this would keep her from falling apart.

"Did she say anything or give you any hint as to where she might go or what she was going to do?" Mango asked, his voice rising slightly

"Nothing," Randi lied. "I told you how upset she was. I fed her and then she wanted to take a nap. When I left, I assumed she fell back asleep. But I told you, I don't think she believed me when I said I was going to run errands."

"You know she's now considered a strong person of interest *and* a suspect in the theft of a firearm, which is a felony," Mango fumed.

"She didn't know I owned a gun! She got scared and went looking for something to write on, took the gun because she found it by accident and ran," pleaded Randi.

Reading Mango's face, Kiana spoke softly, "We couldn't have anticipated this. Regrouping at the station wouldn't have made any difference, Chief. I bet Clare was long gone from here before Randi got to Dickies. I'll put a BOLO on her, too, and get a warrant for her shack in T-ville," she added.

Ignoring Kiana, He stared down at a trembling Randi, not knowing if he was angrier at her for hiding information, or at himself for not moving more quickly. The delay in tracking Clare was not his finest decision and he would be held accountable if it resulted in another death.

CHAPTER 18

CLARE MEETS A BEAR

She hated breaking a trust, but when Randi mentioned going out, Clare knew it was to talk with Chief Mango. She understood Randi was simply being a responsible adult and needed to report her scruffy appearance and showing up unexpectedly the morning after her fight with Billy, especially since Billy was now dead. She harbored no ill will against Randi, but Clare was tired of playing the victim and made up her mind to run.

Feigning sleep, she bolted out of bed and dressed quickly once she heard Randi motor away, then rummaged through a desk looking for writing materials. Finding the .22 Magnum was an accident. She regretted stealing it, but only for a second. Billy was dead and she was pleased to hear it, but she wasn't going to be held accountable. She figured she had a two hour head start if she hurried. She threw a *borrowed* flannel shirt from Randi's laundry over her sweater and planted a frayed SF Giants ball cap atop her head, which she noticed hanging near the washer in the garage, then over that affixed her bike helmet, also borrowed.

Clare grabbed her trusty backpack and within fifteen minutes was cruising her bike toward Route One, northwest out of Serrano back toward Tranquility. She needed an alibi, hopefully from Tranks and co-workers, but not Harry. “No matter what Randi thinks, I’m done with Harry Henderson,” she seethed. “Far as I’m concerned, he’s dead to me.”

Barely a mile outside town, a Serrano police cruiser whizzed past her so fast its tailwind almost tumbled her bike. Pulse up, breath coming in gasps and heart in her throat, (like after watching a horror movie alone late at night and knowing the inevitable real monster in the closet was gonna get you, no matter how fast you ran) she made it another four miles before deciding to leave the road. She turned off past the lighthouse track and pedaled up one of the lesser used spurs to pop out behind Harry’s house hoping to sneak across the road into Tranquility.

Clare was not in the greatest shape. Peddling up trail and stopping several times to catch her breath, it took an hour plus to cover the hilly terrain. Almost there, walking now, wheezing, pushing the bike a final few hundred yards until she could top the last ridge and coast down, she gulped when she reached the crest and beheld Harry’s property; a bucolic spread of porch wrapped house with a barn and tool shed. She also saw two police officers and three parked cop cars, one parked across the highway in T-ville proper. *So much for this great idea. I’ll never be able to sneak back into town this way!*

One officer was walking around the back porch taking pictures while another clinked glass bottles into bags. Scanning further, Clare noted yellow police tape blocking the driveway to the highway and around the property. She slipped carefully off trail and hid behind scrub brush, waiting for someone to speak up and state why they were there. That never happened, just a bunch of garbled radio talk. Clare waited and watched, spending the next couple hours hidden on the hill.

Dusk was an hour away when Clare decided to decamp. She crawled slowly out of her hiding hole, collected the bike and crept down the backside of the hill, thoughts churning, thinking, "The hell? Cops climbing all over and crime tape up? Wasn't that only for when people died? Shit, Harry looked pretty messed up last time I saw him. They gonna think I killed him, too?"

Clare peddled back the way she had come. Not the most proficient rider, she crashed and wrecked almost twice from the adrenalin inducing blast downhill. She veered away from the fork to the eucalyptus grove and headed to the lighthouse, arriving at the bluff just as the sun was disappearing into a watery horizon.

Catching her breath, she watched as flocks of gulls migrated to cliffs north of the lighthouse to bed for the evening, their calls mingling with the faint echo of elephant seals, sounding like a cross between cats hacking up hairballs and baying bloodhounds wearing too tight collars. Pounding surf on rocks aggravated her unease as a light breeze ruffled her hair.

Walking her bike closer to the edge, squinting from the diminishing glare, she noticed a large panga boat listing on its side in the low tide. Goosebumps stippled her arms as her heart resumed its pounding. Worried she had stumbled upon drug runners and would be murdered for it or worse, she glanced wildly all around, getting ready to bolt. It took a couple seconds to realize the boat had been there for a while and no one was near.

Trembling, Clare inhaled deeply and blew it out. *What the hell is going on around here? Everything's falling apart and now someone's dropping drugs between Serrano and T-ville. Fucking world's going to pot.* She giggled aloud at the pun, then froze, hearing what she thought were twigs breaking behind her. *Shit! I'm so spooked it feels like Jason in his hockey mask is about to grab me.*

Clare snatched her bike and headed to the lighthouse hoping for shelter from another damp, murky night near the coast. She had a few clothes and toiletries inside her pack but not enough to make for comfortable sleeping. One night outside was enough and she didn't want to start making it a habit. Plus, in her hurry to leave Randi's she hadn't thought to grab any water or snacks.

The stately Serrano Lighthouse stood on a rocky promontory, a now vacant, yet noble monolith to lives lost and saved. Originally constructed in the late 1880s to guide ships safely into Serrano Bay, it had been decommissioned towards the end of the Great Depression, as trade-by sea had decreased to a mere dribble. Refurbished briefly into a World War II military listening station, the Coast Guard eventually shut it down in 1979. Yachting groups over subsequent years pushed for renovating the grand beacon outright, but an accumulating state deficit curtailed its restoration. It now stood as a lone, crumbling sentinel guarding naught but the past, a decaying orphan of the state parks system which conducted skeleton tours once a month hoping to raise money for its salvage.

Vandals avoided the aging pillar, loath to deface with graffiti and senseless destruction an edifice steeped over the ages in spectral myth. No attendant manned the grounds; the keeper's cottage empty for decades, another dying symbol of days gone by.

Clare had just reached the monument's base when another twig snapped, (or so she thought), making her flinch. She quickly slid the knapsack off her shoulders, reached in and groped for the snub nose pistol.

"I hope this thing is loaded," she thought, realizing she didn't know how to check for bullets and it was too dark to figure how. *It's gotta be loaded. Why in hell would Randi keep an empty gun in her house?*

Clare quietly leaned her bike against the massive concrete foundation. Holding the gun in both hands, she wearily climbed disintegrating steps hoping the entry was unlocked. She was shivering; from the chill damp air or because she was simply scared to death. The one enormous rusted steel door was heavily barred and padlocked. Cursing, she turned and spied the keeper's house further up the rise. *Damn, I really wanted something more stable than an old shack.*

Leaving the bike, Clare trudged up the incline toward the hovel and beheld its façade, two windows separated by a door, evoking a variation of Edvarch Munch's *The Scream.* White-knuckling the pistol, she couldn't shake the feeling she was being watched. "I should have stayed at Randi's," she moaned silently.

Surprised to see the loosely hung door slightly ajar, she pushed on the peeling wood anyway. Rusty hinges rasped stubbornly, squealing like a wounded animal crying for comfort. Clare unconsciously backed up a step, breath held, probing eyes searching the pitch interior. Seconds dragged like hours as she waited on the threshold to be yanked violently inside. Standing frozen, legs shaking, she forced an exhale and shook her head in relief. *Silly! Get the bike and hide inside the shack.*

Assured, she hurried back to the lighthouse only to find the bike gone. Time stopped again. Arm slightly raised, right index finger firm on the trigger, unsure how much pressure would fire the gun, Clare stood mannequin-still staring at the void where her transport should have been leaning.

"Careful, *Chica*," a deep, heavily accented Hispanic voice intoned.

Seeming to occur simultaneously, finger jerking, Clare shrieked and jumped, firing a .22 mag hollow point into the ground. Shocked not so much from the explosion but from the unexpected percussive ear pain, she briefly thought she had shot herself then realized she had peed her panties.

In the same instant, she was knocked from behind and slammed to ground. Gun easily ripped from her grasp, Clare watched as it arced in slow motion above and behind her vision. What felt like a sack of grapefruit pinned her body and appendages. She lay face down, the left side of her head pressed into grass and grit. One horse-eye rotating to see who had attacked her, she could see only the lighthouse looming above her, appearing to sway as clouds and mist swirled around its peak. Stuck prone, scared for her life, Clare felt ridiculously relieved it wasn't blood from a gunshot, glad to be embarrassed by the urine seeping between her thighs.

"Don't move," her attacker rumbled into her right ear, stale breath washing her face. "I will not hurt you, unless you try shoot me again. I wish you no harm, *mi amiga*."

"Let me up. I can't breathe!" she wheezed.

Her assailant eased the pressure from her upper torso, allowing lungs to fill.

"Are you—going to kill me?" she stuttered, leaking tears to complement the liquid seeping at her crotch, fighting to keep from vomiting. "Don't kill me, please," Clare's voice broke.

"I kill no one! You the one with a gun. You one *loca guera*! What you do if I let you up? Be good? No? Then I hurt you bad, *Chica*."

"I'll be good! Real good," she now cried, no longer concerned with anything except staying alive, "Just let me up."

"Okay, but you know what I do to you, try something *loco*."

The coarse voice receded, and although weight lifted from her body, a large hand kept hold of her scruff and one leg held hers to the ground. Clare twisted her torso to view the beast mounted atop her, who deliberately and gradually released his grip to stand straddling her body. Flat on her back, Clare blinked up at the man who looked equally as tall and massive as the lighthouse behind him.

A giant of a man towering well over six feet stood above her. Dark, flowing shoulder length hair framed an equally dusky complexion accented by round, white eyes and similarly florescent teeth. Reaching down, he offered a large, rough hand to help Clare stand. His thumb and index finger wrapped around her whole hand and gently pulled her to where she stood, face level with his chest. Shivering and hiccupping, she raised her chin to stare up at his face.

"Who are you?" she whispered, summoning the courage to speak, "And where did you come from?"

"I come from boat. My crew," he paused, searching for the right word, "*Como se dice*. Mutinied. Now, I try stay alive and find *mi gato*."

"But who are you?"

"Oso. *Mi nombre* Oso. It mean *bear* in English."

"I believe you," replied Clare, unable to hide her smile.

CHAPTER 19

WHAT'S UP, DOC?

The teams gathered back at Serrano's police station just after sundown. Chief Mango had requested Dickies cater two dozen mahi sandwich plates, along with a couple quarts of Mr. Lee's special sweet and sour coleslaw with plenty of iced tea and coffee. The briefing room was filled with cops, computers, cameras and cell phones; everyone scrambling to process and review the electronic evidence.

Taking a bite of the unparalleled fish sandwich, Mango surveyed the room of true professionals still working hard with little or no sleep. It entertained him to reflect upon people who assumed small town cops led boring lives, and thought back to his Los Alamos Department days and his exceptional co-workers. Any of these officers were of equal or better quality and he humbly thanked his good fortune to be leading them.

Kiana broke his contemplation by walking in behind the last set of stragglers to arrive; Officer Joe Skibitski, Deputy Christi Cervantes, and miscellaneous Sheriff's deputies and CHP troopers, back from searching Harry's house and the Tranquility area. The additional hours to find a judge to sign warrants added a delay to already lost time. Mango's forethought to secure Harry's house prematurely forestalled contamination and allowed officers to peak through windows to prevent extra surprises. They also used the time to question employees and the few Trank residents living across the road, although this produced no case-busting information. The warrant to search Clare's residence would not arrive until tomorrow morning.

Mango stood and waved them to the buffet arranged on a credenza in the back of the room, but shepherded Kiana to the side. He said in a low voice, "Hathaway wants me to hold a media briefing in our lobby. Of course, he won't stand with me until someone's been arrested so he can smile and shine. Tell me some good news, because if it weren't for bad news I'd have no news at all. Reporters from every metro area within two hundred miles will be here shortly and I have shit to tell them besides two dead, two persons of interest and 'evidence' we're analyzing."

"Nothing. We found women's clothes in Harry's closet, presumably Stella's, and good prints off a tumbler or two. But even if they're her prints, it shows she visited at some point and hardly a crime," she answered. "We're still checking on Harry's bike info, matching serial numbers and running down different shops in the area."

"At least Hathaway can't accuse me of releasing too much information. Defense attorneys won't be able to accuse me of fanning the flames or griping that the jury pool is tainted from unproven conjecture," Mango sighed, stroking his goatee.

"One thing may help, Chief. Cervantes spoke with a couple of employees who remembered seeing a red Ford Taurus cruising Tranquility late afternoon yesterday. It turned around in front of the old post office, then drove across the highway and pulled into Harry's driveway. The description they gave points to Stella as the driver. It was a little before dusk, but no exact time."

"That may be significant since Stella told us she drove straight home and nowhere else after she finished cleaning Randi's rental," Mango mused, eyes flickering with a sign of hope.

"She knew Harry well enough to know his regular riding route, then drove over the Lighhouse Trail to wait for him. I'm curious to see if the bolt cutters in her Taurus match against the busted lock at the trailhead. Thing is, I don't remember seeing other car tracks except for the drug vehicle, so she didn't drive in. And how did she surprise Harry and overpower him so easily?" Kiana added.

"That's easy. The old 'What brings you here, Stella?' set-up."

Kiana nodded in agreement. "Harry wouldn't have felt threatened."

Dora slipped into the room and sidled up to them. "Doc Kno's on the phone for you, Chief, and has preliminary reports on both victims. Also," addressing them both, "No registry matches on that stolen bike. The owner says he bought the bike used and can't find the paperwork to give me a serial number. The good news is Harry's bike *is* registered."

Mango nodded at the info. "I'll talk with him in my office. Be right back, Lieutenant," he said, carrying his half-finished meal with him.

"What have we got, Doc?"

"Billy Morton first. Neck was broken, but technically that only contributed to his expiration. Third and fourth cervical vertebrae were snapped but death was not instantaneous. The phrenic nerve derives from that part of the spine which controls breathing. The breaks caused complete denervation of the diaphragm and led to asphyxiation, though it took three to five minutes for him to die. He was like a beached tuna, mouth working for air but nothing getting in. Because of paralysis he could only lie there and wait, but probably didn't feel pain; basically from the neck down he was numb," narrated Dr. Novak, speaking in layman's terms. "Time of death is estimated late afternoon, prior to the morning he was found, and he was definitely moved to his resting place."

Brushing crumbs off his chest, Mango asked, "Would the perp have needed a tremendous amount of strength to pull this off?"

"No. The hanging analogy, where a quick, clean snap from left to right would do the trick without needing much strength, would be quite easy. A jolt like that on the side of the neck immediately causes multiple fractures to the C-3, C-4, and a slight displacement to C-5. I've seen suicides hang themselves with the rope knot on the back of the neck; poor bastards hang there and slowly suffocate, living their last minutes in complete agony. Actually, kind of the way Harry Henderson died."

"What? You saying Harry was killed by a different person?"

"Not at all. Mr. Henderson died by a different technique. It could be Billy was simply surprised and then helpless to defend himself, while Harry was allowed to struggle, for whatever reason. Maybe Harry wasn't surprised or just in better shape and struggled longer before dying," hypothesized Novak, "But cause of death was also asphyxiation."

"Are you saying the same person killed both men?"

"I'm saying Henderson did not have a broken neck. He died from blunt force trauma to the trachea and larynx. The larynx is naturally protected by the jaw, clavicles and breast bone, and also protected by thyroid and arytenoid cartilages; Harry's thyroid cartilage, his Adam's apple, was crushed. This caused his airway to collapse, ergo asphyxiation. There was also a slight amount of separation between the larynx and the trachea."

Mango rubbed a hand down his face. "So both Harry & Billy died violently, literally hand to neck, but by different mechanisms still resulting in suffocation?"

"Good thing the body was found before scavengers ripped his neck open, too, as Henderson presented much more neck and throat bruising than did Morton. Took him longer to die, with time of death around early evening. If he was moved it would have been shortly after death. Once Harry's thyroid cartilage was crushed the game was pretty much over. He would have experienced stridor, coughing up blood or bubbles, and a hell of a lot of pain if he tried to swallow."

"You lost me on *stridor*," confessed Mango.

"Harsh or shrill breathing. Us doctors like to use specific Latin terms to describe bodily functions, but can't write a legible prescription to save our lives," Novak joked.

"Again, would Harry's injury be indicative of strength or technique?"

"Henderson's may be more suggestive of strength, but the perp, with good positioning, could have merely pressed his radius firmly against the throat. The high amount of bruising, in my opinion, indicates a struggle; therefore, they were of equal ability or stature, so incapacitating technique more likely," Novak theorized.

"Anything else?"

"Yes. Dirt and sand particles were found inside Mr. Henderson's esophagus, further confirming the struggle premise, happening at some time on the ground before his throat was completely compressed."

"Additional physical evidence off the bodies? I'm a drowning man grasping at straws here, Doc."

"Not one extraneous fiber, fingernail picking, blood smear, or anything out of place from their environment. We found what looked to be carpet fibers and paint spots off Morton's arms and hair, but we know he was in a house with carpeted bedrooms and actively painting the place, both which are easily matched. The dirt in Henderson's throat also matches his surroundings, and only *his* blood is on his shirt, the result of the fatal injury. The toxicology reports probably won't help much, either, when they come in. It did look like he'd fallen multiple times earlier that day, by the various contusions on his arms, back, legs, and even his scalp. Wish I had a game breaker for you, something definitive," Novak lamely finished, but there just wasn't more to say.

"Thanks anyway. I do appreciate your quick work. Fax the reports to Dora and call if you find anything more," Mango said, replacing the receiver softly. He sat in office solitude, fingers rubbing small circular patterns around his temples, eyes closed, breathing slowly through his nose.

Not one stinking clue. Only thing I have are two women who hated him, both with opportunity. Stella working with Billy doesn't make her a killer. Lying about going to Tranquility to Harry's house is suspicious, and witnesses seeing Stella's car doesn't even rate as circumstantial considering how close everything is around here. And who the hell knows where Clare went after leaving Tranquility, and after running away from Randi's?

Dora knocked and stuck her head in the door. "Mr. Lee just called and reported a couple hikers at the bar talking about seeing what looked like a homeless woman up on Ridge Trail, couple miles above Serrano Canyon. Said she didn't look like the outdoorsy type and refused to return a greeting. Think it could be Stella?"

"My luck it'll be Kate, wandering around deciding whether she wants to stay with me or not. Call Mr. Lee, have him ask them to stick around and make them comfortable in The DP. Send Lt. de la Cruz and Deputy Cervantes over for an interview, but make sure they enter via the back deck door. Keep it low key. I'll head that way in a few. I need to call Kate. Thanks, Dora."

CHAPTER 20

DEA CALLING

Before heading for Dickie's, Mango addressed the remaining officers. "Start wrapping this day up. We'll need you in rested boots on the ground tomorrow, so plan to be here at o-five hundred and ready to work. I'll supply coffee and breakfast rolls. If Stella is up in the hills, we'll be fresh and she will not," he encouraged.

"Fairly steep up there until you top out. We gonna use choppers?" Jorge asked.

"I'm thinking horses. A helicopter or two would be nice, but will cost someone money. Plus, we don't know if it really is Stella the hikers saw. I'll ask Sheriff Sederwall to contact the 155th Aviation at Hunter Liggett and see if they'll be on standby for us, if the need arises. Even if it's not her, we may still ride the ridge and check a few oak and eucalyptus pocket valleys, make sure we clear the area. Then we can start narrowing our field of operations for Stella and also Clare," Mango postulated.

"We're in on this, Chief!" piped Cormac, "Buster and I want another shot at tracking Stella. I'll get a few more pieces of her clothing, check with Randi to see if she has anything more of Clare's and head out with you to cut a trail."

"Good. I'll call Kate and ask her to drive down with two horses. We'll take my two, plus one as an extra," answered Mango.

Jorge spoke up, adding, "There are caves up in the hills and a few others along the coastline. Not big, but large enough to hide a couple people for a few days."

"Heard that, too. Hiked around but never saw any caves, though I have seen possible locations on the coast cliffs north of the lighthouse," agreed Mango.

"Smitty, tomorrow, you and your troopers canvas north of town up through Cambria, and branch out down toward Morro Bay and beyond. Officer Skibitski, check out grocery and quick-stop stores, laundry mats, restaurants, and other businesses in town. Without either of them having wheels, I'm laying odds they're both still in the general area," Mango proposed, just as his cell phone rang.

"DEA Agent Levi Craig on the phone for you," relayed dispatch, "About the panga boat."

"Call Kiana and tell her I'm running late. Transfer Craig to my office," Mango instructed. "Guess Kate will have to wait; again," he thought. Heading from the briefing room, he called out, "Get some rest people. Marshall and Jorge, come ready to ride in the morning."

"Agent Craig," quipped Mango into the receiver while swinging his chair around and propping lanky, tired legs along the top edge of his desk, "To what do I owe this honor?" He felt the blood drain from his feet and sighed gratefully.

"Spreading sunshine and rainbows your way," came the reply. "Haven't heard from you in a while. Thought you were gonna become a rancher brandin' cows on the north forty under a full moon, singing "git along little doggie" and eatin' pinto beans off chuck wagons."

"Not yet, but if it was up to Kate that's exactly what I'd be doing," Mango laughed. They had met in Phoenix, three years before Mango was plugged by the bullet aimed at Governor Hogan. Agent Craig, teaching behavioral science at a drug enforcement conference, had tried to recruit him into the DEA but failed. Comfortable with his life, Mango had no urge to move his family and start over. After Mango was shot, Craig was one of the first to call and offer assistance, as well as helping later at Nancy's funeral.

Levi Craig, an unassuming man of average height and weight, nondescript and forgettable visually, which is how he liked to be remembered by criminals, had a mind sharper than a samurai's sword. Currently assigned to the San Francisco office, he was the Agent in Charge of drug task forces for Santa Cruz, Monterey, and San Luis Obispo counties, overseeing and coordinating their multi-agency cooperative operations. With increased drug boat activity along California's central coastline, both enjoyed the opportunity to lunch together after attending quarterly inter-agency meetings.

"Tell me something good, Craig."

"Your panga boat captain may still be in your jurisdiction. We caught his two accomplices after they crashed a cargo van this afternoon. The F-350's brakes failed and the yahoos went horizontal into an embankment on that sharp, left downgrade curving into Los Gatos from Santa

Cruz. Too much weight tipped it right over. They barely escaped decapitation when a pine tree peeled the cab's roof back as it slid down the mountain. Banged them up pretty badly and took an hour for EMTs to cut them out. Van was crumpled up like a Coor's can with marijuana strewn all over the place. Lots of mellow surfers in Santa Cruz tonight," Craig chortled.

"How does Serrano play into this?"

"Their 'Jaws of Life' experience precipitated an epiphany. The minute they cleared ER, the two dumbos sang like parakeets. Said the cargo originated in Ensenada, Mexico, where it was transported by trawler fifteen miles out to sea, then transferred to the panga. They landed near the lighthouse where the van had been left by prearrangement. When they were almost finished off-loading the ganja into the van, the captain walked back to the boat to collect his cat. The two thieving *vaqueros* decided to skedaddle without them. I know it sounds nutty, but that's what they said."

"Did they tell you the cat's name?"

"Why?" asked Craig.

"Because it's curled up on a leather chair in my office watching me as I speak."

"No shit! Those two *vatos* said the cat understood Spanish *and* English, with the skipper claiming it had sailed with him for years bringing good luck. They were more scared of the cat, calling it *El Diablo Negro,* than the captain. Said the dude stood over six feet, solid as a brick chimney, and navigated like an old salt while the cat perched on the bow like a figurehead, claws dug into rope, howling like a banshee from hell as they crested each wave. Said they never met the guy before this run and never want to see him and his devil cat again. Man's name is Oso Barranco and calls his cat *Taco Gato*.

"Any history on him; charges, arrests, weapons, temperament, etcetera?" Mango asked while eyeing the feline with new respect. "I mean, the guy zoomed into a fifty foot wide cove at shallow low tide with rocks lining both sides of the entrance, which by the way would be hidden at high tide, and beached the sucker without cracking a spar. He knows his boats!"

"Fearless or stupid, but who cares if he crashes? The product gets delivered, everyone gets paid, and it's just another day in paradise. What doesn't make sense is that he's off our radar. Nothing. First time our agency has ever heard of this Oso. From what little we can glean, he was born legally in California to Mexican Nationals in 1974 and runs a little tour-cum-fishing boat down by Long Beach. Divorced and up to his eyeballs in debt, but other than that an upstanding citizen."

Taco jumped off the chair and up onto the desk, marking territory by rubbing his cheeks against Mango's brown hiking boots, then sat primly on a desk calendar. Questioning jade eyes, blinking occasionally, stared at Mango like a child waiting for news about what time Dad will be home. Mango reached over and scritched the dark head.

"He could be a virgin," Craig continued. "A first-timer needing quick cash or owing a favor; although *los dos vatos* said Oso brought the panga onto the beach at full throttle in the dark, dodging rocks and swells like a pro, though he did have an almost full moon to steer by."

"Knows his ocean; maybe he's a fisherman caught up in something beyond his control," countered Mango, "Mexico's gone insane with death squads and drug cartels running amok, so maybe he was paying off a ransom on a relative from there."

"This was a first delivery with Oso, but third run for the duo, who gave us a final destination for the weed. If it is his first, he may want to cut a deal and give up names instead of doing hard time. Give us a starting point or the person who set this delivery in motion; especially if it lands us a big fish, the DEA would work to ensure him a lighter sentence."

"Maybe we're all fishermen and we just use different bait," Mango contemplated, moving his fingers in response to a gentle nudge, to massage the underside of the Taco's chin.

"Funny thing; even if the shipment originated in Ensenada or the Baja, the main distributors may be from the U.S. with connections in Los Angeles, who may not be Mexican. The *vatos* are hearing rumors of an Eastern European boss and that a woman could be involved."

"A woman? From LA or Baja?"

"They're not sure, but they've been around long enough to pick up on gossip. We were hoping Oso could provide a little more intel. So," Craig changed topics, "What's with the cat?"

"Found him at the panga scene near where we also found a dead body, which looks like a homicide." Mango swung his legs off the desk.

"Heard you've been busy."

"More than. That's the second dead person we found on or near two of our beaches and could be connected. One possible suspect and another person of interest have both disappeared. We have no real evidence except for a pair of bolt cutters, on which we are still waiting for a match to connect to one of the scenes. And, Taco knows something but isn't talking." Mango picked up a pen and absent mindedly doodled on a legal pad.

"Anything on the body near the panga, and could Oso be the perp?" asked Craig.

"Nothing. Victim was discovered a hundred feet or so from the van's tire tracks, likely where they loaded. Unfortunately, preliminary M.E. workup indicates he'd been dead quite a few hours before your crew even landed on the beach. The victim was only a possible victim until a half hour ago, as half his head was missing."

"Somebody erase it with a shotgun?"

"Coyotes and such enjoyed an evening snack. When we showed up, *el Taco Gato* was inspecting the crime scene but not interfering. Watched every single thing we said and did, and when my lieutenant and I left, the cat followed us and then jumped into my jeep as soon as I opened the door. Acts like a well-trained hunting dog. At the station, he climbed out and walked with us to the front door. He paused to spray a hedge, and when we held the door open he walked ahead of us inside to Dora's office for a nap. He's sniffed all over the station, found my office and hasn't left since."

"Amazing. So, what's your plan for tomorrow?"

"Comb the Ridge Trail in the morning for one suspect who may have been spotted there by hikers. Maybe ride north then cut back toward the lighthouse and look for your Oso. While three of us are doing that, other units will be searching from Cambria to Morro Bay. Unless they nabbed a ride, we don't think either left by vehicle, so they're probably on foot or pushing pedals. Other than what I've told you, that's it. I will be leaving a message with the DA to get an arrest warrant on bolt cutter woman. We also have her apartment taped and an officer guarding the place until we get legal entry."

Mango suddenly sat straight up in his chair. "Speaking of rides, your guys didn't happen to find a bicycle in that van."

"Don't know. I'll check the inventory sheet. Why?"

"If you do, I need the serial number and a photo, especially a good shot of the tread. Too complicated to explain but I'll fill you in if you find it."

"Big secret, huh? By the way, I have two guys in the Monterey office who'd love a drive down the coast to hang for a couple days. Let me know if you need them."

"Thanks, but right now I don't even have enough evidence to justify my own department overtime, much less the county and state manpower I'm sucking up. Maybe if things pick up tomorrow." Mango swiveled in his chair to watch Taco Cat grooming. "Although, if you can dig up more info about that woman possibly involved in the panga shipment . . ."

"Anything else you want to share?"

"Not just yet. Only hunches." Mango looked at his doodles. "One more thing. You know Taco Cat spelled backwards is Taco Cat?"

"I will sleep much better tonight knowing that fact, Chief Mango."

CHAPTER 21

THEY ONLY COME OUT AT NIGHT

Mango stood beside his Jeep, parked against the seawall behind Dickies, one hand resting on the hardtop. The media briefing had not gone well and he was long past exhausted. He checked his Glock 9mm, making sure it was covered by his jacket and readjusted a Model 42 Glock .380 at his ankle before arching his back to a popping point. "You stay here," he said to the virtually invisible Taco, curled up on the passenger seat.

Lee waved at Mango in greeting. Mango studied the dining room patrons to his right and bar flies on his left as he passed, nodding in return, pausing to note The DP door partly open. That meant the social hour (many hours, actually) was in full swing and local townspeople could mingle. Anything confidential could always be discussed on the enclosed patio or with a stroll down the quiet, dark beach. Most of his team was in attendance, except Jorge, who was home with family. He was the only one besides Dora who was married. Mango, Kiana and Skibitski were single, with Ski to be wed who knew when. *His* fiancé kept pushing the date back. Marshall, divorced from his wife and eternally married to his job, kept his time filled with cops, robbers, and doggie training.

Randi, Hathaway and three town councilors were also there, hoping to catch up on juicy chatter regarding the biggest local event in two years. Not since a family of four was killed on the grade between Paso Robles and Tranquility, a drunken father behind the wheel and none wearing seatbelts.

Randi, dressed stylishly as always in gray cashmere, wore skin tight jeans accentuating every curve. The black walnut paneling and polished antique brass lamps accented her Tahitian earring and necklace, set in nothing less than 18k gold.

Kiana, looking as drained as Mango felt, still in her black jumpsuit, sans Velcro detachable police insignias and badge, was cornered by the mayor and two councilmen, being pumped for information. Her sultry brownish-green flecked eyes and long, wavy hair against coffee Polynesian skin equaled or exceeded Randi's chic. Kiana jerked her head at Mango with a look that screamed, "Get me out of this!"

"Hey, Mayor; council members," Mango greeted the knot encircling Kiana. "Mind if I borrow my Lieutenant for a few minutes?"

"Course not, Chief. Not gettin' much inside info outta Ms. Cruz anyway. But it doesn't matter; she's pretty enough to stand there mute and I'd still be interested," Hathaway leered as Kiana ground her teeth in a fake smile while widening her eyes at Mango.

"Yes, sir. We try not to talk about ongoing investigations in public," Mango intervened, giving Kiana the opportunity to retreat. "Plus, we don't have a lot of leads, but now is not the time or place to discuss them."

"You mean you haven't arrested or even found Stella?" he bristled, ignoring Mango's cautionary remark.

"Correct on both counts."

"Summer season starts next week. We can't allow this to hurt Serrano's image." Hathaway's posture stiffened, chest sticking forward unnaturally.

"No, sir. We keep our dirty little secrets, secret. Don't want people thinking crime happens here."

"I am the mayor of this community."

"Of which you remind me every time I see you. Please excuse me. I have town secrets to discuss with Lt. de la Cruz." Mango turned abruptly to follow Kiana outside to the patio deck and beyond.

"Chief Mango," Hathaway addressed Mango's retreating back. "I will be calling you after viewing the newscasts tonight, to discuss how our town was portrayed and your role in the presentation."

Without turning around, Mango raised a hand over his head, waving to show he had heard.

"He's such a puffed up little man at times," Kiana grumbled as they left Dickies and crossed the street to the seawall. "See how *he* likes it, if I were to stare at his crotch like he stares at my boobs!"

"Glad you didn't. I bet he'd raise your salary and you'd end up earning more than me. If I still have a job in the morning."

"Yeah, he does sign our paychecks and not all men are as politically correct and perceptive as you."

Mango snorted. "Always knew you were a smart-ass."

They sat, dangling their legs over the seawall in front of his Jeep. Taco climbed out the Jeep and sat beside Mango.

"What did the hikers say?" he asked.

"Sure sounds like Stella. Clear down to the brown bird's nest hair and derisive stare we've all come to appreciate."

"Tell me how you really feel."

"She's out of her gourd. She damn neared encouraged, if not permitted, the molestation of her adopted daughter and she now may have murdered two people. I don't have to like her, though I am sorry she's a wrung out mental victim of Billy's charades," Kiana huffed.

"Rhetorical Question. Back to professional detachment?"

"Right. The hikers, two kids from Monterey, said she must have been hiding in the area. They could see hundreds of yards in front of them up the trail and hillsides, but never saw her until, boom; there she stood. They assume she continued north opposite their direction, since they never saw her lagging behind, even when they stopped to rest.

"Or she just stayed where she was. What spot exactly?" Mango queried.

"Third valley north of where Serrano Trail connects to Ridge Trail."

"The place where early wanderers used to use some caves for food storage, protection and the Spaniards supposedly hid treasure. Archeologists haven't explored extensively, but local spelunkers claim a system of interconnecting tubes exist. Most people only know about two near the top of the crest. Both of those are blocked and look like simple overhangs; cool areas to sit out the sun, keep dry during a rare shower or a place to camp overnight."

"You can see one from the trail. I know there are more but didn't realize there could be an underground maze," Kiana mused, mentally mapping her previous meanderings through the area.

"Some say the entrances are completely hidden by overgrowth or were purposely collapsed by the local Indians when missionaries, and then the gold rushers, showed up and butchered the native grizzlies into extinction, first for food and then for blood sport. If it's true," Mango added, "The Chumash aren't saying. Los Osos, the town just south of Morro Bay is named for the thousands of bears which used to roam the area and fish the estuary."

"So, we searching on horseback like you planned?"

"Three ATVs would be more practical. I know Kate owns one which can easily seat two extra people; it's like a four wheel drive golf cart with a large back bench seat. I'll call Kate and see if she can gather two more. They're not as quiet as horses but I think our element of surprise is long past. I'd rather Stella hear us and come out to talk."

"She has to know she's in a tight spot, with no escape without being seen. Seems like she wanted to be found. Why show herself then hide from the hikers?" de la Cruz queried, "And what about the risk if she has guns or a rifle?"

"No guns have been used yet, as the method of killing has been by hand using the element of surprise. Even if she is a killer there's no cause to become a *cop* killer. We know most of the people who practice at the shooting range and Stella's name has never popped up. She can't be that proficient."

"All good points, but her elevator may be stuck in the basement and she may be desperate," countered Kiana. "You think Kate can deliver those ATVs on short notice?"

"She's already set up to be gone from the ranch to bring horses on a quick turnaround. I'm hoping she can substitute motorized for hoofed transport."

"It's also a good way for you two to at least see each other; salvage what's left of your auspicious weekend."

"Share a cold bologna sandwich together over a lukewarm bottle of water and a stale bag of chips?" Mango mocked. "Joking aside, it's all the department can afford until our new fiscal year rolls over. The mayor and city accountant have unequivocally stated I need to scale back all costs. Justifying a couple helicopters and a team of state officers would be hard, considering we still don't have any solid evidence linking Stella."

"Be great to see Kate. We haven't talked in months," chimed Kiana. "We actually get along quite well."

"Why wouldn't you?"

"Seeing as I'm the other woman."

"She knows there's nothing between you and me," said Mango nervously. "You know that."

"Trust me. Kate's a woman. I'm the other woman. Leave it at that. You don't understand anything."

"About what?"

"You and Kate, dummy! That's what we're talking about."

"I have no idea what you're talking about. I just want to get some ATVs here tomorrow and spend fifteen minutes with Kate."

"You know nothing about women, no matter how much I try to teach you." Taco, purring loudly, stretched to full body extension using Mango's thigh as a claw anchor. "See, he's agreeing with me," Kiana laughed.

Mango carefully unhooked the talons. "Back in the Jeep, feline. I have work to finish."

Taco yawned in return then languidly ambled to the Jeep and leapt inside. Mango looked at Kiana and smiled, "For what it's worth, you aren't thought of as the other woman."

She smiled back. "Whatever. I'm tired. See you in the morning. Chief."

Mango walked a slow circuit around Dickies to clear his head. Entering via the front door, he was intercepted by Mr. Lee who steered them both into his closet-sized private office.

"What's up, Lee? I've a couple more calls to make before I can crash for six hours, and then play keystone cops all over again tomorrow morning."

"I don't normally get involved in your business unless asked, but Randi is acting weird. She's been here since dinner; didn't eat much, said even less, plus has drunk more than her usual share of vodka. I'm concerned. I've noticed her drifting off, eyes unfocused, and that's just not like her. She's usually hyper-alert and observant, much like you."

"She's had a rough day," Mango reasoned. "Billy conceivably murdered in the rental she owns, her employee under suspicion, and I haven't yet told you how Clare is figuring into this. Which I won't. If I wasn't running this cluster-flog, I'd be sucking down extra brews, too."

"That's not all of it. She's here physically, but it's like a part of her has died and she's been on autopilot. Being involved in this would overwhelm anyone, but we're talking about Randi; the lone survivor and harder than nails. It's been a rough day for her, but nothing like when Emil was killed. I hate throwing this at you now, but you two are close. I think she wants to talk, but so far, not to me."

"Okay, I'll see what I can do."

Mango stepped out of Mr. Lee's office just as Randi walked around the corner from the restrooms. They met at the far end of the bar, near the entrance to The DP. Mango leaned both elbows backwards onto the polished wood, hooked a heel around the brass foot rest and winked at Randi.

"Hey, gorgeous! What's a swanky dame like you doin' in a two-bit dive like this?"

Randi couldn't help but crack a feeble smile, her eyes, though, were empty. Mango pulled her to him in a strong hug and felt her arms tighten around his chest, head nuzzled into the crook of his arm. He felt a tear slide down past his elbow, then another.

"Let's get you out of here," he said quietly as Randi nodded okay.

Leading her discreetly from the bar and out the front door, Jack quickly shuffled Randi around the building, toward his Jeep where he and Kiana had just sat. By the time they reached the seawall, Randi was openly sobbing. Jack helped her down the stairs and led her through the sand down to the water's edge. A lone seal resting on an offshore buoy called across the bay, the sound incongruously similar to Randi's bawling.

Turning, they walked south along the beach past homes perched above them on the cliffs to their left, the incessant lapping of waves sounding like prolonged heartbeats, a soothing rhythm of slow and steady pulses. Morro Bay glowed hazily before them in the distance shrouded in sea fog. Jack waited for Randi to speak as they walked, right guiding arm resting lightly on her shoulder. They finally stopped, and he waited as she disengaged to wipe away tears, then clasped her arms around her chest.

"I'm frightened," she rasped, staring out across the blackened Pacific. "Stella called me this afternoon. Said I've always degraded her by making her clean my filthy toilets, and that she was going to fuck me over for screwing up her life."

"That was ballsy, threatening you. Not only because I've been calling her cell phone hourly, with the number you gave me, trying to get her to answer; but because even I wouldn't ever threaten you. That's like Elmer Fudd threatening Bugs Bunny!"

"I'm not physically worried. I can handle myself but I'm worried she'll try to hurt Clare. Stella's gone nutso. What better way to harm me than to injure Clare, or worse, blame me for everything!"

"Listen, we're heading out early tomorrow to go hunt *Stellas*," he quipped, trying to ease her anxiety. "We'll find her *and* an intact Clare."

"Jack, you don't understand. I showed Stella choke holds. She was asking a bunch of questions after Billy came back, about how to defend herself, so I showed her neck holds and ways to get out of them."

"That doesn't make you an accessory. If you are, Master Lee is, too. You're worrying about something over which you have no control."

"Stella's a conniving sociopath but she's not stupid. She's pure evil. She killed two people and is trying to frame me. She told me there's as much of my DNA on Billy as hers, and that forensic techs will find my hair, fibers, and prints on his body and at the crime scene." Randi had started to hyperventilate. "I spent the whole morning with him before she killed him!"

"You're letting your thoughts control your mind right now."

"Jack, we worked together moving furniture and patio equipment around in my rental. I was with Billy only a few hours before he was killed. There's even a check and receipt in his wallet with my prints on them!"

"You need to snap out of this and get a grip. Doc Kno will find micro-evidence which she can't fake or justify, like *her* skin flakes on *his* neck and shirt collar as well as her hair and fibers."

"She also threatened me with my past and said she knows about me, and how I made a living in LA before moving here. It would ruin me!" She looked wildly up at Jack. "You're the only person I ever told. How could she have found that out?"

"People know you, and have for a long time. They won't hold your past against you."

Randi continued without hearing. "I am over that! I turned my life around. I helped people. I still help people. Just how long is bad karma supposed to last?"

She reached out and gripped him solidly, pressing her chest into his, fresh tears falling. "Jack, I need you with me tonight."

"Randi, you know that can't happen," he chided, untangling his arms from hers. "Go home, lock your doors, set the alarm and get some sleep. If you like, I'll have patrols swing by your house all night."

"I'd rather you come home with me."

"Not going to happen," he answered kindly.

"You're right," she sighed. "Don't bother with the patrols, though. I can handle Stella if she shows up. It's Clare I'm worried about.

Jack leaned over and kissed her forehead. "It'll be okay. I promise."

CHAPTER 22

WALKING THE BEAR

Suddenly aware, not knowing if his eyes were open before or after he realized he was awake, Oso focused on the sounds coming from outside as well as within the small shack. Motionless, he felt the hard core of cool steel, hand gripping the .22 pistol through slumber, now pressed horizontally against his stomach. He peered across the floorboards to his snoring roommate. The bedraggled, crazy white girl, covered by a blue tarp salvaged from the panga's fuel compartment, was crumpled into the opposite corner of the cabin feigning *siesta*. They'd been too tired the previous night to do more than collapse with exhaustion.

Snoozing on cold planks only added to his stiffness. His body ached from two sleepless nights with no food and only a sip of brackish water from a bottle retrieved from the boat. The distant rumble of crashing surf vibrated uncomfortably through Oso's bones. He tasted a salty tang as he inhaled through his nose. The *chava* stirred slightly, rolling over to flat onto her back, eyes closed. Above her, cracked windows refracted grey morning light, a light sheen of moisture coating the glass, condensation from their warm breath.

"Pssst, *Chica*," he whispered in a deep, low voice. "I know you awake."

"Yyyyeahhhh," she answered, barely moving her lips. Clare's eyes remained closed, her breathing slow and measured in the well-practiced game of playing possum.

"What you think, *Chica*? Why you sleep by ocean beside me, while I have you gun. Why you try shoot me? I done *nada* on you!"

Clare's eyes flew wide open as she clutched the tarp so hard it crackled, neck cords bulging to fight off imminent flight.

Oso eased off, quirking his mouth into a half smile. "You treat all *amigos* this way?"

"Long story."

"Not busy."

"Guy I know is dead. Cops think I killed him. I didn't. Think I know who did. My adopted mom. You should meet the bitch, go do lunch. Only person I know who hates kids, puppies, and lollipops. Used to watch her hubby fondle me. Never stopped it or helped me," Clare recited in monotone, staring at the ceiling. "Not even after he raped me. The cops were nice to me. Now they're out to get me."

Oso paused a beat. "This *mujer*. Where she is?"

"Not sure, somewhere in Serrano. Billy, the husband, let outta prison last month. Don't think she liked that. She was having a thing with Harry who I was working for. Two days ago I threatened to kill Billy in front of about thirty people *and* later that day, Harry. They found Billy dead yesterday morning on the beach in town. Today I biked up behind Harry's house. Saw cops crawling all over his place and police tape everywhere. Maybe she framed Harry instead of me?"

"This Harry gringo? How he look?"

"I never saw him."

"No." Oso shook his head. "Tall? Hair? Ahh-hmm?"

"Small guy compared to you, small boned. Thin brown hair, bald spot on the back of his head. Why?"

"I see him. He ride *bicicleta*?"

"Yeah. A green Trek mountain bike. Why?"

"I see him wear *bicicleta la ropa*, clothing to pedal in. No bike. Past my boat, closer to road in trees."

"That's a relief! Could be a bit of a pucker-wad, but he's really not such a bad guy. Kinda weird, though. Never leaves the T-ville or Serrano area, not even to go food shopping, just has it delivered. So what was with all the cops yesterday at his place?"

"*Lo siento,* sorry. Your *amigo* dead. *Mucho muerto*. What I find with smelling, first night after *mis traidores vamos*. I brush my feet from into the sand and hide up coast with the rocks. Then *policia* come. I listen. Think."

"Is he still there?" Clare looked directly at him. "Did you kill him?"

"I tell you again, *Chica.* I kill no one! *Policia* take dead gringo. Late morning. *Es posible mi compadres"* he sneered, "See Harry and make like *la hoja,* they leaf." Oso laughed at his own joke but sobered quickly at the look on Clare's face. "Or *posible* kill him. *Pero, por que*, but why?"

"Your partners didn't kill Harry. He'd have never ridden around here at night, especially in fog; way too dangerous. Now I'm thinking Billy could have killed Harry. But that still leaves *her* and who killed Billy. She goes out to T-ville all the time and Billy was just there." Clare shook her head.

"*Marihuana es uno, asesinato* an other," Oso replied, left eyebrow lifting, the crow's feet at its corner stretching up to his temple. "I do this one time for *dinero.* Pay off *ex-espousa*. Look what I get."

Floorboards complained as the large Mexican extended upward, rising slowly from his prone position. He snugged the revolver inside his belt. Trying to smile benignly, he reached down to help Clare stand. "Come. We are long day planning. Spaces we need. No corners, no walls."

"We leaf, huh?"

Oso nodded, "*Si*."

Her clothes stank and were still damp. While Oso turned his back, Clare changed into an extra pair of pants from her backpack and additional fleece to cut the chill. She rolled the dank clothes into the pack.

"Oso? If I didn't kill anyone, and you didn't either, we're good, right?"

He looked at the waif-eyed face with compassion, thinking her predicament made his own seem small. Assured of his survival no matter the outcome, Oso saw in Clare the frailness of a child, violated her whole life in one fashion or another, running now like a scared field mouse. "What you want do, *Chica*? I help."

"My name is Clare, not *Chica.*"

"And full of grit, too," he thought, suppressing a chuckle. "*Si, Claro.*"

"It's Clare."

"*Si.* Clear."

"No, Clare."

"*Si, claro*."

She glared at him. "You messing with me?"

"*Si, claro* means *yes, of course*, or literally *clearly*."

"So what's with the *Spanglish* crap? You speak better English than you let on, and you make puns with it. Why?"

"Habit. A big dumb Mexican is easier for many people to deal with than a big smart one, though right now I'm thinking I'm pretty stupid to be here. Besides, English is a second language for me."

"You're illegal?"

"I am not!" Oso thumped his chest. "I am Bruce Springsteen!"

"Eh?" Clare looked at him warily.

"Born in the U.S.A."

"So what's your story?"

"My parents snuck across the border in 1974 and ended up in Boyle Heights in LA, the barrio. Six months later, I am born a U.S. citizen. They never did learn English but were smart enough to apply for and receive amnesty under Reagan's 1986 Immigration Act. No lettuce picking! My father, he work the shipyards up and down the coast, where ever he find work. He loved the sea; every chance, off we'd go in a dinghy he built from salvaged wood. Taught me how to steer before I could walk. When I turn twenty, he died. A Maersk container slipped and smashed him flat. He was just a Mexican, so no investigation, no nothing.

"And your mom?"

"She sewed beautiful clothes. So nice the rich ladies sent their Latina maids to her. She could see a picture once and make a copy. You could not tell which was the knock-off except for the missing designer tag."

"She still alive?"

"Gunned down during a drive-by, same year my father died. Walking home from the corner mini-mart after buying lottery tickets, she got caught in crossfire."

"Wow. Sorry. At least you knew your parents."

"They sacrificed to give me a better life than theirs. After they died, I cleaned out their bungalow and found a large metal cylinder; an old exterminator's manual pump canister with the spray wand still attached, hidden in a closet. It had *peligro* and *veneno*, danger and poison, and a skull and crossbones stenciled on it. When I tried to lift it, it was too heavy, even for me. Against my better judgement I opened it. Inside was enough cash to put a down payment on a nice boat."

"So you blew the cash?"

"To honor my parents, I work for fishing companies, boat builders and shipyards until I have a good credit history. Using their money and a bank loan, I buy a boat and start my own charter business. Then I marry and my wife, the *cerda*, the pig, she screw me. After the crash last year the banks give no mercy; no refinance of the boat. I now live the American Dream. I owe, I owe and no way to pay."

"So why help me? Don't you have enough problems?"

"Maybe by helping you, I help me," he shrugged.

"You're a good guy for a bear. I thought grizzlies were mean."

"Some *oso* like to catch the fish and sleep, though all are fierce protecting *los ninos*."

"So, we'll go together. I know a place we can rest for a day and even get food." Clare secured her backpack and cracked open the door, peeking through it at thick fog.

Wasting only enough time to address quick ablutions with saltwater, they hiked quickly up the sparsely grassed ridge behind the cabin. Staying off the trail into Tranquility, Clare led Oso through a maze of arroyos and hills for an hour, angling towards Highway One. They stopped at an embankment to hide and catch their breath, waiting for a chance to cross unseen.

"There's a fork from here we can take into Serrano if we need to, but right now I'm trying to get us into the ass end of T-ville. These trails probably saved my life. I used to hike around here and think about killing myself."

Oso looked down at Clare. Fragile as a young bunny yet as resilient and as calculating as a coyote. "Glad you did not. You don't know what is in front of you. Life is not always bad and sometimes good things happen."

"Hope you don't think this is one of the good times!"

"No. Maybe trouble for me, but we can make you okay." He suddenly stopped and held up a finger as if for her to pause. "You hear?"

"What?"

"No cars. Run!" They scrambled up the bank, slipping on the dry grass, small pebbles tumbling down the slope under their feet. They hopped over the guard rail and sprinted across the blacktop.

From there it was mostly uphill. A couple hours later they topped out, dropping into yet another arroyo to an abandoned cabin in surprisingly fair condition. Sitting beyond the fog line, the wood decayed far less then along the immediate coast.

She needed dry clothes and he desperately needed to eat and drink. Oso stumbled through the door and lay belly down on the floor panting. He'd once survived three days in his boat without food or water, but stomping around parched foothills without provisions was a different can of tuna. Clare's stomach growled. She dumped her pack onto the floor and emptied it, then picked it up again. "We're close. You stay here and I'll sneak back into the village and grab some food. Back in thirty minutes."

"Be careful," he called after her. "And Claro, I no think you *loco* anymore."

"And, I don't think you're a grumpy old bear either."

Oso rested for a moment then forced himself upright and outdoors to scout the immediate area around the cabin. Never liking confined spaces, he always slept on deck of his boat rather than in the cubby below, except when it stormed. Uncomfortable on land and a fisherman by trade, he lived on the sea, a wanderer at heart. Prison was not an option. Choosing death would be preferable to living secured in a ten by ten cell with bars.

Circling the cottage twice, he slowly worked his way up the hillside; first from a hundred yards out, then a quarter mile in the opposite direction from where they had come. Never be unfamiliar with your surroundings, especially when on the lam from the law. He found an outcropping of granite balanced on a rise in a sparse clearing. Climbing to the top of the pinnacle, he could see above the trees to spy buildings below him in the distance; the town of Tranquility, to where Clare had hiked.

A peculiar girl, he thought as he scratched a stubbled chin. A clash of contradictions with too many dark specters surrounding her, but also emitting periodic golden rays of light. It occurred to him that she really wasn't a girl, but a young woman. *A very pretty, young woman.* At age thirty-five he felt more like fifty-five, but with rough times rolled into one lifespan, you damn well *are* older. She, too, had encountered hardships in her life and is maybe of the same mind.

Searching in the direction of the town, he could clearly observe the rusted metal rooftops of old farm houses. He caught a sudden glimpse of someone dashing from a two-story building back toward the tree line and his location. He saw no pursuit of whom he assumed was Clare. He scrambled down from his highpoint and arrived back at the cabin a minute ahead of her, to be standing nonchalantly on the partially collapsed porch when she walked up.

Wearing a fresh Cal Poly sweatshirt and clean, snug fitting cargo pants which accented her hips and thighs, Oso noticed Clare's face was flushed from her sprint. Or had she taken the time to put on a little make-up? *Still fragile, but definitely not a girl,* he thought.

Clare stopped before him and torqued the bulging backpack from her shoulders, letting it fall onto the bottom porch step with a thump. She looked up as he pulled his long black hair back, tucking it behind his ears, a smile grazing the corners of his lips. They regarded each other silently.

Clare broke the hush. "I brought mostly canned stuff; Spam, granola bars and a few avocados from the orchard. I also got a gallon of water." She rummaged through the canvas sack, holding up a metallic square with rounded edges.

"*Spam*, hungry as I am, does not sound like something very tasty," Oso commented.

"A cop in Serrano I know is from Hawaii. She says everybody over there loves it. Soldiers stationed on the islands during World War II ate it as rations. It's made from pork and since Hawaiians are addicted to kalua pig, it became really popular with the locals. You can fry it and serve it with breakfast, or you can eat it cold like sushi, wrapped in seaweed of all things."

"And I thought islanders only ate fish," he chuckled. "We will eat outside so we can hear and see."

They sipped water then munched on the cereal bars as Oso guided Clare to his lookout, long legs outpacing Clare's stride. He looked over his shoulder at her as they climbed and said, "I was up here earlier and saw you come back."

"Aren't you sneaky!"

"Wise. A spot where we can eat and watch." The location offered an unobstructed half mile view as the crow flies, downhill to where the main footpath bent south.

They climbed the knoll and settled into a little cubby on the north side of the monolith. Oso opened two cans of Spam and one of baked beans; not fine dining, but close enough considering how hungry they were. Slurping replaced words. Oso emptied his Spam can in one swallow then glanced at Clare whose cheeks were bulging like a hamster's.

"Delicious taste," Oso said, smacking his lips, "Disgusting texture." Turning serious, he added, "The *policia*, they come today. You know that, *si*?"

"I know. We're going to jail, aren't we?" Clare whispered.

"Best for you to do and safest."

"Jail!" she wailed, voice rising two octaves. "I don't know if I can do that."

"Claro, if all you do is steal *pistola, no problemo.* The *policia*, they know you, and that you are scared. They will help you. Me? This is different. My troubles *muy grande*."

"But you said you've never done anything like this before and those guys abandoned you! That counts for something, doesn't it? They set you up. I'd burn them, turn them in and make them pay. Why not?"

"I will think on this. I am same as you, like a fish with no water. I no breath in jail."

Oso remained silent as they shared the can of beans and avocados. When done eating, he placed all the tins in the carry pack and drank from the water jug. "Rest now. *Policia* will take time, not be here too soon."

Clare walked around to the east side of the rock since it would receive the most sun throughout the morning, stretched out with her shoulders propped against it, hands folded behind her head. "Come join me. This is a perfect spot. Look at how the breeze is lifting the mist up through the trees and pushing it toward the ocean, just floating it up and out like a dream."

"What about the woman, the *puta*?" Oso asked as he folded down next to her, knees bent and arms straight back supporting his torso. He tilted his head backwards. "Should we be thinking about her?"

"Stella? I don't see her being anywhere near here. Why?"

"Just wondering." Oso was also contemplating the possession of the pistol. He knew it would be another charge against him. He also knew he would not be shooting any cop.

There was so much to consider and so little time in which to do it. He lay back against the warming rock and assumed the same position as Clare, his arms folded behind his head, large hands softly cradling his skull. Three weeks ago he was a down-on-his-luck fisherman. Now he was *cojones* deep in a pile of *mierda*.

Three hours later Oso opened his eyes into glaring sunlight to find Clare had rolled over and snuggled against his side, one arm draped across his waist, her face buried in his chest. Staying still, he listened to her steady breathing while her body heat radiated through his left flank, and reflected upon the two years since he'd slept with a woman by his side, at least one he hadn't paid for. His ex-wife when she left had not only vacuumed up his money but sucked any residual love in his heart to empty. Content to live alone while running his fishing business, trying to keep ahead of alimony payments but inept at accounting, Oso had placed his trust in a shady bookkeeper who embezzled the few coins his ex-wife had missed. In desperation, he'd agreed to this one time job. He hoped his boat, *Pico de Gato*, was still moored at the Long Beach marina, but wasn't sure if he still had the papers to prove ownership or if the bank had repossessed by now.

As Clare stirred and squirmed a little more tightly against him, Oso turned his head to study her face inches from his; the texture and fullness of her lips and rapidly moving eyes under thickly lashed closed lids. A long sigh of escaping air through her nose tickled Oso's chin softly.

The distant rumble and vibration was subtle at first, almost imperceptible. Not a physical vibration but a low frequency hum that infested his eardrums. Something or someone was coming.

"Claro!" Oso nudged her. "Time we go! They come."

Clare scrambled upright, unaware of using Oso as a recliner. Immediately awake, eyes large and ears straining to identify intrusion, she shook her head. "I don't hear anything." She was poised in a runner's starting stance.

"They come. Around the curve up there past that hill," he said, pointing. "I hear engines. Too late to hide. I need to figure out our next move," he said, patting the pistol tucked into his belt.

CHAPTER 23

LOOKING FOR STELLA IN ALL THE WRONG PLACES

Chief Mango and Deputy Marshall Cormac parked their matching sunset orange, Arctic Cat ATVs parallel to each other on a wide, dusty spot of the trail. In addition to their service pistols, each carried additional weaponry secured to the front racks of their machines; Mango preferring his mini-14 Ruger Ranch rifle, while Marshall sported a .308 Smith & Wesson MP 10. Both wore black tactical gear with their respective police agency insignias in large orange lettering, front and back.

Gazing down trail south toward Serrano, Mango felt for the ignition key and turned his machine off. "We are following one tough lady."

"Don't you mean one tough old bitch of a mother?" snorted Marshall, imitating Mango's engine silence. "Thought I was gonna pitch over backwards two different times. Not enough elevation change to affect breathing, but a steep grade even for these babies."

"Careful. My mother's tough and not so young anymore."

"I've met your mother and she could probably hike circles around me. Tough doesn't begin to describe her and I have never known your mother to be a bitch, so that makes her one admirable and robust, mature lady," corrected Marshall.

Jack laughed. "I've known my mother longer than you. I try real hard not to tick her off."

"Alexa is a handsome woman. You're lucky I'm too young for her, otherwise I'd propose and then you'd have to call me Daddy," Marshall smirked.

"As opposed to already calling you, 'you mother?'"

Both men were still chortling when Sergeant Jorge Pacheco showed up driving a 4x4 golf cart with a rear bench seat. He parked beside them in shady spot under low hanging oaks, and after setting the emergency brake, palpated his right hand over his heart. Slower and clumsier than the Arctic Cats, it was an extremely quiet electric model with a functional twenty mile range. If they needed to return with a prisoner the extra seat would come in handy.

All three men crawled laboriously off their machines and stretched, turning as one to face the wall of dense sea-mist hiding the town and bay beyond. Barren, burnt-brown hills, wrinkled with ravines filled with groves of Monterey and nine-bark pine, oak, and laurel, emerged out of the grey haze. The morning sky above, a clear blue, allowed the rising sun at their backs to cast long Moai doppelgänger shadows downslope.

"Think Stella's here, Chief?" asked Jorge, surveying the grand tableau. "How in hell could she hike up and simply disappear? Easy once you top the ridge, but was her pappy a mountain goat?"

"If she is part goat, we can't underestimate her. Do you know of any more caves, other than those we've identified one valley over?" replied Mango.

"No, though they all share a series of caves underground. The problem is knowing where the openings are. Most were hidden decades ago and are now either forgotten, overgrown, or so small a man couldn't fit through."

"But a woman could?"

"Good point," Pacheco conceded.

"A few more considerations," Mango added. "We have two females who lived together with a pervert who led a secret life. One, a woman who was at least mentally abused; the other a child who he raped. It's conceivable both know about these caves, as the family house is situated near the main trailhead. Plus, Stella has lived here most of her life. She was also plinking the late Harry Henderson, not playing the damsel in distress patiently awaiting her kiddie-porn psycho-psychiatrist husband's release from prison. When he does get out, wouldn't you have a bolt hole ready, just in case, and even a gun? Same goes for the child, who stole a gun from Randi's *after* Billy's demise."

Hell!" countered Jorge, "If I were either of them, I'd have two guns!"

Kiana and Kate were stationed at the trailhead at the top of Serrano Canyon Road. The department couldn't officially close the footpath, but Kiana could advise hikers it would be in their best interests to find a different area in which to recreate today. Kiana relocked the vehicle access gate, pocketed the padlock key, and watched as Kate secured the tie-downs on the large trailer used to transport the ATVs.

"Thought the Chief wanted to use horses?"

"Well," Kate harrumphed, "Jack isn't the one who has to get them ready. Gassing and charging them up and turning a key is a lot easier than hauling a team of ornery horseflesh. ATVs shit less, too. I talked him into a change of steed since I'm the one doing the dirty work."

"Maybe he wanted to bring them bad gals in just like Wyatt Earp," Kiana joked.

"You're not far off the mark, sister." Kate shook her blond ponytail to swinging. "Man likes to play cowboy but hates doin' the work."

Kiana lined up a topographic map next to her radio and cell phone, all on the hood of Kate's pickup truck, making sure the electronics were charged and in good working condition. In this age of burgeoning global positioning, it seemed like a primitive way to track people, but in small yet affluent towns like Serrano, utilizing helicopters and inter-department support was expensive, and techno-gear purchases were still light years away from being lined-itemed into police budgets.

"I hate being left behind," Kiana groused, "Talk about sexism!"

"I hear you. I can outride and handle an ATV and a horse better than any man, Jack included. Men have always tried to relegate us strong women into the good, little worker-bee roles. Lets them pretend they're better at stuff, and I'm not sure why we stand for it."

"Don't like it, but you're right. But then, what do I know? I'm just a woman!" Kiana mocked. "Seriously, I know Mango wouldn't want to put you in harm's way, both as a civilian, *and* as his sweetheart. If they bring down any prisoners, I'm to make sure you leave and hang out at his place. Here to protect and serve," Kiana saluted her, "Ma'am."

Kate grimaced, turning to the task of latching the small chains and locks of the ramp gate to the trailer. She walked over to Kiana and both women looked up toward the hills hidden behind fog. Standing together, they were a study in contrasts. Kiana's glossy, black hair plaited into one long braid, her shorter physique opposing Kate's equally long, sun-kissed tresses topping a lanky frame four inches taller. Kiana owned smoky, hazel rich eyes and dark, thick lashes opposite Kate's provocatively reflective sapphire irises, rimmed by the daintiest of white flutes.

"Heard anything from the two vacationers?" Kiana idly asked, as she pulled a thermos of coffee and sweet rolls from Kate's truck cab, setting them beside the map.

"About to ask you the same. Hope Jess and Alexa are having fun on the Big Island. Wish airfare was still three hundred dollars a round-trip. I'd like to drag Jack over for a two week holiday!"

"Yeah, prices are getting high. Even with *Kama'aina* rates, it's been awhile since I've been back to Molokai, and I haven't been to the Big Island since way before I moved here." Kiana poured coffee for them both.

The two women enjoyed each other's company and shared an affinity for ranching, although from different angles on the globe. Most people didn't realize the roll *paniolos*, or cowboys have played in Hawaiian history, or that the Moloka'i Ranch was formed in 1897 and still sits on nearly a third of the western side of the island at about 53,000 acres. Kiana's *ohana* have been employed there for more than a century, as well as at the Parker Ranch on the Big Island.

"Hell of a way to spend an anniversary, huh? That's life dating a cop," kidded Kiana. *Slap me! Why did I just say that?* Kiana knew Kate liked to play up the dumb blond shtick, but in reality the rancher's mind was sharper than the Bowie knife she wore strapped to her belt. Kiana vowed to be more careful talking about Jack around her.

"Definitely not what I planned. I keep thinking it'll get easier, but wonder if Jack and I will ever have a normal relationship. As a kid, I had a hard time imagining the *happily* ever after part. Mom and dad married after finishing medical school and had more of an arrangement than marriage, coordinating hectic separate lives around their practices. Maybe that's why I'm so attracted to ranching; I want love like my grandparents experienced, living and working together on the ranch. The ranch to me *is* love, but I need a partner to make that equation work."

"It's hard. I'd like to be in love and eventually have a family, but every guy I date can't handle me being a cop. They run like peckerwoods when they find out I'm a better shot or get offended when I pull a Tae Kwon Do move on them. Men say they want strong, independent women as partners, but secretly still want submissive, simpering subservience!"

"What about dating other officers?" probed Kate.

"I won't date anyone from the Serrano PD. Plus, synchronizing work schedules with someone from a different agency is a logistical nightmare for a stable relationship,"

Kiana shrugged. "And, with another cop there's the constant struggle of whose gonna be the alpha."

"So, does Jack ever talk about me much?" Kate fished, "To you, I mean?"

"No, he keeps his private life private," Kiana lied, answering a tad too quickly. She struggled to keep her face neutral. "This is why I quit playing poker," she thought, trying desperately to look nonchalant.

Kate silently searched Kiana's face for four long heartbeats while Kiana's brain squirmed like a worm impaled on a hook. She managed to not break eye contact first. "Well," Kate said just a little too brightly, "Look at us; a couple of robust, independent, and unshackled broads!"

Kiana wished she was anywhere else at the moment, including last summer's unattended death where the deceased had stewed in bathtub water for a week during a heat wave. Kiana wasn't going to answer the question Kate wanted to ask, unless Kate asked the question first.

"Yeah, and darn sexy ones, too!" Kiana cleared her throat. "I better call the Chief and advise him of Ski's call earlier."

"You do that."

Kiana's phone buzzed. Chief Mango's number was up.

It had taken Mango and Cormac thirty bone rattling minutes to reach the caves with Jorge puttering behind them. Climbing off his rig to stretch and check messages, Mango noticed he still had four bars so he took the opportunity to check in with Kiana.

"How you ladies doing down there?"

"We've been koffee-klatching with little pinky fingers raised and having a grand conversation. Why? Your ears burning?"

"Knew I should have never left you two alone together," he muttered, then cleared his throat. "Say good morning to Kate for me."

Kiana obliged, then continued, "You guys at the caves yet?"

"Roger that, but no sign of Stella. Jorge says that doesn't mean much as she could be standing six feet beneath us and we wouldn't know it."

"Maybe six feet under would be a good place for her."

"Tch, tch. We're going to scout the valley for another good hour by motor and on foot, and if need be, head north and search around T-ville. It would add another two hours, but then we can say we've legitimately searched the whole area. I'm also thinking I want Ski to revisit the lighthouse scene."

"Actually, I was just about to call you. Ski phoned right after you guys left and said he found some interesting video from the Surf Shop's skatebowl cam. At approximately eleven-thirty a.m., two days ago, Billy was caught on tape driving Stella's car into the northside pier parking lot. He parked next to a dark cargo van, exited the car, disappeared from view then reappeared carrying bolt cutters. He climbed back into Stella's car with them and drove away."

"It makes sense. He cut the padlock at the Lighthouse Trail gate then figures he's making good time, so he grabs a latte at the Hill o'Beans where he runs into Clare, and is so addled by their encounter he forgets about the cutters in Stella's car," Mango postulates.

"Description and plates match the DEA's info on the crashed drug van," Kiana added, "And, Ski thinks the van's tire treads from the cam photos match those emailed by Agent Craig."

"Can we ascertain placement of the van into the pier lot?"

"It appeared on video at first light in a parking spot, but it was too dark for the camera to pick up exactly when or who drove it in."

"Do we have an origin?"

"The van was stolen in LA based on the VIN number, and license plates were switched."

"Do we have confirmation on tape as to who moved the van and when, to have it end up off-trail near the lighthouse?" Mango queried, knowing though, if there had been a positive ID, Kiana would have contacted him ASAP.

"Bad luck on that one. Best Skibitski can make out is, the van was moved between 4:30 and 6:30pm. Too much glare angled into the lens at that time prevented him from seeing exactly who moved it and when."

"Of course! Send Ski to canvass the area and see if anyone saw the F-350 arrive or leave and who drove it. Cross your fingers on that one.

"Looks like Billy and Stella were in on this together, though" gloated Kiana.

"Not necessarily. Remember what happens when one ass-umes?"

"Yeah, I know, it makes an ass out of you and me."

"Back to Officer Skibitski, which is why I called. Tell him I've got a hunch and want him back at the lighthouse scene. With his eye for detail, I'd like him to walk the area;

from the trailhead to cargo van and Harry's resting place, to the panga and then over to the lighthouse. I want to make sure we didn't miss anything and that Stella *and/or* Clare aren't backtracking. Oh, and commend him for the info he gleaned from the video cam."

"So, what happens if you don't find Stella?" inquired Kiana.

"We'll cross that bridge if there's water under it. Right now, I want a unit cruising Serrano Canyon Road from the trailhead where you're stationed back to the highway. It's the only way for Stella to hike down into town by trail or bushwhacking, if indeed, it really was her sighted up here yesterday."

"If Stella murdered her husband and her lover, I don't think she'd hesitate adding her kid and a cop to the killing list, holding you both responsible for destroying her dirty little life," Kiana warned, "Be careful—" She stopped abruptly, remembering Kate standing beside her.

"I will. Tell Kate I love her," Mango hesitated. "And you, too." He received no reply as Kiana disconnected.

Two hours of searching yielded no clues to Stella's whereabouts, not even a footprint, even after venturing into some of the larger openings. Marshall and Jorge explored one cave which tunneled a hundred yards into the hillside, but encountered nothing more exciting than scattered beer cans where the passage ended unexpectedly around a bend, egress blocked by a wall of fallen rocks.

Rendezvousing together after a frustrating morning's work, the three men sipped water and nibbled snacks.

Mango texted Kiana, conveying their inability to track Stella, adding they would be continuing toward Tranquility. Mango had initially decided to exclude Buster from the hunt, reasoning that noise and dust from ATVs as opposed to horses would hinder the dog's tracking ability. He now wondered if he should have included the canine. Even with the added inconvenience of carting the exuberant hound in Jorge's cart, it would have been nice to have the additional tracking capability.

Kiana returned his text by phone immediately. "News flash, Chief. Ski called me a minute ago. He found fresh prints near the panga. One set of huge footprints, which match those we documented yesterday, but also another set walking next to them, much smaller ones. He's documented both."

"I knew it! I didn't think he'd leave without his cat. It's gotta be Oso. Any thoughts who the smaller prints belong to?"

"My money's on Clare."

"Why is that?"

"Ski found a yellow bike at the keeper's shack near the lighthouse. It matches the description of the one Clare stole. He swears he's studied the tracks enough, that he's ninety-nine percent sure they match those leading away from the drug vehicle and Harry's murder scene to the highway. Those imprints are Clare's, I betcha!"

Mango ran a hand down his face and frowned. "Okay, have Officer Skibitski visually confirm that both sets match, and not just by memory. Make sure he secures the bike into evidence. Also, if the serial number comes up a negative on the registry, meaning it's not registered to someone else and the owner can't confirm the number, (or he can match the number), then we need expedite the search warrant for Clare's place in T-ville. And make sure the BOLO on her reads armed and dangerous," Mango sighed. "And where the hell is my warrant for Stella's apartment?"

"Got it and officers are tossing Stella's place as we speak."

"What about evidence at Randi's rental house regarding Billy's murder?"

"Inconclusive. It's all been sent on to Doc Kno's office."

"Great," Mango replied sarcastically.

"There's more. We received DEA info on the bicycle with the van wreck. Serial number and description matches Harry's bike and its tire imprint matches those leading from his house up to the donut hole. We have confirmation Harry rode in and that his bike hitched a ride inside the drug vehicle."

"At least we've caught a few breaks. Make sure the bike evidence from Harry's, and what we assume is Clare's, is sent to the *experts* for confirmation, as well as the van treads. When I get back, I'll be able to hold a better briefing with the media jackals breathing down my neck. They raked me over the coals last night. Then when Hizzoner called me later, he threw his scotch into the fire as added fuel, took the embers and shoved them up my ass after ripping me a new one."

"This will cheer you up. The Sheriff's office says the bolt cutters confiscated from Stella are a *possible* match to striations on the gate lock at the lighthouse scene, but can't verify the findings until State examiners give their blessing. No prints, though."

"Speculations?"

"I need to digest the new evidence before regurgitating my opinions. Ski, however, has a fascinating theory in which Billy, Clare, Stella, & Harry were running a drug smuggling ring like those hayseed Kentucky marijuana consortiums. Where it's all in the family but something goes wrong, with no honor among thieves? He thinks Clare and Stella connived together to take over the business and snuff Billy because he was paroled early. Harry laundered the drug money through T-ville but didn't have the stomach for it or for killing Billy, so they offed him, too. The relationships are there. Did Clare and Stella bury the hatchet, double cross Billy, and then one set the other up for murder?"

Mango laughed so hard he dropped his phone. He leaned over and picked it up still wiping tears away. "Tell Ski I needed that. It's as good a theory as any. It fits, though, with what Agent Craig conveyed; an LA connection and a woman involved. Stella's a woman and Tranquility is owned by people from Hollywood. But, why bring a shipment in, so close to home—unless maybe the whole thing was a set up?" Mango scrubbed his face again, thinking maybe he needed to investigate the owners of Tranquility when he got back to town. "On that note, I have a search to finish. Thanks for the updates, Lieutenant. Text me with anything new."

Mango signed off, but texted Kate, "***xoxoxoxo, luv u, miss u, make this up 2 u, promise!***" He stuffed the phone into his breast pocket and repeated the new information from Kiana to his officers.

"Time to move on, guys. You see anything you're not sure of, raise an arm and stop. Jorge, how you doing with the limo?"

"Smooth as velveteen, Chief. Battery gauge shows about six hours of juice left.

"Okay. Off we go in search of Tranquility."

CHAPTER 24

FINDING CLARO AND BEARO

"You must be Chief Mango," the giant called out as he stepped from behind a huge boulder, Clare's pistol in his right hand pointing high to the sky, the granite spiral next to him acting to magnify his large frame.

Mango nodded. "You must be Oso Barranco.

"You know my name. I am impressed," Oso replied, bowing his head once.

"Likewise. How are we doing today?"

"It has been a good day, so far. *We* finished lunch and were taking a *siesta*." Oso grinned down at Mango standing twenty feet below, next to an orange ATV.

"We are a royal *we* or plural *we*?"

"My new friend, Claro." He raised the volume. "Say good morning, *por favor.*"

Clare's familiar voice floated out from behind the stone pinnacle, "Good morning, Chief. Sorry about stealing the gun. I was scared. Oso took it away from me so I wouldn't shoot him—or me."

Mango tried hard not to smile at her remark while studying the big Mexican above him. Jack held his Glock at his side toward the ground in front of him; arm down at a forty-five degree angle, knees slightly bent, feet spaced perfectly in a classic Weaver stance, his voice and breathing smooth and steady. He had made sure Oso had the sun in his eyes before approaching.

"So, what's the deal, Oso? You know what I have to do."

"The second thing I do is throw this gun over there." Oso pointed with his chin to a spot thirty feet to Mango's left.

"What is the first thing?"

"You promise Claro is not charged. She was frightened and made stupid choices, plus she is young. You will also promise to listen to my story before you hand me over to the *Federales*. I think you will like my tale," he added, face devoid of emotion. Oso's black eyes locked onto Mango's and neither man blinked for several seconds.

"If I don't?"

"There cannot be a 'don't'. We must do the right thing, you and me."

"I can promise you one thing. Clare stole a firearm and she is a person of interest in a double homicide. The courts must decide her fate, but you have my word I will present fair and honest evidence. If she is guilty of taking a gun and stealing a bike, I doubt the victims will want to press charges if they get their property back. Also, if she's not involved in these murders, the evidence will show that."

"Oso!" Clare shouted, "Throw the gun down. I know the Chief and you can trust him. Besides, I need a shower," she paused, "And so do you!"

Still holding the .22 high above his head, Oso called, "Chief Mango. You have seen *el gato negro*?"

"*Si*. Taco Gato is asleep in my office and is being well pampered."

Oso raised one eyebrow, and smiled widely, large white teeth gleaming in the sunlight. "*Bueno, Jefe. Muchas gracias.*" He slowly lowered the firearm and tossed it down, then placed his hands on his head as Mango instructed.

Mango slowly and cautiously walked around to the far side of the outcropping, knowing from earlier surveillance it was the only path to their aerie. Clare was sitting on the first level, ten feet up; legs bent and drawn to her chin, head resting atop her knees. She smiled nervously up at him.

Mango held his Glock comfortably at his side, just a little higher than before. Aware Oso might have a second gun; he glanced fifteen feet up to observe the man turning in place to position the sun behind to his back, hands still up.

"Don't move another inch, Oso." To Clare, he said, "Morning. You okay?"

"Yeah. I was scared to death last night but then I ran into Oso at the lighthouse. He took the gun from me, but in a nice way. He's a good guy, Mango, almost as nice as you," Clare said, eyes begging him to understand. "Then he told me about finding Harry. He's been protecting me from Stella." She hesitated. "He's real upset about losing his cat. You sure it's okay?"

Mango knew what kind of difficulties Clare had lived through and it suddenly occurred to him, he had never known her to speak compassionately about anyone or thing. Her cynical behavior and hard-edged mental barriers had cracked, allowing a gentler heart and soul to be exposed. The goliath gazing down at them had most assuredly played a part in her epiphany.

Mango leaned down and murmured to her. She shook her head negatively said, "But I didn't—"

Mango shushed her, one finger to his lips and talked quietly to her again. Finally, Clare stood and reluctantly put her hands behind her, which he quickly shackled while keeping a keen eye on Oso.

"Tell your man up the hill with the rifle I have no more *pistolas.* I want no bullet holes in me."

Mango wondered at the man's acute vision. Maybe he just guessed, or maybe not. Marshall was tucked two hundred yards up behind a dirt mound, holding steady a .308 Smith & Wesson MP 10 with attached scope, the crosshairs focused on Oso's forehead.

"The other *hombre*? The chunky one?" Oso asked.

"Close," Mango answered tersely.

Oso nodded. He asked for permission to climb down off the rock, which was granted. He descended, keeping arms and hands away from his body, as much as the scramble allowed. As soon as he touched soil, Sergeant Pacheco appeared, surprising Oso, who decisively folded his large hands back atop his head. "You are very good, my friend. You must have Mexican blood?"

"Correct, sir. Now, slowly kneel and I will cuff your hands together. *Mucho despacio, por favor*," Pacheco said clearly. Jorge had come prepared with extra flex cuffs just in case standard handcuffs wouldn't fit. Judging by Oso's saguaro imitation, they would apparently be needed.

After restraining his wrists and patting him down, Jorge turned Oso to face Mango. Both men were of almost equal height, with Oso's eyes a bit higher. They assessed each other and Mango sensed a highly intelligent and rational being. Oso's sheer size was impressive, carrying at least two hundred and seventy pounds on his solid frame, eyes projecting awareness of his predicament. Pacheco backed away, skittish, ready to draw down if necessary.

Mango spoke first. "If what you say is true and have information the Feds want, we do this by the book." He read both their Miranda Rights, "You have the right to remain silent . . . "

Oso absorbed each word and dipped his head once in agreement. "Si. I understand." Clare imitated the action and words.

"Oso Barranco, you are under arrest for distribution of marijuana, a controlled substance. Clare Morton, you're being arrested for theft of a firearm and grand theft of a bicycle. Neither of you say a word until you're on video acknowledging you understand your rights, are talking voluntarily and that I am not coercing you. You will also tell the truth. Don't piss on my boots and tell me it's lemonade. No games. *Comprende*?"

"At the ATVs, I'll record each of you being read the Miranda, as well as document your names and why-fors and ask a few simple questions. You then stay silent until we get to the station and we do it all over again inside. Oso, during the trip back, your legs will be shackled but your hands will remain cuffed in front since you'll need to balance on the rear bench seat of Sergeant Pacheco's rig. In the unlikely event the transport rolls, you'll need your arms for protection. There are three of us and we all enjoy a little tussle occasionally. I need your word you won't try any funny stuff; otherwise, we hog-tie you and bring in a helicopter. You really want to get frisky; none of us will hesitate to shoot you. *Comprende*?

"*Yo se, yo se.* I am here to make a deal and help Claro, not make problems," Oso agreed.

"Clare, you'll ride with Officer Cormac. No talking."

"You're not mad at me, are you, Chief Mango?"

"I'm doing my job here, Clare, and don't relish arresting you. I am glad to hear you were finally able to confront Billy head-on, and you got to do it in front of a small crowd," assured Mango. "You get an 'atta-girl' on that one from me and I wish I'd been there so see it. Anything that happened after, well, we'll discuss in Serrano. No more talk."

Once at the ATVs, Mango whistled a staccato cadence, a preset signal directing the sniper Cormac to join them. While waiting, Pacheco recorded as Mango repeated the arrest formalities. Marshall and Clare in one ATV led the caravan downhill, followed by Jorge with Oso. Mango brought up the rear and checked in with Lt. de la Cruz, Sheriff Sederwall and Agent Craig, updating them on the apprehensions, sans Stella. The convoy crawled southbound and down, Marshall stopping intermittently so he could remain within Pacheco and Mango's sight, not wanting to outpace the slower vehicle in case Oso's pledge of cooperation changed.

They stopped at the saddle ridge near a cave access to stretch and rehydrate. It would take another two long hours for them to reach Serrano at their plodding pace. The view to the southwest past golden grassed hills, of deep Pacific water shimmering in the bright afternoon glare, the morning's fog evaporated by a soothing offshore breeze, was an appreciated bonus under the circumstances. A gray whale and her offspring's blow spouts could be seen making progress towards Morro Bay. Two hawks cruised thermals overhead in vast effortless circles while below on Route One tiny specks drove north, silent in the distance. No one felt the need to speak.

Fifty yards to the east, along a ridge which ran perpendicular to the trail, behind a scrubby yet hardy oak, was a small crack in the rock. The tree's roots pierced the stone in a curved grip framing a cavity. Except for a small vent, the entire opening had caved in. Standing on the trail and looking back, it was invisible. Two unblinking eyes peered from the gap and watched the group mount up and ride toward Serrano.

CHAPTER 25

STELLA PULLS THE TRIGGER

Stella snorted the two small piles of powder off the top of her closed fist then rubbed the residue into her upper gums and smacked her lips. *Much better.* She resealed the precious vial and shoved it into the front pocket of her jeans for easier access. It was then that she felt the vibration well before hearing the rumbling ATVs, the pulsating hum through the underground cavern walls crawling along her skin. She cautiously edged her body along one wall, staying shy of the concealed cave entrance overgrown by thick scrub oak and fallen rock. The opening, a tight crevice not more than 20 feet from the trail was little more than a narrow hole. Few people knew the space was connected to a larger opening a hundred yards down the back side of the hill, east of the trail.

Stella cursed, remembering her mistake in allowing the two hikers to see her. Awakening from a drug depleted stupor, she had stumbled up-trail to gaze back at the town below and didn't see the hikers until it was too late to hide. One sitting cross-legged on the ground while her boyfriend snuck a leak some paces into the foliage. Stella knew she looked bad and smelled worse. Her static-electric hair stuck out weirdly and her mouth tasted like rodent poop. It had been two days since she'd showered, not even taking the time to dab her pits the morning she ran from the condo. No wonder the trekkers had disappeared so quickly after trying to exchange pleasantries.

She wasn't about to let the cops grab her, and had taken off before they even considered the possibility she would sneak off. Stella had snatched only a well-worn fleece camo jacket, sweatshirt, two pair of mismatched socks, and sunglasses on a string before being sidetracked with digging a backpack and sleeping bag from the closet. She tossed granola bars, a block of cheese, some crackers, a gallon of water and a bottle of cheap wine into the pack without considering soap or toothpaste. But Stella hadn't planned on a long hiatus from Serrano, so the lack of provisions didn't matter for what she had in mind. There was still one more task to complete.

Snapping back to the present, she squeezed into a gap to watch the convoy mount up and ride off, cackling gleefully once they were out of earshot, "The perfect diversion, concentrating on Clare and that big guy. Whoever he is, he's gonna ruin the springs on that cart and turn it into a low rider before they get him downhill," she snickered. Stella also noted with satisfaction the little hussy was handcuffed. "While the cats are hunting mice, the rats will play. Time to go to work."

As soon as Mango's team and two prisoners disappeared around a bend, Stella snaked her way down a narrow passage that dropped into a lower chamber and gathered the satchel containing her scant possessions, which included a five shot Taurus .38 Special with a two-inch barrel and the last of her cigarettes. She also snatched the nearly empty plastic water jug and patted her pocket, reaffirming the comforting presence of her meth stash.

Stepping slowly into the open, shading her dilated eyes with a hand and grimacing, (pupils engorged more from drugs than the dark), she quickly pulled the dangling shades to her face to block the bright light. Stella paused; listening intently to make sure a second search party wasn't riding the hills nearby. She glanced down at her bruised, scratched hands, and swiped her tongue across pitted teeth, feeling the grit. Stella cursed and spit; her life and humanity ruined by those she despised.

Primordial in reflex, taking advantage of Mango's distraction with his captives, she loped down a slope and east before cutting south, parallel to the footpath. Her destination Serrano, where she could curve her way up a rise to drop directly behind and into Randi Shirazi's neighborhood. *That fake, goody two-shoes whore is gonna pay.* Stella would make sure it hurt, too.

The hiking trails skirting the town's perimeter were used mostly in the mornings by resident dog walkers and happy vacationers. By late afternoon, Stella had worked her way to the apex of a canyon which funneled into Randi's street. Tired and hungry, she hid under a small copse of trees a quarter mile from Randi's, watching the coming and goings of the neighborhood's late afternoon routine. Stella didn't want to arrive too early.

From a house closest to Stella's concealed position, a lithe blonde, dressed in black yoga pants and form fitting yellow spandex top jogged down the front stoop to a black Lexus parked in the driveway, carrying what looked to be multiple garbage bags bulging with clothing. Once the blonde finished loading the bags, she walked around and opened the vehicle's passenger door, then trotted to and opened a gated fence near Stella's hiding spot calling, "Let's go for a ride, Missy! Mommy's dropping stuff off at Goodwill. Afterwards, we'll go to the beach for a walk." A knee-high, white poodle bounded through the gate into the Lexus. "Who's a good girl!" the woman cooed as she slammed the door.

Must be nice to make a goodwill donation in a SUV worth fifty thousand. Bitch. Stella watched as the blond backed from the driveway and drove away. She waited a few minutes then walked at an angle to the backyard, keeping to foliage and trees, taking her time until she was standing next to the sliding patio door. It wasn't completely closed, much less locked.

"Haven't you heard, dearie? There's a crazed murderer on the loose. You must be more careful," she sneered, reaching for the handle. She froze, looking at the woman staring back at her, someone whom she vaguely used to know from her past, now a desperate stranger, a mirror of her future. Stella pulled her sunglasses off and studied the picture of steel-wooled hair and raccoon, grime ringed eye sockets. "Seen better days, girl," she sighed, "You give new definition to rode hard and put up wet. Thank god for the drugs or else I'd be worried!"

Stella broke her gaze to squeeze through the door into a kitchen, stopping to listen for occupants. Relieved, she perused the interior of the fridge and decided upon a ham and cheese on rye. A brown leather sofa in the den beckoned, one facing a hundred gallon saltwater aquarium containing an array of exotic, undulating fish. The gurgling tank was framed by floor-to ceiling mahogany bookshelves, complete with a rolling ladder. "Ostentatious, pretentious pricks. They've got more money sunk into that wall than I've earned my entire life," Stella thought. She chewed another bite of sandwich and reached for the cold bottle of Rolling Rock, making sure the condensation left a permanent ring on a marble end table.

She finished her meal then went back and grabbed two more beers, returned to the sofa, quickly drank one and belched loudly. Stella threw the empty into a fireplace catty-corner from the aquarium. A puffer fish stared at her from behind the glass, oblivious to the crashing bottle, fins fluttering to keep afloat in one place.

Stella stared back and stated, "You can call me Roy, as in Rogers," paraphrasing a line by Bruce Willis's character, John McClain from the movie *Die Hard*. "If I'm Roy, that must make you Trigger," she cackled, slapping leather. "So, how's your fuckin' day going, Trigger?"

The massive aquarium was well lit, a calm and serene hydrosphere of dead bleached coral intermixed with multi-hued faux sea kelp and ceramic hidey holes. A tiny banded coral shrimp scampered in and out of the cavities keeping a wary eye on the puffer. Foxface, clownfish, and butterfly fish circled the tank aimlessly as if sleep swimming. Mindful of the intruder, Trigger stared at Stella intently, its lips puckering over and over, blowing kisses.

Stella glanced down at the beer in her hand and examined the black grunge buried under her fingernails and seated in her cuticles; dried blood mixed with dirt from scrabbling through the underworld. Her arms were encased in layered black streaks of filth ingrained into the creases around her wrists and insides of elbows. She sniffed and analyzed the pungent odor rising from her body and scratched at patterned sweat stains around her armpit.

"You think this is my fault, Trigger? Your type living in big houses with plenty to eat and fancy cars? Your kind running in the same circles, living inside their own little worlds, so us little people can admire and say, 'Wow, see how good you have it? Must be doing something right.' But they don't know the secrets, the lies, and the hurt. There are consequences. No, Randi and your kind look at me and judge! It's not my fault I married a sicko who liked having sex with little girls." Stella suddenly ran out of breath, lifted the beer and chugged it empty. She exhaled, savoring the cool residue of Old Latrobe sliding down her parched throat.

"The only difference between you and me is I know I'm gonna die today." She eyeballed the puffer. "I know this is my last day in the fish tank and it might be yours, too!" Stella tossed the second bottle at the fireplace, this one missing, breaking on the Spanish tile. She pondered the green shards and smiled, turning to face the fish. "It's time," she announced. "Let the games begin!" Stella reached over a sofa cushion and pulled the .38 revolver from her rucksack, turning the barrel to point directly at her face.

She stared down the opening, studying the lands and grooves inside to see which direction the bullet would twist coming out. Looking past to Trigger, she said, "It's not fair unless you have a chance, so we have to change the odds. Today is your lucky day. I'm giving you odds and at the same time I'm giving Randi an out. Bad news; if I win, you and Randi die. Got that?"

Stella pushed on the revolver's cylinder release, tilted the weapon so the cylinder opened, and removed two bullets before spinning it and snapping it closed. "Here's the deal. I really think you're going to like this." Trigger continued to float, staring straight at Stella.

"You see that I took out two bullets and left three. That elevates the game." Stella brought the gun to her mouth and inserted the barrel, licking it with her tongue, sliding it in and out. She closed her eyes and for at least a minute enjoyed the experience before removing it. She spoke softly, "Billy taught me how to do that. Well, it truly wasn't a teaching moment, not when he's gripping my ears and shoving my head. Harry said I was pretty good at it, though. Funny, I never thought I was good at anything."

Stella replaced the barrel between her lips, allowing her tongue to caress the tip, and inserted it as far as she could down her throat, sliding the smooth bottom along the top of her tongue so the front sights wouldn't scratch her throat. After another minute, she felt her nipples tighten under her shirt and a quivering in her groin. She pulled the gun out and shivered. "Wasn't ready for that. Please excuse me, Trigger. I really am a good little girl, but I have a few nasty habits. See what my life has become? I'm playing Russian Roulette with a fish."

Stella put the gun back in her mouth, squeezed her thighs together and carefully placed both thumbs on the trigger, right over left. The front sights rested softly on her upper palate, the barrel pointing directly to the intersection of her brain and upper spine, ensuring instantaneous removal of vertebrae and death. No pain, done and over. She'd been practicing this move for almost two years, never with a chambered round, let alone three. Had profiled herself in the bathroom mirror, perfecting placement and angle of the barrel for maximum impact. She wasn't afraid, but she didn't want to screw this up.

Staring directly at Trigger she squeezed. CLICK!

Gasping, amazed, Stella wasn't sure what she was feeling. "I think I just had the first orgasm of my life. Better than sex with a man; way better! I feel like smoking a cigarette." She pulled the gun out of her mouth, blew on the tip, turned it around and pointed it at Trigger. He floated effortlessly, eyes bulging, still blowing kisses at her.

"You lose, dude. Sorry. It happens."

Stella pulled once. The aquarium exploded in a flood of water, glass and fish. She contemplated the mess then methodically reloaded the three empty chambers.

Stella grabbed two more bottles of Rolling Rock as she breezed through the kitchen, stopping for a moment at the door, listening for any commotion indicating the gunshot had been recognized as such. "Probably not," she thought. "One little bang doesn't draw attention these days, especially from these self-absorbed assholes."

Stella walked through the back yard like she owned the place and quickly disappeared into the ravine out back where she could melt in the flora, rest, and wait until dark. "Time to settle up, Randi. I'm comin' for you, bitch!"

CHAPTER 26

OSO AND CLARE BEHIND BARS

The five rode into the parking area where de la Cruz, Skibitski, Deputy Cervantes, and State Trooper Smith waited, the lot closed to the public by three marked units and a double string of yellow tape. A San Luis Obispo television news vehicle was angled alongside of the road, the ubiquitous blonde primping for her upcoming live broadcast. Two local newspaper hacks strained at the tape, cameras and microphones ready, hoping for their big break, as well as miscellaneous independent media reporters hoping to sell sensationalism on the internet news feeds and a smattering of sticky-beaked Tranks itching to use their iPhones and practice uploading to YouTube.

Mango took the lead into the parking lot and hopped off the ATV to brief with Kiana. "What's in place?"

"The reporters can't get to the prisoners. Dora is set to open the fenced sally-port, and the holding cells are ready plus the interview room. No sign of reporters at the Serrano station; looks like they're all here. No sign of Stella. Hathaway's been complaining to council members about your scenic joyriding instead of searching for killers loose in town. Coming back with a DEA fugitive and a murder suspect should cool their asses down."

Mango cricked his head side to side, placed his hands on his hips and stretched his lower back. He gazed past Kiana at the reporters. "The mayor is notorious for playing arm-chair quarterback. Not an issue." He pointed with his chin at the 4x4. "Wait till you see what I caught when he uncurls from Jorge's rumble seat. I've got Oso in leg shackles and both he and Clare cuffed in front, only so they could hold on and not fall off. We'll need to re-cuff their hands behind their backs before transport to the station. Hate to do it with Clare, but it's important protocol, especially now with conceivable evidence placing her in proximity to Harry's murder site and the drug buggy."

"No trouble from the big guy?" Kiana asked, allowing Mango to reflect upon the danger of redoing his cuffs.

"None. I know what you're thinking, and if Oso has info the DEA wants in exchange for leniency and a plea agreement, I'm betting he'll not want to make things worse by fighting. Although, we could come up with another solution without trussing him up like an animal."

De la Cruz and Mango walked over where the prisoners still sat in the ATVs. Mango instructed Cormac to run extra flex cuffs through Oso's belt and another securing his wrists to it. Oso whispered softly, "*Mucho gracias*."

Mango spoke deliberately to Oso, Clare and the others, "You will both be fed and cleaned up; then we'll interview. But, we'll do it my way. You clearly understand your rights, and that if you decide to talk you will be recorded. Agreed?" Clare and Oso assented.

Mango tipped his head to the road, "Walking near them isn't going to be pleasant. I'm assuming you're both smart enough to not talk to the reporters?"

Mango addressed the waiting officers. "Smitty, you bring Oso. De la Cruz, Clare rides with you."

Oso and Clare maintained their silent, bowed posture, staring at their shuffling feet as they were escorted to the police units and helped inside.

Shouted questions pelted them like rocks, echoing off the canyon walls: "Did you kill them both? Did the giant rape you?" (Clare visibly flinched at that one.) "Did you kill them with your bare hands? Why did you do it? Are there other bodies? Is this a Manson copycat murder spree?"

Oso and Clare were booked, showered and fed. Mango instructed Jorge and Kiana to write up the arrest reports while he double checked the interview room was set up and audio/visual equipment was working properly. He also had Dora run down to the Quik Pik and buy Oso's preferred Marlboros cigarettes, and leave them on the table, smoke free building be damned.

Originally intending to start with Clare, Mango decided interrogating Oso first would score more points with the Feds, accelerating the time in which they could take custody. Besides, it never hurt to have leverage, with information trickling up rather than down, and be credited as the department cracking a smuggling ring. Once they finished with Oso they could concentrate fully on Clare and the murders, and see if any of it tied together.

Officer Skibitski escorted Oso into the stark room where Chief Mango and Sergeant Pacheco waited. Oso's hands were restrained in front by leg shackles, the longer chain shortened by crimping the links, preventing him from using the longer chain as a weapon. The leg hardware Skibitski clipped discretely to a bolt in the floor next to a table leg.

Mango and Pacheco rose from behind the metal slab centered in the room, the large clichéd mirror behind them reflecting their wrinkled, sweat stained uniformed backs. The mirror's placement was obvious, allowing recording devises and additional people to view the suspect's face, posture and gestures safely from a separate area.

Officer Skibitski was given the honors of reciting the Miranda Warning to Oso one more time for the cameras, adding logistical information about those in attendance. Oso stated he understood the ramifications of talking without an attorney.

"You want me to stay, Chief?" asked a nervous Ski, trying to hide sweaty palms inside his pant pockets. As a young rookie caught up in not one, but two murders plus a major drug bust, every action and sound seemed amplified, the colors brighter; like a talking part in a slasher movie for the first time. Skibitski had found one of the bodies and been a catalyst in discovering key evidence.

"That won't be necessary, but I'd like if you didn't stray too far," replied Mango, tipping his head unperceptively at the mirror, wondering how the kid would be able to fit, given that all the players, most of the department and then some, were packed in the tiny viewing room like smelts.

Ski discreetly lifted his chin at Mango.

Suppressing a smile, Mango knew that Ski would figure it out.

"You treat him with respect. We were young like that once, no?"

"Once. I think we grew old too fast. Leg cuffs working better on your wrists?" asked Mango, changing the subject.

"*Si.*" Oso pointed an index finger at the pack of cigarettes and looked across the table at Mango.

"Go ahead. We won't arrest you for smoking in a non-designated area, just don't blow it on Sergeant Pacheco; makes him mad."

Jorge sat motionless, large forearms folded across his chest, staring at Oso across the table poker faced. All part of the game.

Mango lost the coin flip before the interview, so he was playing nice. Both had wanted to play the bad cop, especially in a case like this, so the only way to settle it without Mango pulling rank was a coin toss. So be it, though Mango felt the charade would be wasted as Oso had continued to express interest in trading intelligence for leniency.

This was Mango's forte, which he taught his ranking officers to play with a high degree of success. Emotions are kryptonite for criminals. Interrogate a prisoner until their emotions are aroused, positive or negative, to the point where their sociopathic indifference crumbles, and game over. The 'good cop, bad cop' scenario forces emotions to the surface and creates a double opportunity to trick a suspect into answering questions without the veneer of "Spock" logic.

Mango started with light humor. "Your cat is costing me a small fortune in Fancy Feast," he chided, face passive, eyes studying the large man.

"So much for *mi gato afortunado.* What happens to him now?" Oso asked, while pulling a cigarette out of the pack and lighting it, making a point to blow downward and away.

"Normally he'd be taken to the local shelter. Be a shame to do that. I know of a place with some land where he'll be treated well, and can hang with a couple other cats."

Oso looked down at his hand holding the cigarette, and Mango could see the man's jaw working.

"Sergeant Pacheco speaks Spanish if that's more comfortable for you."

"We speak a different Spanish, I think, just as he wears a gun and I have *nada*. English is good, but Spanglish is better. The two will mix someday down the road," replied Oso.

He inhaled deeply and slowly expelled the rich smoke, eyes closed as if in meditation, and then gave a little grunt. "Without *Taco*, this *tabiro* is the only good thing I have left. My boat is going down and I am not going with it. Not yet."

"Then talk to me, Oso, and you may one day get your boat back as well as the cat."

"Talk about what, *Jefe*? I am not *el rata*."

"Tell me how you got into this mess; everything you can think of and more."

Oso snorted. "*Stupido* got me here. My wife left and stole my *dinero*. The judge, he makes me pay more. Probably tapping the *bruja!* I am losing my boat, I cannot do both. I need cash. Two men I sometimes take on fishing trips, always pay cash, I tell them my troubles. They offer me a job." Oso smacked his forehead. "*Estupido*!"

"What did they want you to do?"

"I was to get forty thousand cash for one delivery. Pick up stuff at sea with two other guys. They supply the boat. Then I run it to ground at a certain place. A van waits and gets loaded. They drop me in Monterey and head north. They tell me take a bus back to LA, go to my boat, business as usual. The money will be given to me next day by a 'fishing client.' *Nunca volveré a cometer semejante estupidez!* I'll never do anything so stupid again!"

"I'm wondering why you didn't have a cat carrier for *el gato*," Pacheco asked, glowering.

"I did. One of the *pendejos* threw it overboard. Said it took up too much space."

"Were these guys Mexican?" Mango asked thinking of his conversation with Special Agent Levi Craig.

"In the boat? *Si*, Mexican. *Dos jefes?* No."

"So, what were they?" Pacheco spoke up.

"Middle Eastern?" Oso guessed.

"From what country?"

"How the hell should I know? Those people all look alike to me!"

Mango interceded, "What else can you tell us? The more details, the better it will go for you."

Oso studied the burned out butt clinched between thumb and forefinger, the ash having fallen in one long log onto a makeshift piece of tinfoil supplied by Mango. "*Mierda.* All I know is they are camel jocks and pay good to deep sea fish. When they think I am no hearing, they talk on their phones. They are *malo jodidos*. They hurt people."

"Let's go around again, Oso," Mango urged.

Oso lit another Marlboro and inhaled, scrutinizing the fresh sphere of smoke spiral to the ceiling. "*El dinero malo echa fuera al bueno.* Bad money drives out good," he exhaled. His gaze rotated back to the two cops.

"All of it, Oso. I have two dead guys and a boat load of dope with you right in the middle. You are a major pain in my panga, *señor*," Mango pressed, matching the man's stare without blinking.

"I am sorry to hear your wife died from cancer. *Mi tia,* also."

Mango felt like he'd been slapped, the urge to straighten his spine overwhelming. He squelched it. "I see Clare shared my history."

"She says you are a good man. We will see."

"Clare talks too much."

"She feels I can trust you. It is a big word with small letters."

"I can't make promises. That's the district attorney's call, not mine. If you just delivered the drugs, have no priors, and providing you didn't murder anyone, I have a DEA friend who, just maybe, can encourage the court into clemency if you cooperate. They cut the deals. He and I do have influence, but it all depends on how much and how good your information is. I owe you for bringing Clare back safely, and for that, you have my word I will try to help. You lie, you feed us anymore bullshit or have us chasing our tails, you'll get squat."

Oso sucked on the cigarette and blew out. "*Si.* No bullshit." He contemplated his reflection in the mirror, eyes glazed, seeing beyond. Mango could envision the man standing at the helm of a forty foot trawler riding the swells, feeling the ocean breathe beneath him, adjusting legs and shifting feet to hold steady as the boat rose and fell.

"Let's circle back to the two who hired you."

"I knew the two *pinche cabrones* were dirty, but they pay well to go fish, so I take them. I need money," he said with a shrug of one shoulder, "They pay even more for not fishing.

"You're sure they're *not* Mexicans." Pacheco reaffirmed.

"*Gringos*, to me at least, but not *Americano gringos*. Black hair, dark skin, dead eyes, strange accent."

"You're still thinking Middle Eastern? Muslim or Arab?" Pacheco persisted.

"Thought the two were the same."

"Not necessarily," Mango advised.

"All I know, they wear much gold and smell like Mexican *putas*. Who wears cologne and a Rolex to go fishing?" he answered while grinding out another butt.

"Turkish, Persian, Saudi?" Mango pressed.

"Possible, but not with the wrapped head." Oso shook his head grimly. "They offered. I bit and got stuck on the hook."

"Why here? Who picked this location and why?"

"They are related," Oso said, head jerking up. "I did not know I knew that."

"You sure?"

"*Si, si, Jefe.* Looking at their faces in my head, I see they are similar. They also have a partner here. Maybe more than one. He was *encarcelado,* in prison, for a few years." He hesitated. "There was a woman, *tambien.* Maybe."

"You're not sure?" Mango probed.

"I hear the two Mexicans in the panga. The *culo* who threw *Taco's* cage away say to the other, 'hope *she* bring the truck.' I am sure. Later, he say something more about the woman, but I am running the boat fast and loud, so not sure."

"Any idea who this woman is?" Mango asked, contemplating the odds Oso could be talking about Stella and Billy. He thought of the bolt cutters found in her Taurus; the same car Billy supposedly drove to Tranquility, unexpectedly walking into a hornet's nest named Clare. Stella would've needed money to leave Serrano to start over elsewhere, and the best way to make a lot of it quickly was drug running. Maybe she *had* been blackmailing Billy with knowledge of more victims. That slip of the tongue when he and Kiana talked with her, where she quickly backpedaled, had been a 'tell', one to which he should have paid more attention.

"*No se,* on the woman. The tough wetback, he come to my boat and give me instructions; take a cab to the Vintage Marina in Oxnard and he will meet me at the panga. It's a $300 taxi ride! I took a $15 Greyhound bus to Oxnard, and then took a cab to the boat. It was empty except for a little drinking water stowed and a full tank of gas. He was not happy to see me with *Taco Gato.* With my new *amigo*, we meet a bigger boat offshore, load up, and pick up another Mexican. He never speak; *nunca*! I think he was supposed to kill me but decided not. Maybe he think I do not die so easy." Oso cracked a broad smile.

Pacheco couldn't help but smile back. No two ways about it, if you planned on whacking Oso, you'd better have your shit together.

"I land the boat and help load a dark van parked in sandy dirt near rocks. They send me back to panga for the last bales and leave me. I thought they took *Taco*! I run back and no

Mexicans, no van, no *gato*. Fucking *hijo de putas!* I find one dead gringo under trees where I try to sleep, so I run quickly and camp near lighthouse. I look for *Taco* at dawn.

"But then the cops showed up," Mango empathized.

"*Si*."

"The two fishing dudes back in LA, do you know how to find them? Can you identify them?"

"They have a business. I have their card with a phone number on it, on my boat in Long Beach. And I will never forget the two Mexicans," he rumbled.

"Did you or your two boat buddies kill the guy near the lighthouse?"

"Not me, *Jefe!* The others? I do not think so. I hear no screams or fighting. But *el viente,* that night the wind was strong, making much noise and why *el gato* did not hear me when I call. He comes for no one but me. But the dead *gringo*, he already smelled ripe when I lay beside him."

"Nothing more about the woman?" Mango asked again, just as a small red light bulb mounted on the wall behind Oso pulsed on and off. "Think on that. I'll be right back." The light was used sparingly during interviews, but was there to signify something urgent needed to be conveyed.

Dora, Kiana, and Skibitski were standing in the hallway waiting for Mango. Dora's enlarged eyes, their whites glowing under hallway lights, spoke first, "I just received a 911 for multiple shots fired. A neighbor says she thinks they came from Randi Shirazi's house. Right after, Randi called 911 from her cell requesting an ambulance. She was incoherent, but I think I heard her say Stella tried to kill her in her kitchen. She hung up before I could tell her to stay connected. I've tried to reverse call. It rings but goes to voicemail."

"Skibitski, you and Trooper Smith hustle Oso into a locked holding cell. Tell him something came up and the interview is over for now. Check one more time as you tuck him in, and see if he remembers anything about the woman he mentioned. I'm thinking it's Stella, but I need more than circumstantial hearsay. If she's dead, she's not gonna be talking. Kiana, you and Jorge meet me in the parking lot," Mango directed. "Ski, once you've secured Oso, check the radio chatter, then you and Smitty follow. Dora, find Cormac and Buster and send them after us. Also, have Deputy Cervantes on standby, just in case. Have her look in on Clare, and let her know her interview is postponed until tomorrow. And keep me posted if anything changes."

"What else?" asked Jorge, prompting Mango, who had gone quiet.

"Okay. We go in separate cars. I go in the front door with Kiana right behind me if it's not locked. If it is, we'll figure out entry when we get there. Jorge, you'll cover the back with Cormac and the dog. Ski can man the street and coordinate EMTs and additional units, with Smitty backing up *everyone*. Use extreme caution and don't assume. If we have a challenger, keep your fingers out of the trigger guard until you come up on target, but remember my old academy motto, 'always cheat, always win.' Use every trick you know so we all go home alive."

"Yes, sir," the three sounded in unison.

"Let's move. No sirens, no code, no rotators, and Dora, that means the ambulance, too. Keep this as low key as possible," instructed Mango, "And if the mayor shows up, no matter how much you'd like to, don't shoot the man."

CHAPTER 27

SHE BE COMIN' ROUND THE MOUNTAIN

Stella jerked awake, eyes agape and mouth open, breath held captive in her lungs. She relaxed once she recognized the blare of a distant car horn and babble of happily screeching children, though not enough to release the tightly gripped revolver. Sitting up, she felt the stiffness in her body hampering movement and was relieved to see it was near dusk; time to get the kinks out.

Concealed in an arroyo under some brush, she heard not a peep from Trigger's house, two hundred yards away. "Guess poodle woman isn't back yet. I got careless," she thought. "Need to stay focused."

"Where's my magic dust?" Stella said aloud, frantically rooting through her pack, then slapping at breast and jacket pockets. She was half a block from turning the corner on hysteria when she felt the bulge under the front pocket of her jeans. *Ahhhhh.*

She crawled behind a tree and emptied the remaining powder into her palm. Unfolding an old straw from her other pants pocket, she snorted the remaining methamphetamine. The intensity of the hit burned through her nostrils and down her throat, setting limbs to twitching and body shaking. Once the convulsions stopped, she stood and stretched, invigorated.

Jogging briskly along the perimeter trail leading to Randi's, Stella's overstimulated brain relived her wasted life, circling through flashbacks worse than an acid trip gone wrong. Graduating at the top of her class from Paso Robles High, quiet and introverted, she'd never learned how to socialize. With few friends to buffer her awkwardness, even the brainiac clique had hurled ugly, hateful epithets, cutting her soul to the bone.

In her freshman year at community college she met a somewhat attractive older guy in a downtown San Luis Obispo bookstore. Billy Morton, an up and coming psychiatrist in his late twenties, asked her out for a coffee, like a spider into his web. Shy and giggly, she of plain flowered dresses with thick bookworm glasses perched on an off-centered nose, never having dated anyone before, much less a *real* man, said yes. One year of chaste courtship later they married.

Having no experiences to compare, Stella wasn't sure what to make of marriage when Billy required she keep her body shaved; all of it except her head. Plus, Billy couldn't keep an erection. He claimed medical complications, but she knew it was because she was physically repulsive.

She tried to resume college classes, but for the most part, she played stay-at-home-mommy with Billy, cooking his dinner, ironing his clothes, and submitting to his increasingly bizarre sex games. He told her the costumes, the weird toys and restraints helped to alleviate his medical problem, and besides, it was natural when in connubial circumstances.

What did she know? He was the learned psychiatrist and she was barely out of her teens when they wed.

After ten long years of perpetual depression, Stella finally figured out Billy was sick in his head, not in his body. She discovered desires of her own, desires she never knew she had and started refusing Billy's play dates. Hanging out at the Hill o'Beans while her husband was at work led her eventually to Harry Henderson, who while not the brightest bulb, was the opposite of manipulating Billy: compliant, accommodating and appreciative.

When the Wednesday's Child Adoption segments began airing, Billy became obsessed. He argued that since Stella was barren, having a family was their missing link. Raising a child would solve his 'condition' while giving them a rewarding purpose and direction. His attitude immediately changed; coming home from work on time, helping out around the house more and even giving her little gifts. After months of constant wheedling and pestering, Billy won. The adoptee would be a pre-teen girl.

God help her, Stella knew just by the expression on his face the first time he brought it up; the smarmy grin, large eyes gleaming, and arched back, just like after their now-rare conjugal moments. Yeah, he tried to downplay it, to hide it, but she saw. He stank of it like a little boy the night before Christmas.

She had thought about what she could do and where to go. Harry would be worthless for protection, and her father was long dead, mother remarried to an alcoholic used car salesman in Visalia. No going home for Stella, to be welcomed with open arms. She couldn't remember a single time growing up when her parents told her she looked pretty or ever kissed her. "What a corn hole for a life," she silently lamented. Doesn't matter now. She was determined to go out with a bang, and stylin' Randi was going with her.

Randi Shirazi, CASA for Clare, presented much of the testimonial evidence against Billy. Even with Clare interviewed forensically and the rape kit eventually returning a positive, the case was still a fiasco of, she said, 'rape;' he said, 'never touched her.' What Clare confided to Randi not only sent Billy Morton to prison, but allowed the District Attorney to paint a chilling picture of Stella Morton as downright ruthless and brutal, implying but never proving, she helped her husband violate their adopted daughter.

Randi called Stella after the trial to apologize for the part she had been required to play in order to convict Billy, saying she felt responsible for Stella's situation and offered employment. It was the least she could do for an innocent wife of a sexual predator, vilified by the media as an eager participant. Randi also provided her a low rent apartment in upper Serrano Canyon, which Stella found out later, was used as a tax write-off for indigent, employee housing expenses. So, while Billy was incarcerated, Stella toiled, cleaning every toilet Randi owned, year after year, and ate shit every time Randi yelled squat.

Then Billy got paroled early for some fool excuse like prison overcrowding, or the inability of the state being able to afford high security lock-up, the better to keep his sorry ass from being murdered or worse. Besides, Billy convinced the board he was rehabilitated, with a low risk of pedophile recidivism. Serranoans were shocked and disappointed by the early release, none the least Harry, whose main concern, Stella thought sourly, had been whether he'd lose his deviant sex partner; one who enjoyed pain and punishment. She'd told him it was just role playing, to go along with it and enjoy. Moreover, it wasn't his pain.

Thoughts whirling, Stella hadn't realized she'd almost reached her tormentor's house. She quickly crouched and sipped water to quench her cotton mouth, muttering, "Poor sick in the head Billy is dead. Tell ya' what, I'll send Randi down to keep you company. And Harry can go to hell, too."

She stared, watching from a distance as a shape moved past a curtain-covered kitchen window, and the sliding door next to it opened enough to let someone turtle their head out and look around. It was too dark to see who, but when the door smoothly closed, there was no after-click signifying a lock had been thrown. Stella pulled the revolver out of her backpack and rechecked the bullets.

CHAPTER 28

DEAD SECRETS

"We need to *vamoose* if we're going to make our flight to Lima from LAX. Figure we'll spend a few days seeing the sights, make sure nobody's following, then fly to Uruguay."

"Shit! With everything that's happened I never had a chance to arrange for Zeba & Zulu's care. It's breaking my heart to leave them."

"I told you it was a bad idea to adopt them."

"I wouldn't have needed to if you'd been here. This was your idea. Besides, I needed the company."

"Like you needed the Police Chief's?"

"Better to have Mango's sympathy than his suspicion. You know what they say about keeping your enemies close, plus it kept Mikhail and Hafid off my back."

"As opposed to on yours? You didn't have to fuck him."

"Says the man who wasn't here to protect me; yes, I did. You have no idea what my life was like the year or so after you 'died.' They were so infuriated their cash flow dropped, your brothers kidnapped and tortured me twice to make sure I kept buying their black market gems and paying their extortion money. They beat and abused me in places that didn't show, made me suck them off and stuck things where—well, let's just say the second time I couldn't walk for three days without a cane. Once I told them about my new buddy, they quit the physical stuff but still spewed their verbal poison."

"You should have told me—"

"Oh, don't look at me like that. I never told you because I didn't want you going all macho, confronting your brothers and spoiling everything. We worked too many years setting this up and been through so much, all to be free of your family. Nothing, and I mean nothing, is going to ruin this."

"I'm sorry, my love. I don't think either one of us realized or planned for how violently my brothers would react."

"We didn't plan a lot of things that happened. We've been over that. It's done. Our new life is waiting."

"I can't wait to show you the little *pied a terre* I rented for us in Montevideo. The address is in the travel packet I gave you with your E-tickets. Once settled, we can buy a place, or go anywhere in the world your heart desires, though I have spent the last five years learning Spanish. I'm quite fluent."

"Actually, I wouldn't mind visiting some of the places we've stashed our millions and then decide; Canary and Cook Islands, Andorra, St. Vincent, Belize, Mongolia, Turks & Caicos, Czech Republic, and Hong Kong to name a few. They're all so exotic."

"You're the one who managed to get our Serrano real estate sold, the taxes paid and proceeds legally deposited offshore. At least the IRS won't be coming after us."

"For now! I need to make sure I file our tax returns properly from abroad for a couple years and start switching the accounts over to our new identities right away."

"I've been hearing rumblings about something called FATCA?"

"Yeah, just what we need. Money grubbing feds want to pass The Foreign Account Tax Compliance Act to make it easier for them to seize U.S. citizens' foreign bank accounts."

"All the more reason to find a country and become naturalized. I messed up when I chose Uruguay. I didn't realize an FBI statement was required when Americans apply for citizenship there! I'm thinking Brazil, but learning Portuguese is one of their conditions."

"We'll figure it out, sweetie."

"Would have been nice to sell the last two rental properties plus our house. Too bad the market tanked in 2008, but at least you got top dollar for four of them between then and when I died."

"Did I mention you're officially dead? The paperwork came through a week ago Friday, which means your life insurance will payout soon. I'm glad you used your connections to get us two new identities, prior to 911. Who knew? Homeland Security tightening borders, cracking down on identity theft, and making it harder for innocent people like us to disappear. I shudder to think about being stuck here if you'd waited longer. I used one fake passport last year to go overseas a couple times, when a few of the banks required a live body to open an account. You ever have any problems going back and forth?"

"Worked like a 24 karat charm, multiple times. I've walked cash under ten thousand dollars and the majority of our gemstones onto planes without security sounding so much as a peep. It wasn't much of a stretch pretending to be an international jeweler. I'm an established expat running a small business in Montevideo, with a nice nest egg I might add, all stashed in a safe deposit box."

"In your name?"

"I set the accounts up in both our new names. The list is in your packet. All you need to do is walk in, show your ID and sign. You'll have instant access."

"You've thought of everything."

"I do suggest we keep our second aliases in reserve, just in case we need to disappear again. Which reminds me! Will you, Evette Marie Upton take me, John Felix Andrade in marriage, to live in comfort with me, or whomever we shall be deemed, as long as we both shall live?

"Oh, sweetie, that's a three carat diamond in platinum! Our engagement will have to be short, though, so I don't get stuck with my initials reading 'emu'."

"Nothing but the best for you, my love. I've missed you so. Now, let's get out of here. I've got all the luggage packed in my SUV in the garage, bought with cash in Fresno at a used car lot, just like we discussed. I need to take a leak, so do whatever you need to do and *let's go*!

"Use the downstairs guestroom. The cats are locked upstairs with food and water. I'll text my friend at the Humane Society, tell her I've been summoned to the city for an early morning meeting with a cranky client and ask her to stop by for a couple days. Once I don't come back she'll figure it out and find them good homes. I'll text her the access code and leave the key under the front mat where it is. Actually, I think I'll leave the sliders in the kitchen unlocked and the alarm off, too. Who cares if anyone breaks in and steals stuff, but I do want my kitties to be safe. Why do you keep looking at that thing?"

"Apple came out a couple years ago with this iPhone. It's addictive. I can't seem to keep my hands off it."

"That's how you used to talk about me. But, yeah, I'm tired of my Blackberry. Buy me one for a wedding gift when we hit South America?"

Randi fiddled with the kitchen door, turned around and absentmindedly walked past the granite kitchen island as she texted. She whirled in mid-stroke upon feeling a breeze curl past her ankles and gasped at the sight of Stella; not so much from the weapon, but from the woman's wretched appearance. She was covered in filth, the odor wafting from her damp crotch making Randi gag.

Stella scrutinized Randi, the .38 revolver held loosely in her right hand, barrel tip obscenely resting between privates, left hand holding right wrist to counteract the slight tremors manifesting erratically along muscles.

"Pretty sure of yourself, sneaking in like a thief," said Randi. "You really think you can shoot me in cold blood and get away with it? What they're saying is true, you are a ruthless killer."

Stella lifted her arm and leveled the gun at Randi's gut. "If anyone would know, you would," She sneered. "Put the phone down."

Randi complied once she noted Stella's eyeballs rattling around in their sockets like dice on a Vegas craps table. "You're going to kill me, too? That the plan?"

"Spare me the bullshit. You and I know who the real killer is, and she's standing in this room. And by the way, you need to work on your fucking attitude; a little compassion would be nice."

Randi looked at her incredulously. "You're talking to me about attitude?"

"I clean your toilets, pick up your shit and you can't even offer me a shower! I mean, look at me," Stella waived the gun down the length of her torso, "I've had a rough day."

"Excuse me, but you're the one with the gun."

Stella snapped the .38 back towards Randi, hand wobbling. "Our *Miss Manners* conversation is over. Right now, I'm wondering what the cops will think about our little talk."

"You think the police will believe anything you say?"

"Doesn't matter, 'cuz I'm gonna make sure they look long and hard at you. A snapped neck?" Stella pitched her voice an octave higher. "Does it give us a little rushy, a little tingle in the tushy, bitch? Maybe even the ultimate big 'O'?"

"You really are bonkers," Randi said, using her comment to cover a slight shift of stance, adjusting weight onto her right rear foot. She pretended to take a step forward.

Stella straightened her arm as if pointing, waggling the gun. "Keep your distance!"

Randi appeared to stop. Standing at the kitchen entrance, she calculated Stella stood exactly twenty feet away. Stella lowered her gun arm a bit and massaged it above and below the elbow.

"So, what did you have Billy do, and why did you kill him and Harry? Not that I hated to see the perv go, but I am curious." Randi expected a response, but Stella just stood there gawping. Randi was biding her time, waiting for the right opportunity. *No, not quite yet.*

Stella's mouth snapped shut and she waved the weapon at Randi again. "I saw the bolt cutters. Mango took them. I know they weren't Billy's so they had to be yours. I don't know how Harry fits into this, but I figure you, Clare and the big fucking Mexican are in on it."

Randi's left eye twitched. "What big fucking Mexican? And where's Clare?"

"Mango and some other cops brought her and some giant beaner off the Ridge Trail in handcuffs. *That* big fucking Mexican."

"I have no idea who you're talking about." Stella wanted to chat and Randi appreciated that, because it would keep the nutcase in front of her off-kilter. Her left sidekick was deadly, and in class Randi could easily break five inches of wood in a second. Mr. Lee said smashing wood just an inch thick equaled severely bruising or even shattering a person's ribs.

Randi knew the average individual could raise a gun and pull the trigger, with even the slightest degree of accuracy, in approximately one and a half seconds. When a shooter stood within twenty-one feet of an assailant, the shooter lost the race ninety percent of the time. She had practiced this distance attack a thousand times over, ever since Jack explained it to her. Who knew this nifty little skill might come in handy tonight?

Trying to gain an edge, Randi added, "You're not the only one with troubles."

"Cry me a fucking river."

"You don't understand. I'm leaving town. Ever since Emil died, his two asshole brothers have threatened me, and it's been escalating. I know that means nothing to you, but I'm running for my life from them tonight. I don't know what you, your idiot husband and boyfriend of yours have been up to, but I want no part of it!

"So, you don't want to get caught, but you are now. How does it feel? You thought nothing about shredding me in court, then using me to promote your own self-serving ass. Now it's your turn."

"You're judging me?" She shrieked. "You lived a lie pretending you didn't see your husband masturbating your twelve year old daughter on the couch across from you; just like my mother!"

"That little slut wasn't the only victim! You don't know nothin'."

"You could have done something. You were the adult."

"Was I?"

"So what now?" Randi checked her stance. *Wait for it.*

"I'm going to shoot you and then kill myself. I'll make it look like you did it. That's the only way to stop this shit-piece merry-go-round. I tried to a couple hours ago, but missed." Stella giggled and glanced down. "That's how I got all wet down there."

Randi didn't hesitate. She launched.

She didn't realize how cranked Stella really was. Nor did she know Emil had opened the guestroom door and stepped into the hallway behind her, a split second before she attacked.

"Randi?" He called, patting the front left pocket of his tan guayabera shirt where his iPhone nestled. "I thought you were going to text your friend. I keep hearing voices. Why are you on the phone?" Randi's ear rupturing scream drowned out his voice as she leapt forward to deliver a flying kick.

Stella jerked and shot twice as soon as the door behind Randi opened. By the time her eyes refocused, Randi's foot was a fraction of a second away from shattering her second and third ribs.

Randi's scream to distract Stella acted to release energy, adding additional inertia to an already violent side-kick. She knew she had won, but in the nanosecond before her foot connected, she was perplexed as to why the gun fired. There should have been enough time and a few inches to block it with her perfectly executed leg extension.

Stella's body was thrust backward and hit the glass door. It fragmented into a tangle of fractal webs but didn't break. Stunned by the exploding rounds and impact from Randi's kick, lungs pierced by splintered ribs, she collapsed in a heap, firing the .38 one last time into the ceiling as she went down.

Randi immediately recoiled into fighting stance; arms up, knees slightly bent and bouncing ever-so-lightly on the balls of her feet. Convinced the woman was not struggling to rise, Randi stepped near and knelt, listened to Stella's strangled wheezing and noted naught but bloodshot whites filling her orbitals.

Randi wrapped her hands around Stella's cranium, trying to find a grip through greasy hair. "You break into my house and threaten to kill me, I will defend myself. You lose. You die."

Randi raised Stella's skull so high the torso followed with arms dangling limply, then slammed it to tile once. And again. Blood seeped from the back of Stella's head. Breathing hard, Randi stood and kicked the gun away from Stella's right hand.

"Uhhhhhnnn! She fucking shot me!"

Randi spun around to see Emil doubled over clutching his right thigh, blood oozing from between splayed fingers.

"Get me to a hospital!"

"We can't take you; not gunshot. Too many questions! You're not gonna be able to fly like that, are you?" she asked, more to herself than expecting an answer.

"Hurry up!"

"Stay right there. Don't move! Hang on to the door frame if you need to. If the bullet is anywhere near your femoral artery and you dislodge it, you'll bleed out!" she shouted.

Randi knew she didn't have much time. In three steps she swooped, grabbed the .38 Taurus, and positioned her feet where Stella had last stood then turned back to Emil. "Can you stand up straight? Good. Don't put weight on that leg!"

The moment Emil was upright and facing her, mouth contorted in pain and confusion, eyes wide in final understanding, Randi took aim and said, "Sorry sweetie. The best way to keep a secret is to make sure it's a dead secret."

Randi squeezed the trigger. Pleased with her shot to his forehead, she squatted quickly, leaned back and plugged the last bullet into the wall to her right. Standing, she observed her prone husband and waited for his legs to stop flailing.

Silence. Except, of course, for the harsh dentist's drill, whining in her ears.

Think, think, think! Randi went back to Stella, bent and checked for a pulse, fumbled the dead woman's fingers through the trigger guard then replaced the gun to where she'd picked it up.

Think, think, think! Randi looked around wildly and spied her cell phone where she'd put it when Stella showed. She called for an ambulance. She sighed. *In another life, I would have won an Oscar for that performance. Such a waste.*

Think, think, think! Emil! She looked down at the sparkling bauble on her ring finger and frowned, then raced to where Emil's body lay, sat beside him cross-legged and dragged his inert form into her lap, making sure a goodly sum of crimson fluid soaked her clothes.

"Think, think, think," she murmured aloud. "Doesn't matter if Stella's blood is on me. Stella tried to kill us. Crazy bitch shot Emil twice, killed him and would have done the same to me. Had to fight for my life. Self defense. I kicked her down. Doesn't matter if my prints are on the gun. We grappled for it so my prints *should* be on it. Same with powder burn when I grabbed for it. It went off three times before I was able to bang her head and she lay still. If she's dead, I didn't mean to kill her, just disable her. Kicked the gun away. Called for help." She inhaled once, pursed her lips and exhaled slowly. "So, here I am with Emil, willing him to live."

Think, think, think! Randi placed two middle fingers on Emil's carotid, the other hand floating above his nostrils, glad she didn't have to pinch them closed. *Okay. Good.*

Think, think, think! "Tell Mango the truth. Emil faked his death so we could run away together, leave the country, get out of his family's business and be free. Only thing I'm guilty of is owning a false identity," Randi quantified audibly, "Nothing else."

"Huh," she whispered into his left ear. "Bet you thought I was gonna break Stella's neck." A shudder rolled through her. *At least I won't have to share any of it. Once this blows over I can still head for Uruguay and live the good life I've always deserved."*

Silence.

Think, think, think. Randi wrapped her arms around the corpse's waist, its head cradled against her right shoulder. She started rocking. A tear pooled and rolled down her left cheek. She rocked harder.

"About deaf from gunfire," she thought, pitching back and forth, wailing and crying, holding dead Emil tight. "I can barely hear myself. Hope it's loud enough."

CHAPTER 29

DON'T BOTHER KNOCKIN'

Three police units parked, angled in front of Randi's house, yellow lights flashing; the neighborhood quiet except for a tractor trailer shifting gears up the Route One hill beyond her backyard. A dog barked from several streets below. Crystalline stars hung in the purple bruised black sky, twinkling and blinking like a distant carnival ride, while a full moon peeped over the eastern Santa Lucia Hills preparing to outshine her distant sisters.

Mango's phone buzzed. "Go ahead, Dora."

"Cervantes says Clare is insisting she needs to tell you something, but won't talk to anyone but you."

"It'll have to wait. Busy right now? Under no circumstances should Clare make a statement until I'm there. I also need phone silence and minimal radio traffic, unless it's an absolute emergency."

"Got it. Uh, Chief? Break a leg—"

Mango stashed the phone and faced de la Cruz and Pacheco. "Even though Randi made the call, we don't know who's alive, so let's play it textbook. If Stella's still a threat, we take her out in order to secure Randi, then sweep the house and double-check for accomplices. Reinforcements are four minutes behind, but those few moments could make a difference. I'd like to start this now."

"I'm comfortable handling the back alone until Cormac arrives," Jorge offered.

"Excellent. I'll wait for you to set up, then knock and enter. Kiana, you're my shadow. Radios on low and weapons out. Let's roll."

Jorge cautiously walked the fence line and disappeared around a corner, while Mango and Kiana approached the front door. Dim light shone through its high, cut glass insets and a muffled low wailing sounded from within. Mango silently tested the door latch, remembering Randi standing in front of him, clad in a loosely tied robe and not much else, merely two mornings ago.

"Check around for a key," Mango mouthed to his lieutenant.

Kiana shoved the welcome mat aside with a booted toe. "That was way too easy," she hissed, "Feels like a trap—" Before she could continue, their radios squelched. "Slider open and glass cracked. See three bodies. Sightline front door. One's moving."

Mango bent and grabbed the key, plugged it and turned the lock. The door swung open slightly. The low moaning grew into high keening. "We're in," Kiana answered into her shoulder mic.

"Police, Police," he bellowed. "Randi? Say something!"

Standing to the side, Mango reached forward with his left hand and pushed the door ever so gently open. Bringing his Glock up to ready, he sidled gingerly into the foyer with his left foot, taking one more step to his right.

He regarded Randi sitting on the floor just inside the open kitchen covered in blood, head thrown back, arms cradling and rocking what appeared to be a male adult sprawled in her lap. The sounds they'd heard from beyond the threshold resolved into her weeping laments. Stella lay past Randi near the traumatized slider; legs splayed, trunk twisted, left cheek laying flush against the cold tile, right hand outstretched above her head where a puddle of blood inexorably meandered towards an old revolver three feet from her fingertips.

Kiana slithered past Mango to stand angled on his right, gun arm pointed in an optimal Weaver shooting stance at Stella, scanning for hazards from different directions, ready to swivel and fire. The distinctive smell of cordite lingered like the first delicious whiff of a freshly lit cigarette.

"Talk to me, Randi," Mango insisted. "Are you okay? Is Stella dead? Is there anyone else here?"

Randi shook her head, gulped air and panted, anguished sobs quieting to a constant whimper. She cleared her throat. "I can't hear very well," she yelled.

Mango repeated the questions louder and slower.

"I'm alright. I wasn't fast enough!" she cried. "She killed him!" Randi's voice reverberated off the stylish marble and granite décor. "It's just her."

Mango couldn't see any movement much less breathing from Stella. He cautiously lowered the gun barrel halfway to his side, pointing down, knowing Jorge stood just outside the kitchen, primed and ready beyond the glass exit. Randi hiccupped twice then went eerily quiet, still swaying forward and back with the body, as if the motion could jump-start the dead man's heart. He heard the faint scrape of Kiana's boot as she shifted position on the hard flooring, then heard her breathe out, "Holy *lepo*, I swear on *Kamehameha's* grave, that's Emil Shirazi."

Randi's metronomic tempo increased. As she plunged into another bow, Emil's iPhone slithered onto the floor from his shirt pocket and clattered to rest screen up, fairy lights and icons flashing. Rhythm short circuited, Randi's head snapped up and she looked down at the mobile. Once she deciphered what the blinking meant, her left arm shot out, hand reaching for the instrument.

Mango's arm reciprocated, palm out, hand flexed. "Don't touch it, Randi!" he shouted. "Evidence!"

Her fingers hovered over the phone, hand trembling above the illuminated face. Deliberating. Wordlessly, like a recoiling serpent, Randi gradually withdrew and rewrapped her arm around Emil's chest. She had never once looked directly at them.

The radios squelched and Ski's voice lit up the void.

"Chief? You 10-6?" *Are you on the scene?*

After sharing one of those looks with Kiana, Mango rolled his shoulders, pointed his nine millimeter to the floor and grabbed his handheld from his left hip holster. He paced one step further into the foyer and pressed the mic button, "10-4, go ahead Serrano Three."

"Roja, Chief! Our 10-12 at the station remembered. They called her Roja!"

Kiana gasped. "Roja means red," she stage whispered at Mango, who imperceptibly nodded.

They wheeled to face Randi, who had used their distraction to rise and soundlessly glide backwards, left arm outstretched behind her, blind hand searching for a wooden knife caddy atop the kitchen island. Her green eyes wide, unblinking, stared through Mango's soul.

"Not going to prison, Jack." Randi grasped a seven inch carving knife and extracted it, sharp edge glinting. She stepped slightly forward assuming an L-shaped stance, body weight shifting to rear foot.

"Put the knife down. Drug running's bad, but we want the big guys, not the little fish like you. I know the agent in charge. I can help cut you a deal."

"Ahh, Jack." Randi looked across the room at him with pity. "If it were that simple. I can't change the past, even when I was trying to change my future. I was this close." She held up a thumb and index finger.

"Put the weapon down and let's talk."

She shook her head to the negative. "I won't rot in prison, and I'll never go back to being someone's whore, even if that's all I've ever been. Remember twenty-one feet? Well, I've got nineteen on you and I'm faster—"

Randi didn't finish speaking before she rushed, releasing a deafening *ki-up* in midair. Within half an eye blink she was six feet from Mango, knife arcing towards his neck, flaming hair flying behind her like Nike, the winged Greek goddess of victory.

In that same instant, Mango swept his Glock up and fired, the smell of burning powder chasing the slug from its barrel, the percussion followed by a second near-instantaneous detonation. Randi was fast. She was also as quick as she claimed.

Mango was also fast, but not swift enough to land two in her chest. Both bullets were low. The first went into her upper groin, the second straight through her stomach and just missed severing her lumbar vertebrae to paralyze. His rounds weren't enough to stop her airborne momentum. Mango watched as the blade high in Randi's fist began its final down stroke, her nostrils flaring like an angry war stallion, lips curled back in a flesh biting snarl.

Kiana tracked Randi's progress like a veteran duck hunter and pulled. Two blasts daggered into Mango's right eardrum. Randi's kinematic voyage ended, body slamming his chest like a bag of wet cement, the tip of her razor-edged weapon propelled into his supraspinatus muscle.

Her carcass atop his, limbs entwined, they tumbled to tile as Mango looked down and studied Randi's blasted noggin' and dripping grey matter. *If I survive this, I'll never hear out of that ear again.* His head hit the floor. Hard.

Silence.

EPILOGUE

IT AIN'T OVER 'TIL THE BLACK CAT SINGS SOPRANO

"I knew I should never have killed myself until our properties sold."

"If we had waited, we would have been fucked when the market crashed."

"Well, if I had known the cops couldn't identify me by the blood I left, I would agree with you. Didn't plan on waiting five years to be declared dead!"

"The extra blood was an inspired detail and made it more authentic."

"I also hadn't planned on ripping my arm on the windshield metal when I wedged the stick on the gas pedal, put it in gear and jumped away. Hard to see in the middle of the night with nothing for light but stars; at least I could watch for miles down the coast and notice if other cars were coming by their headlights."

"You made it back okay."

"No thanks to you. Had to wrap my arm in a jacket and pedal the bike into San Simeon before I picked up the car you left me at the Best Western. By the time I got to Solvang where no one would recognize me, my jacket was soaked with blood. Had to douse my arm with iodine and buy liquid skin to get the wound to close. Thankfully it didn't get infected. See the scar? You have no idea how I suffered."

"What about me? Every time I turned around, your brothers wanted me to buy more of their gems! I finally got them to realize that without your artistic magic, the store's jewelry didn't sell. Then the bottom fell out of real estate, and I wasn't about to skim *our* money to keep paying those assholes off when a six million dollar house was only selling for two!

"You should have called me to get you out when they dragged you into their pot smuggling scheme."

"They threatened to hurt me if I didn't. It wasn't that big a deal, picking up the vans they left in beach lots near Morro Bay, delivering them to obscure areas between here & up through Big Sur. Coming home, I looked just like any other cyclist out for a jaunt. Besides, I was only going to do it for three months until one more house sale closed."

"You shouldn't have gotten Billy Morton involved."

"He needed money and I saw an opportunity. I didn't want to do this last drop so close to Serrano. It's as if your brothers set it up so I *would* get caught. If Billy had done what he was supposed to, he could have skipped town with fifteen grand in his pocket. But no, he got ice cubes in his sneakers and wanted to back out. He did fine with cutting the chain on his bogus run to T-ville. Leaving the van and pedaling back to town later that evening should have been a no brainer. But no, he got stupid. Only smart thing he did was forget the shears in Stella's car."

"You didn't have to kill him."

"Yes, I did. He would have squealed, or even worse, tried to blackmail me. The world won't miss him."

"And Harry?"

"Him, I do regret. I got antsy and should have waited until it got darker to deliver that stinking van, but I needed to get back and figure out what to do with Billy's body. There Harry was, stalking around like the Ghost of Christmas Present, grumbling it was illegally parked, and how he was gonna call the cops. He would have recognized me!"

"What if he did? He was taking a ride and so were you. It's not like either of you could be connected to the thing."

"You don't understand! I had just dragged my cycle out the back and slammed the door shut. I thought he'd seen and heard me. I panicked. I've been under a bit of stress lately, you know?"

"So, now we have to scramble because you murdered two people. We need to *vamoose* if we're going to make our flight to Lima from LAX. Figure we'll spend a few days seeing the sights, make sure nobody's following then fly to Uruguay."

Mango let the voice file run. He tapped a key on his laptop to stop it just before Randi broke Stella's head, and then leaned back in his office chair twirling a pen between his fingers. He eyed Clare and Kiana sitting across the desk from him. "We all know what comes next. Don't need to hear the actual murders, but figured you deserved to understand what happened, now that the case is officially closed."

Clare returned his gaze, speechless.

"I just violated about ten different state and federal statutes by playing it for you. I trust you to tell no one, and that includes Oso."

Clare chewed her lip and nodded. "So, you're telling me Randi had no idea Emil was recording their conversation until the very end?"

Mango nodded back. "We didn't either, not until we inspected his phone later. You also didn't hear the part when Ski radioed us that Oso remembered hearing Randi's nickname, *Roja*. That and the recording was the final nail in her coffin. Mind-boggling what you can do with an iPhone these days," he added looking deliberately at Kiana.

"So why kill Emil?" Clare asked.

"Thought she could get away with it, especially since she'd just set Stella up for the other two homicides. No way could Emil board a plane; she needed to get out of the country fast and he'd just turned into dead weight. He'd been shot once, so why not? Bad timing on his part, messing up the plan."

"Nothing like men and their bad timing," remarked Kiana, arching an eyebrow at Mango.

"Anyway," he resumed, "I really think she intended to make a fresh start with him until Stella showed up and put a bullet in his leg."

"Why didn't Emil trust Randi?" Clare questioned. "I mean, he gave her a list of where he stashed his part of their loot and they were fleeing the country together."

Kiana sniffed. "Would you trust a woman who'd recently murdered two people, and then a third right in front you? I'd certainly want some type of insurance so I wouldn't be implicated, or be her next victim."

"Lot of good it did him," observed Mango.

"What about Stella?" inquired Clare. "How was she involved?"

"She guessed, but wasn't smart enough to prove, that Randi was setting her up and responsible for Billy's death. She also went looking for Harry the same evening both he and Billy were killed, but never found him. Based on the recording, we don't think Stella knew Harry was dead until Randi told her. Stella was so mentally warped, she believed her only option was to kill Randi and commit suicide, trying to flip the frame job back onto Randi."

They bowed their heads and each said a quiet prayer for the deceased, in remembrance of their squandered dreams and pointless deaths.

Mango broke the silence. "Let's go celebrate the living and join the party down at The DP."

It was early Saturday evening before Memorial Day in 2010, a year later plus a few weeks from Randi's demise. Mr. Lee had decorated The DP with papier-mâché streamers and curly ribbons. Two small cakes centered on the conference table, eaten down to crumbs, were surrounded by the skeletal detritus from heaping platters of boiled crab, corn-on-the-cob, chicken wings, new potatoes, as well as a near empty tureen of Pismo clam chowder. One cake had been adorned with 'Happy Birthday Jessica' and the other 'Welcome Home Oso and Clare.' The invitation-only event included all of the Serrano Police Department, (who rotated through when their duty shifts ended), Sheriff's Deputies Cervantes, Cormac and Buster, State Trooper Dewayne Smith, Oso Barranco, Clare and a few loyal Tranks, and of course, Jessica and Alexa. DEA Special Agent Levi Craig also there, the only non-SLO county guest invited. Taco was back at Mango's Alamosta Rancho enjoying a private seafood buffet with Zulu, Zeba, Pono and Kiawe.

Clare poked Mango playfully in the ribs. "I kept trying to tell you I switched the bikes at Randi's house. I thought it was kinda neat they were both yellow. I assumed she wouldn't mind if I borrowed hers, and that guy I stole the bike from would eventually get his back. You kept blowing me off like I was a kid," Clare accused.

"Didn't want you to incriminate yourself in a murder or two. I was trying to protect you."

"I'm all grown up and can protect myself, Chief Mango." Clare leaned over and kissed Oso's cheek, who was intently immersed in a friendly game of elbow wrestling with Jorge Pacheco. "Especially now that my grizzly's back," she grinned. "If you had listened, maybe you wouldn't have gotten stabbed or conked your head. But I know you were trying to do right by me, so thank you. And for everything else you've done for us."

"If Kiana hadn't been channeling Annie Oakley, I couldn't have done anything," he said, unconsciously rubbing between his neck and collarbone. "She saved my bacon so I can fry it another day," he laughed but immediately threw a sigh. "I just wish we didn't have to kill her."

"It's what she wanted, boss," Kiana interrupted, "Suicide by cop. Her life, if you want to call it that, was over. It was over long before that night, but she did make sure some good came from it. Look at the new start she's giving Oso and Clare. It's why we're here, to celebrate life and family; theirs and yours. I think Randi is here with us tonight smiling in approval. Even with her screwed up existence, her heart was in the right place.

"Jorge," she called over her shoulder, "Give it up before you break your wrist!"

"I'm still mourning Randi's death. But, if it wasn't for a directive in her will, pointing us to her safe deposit box containing signed and notarized evidence, we wouldn't have had enough, even with Oso's testimony, to convict and break up the *Shirazi Mafioso Connection*." Mango turned to Clare. "So, how does it feel be a millionaire? I hear probate is finally finished."

Randi had bequeathed her entire estate to the young woman. The IRS and DEA had fought over the details for months, weighing exactly which assets were legit and which were accumulated by illicit funds, even though Randi's meticulous accounting showed no criminal activity and none could be proved.

To expedite Clare's inheritance, Mango had interceded and phoned Agent Craig, who called in a favor. The callee called in another favor, who called in one more favor. A bargain was struck whereby the federal government would seize all of the Shirazi's foreign assets. The remaining bank accounts, properties, possessions and businesses found or operating on U.S. soil were released to Clare, leaving her with the jewelry store, Randi's home, a vacation management business servicing twenty-seven properties, two rental houses with clear titles, and approximately two and half million in assorted cash investments. The feds ended up with the better deal, realizing more than eleven million in offshore accounts and another six in flawlessly graded and cut gemstones stashed in Emil's Montevideo bank lockbox.

"I'm sorry you won't collect more of what Randi intended. If you fight for it, the government will tie you up in court for years, if not decades," Mango apologized.

"That's okay. I learned a hard lesson from Randi. Don't get greedy and appreciate what you have. Oso and I are thrilled. I'm negotiating with his bank to get the *Pico de Gato* back. "If business is good," Clare giggled, "Maybe I'll buy him a bigger boat!"

"Any luck with the life insurance?"

"Since Emil faked his death with Randi's help and was subsequently killed by her, both committed insurance fraud. She was the beneficiary, which voided the policy. It's understandable they stopped payment on his claim.

"What about her policy? She told me a couple years ago that she and Emil had reciprocal wills and I assumed life insurance."

"They did, but she changed all that and made *me* the sole beneficiary a year after he disappeared. There was a two year waiting clause, that if she was killed in the act of committing a crime, they didn't have to pay. That period long since expired before her death. I've been cleared from any involvement in her shenanigans so the underwriters legally cannot refuse settlement. It's been like trying to pry a dead mouse away from a growling cat. That money I *will* fight for, even if I have to take it all the way to the California Department of Insurance and State District Attorney's Office."

"Need any help?"

"Nah," Clare winked at Mango, "I got this one."

"So, you two gonna live in town? You know he can't leave the state without a lot of red tape."

"I'm selling her house." Clare winced. "I could never live there, not after— We're looking in Los Osos, of all places. He can dock his trawler at neighboring Morro Bay, go fishing, or take tourists sightseeing easily from there. Plus, California's got a long coastline so I don't think he'll get too bored puttering up and down the state."

Because of Oso's willingness to testify, and with the information left by Randi about her brother-in-law's activities, Hafid and Mikhail were sent up for a lengthy stay in Club Fed. Oso spent nine months of a five year sentence in San Luis County lockup on drug distribution charges, with four more years of probation pending. Incarcerating him locally was a gift from Agent Craig. It was still a prison housing violent criminals for rape, robbery and murder, with a maximum security level as high as any state penitentiary's. No one bothered Oso, not after the first day. He spent the majority of his confinement teaching the Hispanic population how to speak better English.

Waiting for Oso to be released, Clare hunkered down in Tranquility, moved back into her cottage and was relieved when Mango offered to keep Taco at his rancho during the interim. She got her old job back at the Hill o'Beans, and helped the owners interview a new foreman to run the town. Her faithful Tranks shielded her from the worst of the media's virulent attention, their exposés spouting sensationalized leading headlines: *Prominent Serrano Business Leader Turns Serial Killer! White Trash to Wealth*

– Carnage for Cash! Local Woman Whacks Husband Twice in Multi-Murder Spree!

Mango also made sure Clare received psychological help. Her biggest complaint being the shrinks had never wanted to listen to her story of abuse and abandonment, and only wanted to know how she felt about it. 'How the fuck do they think I feel,' she had groused. She flourished as she worked through her anger, learning how to cope with stressful memory triggers by joining a group emphasizing exposure therapy. No 'one-on-one' psychiatrists for her!

"Hey, Oso," Mango called out. "Life is finally mellower at my ranch, like in those *Happy Cow* cheese commercials with the cats standing in for moo-ers. I was about to rename Zeba and Zulu to Hissing and Pissing, but without the testosterone, Taco's mellowing into the fold and everyone's getting along. Glad you did the right thing, allowing us to have him fixed. He's doing just fine."

Finished with Jorge, who was massaging his elbow, Oso vacated his position from the opposite side of the table, shambled over and sat straddling a chair backwards, facing Mango.

"How about you?" Mango asked the imposing man.

He brought a level hand up, palm flat and waggled it to and fro. "Not so much."

Feigning shock, Mango asked, "She cut your balls off, too?"

Clare snorted. "After two months of pre-honeymooning at one of Kate's secluded ranch cabins, he's saying the opposite. I'm pregnant!"

Mango heard Jessica and Alexa pig-squeal like only woman can, and watched them scrape their chairs back, to run and lift Clare up and squeeze her between them, all three jumping up and down in unison, the sound now resembling cats fighting over fish guts.

Alexa's salted, dark-haired head popped above the fray. She tossed Mango a stink eye. "At least somebody around here is making babies."

Oso slid a cigar from his chest pocket and slipped it down the table at Mango, who said, "Thanks a lot." He tucked the stogy into his own shirt pocket as he and Oso scrutinized the yodeling women. "If you don't mind, I'll save it for later. Congratulations."

Clare disentangled from the two harpies, moved around the table to rest her chin atop Oso's head and clasped her arms around him. "We're going to be the best parents ever!"

"*Si, Claro*," he answered, extricating one large mitt to hug her back.

Alexa, Jessica, Christy Cervantes, and the Tranks came after Clare, swept her up, and like a receding tide carried her out to the enclosed porch. "You're all invited to the wedding!" Clare hollered as the door swung shut.

"Don't even think about playing copycat, kit-kat," Mango belatedly bellowed after Jessica. "And Oso," he pointed a finger at him, "You ever hurt Clare, you'll get more than a pain in the panga from me."

"*Si. Claro*." He nodded once then cocked his head at Mango, pulled out a safety match, lit it with a thumbnail flick and proceeded to stoke his cigar. "You are a good man, *Jefe*. A very good man."

"The jury's still out on that one." He paused. "You know there's no smoking in here."

Kiana leaned over and nudged Mango's shoulder, angling her head at the exit. "Take a hike with me before we work the festivities?"

He looked over his shoulder as they left, to see Levi and Oso blowing smoke rings at each other.

Babble and merriment radiated from the women on the porch, words like 'diapers' and 'vomit' and 'colic' popping from the hum to hang like cartoon text bubbles as the Chief and his second traversed the sheltered terrace to Front Street.

They stopped at the seawall and surveyed the beach, the party at the pier just starting, everyone waiting for the pyrotechnics, and The Mollys, an eclectic Irish/Mexican touring band based out of Tucson, to play.

"Foggy. Can't see one star," Kiana commented. "Never seen a town that likes their fireworks as much as this one. Every holiday here is like Honolulu's Chinatown on New Year's Eve. Think they'll still set them off?

"Always do, barring thunder, lightning, or high swells or wind. Twenty-five years ago, Serrano's volunteer fire department burned the end of the pier down in an 'oops' moment during a show. From what I've read of local history, took ten years of fund raising to scrape up enough money to rebuild it. Ever since, a professional crew shoots the fireworks from barges moored out on the bay. They know how to deal with all kinds of weather and where to aim. It is a perfectly still night for it."

"The firecrackers must go on, huh? Never seen a display in pea soup before," remarked Kiana. "I've heard it's ethereal."

Mango didn't answer, lost in thought as if mesmerized by the cadence of the waves. As one, they turned to amble south along the wall away from the pier, Kiana sipping at a cola. Smoked fish, the scent wafting from the barbeque shack from around the corner, mixed with the briny ocean air.

"Never had that talk," Kiana opened, "Did we?"

"Nope."

"You know it would never work. It's not like we're two hick marshals stuck out in the middle of no where like Wyoming. Someone's bound to notice and then both our jobs are toast, violating the council's non-fraternization rules. One of us would have to quit, and you know how I feel about that. Besides, we're too much alike *and* married to our jobs. Speaking of which—"

"What about Kate?" Jack finished for her.

"Well, where is she tonight?"

"She'll come down from Brewster Ranch tomorrow. Grant's been ill. And yeah, it's past our third anniversary. We're trying to sort it out. We've been negotiating."

"Sounds more like a business deal than true love."

"Between my knife wound, which wasn't all that serious; to my concussion, which was; to the imperceptible but still annoying buzzing in my right ear; I've been busy recuperating."

"Not much time for wooing?"

"Give me a break, Kiana. You know I also spent months wrapping up the Shirazi case, as well as making sure Clare *and* Oso didn't get shafted by our 'don't worry, we're here to help you' government."

"Just pokin' the wolverine, boss. No offense intended."

Their stroll stopped at the end of the macadam, where Old Serrano Creek, (more of gash in the earth, running wet during only the most extreme of flashfloods) empties onto the beach and blocks the retaining wall and road.

"None taken. I do have a secret. It's why I've been so busy. During my recovery I learned to dance. Thought I better make the most of my down time, especially now, since it looks like I'll be attending a wedding or two in the near future. Mr. Lee and Roscoe taught me."

Kiana choked on the cola she'd been swallowing, spewing brown fizzing snot and liquid out her nose, the spatter mostly ending up on Mango's boots.

"That's attractive."

"Bite me." Gasping and sputtering, she jack-knifed from the waist, long glossy braid swinging, but then came up belly-laughing as she brushed at her treacle streaked uniform. "I would have liked to have been a fly on your wall. Thought you told me you couldn't learn."

"I scammed the insurance. Talked them into letting me use my Tae Kwon Do training as part of my physical therapy to help with the dizzy spells from the concussion. Told them it would make more sense since I already had the muscle memory from my black belt. It would shorten my recovery to work out privately with Mr. Lee, the hook being it would also save them a bunch of money. Snagged 'em and reeled 'em right in."

"So, how did they manage to teach you, 'Mr. I Got No Rhythm'?"

"Once I conceptualized formal dancing is nothing more than a memorized TKD form, it clicked. Bingo."

"You any good?"

"Do me the honor of being the first woman I sashay down the sidewalk, and find out for yourself." Jack bowed formally; arms bent, one in front, the other behind, palms flat against his torso. He then stepped back into classic ballroom posture; one arm up and somewhat bent, the other encircling an imaginary waist.

"What if someone sees?"

"So what? My version of the shag is a dance step, not a sex act. I intend to waltz us down to the pier. If it will make you happy, when we're done I'll dance with every female between five and ninety-five that I can lay my hands on."

Jack stood patiently.

"Come one. Just this once," he urged.

She hesitated. "Just once," she agreed. Kiana stepped into his arms, fitting like the last missing piece of a jigsaw puzzle, its original box having long since been discarded.

Mango swung her around as The Mollys opened their set with Nancy McCallion's *Came for a Dance*. Cannon fire boomed and splintered the low clouds, igniting them into a shrouded kaleidoscope of plummeting rainbows as Kiana and Jack twirled a slow polka down the seawall.

Noise.

ACKNOWLEDGEMENTS

This story was conceived by Al while drinking an early morning coffee on the back deck of a beachfront vacation rental in San Luis Obispo County, on the beautiful Central California Coast; therefore the setting of this novel. We would be remiss in not thanking the Martinus family and Tim McLean for unwittingly planting the seeds of inspiration.

It required one year of tenacious dedication by Al to finish the first draft, and another year for Linda to turn it into a polished cohesive novel, with both parties spending long weekend afternoons and weekday evenings together in brainstorming sessions. We wish we could say it was under the mango tree, but was more like next to the papaya grove.

Thank you, Linda, for helping to make one of my bucket-list dreams come true. You truly are my better half!

Thank you, Al, for being open to all the additions, deletions and changes, and for having the grace to accept when I was adamant about not changing a couple sections. (You really don't know women as well as you think you do!)

A special thanks to Nick Meyer and Brenda Meyer, and to Steve Sederwall for their encouragement to stick with this monumental task to its completion.

A big thank you to Eric Boyd, and to his creative writing students who provided Al with more constructive criticism than he cared to receive, forcing him to expand characters and plot, as well as fine tune his writing.

Much gratitude to Miz Babich for proofing the corrected manuscript for typo's as well as catching those pesky conundrums, and honorable mentions to Dr. Rita Hernandez and Melissa Delgado for your insightful suggestions.

Recognition and credit to Emily Moravits, for the many changes we threw at you while designing the cover.

Sincere thanks to Mr. Ron Geoffrion, Tae Kwon Do Master, who instilled in Al a 'never give up' attitude that transcends into so many aspects of his life.

An honorary salute to Al's fellow detectives of the Los Alamos Police Department for their comradery and brotherhood, as well as humor. You know who you are!

A heartfelt mention to Nancy Spitzer Semon. Al still remembers the day he bumped into you at Yukon Middle School, to remain friends forever more.

Hugs and kisses to Carrie, *The Cat Lady*, Buttler, for the care and feeding of our ever expanding feline menagerie. We have too many strays in our city!

And last but not least, our love and affection to our friends and families, especially the Toths, Nowickis, and McFarlands who have been wondering why they have rarely seen or heard from us for the past two years. Mahalo and aloha.

Made in the USA
San Bernardino, CA
14 October 2016